"You never ⟨ ⟩
me, Elizabeth,"

Ethan said with a smile.

"That's only because I let you talk me into doing foolish things," Elizabeth murmured, looking directly into the dark eyes caressing her face.

"Do you?" Ethan asked softly.

He turned his hand to smooth her cheek, slowly skimming the heated skin. When his finger traced the curve of her lip, a delicious current pulsed through her body. Elizabeth drew a long, uneven breath and managed to loosen her hold on him, resting her hands flat against his chest.

"Elizabeth." Ethan's whisper grazed her forehead like the stroke of warm velvet. "Look at me, Elizabeth." Balancing her chin on his finger, he tipped it upward, gently winning her compliance. Like dark prisms of the soul, his eyes seemed to illuminate the entire spectrum of emotions kindled in his heart. "There's no shame in feeling like this, not for a man or for a woman...."

Dear Reader,

Our featured big book this month, *The Honor Price*, by Erin Yorke, is a stirring tale of adventure and forbidden passion. One of Harlequin Historical's most popular authors, Yorke brings readers the story of Alanna O'Donnell, a young Irishwoman whose flight from her uncle's treachery brings her into an uneasy alliance with Spanish nobleman Lucas del Fuentes— a man she should by all rights hate.

Cheryl St.John's first book, *Rain Shadow*, was part of our March Madness 1993 promotion. Don't miss *Heaven Can Wait*, the gripping prequel to *Rain Shadow*. Heartland Critiques gave both books a GOLD ★★★★ rating!

Aisley de Laci is wed to a knight rumored to be in league with the devil in *The Devil's Lady*, a remarkable medieval by Deborah Simmons. And finally, Laurel Pace's *Winds of Destiny* is the long-awaited sequel to *Destiny's Promise*.

We hope you enjoy all of these titles. And next month, be sure to look for the new Theresa Michaels, *Fire and Sword*.

Sincerely,

Tracy Farrell
Senior Editor
Harlequin Historicals

Please address questions and book requests to:
Harlequin Reader Service
U.S.: 3010 Walden Ave., P.O. Box 1325, Buffalo, NY 14269
Canadian: P.O. Box 609, Fort Erie, Ont. L2A 5X3

LAUREL PACE

WINDS OF DESTINY

Harlequin Books

TORONTO • NEW YORK • LONDON
AMSTERDAM • PARIS • SYDNEY • HAMBURG
STOCKHOLM • ATHENS • TOKYO • MILAN
MADRID • WARSAW • BUDAPEST • AUCKLAND

ISBN 0-373-28842-5

WINDS OF DESTINY

LAUREL PACE,

a native of Little Rock, Arkansas, worked as a producer of radio and television commercials before turning her love of writing into a career. Writing historical fiction has given her the perfect excuse for indulging two of her favorite pastimes: exploring restored houses and reading old letters and diaries. Laurel lives in Atlanta with her husband and their five cats, just a half mile from a house originally built by Cherokees.

For Sarah, who saw me through

Prologue

Auraria, Georgia
April 1837

The doorbell jangled, piercing the silence as violently as a knife's thrust. Elizabeth Merriweather started and looked up from the petticoat she was mending. She tried to quell the vague uneasiness stirring inside her, with little success. At a time that now seemed very long ago, she would have hurried to the door, eager to welcome a visiting neighbor or a client seeking her husband's advice about some legal matter. Recently, however, the doorbell had too often heralded bad news for Elizabeth to greet its clang with anything but apprehension.

"It's probably one of those nice ladies from the church, come to call." Dolly Reed, Elizabeth's housekeeper, smiled reassuringly. She put aside her own sewing and rose, but not before another brassy peal echoed from the hall. Dolly glanced out the window on her way to the door. "Why, I do believe it's Mr. Merriweather!"

As the housekeeper's quick footsteps pattered down the hall, Elizabeth hastily folded the petticoat and stuffed it into her sewing basket. She had just removed her apron when Dolly appeared in the parlor door, followed by a stocky man with muttonchop whiskers bristling on his ruddy cheeks.

"My dear Elizabeth! How good it is to see you!" Josiah Merriweather clamped his hat in the crook of his arm, freeing both gloved hands to clasp Elizabeth's.

"I am pleased to see you, too, Josiah." Elizabeth managed a gracious smile. Although she had never felt close to her brother-in-law, he had been unstinting with his time and energy in the ten months since Samuel's fatal hunting accident. As executor of his brother's will, Josiah had undertaken the not inconsiderable task of putting Samuel's muddled estate in order as well as seeing that his widow's financial obligations were met in the interim.

Elizabeth glanced over Josiah's shoulder at Dolly, who was still hovering in the doorway. "Dolly, would you please make us tea? And slice some of the pound cake," she added before looking back at Josiah. "Please do sit down. You must be exhausted after traveling all the way from Milledgeville." She gestured toward the maroon horsehair sofa and then clasped her hands, hating the nervous gesture as much as the anxious feeling that provoked it.

"I've some business in Dahlonega, so I haven't at all gone out of my way," Josiah assured her.

He eased himself onto the sofa and began to pull off his gloves, one buff kid finger at a time. As Josiah chatted about his ride to Auraria he glanced around the room, his slightly protuberant eyes assessing his surroundings in a single, thorough sweep. When his gaze met Elizabeth's he gave her a bland smile, but not quickly enough to disguise the unfavorable appraisal that registered on his face. Elizabeth could imagine him comparing the modestly furnished parlor with his imposing home in Milledgeville, contrasting the meager fruits of Samuel's struggling law practice with those of his own flourishing business. Since marrying into the Merriweather family four years ago she had frequently sensed Josiah's condescension toward his brother, an attitude that Samuel's unsuccessful ventures had done nothing to diminish. Apparently even death could not exempt poor Samuel from his brother's sense of superiority.

Suppressing her resentment, Elizabeth busied herself with the tea tray that Dolly had just delivered. After placing a plate of cake on the side table within Josiah's reach, she carefully filled two cups with the steaming tea.

Josiah waited until the housekeeper had withdrawn before resuming conversation. "I had a frank and, I fear, disturbing discussion with Mr. Pritchard a fortnight ago," he began, shifting his languid gaze from the tea service to Elizabeth's pale face.

"About the mine?" Elizabeth took a sip of the scalding tea to dispel the dryness in her throat.

Josiah's nod was slow but decisive. "I'm afraid Brush Creek Mine has proved utterly worthless. Save for the initial lode, the site hasn't yielded enough gold to plate a man's watch in the three years since it was opened. As acting director for the company, Mr. Pritchard plans to auction the equipment in hopes of covering the operation's debts." He must have caught the low gasp that escaped Elizabeth's lips, for he put his cup aside and leaned forward to place a comforting hand on her wrist. "You've no idea how it pains me to bring you such unhappy news, my dear."

Elizabeth straightened herself, deliberately withdrawing her arm from Josiah's grasp. Kind as his intentions might be, Josiah nevertheless often struck her as patronizing, swathing each revelation about the disastrous state of Samuel's finances in a sugar coating of tepid platitudes.

"Then I cannot depend on the mine as a source of income." Elizabeth assumed a brisk tone, the better to get on with business. "What of Samuel's other assets?"

Josiah plucked at one of the gloves lying on the arm of the sofa, smoothing a veinlike wrinkle from its buttery surface. "I am confident sufficient funds remain to provide for you until fall, after which time—"

"But that's only a little over four months," Elizabeth interrupted, frowning. "Surely I've more money than that. What of my inheritance? It was not a great deal of money, but Samuel assured me that he had invested it wisely."

A faint smile intruded for a moment on Josiah's placid face. "Ah, me, I fear Samuel placed far, far too much faith in Brush Creek Mine." He shook his head like a physician surveying a hopeless case.

As the full impact of Josiah's remark settled in, Elizabeth felt the color drain from her face. "So my inheritance is gone, too." She forced herself to speak. "I suppose there isn't enough left to pay for this house."

When Josiah tilted his head to one side, his fleshy throat swelled inside his collar, spilling over the high, starched rim. "Perhaps if that was your only debt, but . . ." His voice trailed off.

"I see." Elizabeth stared numbly at Josiah, letting his florid image blur before her eyes.

"There, there, my dear! Although matters are not as we would wish, you have not been left entirely without resources. I am sure I will be able to make suitable arrangements for you."

Elizabeth lifted her head to look Josiah directly in the eye. "I truly appreciate your desire to spare me, but I should like to know exactly how much I have at my disposal."

Josiah hesitated a moment before drawing a resigned breath and fishing inside his breast pocket. He unfolded a piece of paper, scanned it carefully and then cleared his throat. "In addition to some minor items of inconsequential value, you have clear title to two able-bodied slaves as well as to a one-hundred-sixty-acre lot in Indian Territory which Samuel won in the 1832 land lottery. I would strongly advise you to liquidate the better part of those assets. You could, I am quite certain, make do with the services of the female slave alone."

"Jephtha and Dolly are husband and wife," Elizabeth cut in sharply. "Selling either of them is out of the question."

Josiah's mustache-framed lips pursed, but apparently Elizabeth's forbidding expression warned him against arguing the issue further. "Very well. If you wish to feed yet another mouth, you have every right to do so. That leaves the land lot."

"How much is it worth?" Elizabeth asked.

Josiah seemed caught off guard by her blunt question. He stroked his abundant whiskers for a moment before replying. "I truly cannot say. The title lists some improvements, but it is impossible to establish their value without an actual inspection of the property. For all we know, the tract could be an uncleared patch of wilderness, the house on it no more than a pitiful cabin. I assume Samuel at one time visited his lot?"

"Yes, shortly after we were engaged. I remember his saying that the soil appeared fertile. He wasn't able to ride over the property, however, since the Indians were still living there and understandably not very friendly. In any case, he couldn't legally take possession of the lot until the Indians moved away."

"No, of course not," Josiah agreed with the faintest hint of sarcasm. "Did he make any effort to claim it later?"

Elizabeth shook her head. "When we were first married, Samuel occasionally talked of trying his hand at farming, but after we settled here he gave up the idea. He was determined to make the most of what he saw as a great opportunity in Auraria. He remained convinced that the gold rush would make this town one of the most prosperous in Georgia. With a stake in the Brush Creek operation and a law practice catering to miners, he hoped that we would share in that prosperity." She fell silent, unable to continue the litany of once-bright dreams gone painfully awry.

"What is done is done," Josiah proclaimed philosophically. "At least the lot is not mortgaged, so you are free to keep whatever you may get for it."

Elizabeth half nodded, but said nothing. For the moment the prospect of finding a buyer for a piece of land she had never even seen seemed overwhelming.

Josiah took his time finishing the cup of tea, his broad brow furrowed in thought. Then he sighed wearily. "Out of duty to my departed brother and to you, the beloved wife he has left behind, I would be willing to undertake a journey to inspect Samuel's holding in Indian Territory and then solicit potential buyers." He cleared his throat. "Mind you, Elizabeth, I do not wish to raise false hopes. However, *if* the lot proves to be of acceptable value and *if* the Indian tenants are no longer in residence or can be persuaded to vacate without undue effort, I myself might consider buying the land from you."

"Would I receive enough to pay for this house and put a bit aside?" Elizabeth tried to restrain the expectant note creeping into her voice.

"As I said, I cannot, in good conscience, offer you assurances that may later prove to be unfounded," Josiah replied cagily. When Elizabeth looked down at her hands, tightly clasped on her lap, he adopted a more encouraging tone. "There, now, dear Elizabeth. Should the sale be viable, you will have, at the very least, enough to satisfy your remaining debts."

Elizabeth looked up to fix him with her steady gray eyes. "I need enough to buy this house, Josiah."

"I know this was the last home that you and Samuel shared and, as such, no doubt holds great sentimental value for you," Josiah began indulgently. "But as time heals the wounds of your loss, you will begin to feel differently. Surely an accomplished lady such as yourself would be happier living among folk of her own station than in this rustic, backwoods community. You have a sister in Savannah, do you not?"

"I would prefer not to depend on my relatives for my keep."

"You must be realistic, Elizabeth." A distinct edge had abruptly replaced the oily solicitude in Josiah's voice. "I have done my best to hold Samuel's creditors at bay while sparing you the necessities for a decent life. If I may be allowed some modest acknowledgment, it has been a most trying task. Bluntly put, you now have the furnishings in this house, a trap and a sound horse to pull it, two slaves and a land lot in Cherokee territory. Of those possessions, only the slaves and the lot are of any real value. Since you are unwilling to part with the slaves, you are left with the lot to insure you some security in the future. As I see matters, you have no choice but to sell it, if not to me, then to someone who will give you a fair and reasonable price."

"I understand, Josiah." Elizabeth lifted her chin to meet his gaze. Just as he had so often blustered at Samuel, he was now trying to intimidate her, and she was determined not to be cowed. "Before I make any decisions, however, I would like some time to think."

Bracing his hands on his knees, Josiah prepared to rise. "I have offered my help, Elizabeth, and should you desire to accept it, I will make good. But let me warn you, your funds are rapidly diminishing. If you must think, then I advise you to do so quickly." He stood, then collected his gloves and hat.

Elizabeth followed him into the hall. As she held the front door open, she swallowed her annoyance enough to thank Josiah for his call.

"I will write you as soon as I have considered everything carefully," she promised.

Josiah made no comment but only adjusted the brim of his hat to shade his face from the afternoon sun. "Good day, Elizabeth." His parting smile, while cordial, suggested that he considered her logic as faulty as Samuel's had been.

Elizabeth watched the robust figure cross the muddy road and then stride purposefully toward the public house. She closed the door and leaned her back against the cool surface. By now she should have developed some resilience to the effects of Josiah's visits, but his calls never failed to leave her feeling drained, as if her dignity were being eroded along with her meager funds. For all his professions of concern, Elizabeth suspected that Josiah would be only too happy to dispose of her property, parcel her off to her relatives and be done with matters.

Elizabeth pushed away from the door and walked slowly back to the cupboard-size room that had been Samuel's office. Pulling the cane-bottom chair away from the desk, she seated herself next to the window. Through the wavy glass she could see the mountains rising behind the irregular row of unpainted buildings that constituted Auraria's commercial center. The rhododendron and dogwood were at their peak now, embellishing the sober green slopes with flashes of red, pink and the purest white.

She remembered their first spring in Auraria, when life had seemed as full of promise as the verdant earth shaking off its winter mantle. One by one, like fading blossoms, Elizabeth had watched those promises wither and die. The heady gold fever that had lured droves of fortune seekers into the mountains in the early thirties had subsided, leaving a few men richer and many more in debt. Samuel's law practice, which had at first thrived on the legal needs of the prospectors, soon felt the pinch. Brush Creek, like so many of the mines, became a voracious maw in the earth, de-

vouring its owners' funds but offering little in return. Far
from the bustling town that Samuel had envisioned, Auraria had never developed beyond a rough mining village,
its growth permanently stunted when nearby Dahlonega
became the county seat.

Seeing the anguish reflected on Samuel's eternally boyish
face, Elizabeth had countless times longed for magical
powers that could remake the world as he wished it to be,
and reward all his earnest, misguided endeavors. *Bring back
little Ned.* As the memory of the smiling, chubby face intruded on her thoughts, Elizabeth closed her eyes tightly.
She took a deep breath, laying the precious image to rest just
as she had so often tucked her dear little son into his cradle. If she thought about Ned she would start crying, and
she could not afford that indulgence right now.

The stiff black silk of her skirt rasped against the chair as
Elizabeth turned away from the window and pulled a
threadbare ledger from one of the desk's cubbyholes. She
opened the book in which Samuel had recorded everyday
domestic transactions along with comments about the
weather and politics. Leafing through the pages, she
scanned the neat backhand script until she found an entry
dated November 10, 1832.

> My great fortune to win a parcel in the lottery. Land lot
> number 179 near Woodard's Landing. Appears to have
> a favorable share on the Oostanaula River, but cannot
> be certain. With God's grace, I can only hope the land
> will prove productive.

Next to the entry Samuel had sketched an outline of the
surveyor's report that must have accompanied his lottery
winning, noting in his labored schoolboy's hand the loca-
tion of important landmarks.

For a long moment Elizabeth stared at the poignant rec-
ord of Samuel's unfailing optimism. *Land lot number 179.*
The designation was so terse and impersonal she could
hardly believe it described her most valuable possession, one
on which her entire future depended. As she closed the
ledger Elizabeth realized she would not rest if she entrusted

the disposition of the tract to Josiah or anyone else. Daunting as the undertaking seemed, she would travel into Indian Territory and see the land for herself. Beyond that, like Samuel, she could only hope.

Chapter One

⚜

"Whoa up there, Midnight!" Jephtha's resonant voice punctuated the steady rattle of the trap's wheels.

As the carriage rolled to a halt Elizabeth exchanged anxious looks with Dolly, who sat across from her in the stuffy cabin, darning socks. In the three days since they had set out from Auraria, both women had learned to dread any unexpected interruption of their progress. They rarely traveled more than a few miles—or so it seemed to Elizabeth—without stopping to clear the road of a fallen tree or to heave the trap free of the muddy ruts. When Jephtha's lean, dark face appeared in the door's window Elizabeth steeled herself to confront the latest obstacle.

"Is something wrong?" she asked, resting one hand on the edge of the window.

A bemused smile flickered on Jephtha's lips. "No, ma'am, not exactly. Just looks to me like we've gone far enough." Catching Elizabeth's puzzled expression, he unlatched the door and helped her alight. Before turning back to the road he offered his wife a hand as she stepped to the ground. "See, ma'am? That's the river up yonder." He pointed to a gray-green channel just visible through the close trees flanking the road. When Elizabeth continued to frown, he went on. "It's the Oostanaula, sure as anything."

For a moment Elizabeth could only stare at the river glistening in the distance. As she registered the full impact of Jephtha's pronouncement, however, she grabbed the leather satchel lying on the carriage seat and pulled out the ledger tucked inside it. She had pored over Samuel's rendering of the surveyor's plat so often, the ledger immediately fell open to the desired page. Elizabeth studied the inked outline for a few moments before looking up at her companions.

"Woodard's Landing should lie directly ahead. As far as I can tell from the survey, the ferry marks the northwest corner of the lot. The northeast tip appears to be close to a wide bend in the river." Elizabeth felt a flutter of excitement at the thought that only a short distance separated them from their destination. Not waiting for Jephtha's assistance, she scrambled back into the trap, with Dolly close behind her.

As they continued on their way Elizabeth hovered at the window, eagerly taking in the landscape. Presently the wall of evergreen and hardwood yielded to a cultivated field, bounded by a split-rail fence. A breeze blowing off the river gently swayed the green stalks of corn, filling the air with the ripe scent of rich alluvial soil. Not far from the water's edge stood a two-story log building flanked by a rough stone chimney. A stand of pin oaks shaded both the rustic structure and the cattle grazing lazily in a nearby pen. Innumerable hoofprints pocked the bank sloping down to the dock where a large flat-bottomed boat was moored.

As Jephtha drove past the log house a heavyset man dressed in homespun appeared on the front porch. His black eyes narrowed slightly, following the trap's progress with the keenness of a hunter stalking prey. Even from the distance, Elizabeth could read the bitter, unspoken reproach in his gaze. Under the terms of the last treaty the Cherokees had ceded the remainder of their land that Georgia had long contested and agreed to relocate west of the Mississippi River by the middle of next year. Not until her journey into Indian Territory, however, had Elizabeth realized how few of them had yet acted on the treaty. To judge from those Cherokees she had recently encountered, even fewer were happy with the prospect.

When Elizabeth spotted a narrow road curving off from the main thoroughfare she signaled Jephtha to rein in the horse. She consulted Samuel's ledger, still open on her lap, before leaning her head out the window. "Turn here, Jephtha, and let's see if we can find the house."

For a few hundred yards or so the road cut through dense woodland. Elizabeth was beginning to fear, as Josiah had cautioned, that the tract consisted mainly of unbroken virgin land when the road opened onto a clearing. Unlike the well-tended farmland bordering the ferry station, however, the fields were overgrown with brush and sawbriars. On one side of the road a sizable orchard had deteriorated into a tangle of unpruned peach trees choked with vines. Through the screen of fruit trees Elizabeth spotted an abandoned wagon, its wooden skeleton bleached gray by the elements. The remains of a rail fence separated the orchard from the moss-carpeted yard leading up to the house. As the trap creaked to a stop Elizabeth surveyed the two-story building, its once-proud facade now blighted by broken windows and sagging shutters.

"One thing's for certain. Any folks who lived here have been gone a good long while," Dolly remarked, mirroring Elizabeth's thoughts.

Elizabeth nodded in agreement. "It surely appears so." As she climbed out of the carriage she instinctively lowered her voice to avoid disturbing the hush that cloaked the deserted yard.

Turning slowly in a circle, Elizabeth took stock of her surroundings. Although suffering from neglect, the property Samuel had won in the lottery was not only cleared but also had once been an impressive farm. Best of all, its former owners had apparently accepted their compensation and moved on, leaving the place available for occupation. For a moment Elizabeth was unable to believe her good fortune. She felt as if a benevolent hand had suddenly swept down from the heavens and lifted the enormous burden oppressing her.

"Looks like there's a barn and maybe a smokehouse 'round back. Want me to drive on so you can have a look, Miss Elizabeth?" Jephtha asked.

"I'd like to see the house first. Why don't you water Midnight and then see what else you can find on the property?" Elizabeth suggested.

Leaving Jephtha to fill the hollowed-out log anchored beside the well, Elizabeth turned back to the house. Despite the absence of any signs of occupation, she tapped lightly on the door and waited a few irrationally tense seconds before pushing it open. A shaft of afternoon sunlight cut through the gloom, illuminating the thick dust clinging to the air.

With her usual levelheaded practicality Dolly walked quickly across the room, fanning dust away from her nose while she pulled open the drapes that covered the tall windows. As light flooded into the room, Elizabeth was surprised to see a settee and three chairs still arranged in front of the hearth. A Seth Thomas clock stood on the mantel, its graceful black hands frozen at eight minutes past four. Beside the wing chair lay a basket with its lid cocked to reveal neat balls of yarn and a pair of knitting needles.

Elizabeth followed Dolly into the adjacent room to discover yet another tableau preserved beneath a layer of dust. An uneasiness began to creep over her as she walked around the long table lined with ladder-back chairs. It was almost as if she could feel the presence of the people who had once gathered here to share meals, laughter, the ordinary yet precious conversations of everyday life.

"There's a big kitchen, Miss Elizabeth, as fine as you could want!" she heard Dolly call from somewhere behind the house.

Elizabeth glanced out the back door at the square brick outbuilding before returning to the hall. As she gathered her skirts and started up the stairs she tried to shake the somber mood that had gradually supplanted her initial jubilation. Every room held tangible evidence of the previous occupants' lives, making her feel more like an intruder than the rightful owner of the house. According to the treaty's advocates, of whom Samuel had been an enthusiastic if passive member, the Cherokees who had agreed to relocate had received generous compensation for their property. To judge from the quantity and personal nature of the possessions these people had left behind, however, their departure could not have been free of heartbreak.

The upstairs bedrooms had been stripped of their essentials, with only easily replaced items or those too bulky for transport remaining. When Elizabeth spied a doll lying facedown beside a washstand, she knelt to examine the cast-off plaything. The heart-shaped lips and one of the eyes painted on the porcelain face had almost disappeared, erased, no doubt, by the loving touch of small hands. Elizabeth rested the sawdust figure on her lap and gently smoothed its white muslin frock. A cavalcade of wrenching images flooded her mind, of a little girl too young to understand the turmoil engulfing her family, of beds dismantled, dressers emptied, the accumulation of a lifetime reduced to what would fit on a wagon or two. In the harsh process of separating the necessary from the expendable, or perhaps only in the haste of departure, the child's doll had been left behind.

"What are you doing here?" a masculine voice suddenly demanded from behind her.

Elizabeth started, almost losing her balance. As she scrambled to her feet the doll fell to the floor, its china head rattling against the bare wood. Her heart still racing, Elizabeth faced the tall man standing in the door. Although anyone in possession of his senses could see that he had frightened her out of her wits, the stranger's uncongenial expression suggested that she would wait in vain for an apology.

"I might ask the same of you, sir." Elizabeth lifted her chin, the better to meet the man's cold, appraising gaze.

For a scant second a flicker of surprise broke the opaque dark surface of his eyes. He made no reply, however, only continuing to regard her as if she were a thief caught in the act. Although annoyance had momentarily overridden her fright, Elizabeth noticed, with some uneasiness, how his lithe, well-proportioned figure filled the doorway, effectively preventing escape. The man's strong features and warm complexion readily identified him as a Cherokee, and, to judge by his unfriendly mien, one who resented her presence in his country. Telling herself that Jephtha and Dolly could not have wandered too far, she fought back the nervousness threatening to undermine her defiant expression. When he abruptly pushed away from the door she forced herself to stand her ground.

With deliberate, even steps, the man slowly circled her. Elizabeth turned to follow his movement. Despite his un-gentlemanly manner, there was nothing coarse in his appearance. A straight, high-bridged nose, well-defined cheekbones and a firm chin were arranged in classical symmetry, lending his face both strength and refinement. His eyes were wide set, their sable depth matched by the luxuriant hair brushed carelessly back from his brow. With his sculpted features and copper-hued complexion he reminded Elizabeth of a graceful bronze statue, the work of a Renaissance master come to life.

Elizabeth caught herself and then glanced at the door, calculating the distance. When she suddenly dashed toward the hall, however, the man cleared the room in a few agile strides to block her exit. Elizabeth stared at the arm braced in the doorway, and for a brief moment she considered trying to shove past him. The taut muscles bared by his rolled-up sleeve warned, however, that her attempt would be futile.

He was standing so close to her Elizabeth feared he could detect the furious pumping of her heart. Sensing that he would be quick to exploit any sign of weakness, she managed to mask her tension behind a glare. "I will thank you, sir, to step aside and allow me to pass."

The sturdy arm relaxed slightly, albeit without surrendering control of the door. "And I will thank you, madam, for a civil answer to a civil question," the man retorted without the slightest hint of contrition.

Elizabeth drew herself up and succeeded in bringing her eyes to his broad chest. "This house belongs to me. And the one hundred sixty acres surrounding it," she added, trying to lend weight to her authority.

"By way of the land lottery, no doubt."

Elizabeth stiffened at the contempt in his voice. "Sir, I am accustomed neither to receiving strangers in my home nor to tolerating their insults. If you do not comport yourself as a gentleman, I shall have to see you off my property." She made the threat without the faintest notion of how she might carry through with it. To her relief, however, the vague hint of a smile eased the implacable cast of her opponent's face, and he dropped his arm to his side. Rather than bolt and risk another confrontation, Elizabeth decided to press her momentary advantage. "I should like the courtesy of an introduction."

"Please forgive my lapse." Although his tone had lost none of its mocking undercurrent, the man's dark eyes betrayed a newfound respect. "Ethan Woodard, madam. I farm the spread just to the south of yours, so I suppose that makes us neighbors." He affected a polite nod, along with another half smile. "May I have the pleasure of your acquaintance?"

"Mrs. Samuel Merriweather," Elizabeth replied primly, feeling as if she was making a major concession. "Now if you don't mind, Mr. Woodard," she continued in an effort to regain ground, "I have business to attend to."

"So do I, Mrs. Merriweather." When she made for the hall, Ethan Woodard shifted to rest one shoulder against the door. He left enough room for her to sidle past him, but only if she was willing to wedge herself between his muscular body and the doorframe. "If you can direct me to Mr. Merriweather, I shan't trouble you further."

"My husband is deceased," Elizabeth told him.

Woodard straightened himself. "I'm sorry." To Elizabeth's surprise he sounded as if he meant it. He hesitated a moment, as if he were unsure of what to do next. "And you've inherited his lottery winning," he murmured, almost to himself.

Elizabeth nodded briefly. "Mr. Woodard, I assure you I have no interest in any land other than that which my late husband won in the lottery," she began, anticipating the issue Ethan Woodard had come to settle. "I only wish to assess my property and then return home to dispose of it." When Woodard said nothing she glanced around the barren room. "My husband was careful to abide by the terms of the treaty, but by all appearances the people who lived here moved away some time ago. While I can certainly understand your feelings—"

"Can you, Mrs. Merriweather?" Woodard cut in, the caustic edge in his voice honed anew. "The man who lived in *your* house and farmed *your* land was my cousin. We grew up together here, just as our fathers had before us. My ancestors knew *your* fields when they were still covered with forests full of game, before the trappers and soldiers and settlers swarmed into this country." He shook his head, his shapely mouth drawing into a humorless smile. "No, Mrs. Merriweather, I don't believe you can understand how I feel."

Elizabeth felt the color rise to her face at his accusation—all the more so because she knew it was true. She wanted to say something that would exempt her from Woodard's sweeping condemnation, make her own role in the terrible, tragic story of relations between native Indians and white settlers seem less contemptible. But what could she say? Argue as she might about Samuel's scrupulous adherence to the treaty's terms or her own desperate need, one undeniable truth remained—given any real choice, Ethan Woodard's cousin would never have abandoned his farm.

Woodard cleared his throat, causing Elizabeth to brace for another diatribe. To her relief, however, he turned to go. Pausing in the hall, he looked back at her. "How long will you be here?"

"At most, another day," Elizabeth replied, although now even that brief time seemed far too long.

"Then we must settle our business tomorrow."

Elizabeth frowned. "What business can you mean, Mr. Woodard?"

Woodard tilted his head to one side, regarding her dubiously. "Why, the ferry, of course."

Elizabeth shook her head. "I am afraid I don't know what you mean, Mr. Woodard." Although she had quickly connected the handsome Cherokee's name with that of the nearby landing, she was at a loss to understand what bearing the ferry could have on Samuel's land lot.

"Perhaps you've been misled by the surveyor's plat, Mrs. Merriweather," Woodard suggested with undisguised skepticism. "I hate to disappoint a lady, but you are mistaken on at least one count. Not all of your lottery win has been abandoned by the original occupants."

"But you just told me that your cousin moved away," Elizabeth protested.

"Jonathan did, but I am still here." Woodard smiled, taking obvious pleasure in her consternation. "And as long as I remain, the ferry is not entirely yours."

"I don't know anything about a ferry," Elizabeth sputtered in exasperation. "Would you please explain what you're talking about?"

"Prior to the land lottery, the state of Georgia dispatched a team of surveyors to the Cherokee Nation to divide the land into precise one-hundred-sixty-acre lots," Woodard began in the perfunctory tone of a weary educator. "The process took no account of existing boundaries, the only consideration being to cut the land into neat parcels. By chance one border line of your land lot happened to fall across a certain ferry, commonly known as Woodard's Landing. That means, Mrs. Merriweather, that part of *my* ferry is sitting on *your* land lot."

Elizabeth was so stunned by the revelation she could only stare at Woodard in disbelief.

"Don't worry," Woodard assured her. "I will be more than happy to sell my portion to you. We need only establish a fair price."

"But I don't have any money," Elizabeth gasped without thinking.

The hint of a smile creased Woodard's lean face. "That, Mrs. Merriweather, is your problem." Without another word he turned and disappeared down the hall.

"There, now, don't fret so, ma'am." Dolly put aside the pillow she was fluffing to lay a comforting hand on Elizabeth's arm. "Mr. Merriweather can surely settle this matter with the ferry."

"Yes, I suppose so," Elizabeth conceded. She sighed as she smoothed the folded quilt that would be her bed for the night. "But I did so want to manage the lot without having to ask Josiah's help," she added wistfully.

"Will you be needing anything else for the night?" Dolly asked, holding her candle aloft to survey the empty bedroom.

Elizabeth shook her head. "No, thank you, Dolly." She smiled at the young woman standing in the half-open door. "Good night."

The candlelight softened the angles of Dolly's thin face. "You sleep well now, Miss Elizabeth, and don't worry about that ferry. Everything will work out fine in the end."

Elizabeth gave Dolly an assuring nod. Long after the housekeeper's light footsteps had disappeared down the hall, however, she sat on the folded quilt, her back propped against the wall. Elizabeth stared at the quivering aureole of candlelight spreading across the floor, trying to sort through her problems.

Dolly, of course, was right. With the lot indisputably valuable and available for sale, Josiah would be more than happy to step in and handle the affair for her. As a successful attorney, he possessed both the negotiating skills and the necessary funds to see the matter to a satisfactory conclusion. He had managed to navigate through the financial morass surrounding Brush Creek Mine, and Elizabeth was certain he could come to terms with Ethan Woodard. For some reason, however, she was reluctant to surrender the land lot's fate into her brother-in-law's hands.

Although Elizabeth hesitated to suspect Josiah of outright duplicity, her conversation with Ethan Woodard had raised troubling questions in her mind. Since Josiah had possession of all Samuel's financial documents, he had surely seen the original land lot title. Why, then, had he cast doubts on the value of the property and its improvements? According to Woodard, the ferry was plainly indicated on the survey. Try as she might to give Josiah the benefit of the doubt, Elizabeth could not believe that such an astute businessman would overlook one of the lot's most valuable features.

Elizabeth was faced with a conclusion that was as inevitable as it was disconcerting: Josiah had deliberately kept her in the dark regarding the land lot's value. And had she not visited the property herself, she reflected, she would have remained ignorant, dependent on his appraisal and advice. Josiah would have gallantly stepped in and taken the lot off her hands, and she would have been grateful for whatever pittance he chose to give her for it.

Pulling her legs up beneath the skirt of her nightdress, Elizabeth rested her chin on her knees and considered her dilemma. She could enlist Josiah's aid in settling with Ethan Woodard, knowing full well that he would put his own interests above hers. Or she could deal with Woodard herself. If their first encounter was any indication, he would drive a hard bargain. He seemed honest, however, direct to a fault, and Elizabeth sensed that despite his abrupt manner, he was not an unkind man. For a moment she conjured the memory of his lean, handsome face, and the gentle look in his dark eyes, as fleeting as it was intense, when he had learned that she was widowed.

Turning to one side, Elizabeth cupped her hand around the candle's flame. She had followed her intuition and traveled into Indian Territory to see the lot firsthand. In that instance, her impulse had been for the better. Now she would simply have to trust her instincts once more. Tomorrow morning she would speak with Ethan Woodard and try to strike a bargain concerning the ferry. Leaning over the fluctuating spark, Elizabeth blew softly and plunged the room into darkness.

Chapter Two

"You're sure you don't want me to come along with you, ma'am?" As Jephtha tethered the reins to the trap's whip-stand, he eyed the two-story frame house with undisguised misgiving.

Elizabeth shook her head. "No, that won't be necessary. And in any case, I shan't be long. Either Mr. Woodard and I will be able to reach an agreement, or we will not."

Privately, Elizabeth wished the challenge of dealing with Ethan Woodard was as simple as she had made it sound. She gave Jephtha a quick smile, as much to bolster her own confidence as to reassure him, before walking resolutely up the path to the house. As Elizabeth mounted the steps to the veranda she tried to ignore the tickling sensation inside her stomach. Perhaps she should have yielded to Dolly's urging and had some breakfast before setting out for Woodard's farm. She had been too eager to approach him as early as she decently could, however, to squander time eating. In truth, she doubted if even Dolly's biscuits and grits could have stilled the nervous flutter nagging her.

Elizabeth tightened the bow that secured her black velvet bonnet before rapping on the door. She inclined her head slightly, straining to detect any sound inside the house. Nothing stirred on the other side of the door. Frowning, Elizabeth hesitated a second before knocking once more. She was beginning to fear that Woodard had already embarked on his daily chores when she heard booted feet charging down stairs.

The door flew open so abruptly Elizabeth flinched in spite of herself. For a very long moment she could only stare at Ethan Woodard, stripped to the waist with water dripping from his black hair down his shoulders.

To judge from the look on Woodard's face, he was equally surprised by the apparition he had discovered framed in the doorway. "What are you doing here?" he blurted out.

"I thought I answered that question yesterday, Mr. Woodard." Elizabeth glanced down, in part to conceal the smile that threatened to undermine her serious expression, in part to focus on something other than the broad, well-muscled chest that stood in her direct line of vision. Forcing her eyes to skim over the tanned skin glistening with moisture, she looked up into his face. "I came to discuss the ferry. If you would prefer, I can return at a more convenient time." Her gaze traveled inadvertently to his taut midriff, and she caught herself.

Woodard blinked as only a man who is rarely caught off guard can. "No, no need for that. Uh, come in. Please." He stepped back, gesturing toward the room behind him. "If you could give me a minute—" He broke off to brush a lock of wet hair from his forehead.

Elizabeth nodded. "Certainly, Mr. Woodard."

Ethan Woodard took a few steps backward before wheeling to dash up the stairs. As his hurried steps sounded overhead, Elizabeth took the opportunity to survey her surroundings.

The room was so large that Elizabeth guessed it had once comprised the entire house, with additional rooms added to the original structure over time. A wooden settle and three chairs were arranged in front of the hewn-stone fireplace that filled almost an entire wall. To judge from the articles displayed on the hearth—a three-legged Dutch oven, a coffeepot resting on a trivet, and a tangle of leather and chain that must have been some sort of harness—the room accommodated a number of activities. In contrast to the rustically utilitarian appearance of the hearth area, the opposite end of the room was furnished with a fine cherrywood desk, two glass-fronted bookcases and a wing chair upholstered in an English screen print. Elizabeth was stooping to examine the volumes lining the bookcase shelves when she heard Ethan Woodard on the stairs. She turned just as he appeared in the door.

"I'm sorry to have kept you waiting, Mrs. Merriweather." Woodard adjusted the open collar of his blue linen shirt as he walked across the room.

"You've no need to apologize, Mr. Woodard." When he joined her beside the bookcases Elizabeth took a small step back, lifting her chin to compensate for the considerable difference in their respective heights. "I would like to make you an offer concerning the ferry."

Woodard's smile revealed a narrow sliver of perfect white teeth. "And what might that be?"

Elizabeth was clutching her purse so tightly her fingers were almost numb inside the tight kid gloves. She took a deep breath, willing her hands to relax. "I should like to sell you my share." When Woodard began to shake his head she quickly went on. "I would be willing to part with it for a very reasonable price."

Woodard's low chuckle was more bitter than amused. "I've made some foolish decisions in my life, Mrs. Merriweather, but I've more sense than to buy a piece of property to which I'll have no legal claim after May of next year. No, ma'am, I fear any buying is going to be on your part, not mine."

Elizabeth licked her lips. "I see. Then how much do you want for your part of the ferry?"

"I've no wish to inflate the worth of my property, Mrs. Merriweather," Woodard replied. "I'm willing to accept the value established by the government's appraiser."

"And how much is that?" Elizabeth prompted.

"Come now, Mrs. Merriweather," Woodard chided. "Surely you've examined your own lottery papers more carefully than that."

Elizabeth bristled at his cynical tone. "I have never even seen the lottery papers."

Woodard regarded her skeptically. "Somehow you found your way to the lot. You had to have had some indication—"

"My brother-in-law is executor of my late husband's will and, as such, has possession of all his important papers," Elizabeth interrupted. "I was able to locate the lot by referring to a sketch that my husband had drawn in his personal ledger."

For a moment Ethan Woodard only stared at her in disbelief. "So you really had no idea that part of the ferry was on your lot?"

Elizabeth shook her head. "Not until yesterday."

Still frowning, Woodard ran his fingers through the damp hair falling over his brow. Then he turned to the desk and opened one of its drawers. After riffling through a few papers, he pulled out an official-looking document and handed it to Elizabeth.

"You can see where the federal appraiser stated the value of the ferry. Ten thousand dollars." Elizabeth could feel the warmth emanating from Woodard's robust body as he leaned over her shoulder to point out an entry on the list of improvements. "For all practical purposes the land lot boundary cuts the landing in half."

Elizabeth studied the document for a few moments before handing it back to Woodard. "How much are you asking for the portion on your land? Five thousand dollars?" She felt bound to ask, although she already knew the answer.

"That's what the property is worth." Woodard was bent over the desk, his back turned to Elizabeth as he returned the appraisal to the drawer.

"I cannot afford to buy it." Elizabeth was startled by the effort required to utter those six simple words.

Woodard straightened himself abruptly, wheeling to face her. Beneath the wave of black hair his brow furrowed in frustration. "That ferry sits on one of the busiest roads in the Territory, Mrs. Merriweather. After next year this country will be flooded with settlers, and whoever owns the ferry stands to profit handsomely by seeing them safely across the Oostanaula. Whatever you pay now, rest assured you will more than recover it later."

"That may well be true, Mr. Woodard. But the fact remains. I do not have any money. The land lot is all I have."

Elizabeth instantly regretted the admission she was now powerless to retract. She had come to bargain with Ethan Woodard, not beg for his sympathy, and she was determined to conclude their discussion with her self-respect intact. She looked away before her eyes could betray her wounded pride.

Ethan Woodard took a step toward Elizabeth and then hesitated. He seemed as confounded as she by the impasse in their negotiations. No doubt he had been counting on selling his part of the ferry for a tidy sum to help establish himself in the West. That the land-lot's owner had proved to be an impecunious widow must have been a sore disappointment to him.

"I can't afford to sell my share for less than it's worth." Woodard sounded annoyed, whether with her or with the defensiveness revealed in his voice, Elizabeth was uncertain.

"Nor would I expect you to." Elizabeth tugged the drawstring of her purse, pulling the woven cord into a tight knot. She looked Woodard directly in the eye. "I will not waste any more of your time. Good day, Mr. Woodard." Gathering her skirts, she turned and walked out the door before Ethan Woodard could say another word.

"This whiskey is sour enough to poison a hog!" Ethan recoiled from the demijohn he had just uncorked, scowling in disgust.

Gray Bear stooped to sniff the open decanter before delicately skimming the bottle's neck with one callused finger. He tasted the film of amber liquid clinging to his finger, his lined face a study in concentration. Then he shrugged. "Bad whiskey, but not the first old Gilmer has sold you."

"It will be the last," Ethan vowed. He replaced the cork in the demijohn with a firm smack, not unlike the treatment he would have relished giving the scurrilous peddler's balding head.

Gray Bear reached for the broom he had propped beside the public house's bar. "Gilmer is a cheat, but at least he is fair. He cheats white folks and Indians all the same," he commented as he resumed his task. "What kind of woman is this one?'' Gray Bear's head jerked in the general direction of Jonathan's abandoned farm.

Ethan grimaced at the tub of unwashed tankards and dishes that had been accumulating beneath the bar for the past several days. ''Decent enough. She's widowed, claims to have no money. I don't know.'' He broke off, annoyed with himself for indulging Gray Bear's sly curiosity. He rounded the bar to boot a discarded bone in front of his helper's broom. ''This place is a disgrace. No wonder Gilmer thinks he can unload his rotten mess on us.''

Gray Bear obligingly swept the bone aside, but his stoic expression remained unfazed. ''When Chewani worked for you, this was a fine public house. Too bad she moved west. I am a ferryman, not a barmaid.'' He gave the pile of debris another nudge toward the door. ''What will happen when this woman buys the ferry?''

''Nothing. She isn't going to buy it.'' Ethan was crouched behind the bar, wrestling a keg into place. When the even scratching of Gray Bear's broom abruptly ceased, he peeked over the edge of the bar. ''I'll finish up here. Why don't you see how much damage Major Culley's bull did to the boat when you ferried it over yesterday?''

Gray Bear hesitated for a moment, torn between the appeal of more agreeable chores and the opportunity to glean further gossip from Ethan. Apparently Ethan's forbidding expression was enough to convince him that the latter was now a lost cause. After parking the broom beside the door, he trudged out of the tavern.

Of course, Gray Bear had every right to wonder about the future of the ferry, Ethan reflected as he cut the rope securing a smoked ham to one of the rafters. His old friend had overseen the ferry's operation for years, since the days when Ethan's father had returned from the Creek wars to build his homestead into one of the most prosperous farms in the Cherokee Nation. Ethan suspected that for Gray Bear, as much as for himself, the ferry was more than an improvement, reduced to a crude dollar value by the white man's appraiser. Woodard's Landing represented a way of life, a history they both shared, one that was now threatened with oblivion. They had both dreaded the inevitable day when a white settler would arrive to lay claim to his lottery winning.

Ethan and Gray Bear had often discussed the matter, sitting on the public house's sagging steps while the older man smoked his evening pipe. For a long time Ethan had prepared himself to face down any ruffian bent on harassing him from the land. He had not, however, been prepared for Mrs. Samuel Merriweather.

Ethan frowned as he placed the salt-caked ham in a crock and then poured cold water over it. For some perverse reason he almost wished that Mrs. Merriweather had descended on the land with a retinue of armed male relatives, ready to do battle. At least then he would have known exactly what she had in mind. Instead, she had arrived without fanfare or arms, accompanied only by her driver and a maid. Her reaction to his challenge had been equally unexpected. She had neither scoffed at his claim nor retreated in fear, but had heard him out and tried to reach an agreement. Looking into her earnest gray eyes, he could almost believe that she took his land rights as seriously as those of any white man.

Without prompting, Ethan's memory invoked the perfect oval of her face, set like a delicate ivory-petaled flower against the black velvet bonnet. Not that anyone could accuse Mrs. Merriweather of insipid fashion-plate beauty; her features were far too distinct, too full of character to condemn her to mere conventional prettiness. Everything about her appearance—the wide, expressive mouth, the rich chestnut-brown hair and, most striking of all, those intense, deep gray eyes—seemed unique to her.

As if to extinguish his reverie, Ethan slopped the remaining fresh water onto the bar and began to scrub the scarred surface with a rag. He would do well not to waste time pondering Mrs. Merriweather's beauty—especially at the risk of clouding his judgment. Already he was reluctant to doubt her honesty, but her claim of being a poverty-stricken widow might be only a ruse designed to win concessions. Still, she had looked so sincere, so vulnerable when he had told her about the appraisal. Perhaps she really had been deceived by her husband's brother. Ethan had seen too many land-hungry opportunists to find that part of her story incredible. He could imagine the scoundrel counseling the desperate widow, feigning sympathy for her impoverishment while he schemed for possession of a land lot worth a small fortune.

Ethan wrung the dirty rag dry, venting his annoyance on the hapless piece of cloth. How much less worrisome everything would be if Mrs. Merriweather had simply paid him for his share of the ferry and been done with it. But she had not. Tomorrow she would drive back to her home, a sadder woman than when she had arrived, and he would be left to wait for the unprincipled in-law or speculator who managed to dupe her out of her title.

Throwing the spent rag aside in disgust, Ethan shoved open the bar's wooden gate and stormed out of the tavern.

"I'll have supper ready in no time, just as soon as I finish cleaning these fish Jephtha caught." Seated on the kitchen steps, Dolly looked up from the plump bass she was scaling to call to Elizabeth.

"I won't wander far," Elizabeth promised. "I just want to see a bit more of the land before we leave, and there will be no time tomorrow morning if we get a proper start."

Her exploration sanctioned by Dolly's good-natured nod, Elizabeth gathered her skirt and set off across the yard. She paused at the fence separating the derelict orchard from the road and considered the possibilities. Jephtha had returned from his fishing expedition to describe a lovely spring-fed pond frequented by numerous waterfowl. Without giving the matter further thought, Elizabeth climbed between the fence rails, intent on finding the pond. She waded through the high grass, forging a path across the overgrown pasture, until she reached a small knoll. Shading her eyes with one hand, she stopped to survey the rolling fields stretching down to the wide river.

It was hard to believe that this entire, great, fertile expanse of land, for as far as she could see, belonged to *her*. That only tomorrow she would be forced to abandon it forever struck her with such impact that she winced. Elizabeth pressed her lips together to quell the tremor that had seized them without warning. It served no purpose to let her thoughts linger on what might have been, she told herself sternly. She had done what she had set out to do—see the land lot and determine if it was vacant. With Ethan Woodard still occupying the tiny but critical corner of the lot, she now had no choice but to place the matter in Josiah's hands.

In spite of her resolute intentions, Elizabeth could not hold back the tears welling in her eyes. If she must cry, then best to do it here where no one could see her, she thought, fiercely wiping the moisture from her cheek. As a painful lump began to fill her throat, she almost choked in her determination not to sob. She covered her eyes with both hands and took a deep breath, then held it a moment to calm herself. She was digging a handkerchief from her pocket when she noticed a man striding through the high grass toward her.

In the split second that Elizabeth recognized Ethan Woodard she almost turned and ran. His long legs had cleared the field so quickly, however, that she could not hope to flee without making a fool of herself. Resigned to facing her adversary once more, Elizabeth hastily blotted her face with the handkerchief and tried to compose herself. She managed to slip the wad of damp linen into her pocket just as he reached the knoll.

Woodard pulled up a few paces short of Elizabeth, too close not to notice her reddened eyes. To her surprise he looked embarrassed. "I wanted to speak with you again," he began, looking away from her streaked face to the open field behind him. "Your maid said you had gone for a walk, and I was hoping to catch up with you."

Elizabeth nodded curtly before daring to test her voice. "Well, you have, Mr. Woodard."

Woodard frowned, cutting his eyes at her briefly before gazing off into the distance again. "I wanted to conclude our discussion this morning, but you marched out the door without giving me the chance." He had adopted an accusing tone, as if Elizabeth were somehow to blame for the awkward situation in which they now found themselves.

"I left because there was nothing further to discuss," Elizabeth told him flatly.

"No?" Woodard gave her an exasperated look.

"No." Elizabeth looked back into his dark eyes without blinking.

Woodard raked one hand through his thick hair and then jammed the hand into the pocket of his breeches. "For the life of me, Mrs. Merriweather, I can't understand why you don't want to reach some kind of agreement about the ferry."

Elizabeth was beginning to feel genuinely annoyed, a welcome sensation in the wake of her tears. "What I want has nothing to do with reality. Perhaps you do not believe me, but I have no money."

"I believe you," Woodard interposed hastily. "I'm surprised, though, that you haven't considered other possibilities."

Elizabeth's eyes narrowed in suspicion. "What do you mean?"

"Make the land earn money for you." Before Elizabeth could interrupt, Woodard went on, his handsome face suddenly earnest. "Think of it, Mrs. Merriweather. Why would anyone want this land?" His arm swept the air in an expansive gesture. "To farm it, fill these pastures with stock, reap its bounty."

"I know nothing of farming, Mr. Woodard." Elizabeth regarded him as if he had just suggested she sprout wings and take flight.

"Perhaps not," Woodard conceded. "But you could easily hire someone who did to manage it for you."

Now it was Elizabeth's turn to glance away to the far horizon. There must have been at least one hundred solid, irrefutable reasons to reject Ethan Woodard's preposterous suggestion, but for the moment she could think of only one. "Even if that were so, I still would not be able to pay you for the ferry for some time."

"Money isn't the only means of payment, Mrs. Merriweather," Woodard informed her.

Elizabeth's eyes darted from the shadow-mottled pasture to fix uncompromisingly on Woodard. "I am afraid I don't understand, Mr. Woodard."

A faint smile softened the lean angles of Woodard's face. "Have you never heard of barter?" An emotion Elizabeth preferred not to plumb surfaced in his dark eyes, a glimmer that was as brief as it was elusive. When she said nothing, he folded his arms across his chest in a matter-of-fact fashion. "I'll be frank with you, Mrs. Merriweather. I have a public house that is sadly in need of proper management. In truth, I doubt a respectable traveler would cross its threshold were he not in need of the ferry. My ferryman does the best he can with the place, but he's a fellow more accustomed to hard work in the outdoors than to cooking or seeing to the finer details of hospitality."

Woodard shifted his stance, hinting that he was about to get to the point. "Since neither of us can buy the other's share of the ferry, it seems to me we should make the best of owning it together. If you would be willing to manage the public house, I would apply your share of the profits to an eventual purchase of my part."

Elizabeth opened her mouth to speak, but appropriate words failed to materialize. She gave a short laugh for want of any better response. "What do I know about managing a public house?"

"More than Gray Bear, I'll warrant," Woodard retorted dryly.

Elizabeth's gaze darted around the dusky pasture, searching for some mooring to stay her rampant thoughts. Ethan Woodard must have lost his senses to make such an outlandish offer—and she hers for considering it. Yet, try as she might, Elizabeth could not think of a single reason to reject the prospect out of hand. She had kept a home running smoothly. Surely the same skills applied to operating a public house. And even if she proved woefully inept, what was her alternative? To take whatever Josiah saw fit to give her and then rely on relatives to keep a roof over her head.

"I cannot make any promises other than to do my best." Elizabeth almost could not believe what she had just said.

"That is the best anyone can do." For the first time since she had met him, Woodard's face broadened into a smile untinged by mockery. "So I have a partner?"

"I suppose so." Elizabeth felt a smile slowly replace the uncertain expression on her face.

"I'll take that to mean yes." Woodard stooped slightly to look up into her face. "I've only one other question, Mrs. Merriweather, but I fear I must have an answer before we can close our deal."

Elizabeth stiffened in surprise. Now that she had taken the leap of faith, she was dismayed to hear that a hidden obstacle loomed in her path. "What is that, Mr. Woodard?" she asked warily.

Like a single star against a midnight sky, a twinkle sparkled in Woodard's dark eyes. "Do you have a given name?"

"Elizabeth." She felt her own smile widen in unison with his.

"Very well, Elizabeth Merriweather. Are we in agreement?" He extended his hand, not taking his eyes from her face.

Elizabeth surrendered her hand to his warm, firm grasp. "Yes, Ethan Woodard. I think we are."

Chapter Three

"Steady, Belle! There's a lady." Ethan stroked the restive filly's neck, smoothing the tense muscles knotted beneath the silky bay coat. The young horse regarded him warily, her eyes rolling to reveal a wide rim of white, but she offered only slight resistance when he lifted her left foreleg. Bracing the animal's leg between his knees, Ethan placed the iron shoe on the neatly trimmed hoof and checked the fit.

"I've never seen a horse that could throw shoes faster than this one." Martin Early leaned against the stall partition and relaxed his hold on the filly's leather halter. "Trot her four miles, and she'll leave as many shoes along the way."

Ethan glanced up at his brother-in-law. "If you're thinking of selling her, I'd be happy to take her off your hands," he offered through the row of horseshoe nails he held clamped between his teeth.

Martin chuckled. "I'm sure you would, Ethan, you and every horse trader this side of the Oostanaula, but this beauty isn't for sale. I figure by the time she's learned her manners, Rebecca will be up to handling her."

Ethan tightened his grip on the filly's foot as a little girl dashed through the stable door, long dark braids swinging freely behind her. "That may be sooner than you think," he remarked with a smile.

Clambering onto the stall partition, the child rested her arms on the top rail. "There's a wagon coming up the river road, Papa! Ben and I saw it from way up in the apple tree," she announced proudly. "If it's Mr. Gilmer, maybe he'll have ribbons this time. You said I might have a new one."

"So I did, Rebecca. A satin ribbon, if you like," Martin agreed. When he reached to brush a stray wisp of hair from his daughter's brow, a tender expression relieved the strong angles of his face for a moment. "Why don't you see what sort of frippery old Gilmer has among his wares today? We'll be along as soon as Belle is shod."

Ethan glanced over his shoulder to see his niece swing to the straw-littered floor and scamper toward the door. "Let's hope Gilmer's ribbons and bows are a good bit finer than the whiskey he's stocked of late," he said.

"Gilmer's been peddling bad whiskey again?" Martin asked.

Without looking up from his task, Ethan nodded. "A mule skinner dying of thirst wouldn't drink the last lot he sold me."

Martin gave the halter a tug to quiet the restless young horse. "Noah Gilmer is no different from any other white man. He doesn't think he's made a good deal with an Indian unless he's managed to cheat." A biting edge sharpened his low-pitched voice.

"Perhaps, but the next time he leaves this ferry station, he's going to be carrying more whiskey and less money than when he arrived," Ethan vowed before expertly tapping the remaining horseshoe nail into place. As he released the filly's leg and straightened himself, he patted her shoulder. "She's ready to kick up her heels again," he declared, reaching for the waistcoat he had draped over the stall door.

Ethan pulled on his waistcoat as he followed his brother-in-law out to the stable yard. Rebecca had posted herself on the hitching rail to await the peddler's arrival. At the rumble of approaching wagon wheels, she jumped to the ground and rushed to the road's edge.

"Ben!" Rebecca waved to the flush-faced boy racing along the rutted thoroughfare. Her excited smile faded when a wagon drawn by a sleek black horse and a mule rolled into view.

Although the wagon was clearly not Noah Gilmer's lumbering conveyance, its bed was piled with an assortment of goods that rivaled the peddler's stock, both in variety and in their haphazard arrangement. Two bedsteads stood wedged between an upended rocking chair and a stoneware butter churn, buttressed by several barrels and an armoire. As the wagon's wheels bounced over the corrugated road, the armoire's door tipped open to reveal an interior crammed with cast-iron cookware and feather pillows. With every inch of the wagon bed devoted to cargo, the vehicle's human occupants sat squeezed together on the narrow driver's perch. A slender black man plied the reins with care in an obvious effort to spare his two female passengers unnecessary jolts. Even from the distance, Ethan immediately recognized the woman clad in widow's weeds as Elizabeth Merriweather.

Skipping to catch up with her brother, Rebecca retreated to the stable yard. "It isn't Mr. Gilmer after all," she told them with undisguised disappointment.

Martin scowled at the wagon slowly wending its way along the road. "Don't fret, Rebecca. Gilmer will be by any day now." He rested a hand on his daughter's shoulder, but his narrowed eyes remained trained on the interlopers.

"They're folks who have come to live in Cousin Jonathan's house," Ben provided, his brown eyes still bright from exertion. "The lady in black told me so." As the wagon drew even with them, he started to wave, but his father seized the child's hand in midair.

"Those who steal our land deserve no welcome," Martin reminded his son. Catching the bewildered look in the boy's eyes, he followed his gaze to Ethan who had just thrown up his hand to the passing wagon. "What are you doing?" Martin demanded.

"Waving to the tavern's new barmaid." Slowly lowering his hand to his side, Ethan faced his brother-in-law.

A man of strong opinions and equally formidable will, Martin Early was rarely at a loss for words. Ethan's unexpected revelation, however, had rendered him dumbfounded for the moment.

Not waiting for Martin to recover himself, Ethan loped across the yard to the road. When Elizabeth saw him, she

leaned to touch the driver lightly on the arm, signalling him
to halt.

"Hello, Ethan." She smiled, prompting him to wonder
how any woman could manage to look so shy and yet so
captivating at the same time.

"Hello, Elizabeth. I was wondering when you would
come back." Ethan's gaze followed her hand as she reached
to tuck in a lock of burnished chestnut hair that had escaped from the severe black bonnet.

"Setting my household in order required a few weeks."
Elizabeth glanced at the log building facing the road. "This
is your public house, then?"

Ethan nodded. "And yours to manage, whenever you're
ready."

Elizabeth straightened herself. "I can begin tomorrow, if
you like."

"If that suits you." Considering the many arduous miles
she had just traveled, Ethan had hardly expected her to
plunge into her new duties without delay. To judge from the
determined look in her gray eyes, however, Elizabeth would
have resisted any arguments to the contrary. "I'll tell Gray
Bear to expect you in the morning."

Ethan backed away from the wagon, still smiling up at
Elizabeth. He waited until the driver had urged the team into
a walk before returning to the stable yard. Martin was still
standing by the hitching post with the two children, watching the scene with unsmiling eyes.

"What can you be thinking, Ethan?" Now that he had
regained his tongue, Martin made no effort to conceal his
outrage.

"How best to protect my interest in the ferry," Ethan told
him evenly. "When Elizabeth Merriweather arrived last
month to look at Jonathan's land, I explained the problem
with the surveyor's boundary line. She's a widow with very
little means, but she agreed to manage the tavern as a way
of paying for her share of the ferry."

"You said nothing to me about this arrangement." Martin's low voice bristled with disapproval.

Ethan met his brother-in-law's accusing eyes. "I didn't see
any need to." In truth, the censure he had anticipated from

Martin had prompted him, at least in part, to keep his agreement with Elizabeth Merriweather to himself. He had no intention now, however, of apologizing for what amounted to a practical business decision. "You know as well as I that the public house has suffered since Chewani left," he went on. "This woman impressed me as hard-working and honest."

"Honest?" Martin spat the word in contempt. "You call the woman who steals your cousin's land 'honest'?"

"Jonathan accepted the government's compensation for his improvements and moved west of his own accord," Ethan reminded him. Seeing the angry white line etched around Martin's set mouth, he hastened to move beyond an issue that always placed them at odds. "In any case, what was I to do? Simply give her my share of the ferry?" When Martin only continued to glower at him, he went on. "For now, I've managed to keep control of the ferry and gained some help in running the tavern. To my way of thinking, I've gotten the best part of the deal."

"No Indian ever gets the best part of a deal with the *Unakas*." Martin's tight lips quivered at the bitter flavor of the Cherokee word for white people.

"Then why are you building a schoolhouse on your land for Abigail Ballard?" Ethan retorted.

"I build the school for *my* children," Martin insisted. "You know that after the Foreign Mission Society withdrew their people from the Cherokee Nation, it was the only way to keep a teacher."

"A teacher who fills your children's minds with the white man's learning." Ethan's eyes remained locked with Martin's dark gaze, driving his point home.

"Do not taunt me, brother." The low tenor of Martin's voice made it all the more ominous. "Mark what I say. In the end, this woman will take everything, and you will be only another wretched Indian, driven from his land with a few pennies for his misery." Without another word he turned abruptly and strode to the stable.

Ethan watched Martin's rigid figure disappear through the stable door. The touch of small fingers weaving through his own caused him to look down into Rebecca's wide, dark eyes. In the heated exchange with Martin he had almost forgotten that the children had been watching their elders' dispute.

"Is that lady going to make you move away?" the little girl asked, her hand curling tightly around Ethan's much larger one.

Ethan sank into a crouch and placed a hand on Ben's shoulder, drawing both children to him. "No, of course not. I'm going to stay right where I am for a long, long time." In the present climate, such assertions bordered on bravado, but Ethan could see no value in further distressing the children. It was bad enough that they had witnessed the strife between him and their father. When Martin appeared in the stable door with the filly in tow, Ethan rose. "You'd best not keep your father waiting." He gave each child's back a gentle pat to propel them toward the stable.

Watching the two youngsters run across the stable yard, Ethan imagined that Sally and he must have looked that way some twenty years ago, she a tall, fresh-faced girl with a laugh as musical as a mountain stream, he the younger of the two, sturdily built and determined not to be left out of any scrape. He had known Martin in those days, too, long before his friend had grown into the impetuous young farmer who would ask for Sally's hand in marriage.

The two men's friendship had endured over the years despite their dissimilar temperaments. In fact, had the Treaty of New Echota never been ratified, Martin and he would have had few differences, Ethan reflected as he walked to the tavern. The wretched treaty had changed everyone's life, however, dividing families and turning once-stalwart friends into bitter foes. Like Ethan, Martin regarded the treaty as illegal, but he carried his condemnation further, branding any Cherokee who abided by its tenets a traitor to his people. Martin had never accepted Jonathan Woodard's decision to voluntarily relocate his family west of the Mississippi River, and the issue had continued to be a source of friction between him and Ethan.

If Sally had lived, perhaps Martin would have grown milder in time and found some way to temper the consuming rage festering inside him. A profound sadness welled in

Ethan at the memory of his sister's gaunt face lying against the pillow, its beauty ravaged by fever and pain. He remembered her summoning what little remained of her wasted strength to smile for her children and kiss each of them in turn. Once the house servant had ushered Ben and Rebecca out of the room, however, Sally had beckoned Ethan to her bedside. She had been almost too weak to speak, but she had made him promise to look after her little ones as a brother should in keeping with Cherokee custom.

"Take care of Martin for me, too, Ethan," Sally had whispered, her thin hand clinging to his. "He'll need someone to help him go on alone."

"I will, Sally. I give you my word." Ethan would never forget how his throat had constricted, rebelling at the words that at last acknowledged the young life slipping inexorably away from them.

In the four years since that bleak day, Ethan had done his best to keep his last promise to his sister. He often took comfort in the thought that Sally would have been proud of the happy, inquisitive children that Rebecca and Ben had become, and pleased to see that Martin's modest homestead had blossomed into the thriving plantation of his dreams. At the same time, Ethan prayed that Sally would never glimpse the ugly clouds that gathered over the once-peaceful valley, would have no hint of the forces threatening to end their way of life forever.

From the shadow of the tavern's door Ethan watched the two horses trotting past. To the fore, Martin rode on his big-boned gray mare with Ben mounted pillion behind him. Rebecca sat astride the filly that jogged on the end of the lead line, small hands clinging tenaciously to a tuft of the animal's mane. Ethan rested his shoulder against the door frame, his eyes following the little party until they had disappeared among the trees. Then he turned and slowly walked inside the tavern.

Gently seesawing the reins through her hands, Elizabeth leaned back in the wagon's seat. Midnight tossed his head in protest, but he yielded to the bit's pressure and halted in front of the tavern. It was quite early still, the dawn only a pale halo glowing behind the tops of the tall trees. For a few moments Elizabeth studied the log house and the empty yard surrounding it. Then she collected the basket she had stowed under the seat and climbed to the ground.

Elizabeth patted the horse's glossy neck as she clasped the reins and led the animal to the stable yard. Never an even-tempered horse, Midnight had seemed to bear a grudge toward her since she had sold the trap before their departure from Auraria and acquired a far more practical wagon. He jerked his head and pawed the ground now while she struggled to unhitch the wagon and remove his harness. Elizabeth's black frock was speckled with horsehair and wisps of straw by the time she had backed the unruly creature into a stall. After tossing the horse a block of hay she dusted her skirt and headed for the tavern.

She gingerly mounted the uneven stone steps leading to the porch and then paused to glance through one of the uncurtained windows. A thick film of grime covered the glazing, preventing all but the sketchiest reconnaissance of the tavern's interior, but Elizabeth determined that the public room was unlighted and, to all appearances, unoccupied. Nonetheless, she knocked on the rough wooden door and pushed it open.

"Is anyone here?"

Receiving no response, Elizabeth squinted into the cloud of greasy smoke that seemed to fill every cranny of the room. As her eyes adjusted to the meager light, she ventured farther.

A massive stone fireplace took up the better part of one end of the room while a bar and shelves laden with bottles and flasks occupied the opposite wall. A hodgepodge of tables and chairs, arranged in careless order, filled most of the remaining space. To the rear of the room a wooden staircase leading to the upper level flanked the narrow back door.

Lifting her skirts clear of the litter scattered underfoot, Elizabeth picked her way between the tables to peer up the stairs. "Hello?" she called on the chance that an unsuspecting traveler lay slumbering overhead. When no one answered she retreated to inspect the hearth.

Several inches of ash had accumulated in the grate, piled in little drifts around the cast-iron kettle and Dutch oven. Elizabeth lifted the lid of a pot hanging from the crane to discover the remains of a stew, now blanketed with congealed grease. Turning her back on the ill-tended hearth, she collected three empty tankards left on the tables and walked to the bar. When she placed her basket and the tankards on the counter, she was dismayed but not surprised to hear a considerable number of mice scurry for cover behind the bar.

Elizabeth drew as deep a breath as the smoky air permitted and surveyed the untidy room. Her inspection of the tavern, brief as it had been, had established one incontestable fact. When Ethan Woodard had said his public house was in desperate need of proper management, he had certainly not exaggerated. Although Elizabeth had hoped to receive more specific direction from him regarding the labor he expected of her, she now felt certain that nothing could be accomplished until she had brought a semblance of order and cleanliness to the place. To this end she pulled her apron from the basket and rolled up her sleeves in preparation for the daunting task before her.

Bending over the fireplace, Elizabeth scooped the ash into a bucket and carried it to the porch. She selected a couple of logs from the woodpile, along with a handful of kindling, and then returned to the house. As soon as a fire was blazing in the grate, she drew water from the well in the yard, filled the largest pot she could find and set it to heat over the flames. While Elizabeth waited for the water to boil she rummaged behind the bar and located some rags, a sturdy brush and a cask of lye soap.

As she began to wash the filthy windows, Elizabeth frequently glanced across the yard, half-expecting to see Ethan Woodard striding toward the tavern. She had no idea what sort of schedule he maintained, but his day surely included a visit to the ferry and the public house. By the time she had cleaned the windows, swept the floor and scoured the cookware, however, neither Ethan nor his ferryman had appeared.

After throwing an extra log onto the fire, Elizabeth paused at the bar to splash cool water on her face and then headed upstairs. She was surprised when she opened the first door in the narrow hall and discovered a simply furnished room that was both neat and clean. Seeing a pair of home-spun trousers hanging on a wall peg, Elizabeth withdrew into the corridor rather than risk intruding on some travel-er's privacy. None of the remaining three rooms was occu-pied, but unfortunately their condition was as deplorable as that of the ground floor. Most of the linen was dingy and tattered, the straw filling the mattresses compressed to a hard mat. Elizabeth was dragging one of the shabby mat-tresses onto the landing when the sound of spirited whis-tling drifted up the stairs from the public room.

The whistling abruptly ceased. "Damn, but it's hot in here, Gray Bear! We're nearly into summer, and yet you've built a fire that would do the devil himself proud."

Resting the unwieldy mattress against the wall, Elizabeth leaned over the stair rail to find Ethan Woodard frowning at the crackling blaze. His fists were propped on his hips, emphasizing the flare of his broad shoulders.

"I needed hot water to clean properly," she explained in a quiet voice.

Ethan started with such surprise Elizabeth almost feared that he would stumble into the fire. He spun around and blinked as if an apparition had just materialized in front of him. "Elizabeth Merriweather! For a moment I thought you were my ferryman." His eyes drifted slowly down her form as she descended the stairs. "But only for a moment," he added with more than a hint of a smile.

"I've begun tidying the place." Elizabeth adopted a se-rious expression, trying to ignore the unapologetic assess-ment of those brazen dark eyes. She could not decide if Ethan's audacious gaze was deliberately fostered to tease her or was simply a matter of habit, but in either case she had no intention of shrinking from its bold appraisal. "I be-lieve I have made some small progress."

Ethan's eyes lingered on her face as if they were loath to move on to more mundane observation. Then he turned to scan the room. When he faced Elizabeth once more, he looked frankly amazed. "Indeed you have."

"There is still much to be done," Elizabeth countered modestly, clasping her hands in front of her. "Cleaning is all the same, be it a tavern or a home, but perhaps you can tell me a bit about managing your establishment."

Ethan folded his arms across his chest as he walked to the bar. "This is the first place most folks head when they stop by here. Some expect a bite to eat, as well. Occasionally a traveler will elect to spend the night. Your job is to handle the bar trade, cook and generally see that the place is clean and presentable. Gray Bear makes his home in one of the rooms upstairs, so you needn't worry about minding the place of an evening. He'll also draw water and keep you supplied with firewood."

Bracing both hands on the counter's edge, Ethan leaned back against the bar. "You'll find most customers to be ordinary, decent people, but now and then some fellow will drink more than his share and make trouble. There's a long rifle in the corner behind the bar, but if you notice a fight brewing, I'd advise you to let Gray Bear or me settle it."

Elizabeth nodded, doing her best not to appear as uncertain as she felt.

Ethan must have glimpsed a trace of her apprehension, for he was quick to add, "Don't worry, Elizabeth. Not everyone who frequents this tavern would pass muster in a Savannah drawing room, but the ruffians soon learn they're not welcome and take their business elsewhere."

"My last home was in Auraria, not Savannah," Elizabeth told him. "Although no guest ever resorted to fisticuffs in my parlor, I am familiar with frontier manners."

Ethan chuckled, apparently pleased with her response. "Then you should have no problem overseeing the tavern."

During their conversation Elizabeth had been aware of a vague clamor in the distance, squealing mixed with noisy scuffling. As the commotion grew louder, Ethan pushed away from the bar and walked to the window. Elizabeth

peered over his shoulder to find the yard filled with pigs.
The animals grunted and nudged one another, some vying
for position at the water trough while others rooted through
the refuse heap in search of an edible morsel. Two unshaven men wielding staffs moved through the herd, seemingly indifferent to the chaos around them.

"Gray Bear is going to need an extra hand getting this
herd penned and ferried across the river," Ethan commented. As he started for the door, he grinned over his
shoulder at Elizabeth. "I'll leave the drovers in your care.
I'm certain they'll want to fortify themselves while they have
the chance."

Elizabeth cut an anxious glance at the bar. "But you
haven't told me what to charge for anything. How much is
a glass of whiskey?"

Ethan paused in the door and scowled. "We should pay
anyone willing to drink *that* whiskey. If by any chance a
peddler named Gilmer stops at the tavern, don't let him
leave until I've had a chance to talk with him. He's going to
give me my money back on that rotten slop if I have to pour
it down his sorry gullet."

Ethan's expression was so forbidding Elizabeth felt bound
to nod her agreement. "I understand." As he hurried outside she dashed after him. "What should I ask for the
brandy?"

Ethan shrugged. "Whatever you think it's worth. And
you'd best cook something while you're at it. It's nigh on
midday already." Without giving her a chance to protest, he
plunged into the herd of milling swine and began to push his
way toward the landing.

Elizabeth hesitated on the porch, frowning at the tall figure carving a path through the grunting livestock. She had
never bought a glass of brandy in her life, much less sold
one, nor did she have the vaguest notion what people normally paid for such refreshment. And what on earth did
Ethan expect her to cook? From what she had seen so far,
the tavern stocked a quantity of spirits and little else. Heaving a sigh, Elizabeth straightened the sash of her apron and
returned to the public room.

A thorough search of the various crocks and bins behind the bar yielded a good-sized chunk of smoked ham, a few shriveled but edible turnips, some potatoes and an onion. Luckily the mice had not yet discovered the bag of corn-meal stored in the tin-lined larder. After concocting a stew of the meat and vegetables, Elizabeth prepared corn pone in the cast-iron spider. She had just set the three-legged pan of bread to bake over the coals when the two drovers appeared in the door.

The taller of the two, a strapping fellow with hair and whiskers the color of Georgia clay, seemed startled to have found a woman presiding over the bar, and he hastily removed his hat. He nudged his stocky comrade, prompting him to follow suit. Self-consciously clutching their hats by the brims, the drovers reminded Elizabeth of wayward schoolboys as they approached the bar.

"Mornin', ma'am," the tall drover greeted Elizabeth while his partner contributed a bashful nod. "'Scuse me for starin' like that, but for a moment there I thought Chewani had come back." Catching the puzzled look on her face, he went on. "She used to run Ethan's place for him, pretty as a picture, too, she was. Not that you ain't," he was quick to add. "Anyhow, me and Elisha'd like some whiskey, if you please, ma'am."

Elizabeth winced inwardly. "I'm afraid the whiskey we have right now isn't fit to drink. Perhaps you'd like brandy instead?"

The drover cast a wistful glance at the whiskey barrel resting on the far end of the counter. "Peach brandy'll do, then, I guess," he told her in a voice heavy with resignation. "And while you're at it, how about some of whatever you got cookin'?" He cut his eyes toward the hearth, licking his lips in anticipation.

Elizabeth placed the bottle of brandy on the counter, along with the two cleanest-looking glasses she could find in the hutch. As the men shambled to one of the tables with their bottle, she carried two plates to the hearth and dished a generous portion of stew onto each. The two men sprawled comfortably in their chairs, speculating on the weather and guffawing over each other's jokes, but they straightened themselves when she arrived with the food.

"How much would that come to, ma'am?" the tall drover asked, shifting his husky frame to fish in his pocket.

Elizabeth thought quickly. "We haven't raised our prices since Chewani left." She made a show of counting the coins the man handed her before slipping them into her apron pocket and returning to the bar.

Shortly after the drovers had finished their meal, a stocky Indian appeared in the doorway. Elizabeth immediately recognized the man from her first visit to the land lot. Recalling the Cherokee's unfriendly mien as he had watched her trap drive past the tavern, she felt a little uncertain. He now nodded to her politely, however, before turning to the drovers.

"Your stock have drunk their fill," he announced. "We can start to ferry them across the river when you are ready."

The drovers drained their glasses before plugging the bottle and gathering up their travel sacks. They paused in the door to bid Elizabeth a good day and then followed the gray-haired Cherokee into the yard.

After eating some of the stew and a piece of warm corn pone, Elizabeth decided to resume cleaning the upstairs rooms. Although she had allowed the fire to subside, she was startled by the cloud of heat that greeted her at the top of the stairs. She hurried to throw open the windows and admit a welcome rush of cool air blowing off the river. One of the rear windows offered an excellent view of the ferry, tempting her to interrupt her work to watch the men transporting the great herd across the river.

The landing was teeming with raucous activity. Pigs jostled one another and bawled their protest at the drovers prodding them onto the flat-bottomed boat. Elizabeth watched Ethan as he sprang nimbly back and forth between boat and dock to direct the operation. Perspiration dampened his shirt, plastering it to his back in a dark patch that revealed the muscles straining beneath it. His black hair shone in the midday sun, its hue as rich and deep as polished ebony. He seemed to relish the hard labor, for his generous smile flashed frequently as he cajoled the animals and shouted to the men.

Elizabeth was so enthralled by the lively scene, she started when she heard glass clink in the public room below. Gathering up her skirt, she hurried to the stairs. The pudgy little man standing behind the bar wheeled, but not quickly enough to conceal the open flask he held in his hand.

"And a good day to you, ma'am!" The man tucked the bottle beneath the counter as slyly as if he were dealing a card from the bottom of the deck.

"Good day to you, sir," Elizabeth replied without smiling.

As she stalked across the room she kept her stern gaze fixed on the squat figure that seemed divided into three equal portions of stubby legs, barrel-like torso and ridiculously tall hat. Not taking her eyes off the intruder, Elizabeth reached behind the bar and seized the open flask. She placed it on the counter so solidly the man flinched.

"You wish to purchase a drink, sir?"

"Why, yes, indeed! I am a connoisseur of fine spirits, especially when they are served by a lady as lovely as yourself," he added, an unctuous smile playing on his plump face. When his flattery failed to dispel Elizabeth's severe expression, the man swept his hat from his head and bowed to reveal the bald spot in the middle of his well-oiled pate. Straightening himself, he adjusted the lapels of his frock coat. "Noah Gilmer, at your service, ma'am."

Noah Gilmer! So this slippery little man she had caught helping himself to a drink was the peddler who had sold Ethan bad whiskey!

Gilmer smiled, misreading the recognition reflected on Elizabeth's face. "And who might be the charming lady whose acquaintance I have had the good fortune to make?"

"*Mrs.* Merriweather," Elizabeth told him primly.

She glanced toward the door. To judge from the racket coming from the yard, a substantial number of pigs remained in the pens, awaiting transport across the river. Ethan would be occupied with the ferry for some time yet, perhaps longer than Gilmer intended to tarry at the tavern. She could, of course, run and fetch him from the landing,

but only at the risk of allowing the peddler to slip away. As
she considered the matter, Elizabeth realized her only choice
was to deal with Noah Gilmer herself.

She cleared her throat as she rounded the bar. Glaring at
the peddler, Elizabeth waited for him to scoot to the other
side of the counter. Then she took a large glass from the
shelf. She recorked the flask before reaching for the demijohn standing beside the whiskey barrel. She filled the glass
to the brim with whiskey and then shoved it toward him.

"This one is on the house," Elizabeth told him with a
cold smile.

The peddler regarded the drink uneasily. "I do believe I
would prefer a glass of brandy, ma'am."

"And why would that be, Mr. Gilmer? Because you know
this whiskey you sold Mr. Woodard is unfit to drink?"
Seizing the glass, Elizabeth tossed the whiskey into the refuse pail beneath the counter. The peddler watched in
openmouthed amazement as she imposed the same fate on
the demijohn's contents. "You owe us money, Mr. Gilmer,
every penny Ethan Woodard paid you for your poisonous
liquor."

Gilmer attempted an offended look, fat hands smoothing his garish yellow waistcoat like a bloated canary preening itself. "With all due respect, Mrs. Merriweather, you are
mistaken if you think that *I* would tender spirits of inferior
quality."

"Then why wouldn't you drink the whiskey I just served
you?" Elizabeth retorted. She shook her head in disgust.
"No, Mr. Gilmer, it is you who are mistaken."

The peddler squirmed inside his stiff suit. "Perhaps I
should discuss this misunderstanding with Mr. Woodard
personally. Unfortunately, he appears occupied at the moment, but the next time I pass this way—"

"Mr. Woodard will only tell you what you've heard from
me already—take your whiskey and give us the money
back."

Gilmer thoughtfully scratched his bulbous chin, and
Elizabeth could imagine the wily calculation taking place
beneath his shiny bald dome. "How would it be if I were to

rade you new stock for old?'' Seeing Elizabeth's skeptical
ook, he went on. "You can sample the barrel, if you like.''

Elizabeth considered his offer for a moment before nod-
ling. She followed the little man outside to a wagon piled
vith boxes, crates and barrels. Surrounded by his wares,
Noah Gilmer quickly recovered his smooth manner. He
made a show of selecting a cup from a crate of china and
plugging the whiskey barrel with a spigot. The peddler pre-
ented the cup of whiskey with a flourish, hovering with
eigned expectancy as Elizabeth took a small sip.

Although she rarely drank spirits, she trusted herself to
udge Gilmer's present batch of whiskey palatable. "This
vill do," she conceded.

Elizabeth was watching the peddler load the barrel onto
a wheelbarrow when Ethan and the stocky ferryman appeared from behind the public house.

"Good day, Ethan!" Gilmer paused to mop his brow with
a handkerchief that reeked of cheap cologne. Catching
Ethan's dark look, he hastened to ingratiate himself. "Mrs.
Merriweather has brought to my attention the disappoint-
ng quality of your last whiskey purchase. I was most
pleased, of course, to replace the unacceptable liquor with
his fine whiskey, which Mrs. Merriweather has already
ampled and approved."

Ethan's eyes slowly traveled from Noah Gilmer's glisten-
ng face to Elizabeth as if he were uncertain what to make
of the unlikely scenario.

"I think you'll find the whiskey quite satisfactory," Elizabeth told him, suppressing a smile.

"I'm sure I will," Ethan returned with a twinkle in his
ye. He winked over Gilmer's head before turning to his
companion. "Gray Bear, maybe we'd better give this gen-
leman a hand, just to make sure he doesn't get confused
and leave us the wrong barrel the way he did the last time."

The two men rode herd on Noah Gilmer as he trundled
he wheelbarrow to the tavern. Leaving the peddler to fan his
reddened face, Ethan and Gray Bear installed the new bar-
el of whiskey while Elizabeth looked on. After the trans-
ction was completed, Gilmer spent a few minutes inquiring
bout business and the latest crop forecasts. He was clearly

relieved, however, to return to his wagon and drive away with his hide still intact.

Ethan stood in the door and watched until the peddler's wagon had lumbered out of sight. Then he clapped Gray Bear on the shoulder. "Well, my old friend, shall we see if Elizabeth Merriweather cooks as well as she bargains? I don't know about you, but I'm starving."

Nodding his agreement, the older man accompanied Ethan to the bar. Elizabeth had busied herself washing dishes, but she quickly reached for a cloth to dry two plates.

After introducing her to Gray Bear, Ethan rested one arm on the counter and grinned. "I don't know how on earth you persuaded that old scoundrel to make good on his four whiskey, but I would have given something precious to see it." He glanced at the other man. "Wouldn't you, Gray Bear?"

"Yes, I would," Gray Bear said quietly, but his lined eyes looked merry.

"I offered him a glass of it to drink," Elizabeth explained with an unassuming smile.

Ethan's hearty laugh filled the public room. "I can just imagine the look on Gilmer's face." He straightened himself and took the plates from Elizabeth. "You must be hungry. You're more than welcome to join us."

"Thank you, but I've already eaten."

Ethan looked a trifle disappointed, but he only shrugged before walking to the hearth and ladling two large servings of stew onto the plates. Then he joined Gray Bear at the table nearest the door.

Elizabeth resumed her chore, but she could scarcely avoid overhearing the two men, laughing and chatting over their meal. They seemed so at ease with each other that she secretly wished she had bent the truth and accepted Ethan's invitation to eat with them. Unlike most of the men she had known, Ethan seemed to subscribe to a single code of etiquette, employing the same direct, outspoken manner with her that he presented to Gray Bear. A lady could expect little in the way of flowery language and flattery from him. By the same token, however, Elizabeth sensed that he would never make light of her opinions or penalize her for speaking her mind.

She felt slightly embarrassed when Ethan glanced over Gray Bear's shoulder and caught her watching them. "The stew is very good." He gestured appreciatively with his fork.

Elizabeth managed a gracious smile, but she made short work of the remaining dishes before going upstairs to continue her cleaning. When she returned over an hour later, the stew kettle was empty and the men had disappeared. She was scrubbing the last of the crockery when Ethan appeared in the doorway. He stood there for a moment, watching her with a whimsical smile on his face, before ambling to the bar.

"So you threatened to poison Noah Gilmer with his own whiskey, eh?" Ethan leaned back against the counter, bringing his head almost level with hers as she bent over the dishpan.

"That is one way of looking at it, I suppose." Elizabeth gave the dishrag a brisk shake, in part to distract herself from the handsome face looming not more than a handbreadth from her own.

"You're too modest, Elizabeth." Ethan chuckled as he turned to reach across the counter and give her wrist an impulsive squeeze.

Momentarily caught off guard, Elizabeth could only stare at the strong, tapering fingers closed around her arm.

"Come now. You've worked enough for one day. Why don't you fetch us a couple of those glasses—" Ethan nodded toward the sparkling glassware Elizabeth had just arranged on the shelves "—and we'll have a bit of the whiskey you acquired for us." When she hesitated, he gave her wrist a light shake. "I'll take no excuses from you this time, Elizabeth," he warned with a twinkle in his eye. He tugged the end of her sash with his free hand, removing her apron with a deft pull.

"Then I'll offer you none," Elizabeth replied, winning control of her wrist once more.

Ethan grinned as he took the glasses she placed on the counter. He dispensed a scant inch of whiskey from the barrel into each and then led the way to one of the tables. He held a chair for Elizabeth before settling himself comfortably across from her.

Ethan held his glass aloft. "To health and good fortune."

Elizabeth smiled as she nicked the edge of his glass. "Good health and good fortune." Following his example, she took a sip of the whiskey that, for some reason, tasted even better than it had earlier that afternoon.

They sat without talking for some time, enjoying the light breeze and the muted cooing of the mourning doves nesting in the pin oak outside the window. Ethan at last broke the silence.

"So how was your first day running the tavern?" He smiled over the rim of his glass, and Elizabeth could tell he was gauging her reaction.

"Since I've no experience for comparison, perhaps I should ask you," she returned, meeting his direct gaze.

Ethan leaned back in his chair, his dark eyes regarding her with gentle curiosity. "Considering that you've managed to make the place look respectable and to outwit Noah Gilmer in one day's time, I'd say you're off to a very good start."

"I hope so," Elizabeth said, more fervently than she had intended. She hastily picked up the conversation to cover her lapse. "This valley is so beautiful, even prettier than the country around Auraria. Have you lived here all your life?"

"Most of it, save for the year I went away to school." Ethan took a slow drink of the whiskey. "How long did you live in Auraria?"

"A little over three years, although often it seemed a far longer time."

"You weren't happy living there?"

Elizabeth reluctantly shook her head. "My husband thought he would find great opportunity in the gold country, but he never realized his dreams." She sighed, looking down at her glass to evade the intense dark eyes searching her face. "So many things went wrong in Auraria it was hard to think of it as home."

"Where do you call home, then?" Ethan asked.

Elizabeth studied the pale amber film clinging to her glass. "I know it probably sounds strange, but that's hard for me to say. I was born in Savannah, but after my sister and I lost our parents we went to live with our uncle on his plantation near the Oconee River. The country life didn't agree with Miranda, I'm afraid, and she was only too happy when Uncle arranged for her to attend boarding school in Charleston. I loved living on the plantation, though. I suppose when I think of home, Prospect is the place that comes to mind."

"Do you ever go back there?" Ethan leaned forward to rest both arms on the table.

Elizabeth nodded, a wistful smile drifting across her face. "My cousin and his wife inherited the place. They begged me to come live with them after Samuel passed away."

A flicker of surprise stirred in the mahogany depths of Ethan's eyes. "But you chose not to?"

Elizabeth hesitated. "Charles and Lucinda are both very dear to me, but I didn't want to spend the rest of my life as a burden to them."

Ethan laughed softly. "That's a rather bleak view of the future, don't you think? After all, it's highly likely that a woman as young and pretty as you are will marry again."

Elizabeth felt the warmth rising in her cheeks. "I'm nearly thirty years old, Ethan," she countered, avoiding his eyes. "And . . . and I'm sure most people consider me quite plain."

"How on earth did you ever come by such a ridiculous notion?" Ethan interrupted with such vehemence that Elizabeth was forced to look up at him. "There's nothing plain or ordinary about you, Elizabeth." His voice softened, and a tender expression tempered the smoldering fire in his dark eyes. "You'll meet another man you can love someday, and if he has any sense at all, he'll tell you the truth about the way you look."

"You make a complicated matter sound very simple." Pushing her chair away from the table, Elizabeth tried to conceal her awkwardness behind a smile. "I should probably start for home. Dolly will be wondering when to serve supper." Without giving Ethan a chance to counter her decision, she rose and hurried to the bar.

As Elizabeth stuffed her apron into the basket, she berated herself for having been foolish enough to drink more than a swallow of whiskey. Had the liquor not loosened her tongue, she would never have revealed such personal feelings to someone she scarcely knew. That Ethan Woodard was not in the least shy about asking questions was no excuse for her to answer them so freely. In fact, she had probably allowed him far more familiarity than their brief acquaintance warranted. He meant no harm, she was certain, but she was a widow still in mourning. Her back stiffened at the somber reminder.

Elizabeth wheeled to find Ethan waiting for her in the doorway, but he stepped aside as she approached. "I'll hitch your horse for you," he offered.

As they crossed the yard, Elizabeth quickened her steps to match Ethan's rangy stride. She waited by the watering trough while he led Midnight out of the stable and backed him between the wagon's traces. The temperamental animal must have realized that he was in the hands of a seasoned horseman, for he submitted to the harness with only a perfunctory snort. Ethan looped the reins around the whip stand and then helped Elizabeth climb onto the driver's seat. He held on to her hand for a moment, giving her no choice but to look down at him.

When Ethan smiled, his face seemed to capture the glow of the fiery sun sinking toward the horizon. "I like the way you manage my tavern, Elizabeth," he said simply.

Without thinking, Elizabeth felt her hand tighten around his. "And I like the way you manage our ferry." Her eyes still lingering on his face, she withdrew her hand and seized the reins. "Good evening, Ethan." Slapping the lines against Midnight's back, she set the wagon in motion, leaving Ethan standing in the stable yard.

Chapter Four

"Good afternoon, Gray Bear!" Elizabeth looked up from the pan of blackberries she was sorting and greeted the ferryman, who had just appeared in the tavern door. "Surely you have time for a cup of coffee. The pot I brewed is still fresh."

"I will take time if you will." A slow smile stirred the wrinkles lining Gray Bear's face as he pulled his favorite cane-bottom chair up to the table where Elizabeth was sitting.

After wiping her hands on her apron, Elizabeth collected two cups from the hutch and then hurried out the back door to the kitchen where the summer heat now forced her to do most of the cooking. She filled both cups to the brim with rich dark brew, paused to add a liberal chunk of sugar to Gray Bear's coffee and joined him in the tavern.

In the three weeks since she had taken charge of the public house, the kindly ferryman had proven to be an invaluable mentor, never failing to offer advice or help when she needed it. In addition to keeping the woodpile stocked for her, Gray Bear acted as interpreter with patrons who spoke only Cherokee and discouraged the occasional drover whose attention threatened to exceed gentlemanly bounds. Elizabeth had quickly discovered the aging Cherokee's weakness for strong, sweet coffee, and the daily treat they shared had become something of a ritual.

Gray Bear inhaled the fragrant vapor appreciatively before taking a slow sip. "You make very good coffee, Elizabeth,'' he complimented her solemnly, just as he did every day.

Elizabeth smiled through the steam rising from her cup. ''Thank you, Gray Bear.'' She glanced toward the open door, her attention diverted by the drum of cantering hooves growing louder by the second. Pushing up from the table, she motioned Gray Bear to keep his seat and then walked to the door. ''I believe it's the stagecoach,'' she announced, trying not to sound disappointed.

In truth, she had hoped to find Ethan galloping along the road on his handsome bay gelding. Even with the burgeoning crops now demanding most of his attention, a day rarely passed without his coming by the ferry, and Ethan never rode off without stopping in the tavern. Elizabeth had grown to anticipate those visits more than she would have openly admitted. Sometimes Elizabeth and he would discuss the purchase of supplies or a necessary repair, but more often they simply enjoyed a pleasant break in the day's labor, a chance to share laughter and the abundant gossip that inevitably circulated around the busy crossroads.

''The stage horses will need water,'' Gray Bear remarked as he scooted back his chair. He drained the last of his coffee before ambling to the door.

Elizabeth followed him onto the porch to watch the driver rein his lathered team in the yard. In theory, a stage stopped at Woodard's Landing every week, but inclement weather, lame horses and broken wheels imposed a more erratic schedule on its visits. Today was only the second time since Elizabeth's arrival that the stage had appeared to collect and dispense passengers and mail. Shielding her eyes from the sun with one hand, she peered across the yard to see how many travelers would require food and drink in the tavern.

The driver, an angular fellow with a stiff leg, talked with Gray Bear as he limped around the coach and unlatched the door. He helped a small woman clutching a carpetbag alight and then collected the leather mail pouch from beneath the driver's seat. As the driver and the woman approached the tavern, Elizabeth smiled in greeting.

"Afternoon, Mrs. Merriweather." The driver removed his broad-brimmed hat and slapped it against his knee, releasing a puff of road dust.

"Good afternoon," Elizabeth returned. She made a point of nodding cordially to the little woman as she led the way into the public house. "Would you care for something to eat or drink?"

The driver dropped onto the chair that Gray Bear had recently vacated, raising another small cloud of nose-tickling dust in the process. "If you got any eggs, fry up a half dozen or so o' them. And some bacon or ham with 'em—it don't matter which. And I'd like biscuits with plenty of butter, if it ain't too salty. And..." Catching Elizabeth's pointed look, he broke off. "'Course, maybe you ought to see to Miss Ballard here first."

Elizabeth managed not to smile as she turned to the petite woman who hovered on the threshold like a nervous wren. "What may I get for you, ma'am?"

"Some cool, fresh water will be sufficient, thank you," Miss Ballard informed her in an accent whose broad vowels testified to a New England upbringing. Her lively dark eyes scoured the room, finally settling on a table situated an acceptable distance from the stagecoach driver.

Guessing that a not-ill-founded fear of public house cookery might have inspired the woman's Spartan order, Elizabeth followed her to the table to offer reassurance. "The eggs are quite fresh. I also have dried peach turnovers that I baked just this morning. They'll keep well, too, if you'd care to take some with you for the rest of your journey."

Miss Ballard's smile was as spare as her unadorned brown traveling suit. "Thank you, but I shall be traveling no farther than Mr. Early's farm. By good fortune, he was tending his field near the river and noted the stage as we drove past. I expect he will arrive presently to fetch me. And my boxes of precious books," she added with an anxious glance toward the door.

"You have a quantity of books?" Elizabeth could not resist asking.

"Yes, indeed. You see, I have come to educate the children of this valley," Miss Ballard announced, so solemnly that none could mistake the gravity of her mission.

Elizabeth would have enjoyed learning more about the middle-aged schoolmistress's plans. Unfortunately, the stagecoach driver looked ready to devour the handiest piece of furniture if his meal was delayed much longer. After providing the cup of water that Miss Ballard had requested, she rushed to the kitchen to prepare his order. No sooner had she served the driver than four cattle drovers arrived, hot, thirsty and ravenously hungry. Elizabeth scurried back and forth between kitchen and tavern, pausing to sell a woman a card of pins and pour brandy for an itinerant tinker on his way to Tennessee. She was delivering a second platter of biscuits to the drovers when the coachman beckoned to her.

The driver devoured the better part of a biscuit in one bite and wiped his mouth on his sleeve. "'Fore I forget, I think I got somethin' for you here," he mumbled through a full mouth. He dug in his mail pouch and produced a folded and sealed letter. Holding the letter at arm's length, he squinted at the inscription before handing it to Elizabeth. "Mrs. Samuel Merriweather, Woodard's Landing. I reckon that's you."

At the sight of Josiah's bold script, Elizabeth felt an unwelcome twinge in the pit of her stomach. Shortly before leaving Auraria she had written to inform him of her plans. Until now, however, she had received no answer from him. Whatever Josiah had to say in his letter, Elizabeth felt certain it would not be encouraging. Preferring to face his dire predictions in private, she slipped the letter into her apron pocket and headed for the kitchen.

As she entered the kitchen she was surprised to find two children hovering by the oak worktable. When they spotted Elizabeth, they hastily retreated from the basket of peach turnovers that had been the object of their attention. Elizabeth regarded the two pairs of wide, solemn eyes fixed on her, and did her best not to laugh.

The little girl she judged to be not more than seven years old, with glossy black braids and eyes the color of melted chocolate. The boy, who was probably a couple of years younger, possessed the same sun-warmed complexion and comely features as his sister, albeit with a decidedly more impish cast. Elizabeth immediately recognized him as the youngster who had run alongside her wagon the day she had arrived in the valley.

Small hands clasped in front of her starched pinafore, the little girl was the first to step forward. "Please, ma'am, may we have a turnover?"

Elizabeth smiled. "I don't see why not."

A grin that was both shy and coquettish dimpled the child's pretty face. "Ben already had one, but I said we should ask first," she explained in a very grown-up voice.

"It wasn't a very big one," Ben protested in his defense.

"I remember you. You managed to outrun my wagon," Elizabeth told him with a knowing twinkle in her eye. "So your name is Ben?" When he nodded, she turned to his sister. "And what is yours?"

"Rebecca."

"Well, then, Ben and Rebecca. I am Mrs. Merriweather, and I'm very pleased to meet you." Elizabeth reached for the basket of turnovers and held it within the children's reach. "You may both have one."

Rebecca thanked her and prompted Ben to do likewise as only an older sister can. Having escaped Elizabeth's censure for sampling the turnovers, the children seemed happy to linger in the kitchen as she went about her work. When she returned to the tavern they tagged along, Ben carrying a stoneware bowl for her while his sister bore a fresh cone of sugar. The public room was empty now and quiet, save for a hound snoring on the cool stone hearth where it had sought relief from the afternoon heat. While the children helped her sort and rinse blackberries, they regaled her with stories about the barn cat that had just had kittens and the special stream where they swam now that the weather was warm enough. Elizabeth was sprinkling sugar over the berries when Rebecca suddenly pushed away from the table.

"Uncle!" she cried as she dashed to the door with Ben close on her heels.

Elizabeth turned in her chair and saw Ethan sweep Rebecca into his arms. Balancing the little girl on his hip, he stooped to ruffle Ben's thick black hair. He smiled broadly as he carried Rebecca to the table with Ben in tow. Ethan seated the girl on the table and then lifted her brother alongside her.

"Mrs. Merriweather, may I have the pleasure of introducing my favorite niece and nephew?" Ethan began with mock formality.

"We've already met, thank you," Elizabeth informed him.

"So I should have guessed." Ethan grinned as he brushed a crumb of turnover pastry from the corner of Ben's mouth. "Have you children been pestering Mrs. Merriweather?"

Both youngsters shook their heads emphatically.

"We've been helping her," Ben corrected him.

"You certainly have, both of you." Elizabeth offered immediate corroboration. "And I've enjoyed your company very much."

Rebecca gave Ethan a triumphant smile. "See my new ribbons?" She lifted one of her braids to display the lavender satin bow binding it. "Mr. Gilmer had pink and yellow ones, too, but I liked these best."

"They're very pretty," Ethan commented. "Mr. Gilmer stocks some fine things on his wagon if you know what to look for." He gave Elizabeth a surreptitious wink.

Elizabeth smiled, unable to resist Ethan's infectious good spirits. Humor had eased the lean angles of his face, infusing it with a gentleness she had only rarely glimpsed. Watching him listen to Ben and Rebecca's innocent chatter, his dark eyes full of warmth and affection, Elizabeth had little difficulty imagining him with his own children. A daughter of his would grow up knowing that she was the most beautiful, charming girl in the world, while a son would never doubt his father's pride in even his smallest achievements. His children would feel safe sharing secrets with him, could rely on him to soothe a hurt, brush away tears and cajole a smile in their place. Best of all, they would always be certain that he loved them with all his heart.

"I see that Miss Ballard arrived on the stage today," Ethan commented, helping himself to a couple of the blackberries.

Rebecca nodded. "Papa says she brought lots of books with her."

Elizabeth interrupted Rebecca's cheerful narrative. "So you and Ben are going to attend Miss Ballard's school?"

"After the harvest," Rebecca told her. "We can see the school from our house. Papa's building it in the apple orchard. Miss Ballard is going to live with us, too, in the room right next to mine."

"I imagine Miss Ballard will be very happy to set foot in that room after traveling all the way from Connecticut," Ethan remarked. "Perhaps we should see if your father is ready to take all of you home."

Ethan scooped Ben off the table, winning a giggle from the little boy. He swung the child in a circle before lowering him gently to the floor. Rebecca extended her arms to demand the same treatment. She was still trying to catch her breath through her laughter when a man dressed in close-fitting breeches and a gray shirt appeared in the doorway.

Although the doorframe was more than adequate for a man of even Ethan's considerable stature, the newcomer stooped slightly as he entered the public house, a habit his exceptional height had no doubt forced him to cultivate. An aquiline nose and bones unobscured by any excess flesh gave his face a look of solemn dignity. Most striking of all his features were his piercing eyes, hard and black as obsidian. Elizabeth could almost feel those dark eyes graze her face as they surveyed the tavern and its occupants.

Ethan released the little girl's hand to beckon to the man. "Martin, you haven't met Elizabeth Merriweather yet." Still smiling, he turned to Elizabeth. "Elizabeth, my brother-in-law, Martin Early."

"Mrs. Merriweather." Martin Early nodded curtly to Elizabeth.

"I'm pleased to meet you, Mr. Early," Elizabeth replied. "You've two delightful children—" She broke off when Early turned toward the door. Feeling the color rise to her face at the snub, she pretended to tidy the table while the children trooped behind their father.

"Don't forget to tell Mrs. Merriweather goodbye," she heard Ethan remind the youngsters from the doorway.

When Ben and Rebecca followed their uncle's prompting, Elizabeth glanced up and managed a smile for them. She avoided Ethan's gaze, busying herself with collecting dirty tankards and dishes from the tables until he had disappeared through the door. As she walked to the bar, she could hear him talking with his brother-in-law in the Cherokee language. She had been fascinated the first time she'd heard Ethan and Gray Bear converse in their native tongue, intrigued by the rhythm and inflection of the unfamiliar language. Now, however, the unintelligible words, like Martin Early's thinly veiled hostility, only reminded her of her alien status in this troubled country.

Stung as she had been by Early's rebuff, she could hardly blame him for his feelings, for who would look kindly on an intruder who had come to dispossess his people? *An intruder.* Even as she cringed from the distasteful label, she forced herself to admit that she was nothing more than a flagrant trespasser in the eyes of Martin Early and most of his fellow Cherokees. She had allowed her increasingly comfortable rapport with Ethan to distract her from that unpleasant fact.

Elizabeth stared across the empty room and imagined Ethan standing in the doorway, his tall, lithe figure sculpted by the light behind him. It was impossible to conjure him without his smile, the slow, insinuating way his wide mouth curved when she would at last look up from her work and notice him watching her. She was startled by how vividly she had etched her impressions of him in her mind, the luster and depth of his dark eyes, the exquisitely chiseled angles of his tanned face, the scent of sun and windswept pine in his hair. She had glimpsed, too, a generosity of spirit, a kindness in Ethan commensurate with his splendid physical attributes. Since they had reached their agreement, he had never reminded her of the unhappy circumstances that had prompted it. Nonetheless, he surely shared his brother-in-law's bitter awareness that her gain was ultimately to be his loss. She winced at the thought as she carried the tray of dirty crockery to the kitchen.

Elizabeth was bent over a tub of hot, sudsy water, scouring dishes, when she heard a light tap at the door. Still clutching a plate, she looked up to see Ethan standing with both hands braced against the doorframe. He smiled, pushed away from the door and walked to the table.

"It's a regular inferno in here, Elizabeth. I'm surprised you haven't roasted to a fine crisp by now."

"I'm very nearly finished washing up." She gestured with the plate, trying to quell the awkwardness that had replaced her normal ease around him.

"What isn't done can wait." Ethan grabbed a rag lying on the table and tossed it to her. "Come sit on the landing for a while. There's a cool breeze blowing off the river."

Elizabeth blotted her hands and removed her apron before accompanying Ethan out of the kitchen. He had adopted a more leisurely stride than usual, allowing her to keep pace as they followed the footpath leading down to the river. Ethan climbed onto the dock and then caught her hand to help her bridge the eddies of black mud surrounding the pilings. He seated himself near the edge and beckoned Elizabeth to join him. Gathering her skirts against the stiff breeze, she sank onto the rough wooden floor a few feet from his outstretched legs.

"Isn't this better now?" Narrowing his eyes against the sun filtering through the trees, Ethan leaned back on his elbows and smiled at her.

Elizabeth nodded and fanned her face with one hand. "You were right," she conceded, venturing a small smile.

Pushing himself up, Ethan loosened several buttons of his shirt, then leaned over the side of the dock. He splashed water on his face and neck, careless of the wet streaks darkening his blue shirt. Elizabeth caught her eyes traveling to the open cleft of his shirt, following the rivulets trickling over the hard muscles, and she quickly turned to face the river. She started when she felt a cool, wet hand against the back of her neck.

"Goodness!" Trying to collect herself, Elizabeth glanced at Ethan, who was kneeling behind her. "You startled me," she added in an effort to conceal the unsettling effect of his touch.

He scooped another handful of water from the river and splashed it on her neck. "Doesn't that feel good?"

"Yes." Her voice sounded far more timid than she had intended. She clutched her elbows, watching Ethan as he moved to face her.

"Hold out your hands." When Elizabeth complied, he slapped water on her wrists, his strong fingers lightly chafing the pulse throbbing beneath the warm skin.

A faint smile playing on his lips, Ethan reached to touch her face. Elizabeth sat stock still, insensitive to anything but the cool fingers patting water on her cheek. When his palm rested against her cheek for a brief moment, she wondered if he could feel the blood rushing beneath it. His thumb gently smoothed a drop of water from the curve of her cheekbone. Then he sat back on his heels, regarding her with a mixture of amusement and some other, less readily defined emotion.

In an attempt to evade his disconcerting gaze, Elizabeth dug a handkerchief from her pocket. Turning toward the river, she dabbed her face with the linen square. "It's so beautiful here, so peaceful," she said at length.

"I've always loved the river." Ethan's voice was as muted as the water gently lapping at the dock. When Elizabeth risked a glance at him, she found him sitting cross-legged not far behind her, his eyes fixed on the dense green curtain rising from the opposite bank. "See that big pin oak, the one on the very tip of the bend?" He pointed across the wide stretch of water. "When Martin and I were boys, that was our favorite tree for jumping into the water. It was a game to see who could climb the highest."

"Martin and you have been friends for a long time?" Elizabeth asked softly.

Ethan nodded without looking at her. "We grew up together, just as his father and mine did." He paused for a moment. "Martin is a good man, Elizabeth. No one could have loved Sally better than he. They both had such plans for their life together, for Ben and Rebecca." Ethan drew a deep breath, suddenly looking down at the dock's weathered surface. "Martin once told me that having Sally taken away from him was like giving up part of his soul. I believe that's why he can't bear to think of losing the home they shared, why it's so hard for him to accept anything that reminds him he might," he added in a very low voice.

Elizabeth swallowed hard, summoning the courage to speak. "Martin is right, Ethan. I've no right to be here. This land belongs to you."

Ethan shook his head. "No one can own the land. At least, that's what we believe." His dark eyes skimmed the uneven silhouette of the trees lining the far shore. "The treaties always speak of land as if that were all that mattered, so many acres worth so many dollars. But for us, something very different is at stake." He hesitated, and it seemed to Elizabeth he might be struggling to find words adequate to his feelings. "I want to live in this place where my ancestors lived before me, among these mountains and rivers. When I look up, I want to see the same patch of sky that they saw long ago. And when I die, I want my spirit to rest with theirs." A cloud gliding across the sun cast a shadow on Ethan's handsome face, intensifying its pensive aspect.

Elizabeth stared at her hands tightly knotted on her lap. "Ethan, I don't know what I can say." A painful tension clutched her throat, reducing her voice to a hoarse whisper. "What is happening to you, to your people, is so horribly unfair, and I, as much as anyone, am guilty of bringing that fate upon you. You ask nothing but to be left in peace to live out your life, and yet—" She broke off, unable to trust her trembling lips.

Ethan turned to face her, shifting so close that his shadow fell across her. "Isn't that all you're asking, Elizabeth, just for a little peace and a place to call home?" he said softly. "Just like us, like our country, you're caught up in a fate that you didn't choose. How could I blame you for that?" When she refused to look up at him, he reached to lift her chin gently, holding it poised on his fingertips. Through the damp curtain blurring her vision, Elizabeth met the eyes that now seemed to peer into the deepest recesses of her soul. "You are as good as you are beautiful, Elizabeth. What-

ever may happen, I will always know that." His finger
drifted slowly along the curve of her throat to rest against
her cheek for a moment.

Without warning, Ethan dropped his hand to his side and
stood. He hesitated, a faint quiver pulsing beneath the
tanned skin of his jaw as his gaze lingered on her damp face.
Then he turned and sprang from the dock to the shore.
Elizabeth watched him hurry up the path. She waited until
he had disappeared into the stable before rising and climbing off the landing. She walked back to the kitchen slowly,
to give herself time to sort through the complex emotions
still stirring inside her.

Ethan's halting attempt to explain the Cherokees' at-
tachment to their land had moved her deeply, not least of all
because she sensed that he was baring a profoundly personal part of himself. Yet as passionately as he felt about his
country, he was still willing to understand her plight, ab-
solve her from complicity with the forces seeking to drive his
people from their hereditary home. His eyes had been full
of tenderness when he tried to reassure her, as if he truly
cared about her. And when he had touched her, she could
almost believe—

Elizabeth pulled herself up short, retreating from the
treacherous tide of emotion that threatened to engulf her.
Determined to redirect her thoughts to more predictable
territory, she reached for the apron lying on the kitchen table. Only when she was tying the sash did she notice Josiah's letter, still secreted in the pocket.

Sinking down at the table, Elizabeth removed the letter
and slid one finger beneath the wax seal. She drew a long
breath before she began to read.

My dearest Elizabeth,
It was with great alarm that I read your letter of April
27 in which you informed me of your intentions regarding Samuel's land lot in Indian Territory. Although I understand your decision is prompted by a
wish to spare those who love and care for you from
further toil on your behalf, I would be remiss in my
duty, both as a gentleman and as a brother to our be-

loved Samuel, if I were to allow you to continue on such a misguided course. Indeed, my weary mind has enjoyed but little respite from concern since I learned of your unfortunate encounter with the Indian Woodard. I must remind myself that a lady of your delicacy and gentle disposition cannot possibly imagine the deceit and cunning to which the Indian's depraved nature disposes him. I know, dear Elizabeth, you will demur that I have labored too long already to provide for your security. Such unselfish protests must go unheeded, however, when your welfare, nay, dare I say your very safety is in peril. Hence, I stand ready to journey into Indian Territory and obtain from Woodard clear title to the ferry that is rightfully yours. I await your summons.

> Affectionately, Josiah R. Merriweather.

Elizabeth's hand fell to her lap, still holding the open letter. She glanced out the window to the yard that dusk had now suffused with a dusty pink glow. She could see Ethan saddling his horse at the hitching rail, talking quietly to the big animal as he tightened the girths. When a red-tailed hawk suddenly took flight from the pines, he paused, resting one hand on the horse's neck, and watched the graceful bird glide across the sky.

Turning away from the window, Elizabeth folded the letter, then stood. She walked to the fireplace and bent over the grate to stoke the embers. When the fire blazed, she slipped the letter beneath the crackling log and held it there with the poker, watching until nothing remained of it but black ash.

Chapter Five

❧❧❧❧❧

Elizabeth gathered her skirt with both hands, doing her best to rescue the hem from the heavy dew and the inquisitive nose of the hound trotting at her heels. She had not worn the black silk frock since she had left Auraria, but her meeting with Ethan this morning seemed to warrant finer attire than usual. Exactly one month had passed since she had taken charge of the tavern, and he had insisted she join him in examining the ledger.

"Blue! Come here!" When Ethan appeared on the veranda, the dog obediently retreated to his side. The animal nuzzled his master's hand, winning an affectionate pat on the head. As Elizabeth mounted the steps, he gently nudged the hound to make way for her. "I gave Blue strict orders to stay in the yard and bark when you drove up. If I remember correctly, the last time you called at my home he was off chasing rabbits and didn't give me any warning," he remarked with a mischievous twinkle in his eye.

"You should reward him for doing a good job this morning," Elizabeth replied with as even a smile as she could muster. At the reminder of her previous unannounced visit, however, her gaze involuntarily traveled down Ethan's muscular torso, which was now mercifully clothed in an immaculate white linen shirt. Catching herself, she pretended to adjust the drawstring of her purse as she followed him into the house.

Ethan pulled a spindle chair alongside the cherrywood desk, then beckoned Elizabeth to be seated. She watched expectantly as he sank onto the desk chair and opened a cloth-bound ledger.

"I tallied the receipts from the ferry last night," he began, scanning the column of precisely inked notations. "A lot of large herds passed this way last month, so I had expected us to do quite well. But I must say the tavern's earnings really surprised me." He shook his head, still not lifting his eyes from the ledger page.

In spite of herself, Elizabeth edged forward in her seat. "What do you mean?"

Ethan turned in his chair and shoved the ledger in front of her. "You can see for yourself."

Elizabeth reluctantly looked from his solemn face to the row of figures displayed before her. She swallowed hard, steeling herself for the worst. "Perhaps I shouldn't have bought so much sugar from Noah Gilmer the last time he stopped by, but the blackberries were so plentiful it seemed a shame not to make jam with them. I have sold quite a bit of it already." Her finger underscored several entries in her own hand. "And I don't think it was such a bad idea to stock some needles. I know they're dear, but people are always asking for them. We're bound to recover the money sooner or—" Ethan's low chuckle caused her to look up. Elizabeth straightened herself, wishing she could somehow restrain the insidious flush creeping up her neck. "The tavern will do better next month, Ethan. I swear it will."

"Take care that you don't promise too much, Elizabeth. I'll grant that you've done exceptionally well, but there is a limit to how much a backwoods public house can yield."

Elizabeth frowned, still uncertain of his intention. "You mean you're happy with the small profit?" she ventured.

"What do you mean by 'small'?" Ethan shook his head, his eyes sparkling with amusement. "The tavern hasn't earned this well in months," he confessed.

"And all this time I thought that I had failed miserably!" Elizabeth tried to look indignant, a near impossibility in the face of Ethan's contagious grin.

"Forgive me, but I couldn't resist teasing you." Ethan summarily closed the ledger and leaned back in his chair, lapping one arm over the back. "You've done a splendid job with the tavern, Elizabeth.'' His smile did nothing to diminish the sincerity of the simple compliment. ''Perhaps you'll take heart now and try your hand at farming.''

''Jephtha has already planted a few acres of corn as well as a kitchen garden. I should be happy if we could raise enough to feed ourselves.''

Ethan stood and began to put away the pen nibs and papers lying on the desk. ''I'd lay money you'll do better than that.''

Elizabeth smiled, twisting in her seat to survey the room. She enjoyed the chance for a closer inspection of his home, not least of all for the insights it offered into his life. When she noticed Ethan watching her, she gave him an apologetic look.

''Forgive me if I seemed to stare,'' Elizabeth began.

Ethan laughed and shrugged. ''There are worse faults.''

Elizabeth turned back to the room. ''I couldn't help but admire how well everything in this room fits together, so many different things and yet they all seem to belong here.''

''That's what comes of living in one place for a long time, I suppose. My father built this house the year he and my mother were married. She chose the spot because it offered such a fine view of the river. It was only this one room then, of course. The wing and the upper story were added later, after Sally came along.''

''You were born here, then?'' Elizabeth ventured.

Chuckling, Ethan cut his eyes toward the ceiling. ''In one of those rooms upstairs.''

Emboldened by Ethan's willingness to indulge her curiosity, Elizabeth leaned forward to examine the oil portrait of a woman hanging over the desk. ''Your mother?'' When he nodded, she smiled. ''I thought so. You inherited her eyes.''

''She was about your age when she sat for that picture.'' Resting one knee on the desk chair, Ethan gazed fondly at the painting. ''An itinerant painter on his way to Alabama happened to stop at the public house one day. When my father learned how the fellow earned his keep, he told him he could name his price if he would only tarry here long enough to render a portrait of my mother. The painter said she was so pretty he'd be happy to paint her for nothing more than room and board."

Elizabeth studied the full crimson lips and shimmering dark eyes that the artist had captured on canvas. "I can see why he felt that way," she remarked.

She turned slowly and walked to the glass-fronted bookcases. Clasping her hands behind her back, she regarded the sheathed sword hanging on the wall over them. "I remember a sword like this one in our home in Savannah. It was my father's." Elizabeth reached to lightly touch the polished scabbard. "He fell at the Battle of Horseshoe Bend."

Ethan had followed her to the bookcases, halting a few steps behind her. "Then he was a comrade of my father," he said quietly.

Elizabeth looked up at him in surprise. "Your father served under Andrew Jackson?"

"Many Cherokees did. After all, we had been fighting the Creek long before the white settlers arrived. My father saved Colonel Kilpatrick's life during the Battle of the Horseshoe. Kilpatrick had been wounded and his horse shot from under him, but luckily for the colonel, my father was faster with his rifle than the Creek warrior was with his hatchet. As a token of his gratitude, the colonel gave him his own sword." Ethan's face sobered. "After the war my father felt personally betrayed when Andrew Jackson became such a staunch supporter of Indian removal. He had always believed that if we could learn from one another, take the best from each of our worlds, the white man and the Indian could one day live in peace. That was the way he raised Sally and me, to be proud of our heritage and to appreciate what was good in the white man's way of life, as well." He smiled wistfully. "I only missed the Green Corn ceremony once, the year I went away to school in Massachusetts."

"Your father must have been very serious about giving you an education. Did you acquire these books when you were up north?" Elizabeth gestured toward the impressive collection displayed in the bookcases.

"Some of them." Ethan sounded uncharacteristically diffident.

Elizabeth crouched for a better look at the leather-bound volumes lining the shelves. "I don't believe I've seen so many fine books since I left Savannah." She shook her head and laughed. "Uncle had a library, but most of it was devoted to military treatises and books on breeding horses." Elizabeth reached for the brass knob securing the glass door and then glanced up at Ethan. "May I?"

"Of course."

"Homer's *Iliad*." Elizabeth's finger traced the title etched in gold leaf on the brown leather spine. "*The Decline and Fall of the Roman Empire. Paradise Lost.* Now here is something I've loved since I was a girl. Shakespeare's sonnets." She pulled the book from the shelf and opened it on her knee. "Such beautiful poetry—" Elizabeth broke off as her eye fell on an inscription penned on the title page.

"May 1827. For my dearest Ethan. Tho' we be apart, know that I cherish your memory in my heart and live only for the blessed day that will see us united as husband and wife forever. Your devoted Catherine."

Looking at the earnest feminine script, Elizabeth realized that she had blundered into an intensely private realm of Ethan's history. "I'm sorry. I didn't mean to pry," she began.

"You needn't apologize." He reached over her shoulder and gently took the book from her hands. "That was a long time ago." His voice was little more than a whisper.

Staring at the page, Ethan looked so alone with the sad memories it evoked that Elizabeth longed to reach out to him. "You loved her?" she asked softly.

"Yes." Ethan drew a deep breath and closed the book. "But it simply wasn't meant to be." He placed the book on top of the case and then wheeled, in part, Elizabeth guessed, to conceal the emotion betrayed on his face. "If you've time, there's something I'd like to discuss with you," he said on his way to the hall.

Elizabeth scrambled to her feet to follow him. She caught up with him on the veranda. "Certainly I have time. Does it concern the tavern?"

When Ethan turned she was pleased to see that his face had regained some of its familiar amused expression. "No.

I want to talk about your horse and that ungainly wagon you're asking him to pull. I'm fond of horses and, frankly, it pains me to see a high-spirited creature reduced to no more than a plodding nag." He tilted his head, pretending to study Elizabeth. "That smart black trap suited you much better, too."

"Come now, Ethan. I couldn't very well move my household belongings in the trap," she argued. "Besides, I need a wagon if I'm to farm."

"That's true," Ethan agreed. "But surely you'd prefer riding when you've nothing to transport but yourself."

"Yes, but I don't have a saddle," Elizabeth countered.

Ethan ran his fingers through the wave of black hair falling over his brow, shaking his head in exasperation. "Elizabeth, you can think of more excuses than anyone I've ever known. What if I told you that I had a sidesaddle that was yours for the taking?"

Elizabeth fought to control the grin tickling the corners of her mouth. "Then I would have to think hard to find a good excuse not to accept it."

"I won't give you time for that." Tugging playfully at her elbow, Ethan started down the steps.

As if he was intent on keeping his word, he strode across the yard so quickly Elizabeth had to skip steps to keep up with him. She stood to the side and watched while he unhitched Midnight from the wagon and led him into the paddock. Apparently sensing that something was afoot, the temperamental horse pawed the ground when Ethan disappeared into the stable. Ethan reappeared shortly, carrying a sidesaddle with a bridle slung over his shoulder.

"This saddle belonged to my mother, but it hasn't been used in years," he told her as he swung the saddle onto the fence. He patted Midnight's neck and let him sniff the bridle before handily slipping it onto the horse's head. "Has he been trained to carry a rider?"

"The man who sold him to my husband said he was broken to ride as well as to drive," Elizabeth told him. "But we only used him to pull the trap. You think he might act up under saddle?"

Ethan's wide mouth pulled into a wry grin. "There's one way to find out."

Bracing one hand on the horse's withers, he gathered the reins in the other. He swung onto the animal's bare back, so lightly that for a moment Midnight looked as if he was not quite sure what had happened. The gelding tossed his head, pulling at the unfamiliar bit, then took a few testy steps backward. Elizabeth held her breath, waiting for Midnight to buck or rear, two tricks he had pulled on occasion, with unnerving results. Only Ethan seemed unperturbed by the state of affairs. He let the gelding sidle and prance, sitting as easily on the horse's back as if they were molded together. Finally Midnight seemed to realize he had met his match. When Ethan urged him forward he broke into a springy trot, docilely circling the paddock to halt in front of his amazed mistress.

"It looks like that fellow who sold him to you was telling the truth after all." Ethan chuckled as he slid off Midnight's back and tethered him to the fence.

Elizabeth nodded, but she cast an apprehensive glance at the saddle Ethan had just hoisted onto the horse's back. "I hope he will behave as well for me."

"He will," Ethan replied with, to Elizabeth's mind, wholly unfounded certainty. "I know his kind. He snorts and paws for show, but he's really all bluff. Once he realizes you're not taking him seriously, he's as gentle as a baby." He gave her a reassuring smile. "I'll lead him around until he gets used to carrying you sidesaddle."

Ethan clasped his hands, cupping Elizabeth's foot to boost her into the saddle. He stroked Midnight's bowed neck, and talked soothingly to the horse, before backing him away from the fence. The gelding rolled his eyes and balked, rebelling at the lopsided weight he was being asked to carry, but Ethan managed to cajole him into a reluctant walk. When they had circled the paddock twice without incident, Elizabeth reached for the reins.

"You think he's ready?" Ethan kept a firm hand on the bridle.

"There's one way to find out." Elizabeth mimicked his determined tone.

Ethan grinned as he stepped back and released his hold on the horse. Elizabeth had less than a second to smile in return, for that was the scant grace period Midnight was willing to grant her. As if he had decided to vent all the spleen bottled inside him, the gelding reared slightly, then lunged forward. Elizabeth managed to rein the recalcitrant animal, only to have him swing his hindquarters wildly to the side and then buck. When he suddenly bolted, she grasped the pommel with one hand and by some miracle kept her seat. The horse slid to a violent stop just a few feet short of the fence, wheeled and raced in the opposite direction. From the corner of her eye Elizabeth saw Ethan running across the paddock toward them, but she was too intent on anticipating the horse's next move to pay him much mind.

"Whoa, there!" Ethan reached for the bridle only to have Midnight pivot out of his reach and tear off across the paddock.

This time, however, Elizabeth was prepared for her mount's maneuver. When Midnight halted abruptly, she threw her weight back in the saddle as if that was precisely what she had wanted him to do. When he charged again, she nudged him with her heel. Midnight repeated the performance with such fury Elizabeth felt as if she were a rag doll being slung about by a willful child, but she doggedly clung to the saddle. The next time he pulled up short, he surprised her by simply standing still, apparently bored with the game.

"Oh, no, you don't!" Elizabeth muttered between gasps of air. She firmly turned Midnight in a circle, then goaded him into a quick trot. When she finally reined to a stop in front of Ethan, both horse and rider were panting.

"Are you all right?" The utter amazement written on Ethan's face made Elizabeth burst out laughing.

Ethan's mouth slowly widened into a grin, and his shoulders began to shake with laughter. "I don't know who's crazier, that fool horse or you for riding him down."

"What did you expect me to do? Leap out of the saddle?" Elizabeth retorted. She pressed one hand to her side, which was aching from exertion and laughter. "Now that I think of it, that does seem a rather attractive idea."

As she prepared to dismount, Ethan reached to clasp her waist with both hands. He lifted her out of the saddle and then turned in a half circle, causing her skirt to billow around her. When he lowered her to the ground she was laughing so hard she swayed against him.

Elizabeth rested her hands on his shoulders to steady herself. Through the fine shirting she could feel the warmth of Ethan's skin, the superbly defined contours of his hard muscles beneath her fingers. She drew in her breath, trying to subdue her accelerated heartbeat and the rampant emotions fueling it.

Ethan's eyes drifted slowly over her face. Still smiling down at her, he loosened one hand from her waist and reached to brush a damp wisp of hair from her temple. "You never cease to amaze me, Elizabeth."

"That's only because I let you talk me into doing foolish things," Elizabeth murmured, looking directly into the warm eyes caressing her face.

"Do you?" Ethan asked softly.

He turned his hand to smooth her cheek, slowly skimming the heated skin. When his finger traced the curve of her lip, a delicious current pulsed through her entire body. Without thinking, she turned her face to brush his palm with her lips. Elizabeth closed her eyes in an effort to regain her composure, even as her wayward hands tightened around his arms, yearning to draw him closer. She drew a long, uneven breath and managed to loosen her hold on him, resting her hands flat against his chest.

"Elizabeth." Ethan's whisper grazed her forehead like the stroke of warm velvet. "Look at me, Elizabeth." Balancing her chin on his finger, he tipped it upward, gently winning her compliance. Like dark prisms of the soul, his eyes seemed to illuminate the entire spectrum of emotions kindled in his heart. "There's no shame in feeling like this, not for a man or for a woman." He smiled tenderly, his gaze following his hand as it traveled along her jaw.

Elizabeth's lips parted to speak, but the words she sought stubbornly refused to take shape. Glancing down at the deeply tanned hand cradling her face, she reached to cover it with her own. As if he sensed and understood all the confusing emotions brewing inside her, Ethan's hand slipped from her cheek to clasp her fingers tightly.

He frowned when loud and furious barking suddenly erupted in the yard. Still holding her hand, Ethan glanced in the direction of the house. A piercing yelp interrupted the hound's baying, and he gave her hand a firm squeeze before reluctantly dropping it.

"Something's bothering Blue. Wait here while I have a look."

Ethan swung over the paddock fence and dashed around the stable. Clutching both arms, Elizabeth hovered by the fence. She listened to the now-frenzied barking for only a few seconds before climbing between the fence rails to follow him. Rounding the corner of the stable, she saw the frantic dog circling Ethan, its naturally loose gait now hampered by a pronounced limp. She caught up with him as he was crouching to examine the dog's foreleg.

"Is he hurt?" Elizabeth stooped to peer over his shoulder.

"I think his leg is just bruised." Ethan's low voice was tight with anger as he stroked the dog's long, drooping ears. He rose slowly, keeping his eyes on the roan saddle horse tethered to the veranda rail.

"Do you recognize that horse?" Elizabeth instinctively lowered her voice to a whisper.

Ethan shook his head. "I've never seen it before." Turning to Elizabeth, he clasped her wrists for a moment. "I want you to stay here, Elizabeth, and keep Blue with you."

Swallowing to ease the dryness in her throat, Elizabeth bent to clasp the big hound around the neck. As Ethan started for the house, Blue lunged, intent on following, but she managed to restrain the dog. She murmured softly, as much to soothe her own tensed nerves as to quiet the hound.

Kneeling beside the dog, Elizabeth watched Ethan cautiously approach the horse. Still keeping a watchful eye on the front door, he rounded the horse to take stock of its tack and saddlebags. Then he cleared the veranda steps with quick, compact movements calculated not to make a sound. Elizabeth bit her lip as Ethan hesitated by the open door to survey the hall before slipping inside the house.

Blue had apparently been watching his master as intently as she. When Ethan disappeared from sight the dog suddenly broke from her grasp and bolted for the house. Stumbling to her feet, Elizabeth ran after him. She gathered her skirts, climbing the veranda steps as gingerly as possible. From the threshold she could see Blue stationed at the bottom of the staircase. He had resumed his barking in earnest, stiff front legs braced on the bottom stair.

Elizabeth flinched as a coarse voice shouted from upstairs. "Shut your mouth, you goddamn cur, or I'll shut it for you!"

Blue's lips drew back into a snarl at the approach of heavy footsteps on the landing. As a barrel-chested man appeared on the stairs, the dog cowed, but stubbornly held his ground.

The man leveled a kick at Blue, narrowly missing the dog's head. "I'll teach you, you—"

"Kick that dog and I'll blow your leg off." Ethan stepped from the sitting room into the hall, holding a long rifle directly trained on the intruder.

The man teetered on the stairs, caught off-balance with one leg in midswing, but he managed to steady himself against the wall.

"Who are you and what are you doing in my house?" Ethan demanded.

For a moment the ruddy-faced intruder only continued to scowl. When Ethan nudged the air with the rifle, however, he apparently thought better of refusing a man who held a gun on him. "Name's Cephas Johnson." His voice was thick with belligerence. "And I reckon I got a right to have a look at what's mine."

Elizabeth glanced at Ethan. Rage had transformed his face, giving it the appearance of cut stone. "Get out of my house."

Johnson edged down the stairs, his watery blue eyes fixed warily on the rifle pointed at him. When the intruder reached the bottom of the stairs Ethan jerked the rifle toward the door. Keeping his back to the wall, Johnson sidled down the hall. When he glanced at Elizabeth she cringed, recoiling from the hatred reflected in the small, mean eyes. The rank smell of stale sweat and tobacco assaulted her nose as he eased alongside her. She stepped to the side, but Johnson mimicked her movement, taking advantage of the shield her body offered. "Ain't your house no more." He spat the words at Ethan.

"I'm only going to repeat myself once. Get out of my house." Listening to Ethan's low, deliberate voice, Elizabeth felt a chill ripple down her spine.

His threat was not wasted on Cephas Johnson. As Ethan started down the hall, Johnson bolted through the door. He jerked his horse's reins from the rail, causing the animal to start. With one foot jammed in the stirrup, he hopped in a circle, cursing the frightened horse and yanking at the bit.

Ethan halted at the top of the veranda steps, his rifle still propped against his shoulder. His eyes followed the horse shying across the yard, his face set in a cold mask. Only the slight quiver of the tensed muscles cording his neck revealed the emotion roiling inside him.

When Johnson finally succeeded in hoisting himself into the saddle, he reined the horse violently toward the road. He galloped to the bend, then pulled up short and wheeled his mount to face the house.

"This is my land now, redskin," he shouted across the distance. "Jus' 'cause you got yourself a white woman ain't no count for you to think differ'nt. I intend to have what's mine, you hear me? And I will. Can't one filthy Indian hold off the whole U.S. Army!"

Chapter Six

"**A**rrogant bastard!" Martin shoved away from the table so abruptly the chair crashed to the floor behind him. He strode to the window and then back to the table, unable to contain the fevered restlessness tormenting him. "He'll not drive you from your land, Ethan. When he returns, he'll see that quickly enough. I'll take up arms with you. You can count on Gray Bear and Noble, too."

Ethan stared at his hand lying on the table. Like the rest of his body, it felt numb, with no more vigor than the polished wood on which it rested. "How long do you think three Indians and a freed slave can hold off the federal troops?"

"That is what the white men want us to think, that we've no choice but to comply with this worthless treaty. When have we not heard rumors that we would be forced from our land?" Martin braced his hands on the table, leaning to look up into Ethan's face. Urgency had given his low-pitched voice a breathless quality, disrupted its normal measured cadence. "When I was in Walkerstown last month I heard John Ross speak. He's drafting other treaties, using his influence in Washington."

"Do you think anyone in Washington still listens to our chiefs, Martin?" Ethan was surprised by how hollow his own voice sounded, like wind whistling through a cavern.

Martin's black eyes leveled with his. "I believe we must not yield, Ethan—whether they listen or not." He placed a hand on Ethan's shoulder. "You are my friend, the brother of the woman I loved better than life itself. Know that I will stand by you." His hand tightened its grasp. Then he stepped back, his solemn gaze lingering on Ethan for a long moment before he turned to the door.

Ethan listened as Martin's footsteps disappeared down the hall. For what seemed a long time he remained seated at the table, staring blankly across the wainscoted room where he and his family had once gathered to share their meals. The light coming through the tall windows had stretched to long, fading shadows before he at last roused himself from his chair.

As he wandered into the hall he stopped short, jolted by the vivid memory of the morning's confrontation. Cephas Johnson's presence seemed to cling to the narrow corridor, the feral smell of his unwashed body poisoning the air. Revulsion rose in Ethan like a sickness, and he rushed outdoors.

He sank onto the edge of the veranda and rested his back against the column. When a cold nose nudged his hand, he absently stroked Blue's ears, his eyes drifting across the pools of pastel light collecting on the distant river. The trees along the bank were thick with foliage now, screening from view the fields stretching behind them. In winter, however, he could see Jonathan's house through the skeletal forest— the house where Elizabeth now lived.

At the thought of her, the vision of her stricken face rose in his mind, its delicate color blanched by apprehension as she watched him challenge Cephas Johnson. After Johnson had ridden away, the pain had lingered in her deep gray eyes even as she had tried to offer encouragement.

Ethan closed his eyes and tried to evoke a happier recollection. Over the past weeks he had accumulated a cache of memories from his association with Elizabeth, a private treasure that he could recall and savor at will. He was startled by how carefully he had marked even the smallest detail of her person—the way light played on her hair, weaving threads of spun gold through the thick chestnut waves; the color of her eyes on a clear day, shimmering like smooth gray stones beneath a rushing stream; the determined tilt of her chin when she was set on doing something; her smile, at once shy and beckoning; the softness of her skin beneath his hand.

Never had he wanted to take a woman in his arms as badly as he had wanted to hold Elizabeth that morning in the paddock. Not even when he had loved Catherine had he yearned for her kiss with such passion. He had been much younger then, Ethan reflected, scarcely nineteen years of age. With the brash confidence of youth he had believed that love was powerful enough to overcome any obstacle, that it could vanquish prejudice as readily as Dr. Ewing's cherished books dispelled ignorance. He had been foolish enough to think that the distinguished schoolmaster who had fostered his learning with such care, who heaped glowing praise on his young student from the Cherokee Nation, would welcome him with equal enthusiasm as a son-in-law. He could not have been more wrong.

He was an older and wiser man now, Ethan reminded himself, at least wise enough not to repeat the same bitter mistake. However strong his desire for Elizabeth, it could lead to nothing but heartache. He had let the comfortable familiarity developing between them lull him into ignoring that fact. Cephas Johnson's appearance and the vile slur he had hurled in parting had jarred him back to reality. He had no right to draw Elizabeth into his life, not when doing so subjected her to the insults of scum like Johnson. In addition to love, any man worthy of her affection would offer her security and stability, benefits he could not even guarantee himself. If he cared for Elizabeth, the best he could do for her was to leave her in peace.

A heaviness sank over Ethan, dulling his senses to everything but the pain that gnawed deep inside him. Leaning his head against the column, he watched the forest's black wall slowly devour the last of the sinking sun.

"Good afternoon, Miss Ballard! What can I do for you today?" Wiping her hands on her apron, Elizabeth abandoned the beef brisket she was salting and hurried to welcome the tiny woman who had just appeared in the tavern door.

"Good afternoon, Mrs. Merriweather. Gray Bear." Miss Ballard inclined her head to the ferryman, who was seated by the window eating a plate of chicken and dumplings. A reserved smile accompanied her greetings. "I've a letter I wish to post. Do you expect the stagecoach this week?"

Elizabeth laughed. "Heaven willing. The best I can promise is that your letter will leave on the first stage that passes this way."

"Very well, then." Miss Ballard pulled a sealed letter from her purse and handed it to Elizabeth. "My sister will simply have to adjust to the vagaries of frontier postal service, I suppose."

"Just as my relatives must." Elizabeth smiled as she carried the letter to the bar and stowed it in a cubbyhole beneath the counter. Catching the glimmer of curiosity in Miss Ballard's bright eyes, she added, "I have a sister in Savannah and two very dear cousins who live on a plantation in Morgan County."

"At least they are not so very far away. My sister lives in Boston."

Elizabeth nodded sympathetically. "That is a considerable distance."

"Too great when I think of how much I should love to see my precious nephews." Miss Ballard sighed. "But then, I am fortunate to have my children here." For a brief moment two stubbornly pronounced dimples dented her spare cheeks. "You must visit the school when time permits, Mrs. Merriweather."

"I would like that very much," Elizabeth told her. She accompanied the diminutive schoolmistress onto the porch. She was watching Miss Ballard climb onto the driver's seat of Martin Early's wagon when Ethan cantered his horse into the yard.

"Good day, Miss Ballard!" He reined the deep-chested bay gelding alongside the wagon. "Don't tell me Martin has grown so lax that he's left you without a driver!"

Miss Ballard lifted her chin, taking her time gathering the reins. "Not at all, Mr. Woodard. Only a child or an invalid requires a servant to drive him about, and I am neither." She gave Ethan as triumphant a smile as her strict code of eti-

quette would permit. "Good day to you both." She slapped
the lines against the horses' backs with surprising authority
for a woman of her meager size.

Chuckling to himself, Ethan watched the wagon bounce
onto the road before he pivoted his horse toward the tavern
and then dismounted.

"Hello, Ethan." Elizabeth hovered at the top of the steps,
hands jammed into the pockets of her apron.

"Good afternoon, Elizabeth." He glanced up from the
reins he was tethering to the rail and smiled briefly.

Elizabeth licked her lips, hating the awkward feeling that
had suddenly come over her. She waited a few moments in
the vain hope that Ethan would pick up the conversation. "I
haven't seen you in a while," she said at length.

"This time of year, tending the crops keeps me occupied.
I've over one hundred acres under cultivation now," he reminded her, his attention focused on the saddle girths he was
loosening. "How is business?"

"Better than fair, I would say. We had a party headed for
Tennessee that stopped here Monday and spent the night.
Such a clamor, ten children in all and the eldest only eight
years old! I doubt that Gray Bear enjoyed much sleep that
evening." When Ethan said nothing, Elizabeth gestured toward the landing. "Surely Gray Bear mentioned the big herd
of cattle that Noble and he ferried across the river yesterday. Nearly three hundred head, I believe he said."

Ethan only nodded as he patted the horse's neck and then
started up the steps. When he drew even with Elizabeth, he
hesitated as if he were uncertain how to negotiate the last
step with her standing on it. She moved to one side, self-
consciously smoothing her skirt as he brushed past her.
Ethan halted in the tavern doorway.

"After you've finished eating, Gray Bear, I'd like some
help in the stable," he said. "James Birdsong will be by before dusk to fetch his stallion, and he'll expect the temperamental devil to be wearing a new set of shoes. The job will
go easier if you can lend me a hand."

Gray Bear nodded, but did not hasten his chewing in the
least.

"There's plenty of stewed chicken left, if you'd like some, Ethan," Elizabeth ventured, starting for the kitchen.

"No, thank you," Ethan put in quickly enough to halt her in her tracks.

Gray Bear swallowed with care. "You should eat something, Ethan. If this horse is as bad as you say, you will need the strength," he remarked in his unhurried, deliberate manner.

"I'm not hungry," Ethan said, more abruptly than Elizabeth had ever heard him address Gray Bear. "I'm going to fire the forge. You'll find me in the stable whenever you're ready." He stepped back, giving Elizabeth a short nod, before turning and hurrying outside. Through the open door she could see him striding across the yard as if he were rushing to quench a wildfire.

"Ethan will be sorry he did not take my advice," Gray Bear commented, gesturing philosophically with his knife.

Elizabeth forced herself to smile, no easy task given the perverse stiffness afflicting her mouth. "You must eat a second helping, then."

She waited for Gray Bear to spear the last dumpling before taking the plate and heading for the kitchen. When she returned to the tavern she busied herself preparing the corned beef while the ferryman finished his meal. Gray Bear had joined Ethan in the stable by the time she had seasoned the meat and stored it in a stoneware crock.

As Elizabeth cleared the table she could hear snatches of the men's laughter drift across the yard, punctuated by an occasional firm command directed at the fractious stallion. Something about those vague, unremarkable sounds struck her with such poignancy that she paused and sank down at the table. Only a few weeks earlier, Ethan and she had shared that kind of relaxed rapport, bantering and joking as easily as old friends. They *had* been friends, Elizabeth reflected, or so it had seemed until that awful morning when Cephas Johnson had ridden up to Ethan's farm. Since that day she had felt as if they were standing on opposite sides of an ever-widening gulf, one that she was powerless to bridge.

Days now passed without Ethan showing his face at the tavern, and when he did call, he limited his visits to brief discussions of business matters. Although he had always treated her with consideration, an almost stiff formality had supplanted his once-free manner. Now he never teased her, and he took extraordinary pains never to touch even her hand.

At the memory of his touch, Elizabeth pressed her lips together to fight back the unpleasant lump filling her throat. She had no one to blame but herself, of course, for letting herself take playful flirtation far more seriously than it was intended. Yet how could she doubt her deepest instincts when he had whispered her name, caressed her face, looked into her eyes with such tenderness? More persuasive still, Ethan had been willing to reveal to her a deeply personal part of himself, if only fleetingly. As Elizabeth gazed out the window at the sun-stippled yard, she refused to believe she had misread his heart so completely.

Whatever the case, Cephas Johnson's appearance had altered everything between Ethan and her. Perhaps the uncouth intruder had reminded him of the circumstances leading to her own arrival in the valley. Distressing as the thought might be, Elizabeth had to allow for the possibility that Ethan now viewed her as an interloper whose sympathy would inevitably fall with her own people. Even were she to protest to the contrary, an incontrovertible fact remained—unlike Ethan, she need never fear the day when troops would arrive to drive her from her home.

Fighting the soul-deep weariness that had settled over her like a smothering blanket, Elizabeth forced herself to her feet and began to tidy the common room. She tried to concentrate on the simple tasks, numb her mind to its troubling thoughts. While she was sweeping the floor upstairs, she heard a rider in the yard, followed not long afterward by men's voices, Ethan's prominent among them. When she at last carried the bucket of dirty wash water outside and emptied it onto the refuse heap, Ethan's bay gelding was no longer tied to the rail, and the yard was quiet.

Elizabeth dropped the bucket beside the porch and seated herself on the steps. Propping her elbows on her pulled-up knees, she gazed down the shaded path leading to the landing. She was so lost in thought she did not hear Gray Bear behind her until he cleared his throat.

"Would you like a cup of coffee, Elizabeth?"

Elizabeth twisted on the step to find Gray Bear standing on the porch, holding two steaming cups. "More than almost anything I can think of right now." She smiled as she reached to take the cup he held out to her.

"I fixed it the way you like it, with nothing in it," Gray Bear told her, sinking onto the step above her.

Elizabeth took a small sip of the scalding hot brew. "Did Mr. Birdsong's horse behave himself?" she asked, resting the cup on her knee.

"He was stubborn, almost as stubborn as Ethan. I let them wrestle with each other until they were both tired of it. Then everything went fine." Gray Bear fanned the steam rising from his cup, cutting the vapor into shreds that disintegrated in the air. "That is the trouble with Ethan. No one can tell him anything." Elizabeth felt him glance at her. Then he drew a long breath. "He has always been like that. I remember when he got it in his head that he was going to marry that girl up north."

Elizabeth's eyes followed her finger skimming the rim of her cup, not daring to look at Gray Bear. "Catherine?"

"Yes, that was her name. Catherine Ewing. Her father ran a fancy school that Ethan's folks sent him off to when he came of age. Ethan wrote his parents lots of letters when he was away. He was good about that. In most of them he had something to say about this Catherine, how pretty and smart she was, how well she played the piano, how she loved to dance. By the time he came home in the summer he had made up his mind to marry her."

Gray Bear shook his head slowly. "His father tried to talk him out of it, but Ethan would not hear a word against what he had his heart set on. He wrote long letters to her all summer, and she wrote long letters back to him. I guess they were about as in love as two reckless young people can be. Then one day he just got on his horse and rode back to Massachusetts, determined to ask for his Catherine's hand and bring her home with him."

When Gray Bear paused, Elizabeth ventured a glance at him. "What happened?"

"By the time Ethan got to Massachusetts, Catherine's folks had packed her off somewhere. Ethan had looked up to her father, and now this man would not even have him in his home. He met Ethan at the door and told him he could not allow his daughter to marry an Indian. Ethan never saw Catherine again."

"How monstrously cruel!" Elizabeth placed the cup on the step and shifted to face Gray Bear. "Ethan must have been hurt to the quick."

"He was, but he did his best not to show it. He made himself hard on the outside, so he would not ever be hurt that bad again. When his father died he had a reason to work all the time, with the ferry and everything. But it has taken him many years to forget Catherine, I think." Gray Bear's kind dark eyes swept Elizabeth's face. "It was good to hear him laugh again."

Elizabeth looked down at her hands clasped on her knees. "Do you think that Ethan has once more forgotten how to laugh?"

Gray Bear's smile was sad and infinitely wise. "Ethan is stubborn, Elizabeth, but he is not a fool. Be patient with him." Collecting his empty cup, he rose slowly and walked back into the tavern.

"Enough of your mischief, Midnight!" Dolly tugged the reins smartly and succeeded in halting the headstrong horse beside the hitching rail.

Elizabeth smiled as she reached to set the wagon's brake. "Poor Midnight! He's grown so accustomed to carrying me under saddle, I suspect he thought his days of pulling the wagon were over."

Dolly shook her head as she climbed to the ground. "If you ask me, ma'am, I think he's just plain mean." She cast a withering eye at the gelding, who irritably tossed his head and chewed the bit. She walked to the rear of the wagon and helped Elizabeth unload two large baskets of clean linen from the bed. "That's some big herd of cattle penned up over yonder," Dolly remarked as they carried the freshly laundered bedclothes up the path to the public house.

"Gray Bear says we'll see even larger herds if the pastures dry up next month and people start to sell off their stock." Elizabeth clutched the unwieldy basket to her midsection, juggling the weight as she climbed the steps. "I'm glad to see the trade pass through here, but I'd rather we had plenty of rain. Jephtha has worked so hard breaking ground and planting, he deserves to see a good yield for his effort." She dropped the basket onto the tavern floor and scooted it aside with her foot to permit Dolly to pass.

Dolly deposited her basket next to Elizabeth's, then straightened herself, pressing both hands to the small of her back. "My Jephtha has a real feel for farming, that's for sure. Back when we lived on old Mr. Merriweather's big place, he raised corn and cotton and even a little tobacco on his own time. Earned himself some good money with it, too. Once he even approached old Mr. Merriweather with the idea of buying us free by and by. 'Course, Mr. Merriweather had his own ideas." She broke off abruptly and began to sort through the linen baskets. "I expect you'll want these sheets upstairs, ma'am?"

"Just leave them here for now, Dolly. We can take them up after the drovers who have slept over are on their way." Elizabeth hesitated. The revelation that Dolly had let slip disturbed her deeply, for she knew exactly what ideas had been brewing in Elias Merriweather's mind when he had rejected Jephtha's bid for freedom. His younger son, Samuel, would need two reliable servants to see his household properly established, and Dolly and Jephtha had been designated for that purpose. Elizabeth placed a light hand on the young woman's shoulder, relying on a gesture to convey a measure of her feeling. "Let's go to the kitchen and start breakfast. We're going to have five hungry men to feed as soon as the sun is up."

The night breeze blowing off the river had cooled the kitchen, leaving only a remnant of warmth in the brick fireplace. While Dolly revived the fire, Elizabeth fetched butter, bacon and ham from the spring house where perishables were stored in the warmer months. Soon the tiny cubicle was filled with the tantalizing fragrance of simmering coffee and smoked meat sizzling on the grate.

True to Elizabeth's prediction, the drovers descended on the public room with prodigious appetites. Leaving Dolly to manage the cooking, Elizabeth trotted between the kitchen and the tavern, serving food and fulfilling demands for yet more biscuits, eggs and coffee. When the men had eaten their fill they wandered out to the stock pens, leaving a daunting quantity of empty cups and dirty crockery in their wake. Elizabeth collected as much of the debris as she could carry on her way back to the kitchen.

"I can wash dishes later," she told Dolly. "Right now I think we're both entitled to some breakfast."

To that end, she cracked four eggs into the hot cast-iron spider. By the time the eggs were done, the remaining pan of biscuits had baked to a mellow golden brown. Elizabeth had not realized how hungry she was until she was seated at the table with the plate of tempting food in front of her. While the women enjoyed their meal, she entertained Dolly with stories about some of the more eccentric patrons who had visited the tavern since she had assumed its management. She was refilling their coffee cups when Dolly twisted in her chair to peep through the open door.

"Looks to me like Mr. Woodard himself just rode up," Dolly commented.

Still clutching the coffeepot, Elizabeth glanced through the door. "I imagine he's going to lend the men a hand with that big herd." She tried to sound unconcerned, a technique she had as yet failed to master. Fortunately, Dolly seemed too preoccupied with the activity in the yard to take note of her discomfiture.

"My, but he is a fine figure of a man!" Dolly smiled to herself.

"Yes, he is," Elizabeth agreed, not looking up from her coffee.

She drew a deep breath, wishing she could dislodge the heaviness in her chest. In the past weeks she had tried to follow Gray Bear's counsel. So far, however, Ethan had shown no inclination to resume their earlier comfortable association. If anything, he had distanced himself even fur ther, stopping at the tavern less frequently and abbreviating his visits to the bare minimum necessary to conduct business. Innumerable times, Elizabeth had tried to summon the courage to take the first step, to say something that would pierce the barrier between them, but uncertainty had held her back. Gradually she had begun to fear that Ethan now viewed her as only a bitter reminder of old wounds he fervently wished to forget.

Dolly had taken her cup of coffee and walked to the door. "It's going to take some doing to get all those cows across the river."

"Have you ever seen a ferry under operation?" Elizabeth asked as she replaced the lid on the stoneware jam crock.

Dolly shook her head. "No, ma'am, I can't say I have," she confessed.

"Why don't you walk down to the landing and watch, then?" Elizabeth suggested, sweeping crumbs from the table with a folded towel. When Dolly hesitated, she motioned toward the yard with the homespun cloth. "Go on, now. After boiling dirty linen for most of yesterday, you've certainly earned a bit of time to amuse yourself."

"You boiled a goodly share of that linen, too, ma'am, and done most of the ironing," Dolly reminded her, but she dutifully placed the cup on the table and began to untie her apron sash.

"I've seen herds ferried across the river dozens of times," Elizabeth demurred. "Perhaps I'll join you later after I've taken stock of the supplies," she added, giving Dolly the necessary verbal push across the threshold.

In truth, Elizabeth had no intention of venturing near the landing while Ethan was working there. She had devised an appropriately businesslike manner for dealing with him when circumstances brought them together, but the brisk diction and practiced nods did nothing to salve the ache inside her. She still could not look at Ethan without remembering the tenderness in his melting dark eyes, without yearning for a glimpse of his smile, at once teasing and kind. In time, she assumed, her emotions would grow more tractable, their craving blunted by inescapable reality. In the interim, however, she had resolved to avoid unnecessary contact with Ethan and the painful longing it aggravated.

Despite her best intentions, Elizabeth paused on her way to the spring house, her attention captured by the raucous commotion rising from the riverbank. Parting the low branches of a magnolia, she peered between the dense, waxy leaves at the bustling landing in the distance. Dolly had ventured as near the water's edge as her natural reserve and the unruly herd of cattle would permit, and had stationed herself on a stump that afforded a clear view of the proceedings. The drovers were guiding the balky animals into a narrow chute where the stoutly built Noble prodded them, one by one, onto the flat-bottomed boat. When the craft was filled to capacity with cattle bawling their protests, Gray Bear secured the gate and then waved for the ferrymen to cast off.

Elizabeth's eyes followed the boat as it slowly glided away from the dock, yielding reluctantly to the ferrymen's poles. As he often did when an exceptionally heavy load required transport, Ethan was working side by side with his men. Stripped of his shirt, his splendid shoulders glistened under the strong sun as his muscles strained against the pole. She heard him shout to the pilot, then glance behind him to encourage the men engaged at the poles.

Suddenly a loud crack, not unlike the sound of lightning sundering a tree, carried across the water. Bellowing and snorting, the cattle surged toward the breach they had opened in the stanchion. They charged onto the deck, splintering crates and barrels in their path. Ethan braced both hands on the pole and attempted to lever himself away from the panicked beasts, but the overcrowded boat afforded little room for evasive action. Another shattering crash followed, and the boat's rail gave way. Elizabeth watched in mute horror as the frenzied animals plunged into the water, sweeping Ethan in their path.

Chapter Seven

"Ethan!" Elizabeth's cry tore through the humid air. Wrenching her skirt free of the snags catching at the hem, she thrashed through the close branches of the magnolias. She half ran, half slid down the muddy bank, oblivious to everything but the terrifying scene unfolding before her eyes.

The ferryboat was now surrounded by cattle struggling to swim. As the animals battled the current, their terrified bleating egged the stock remaining on board into a panic. Elizabeth's eyes scoured the churning water in a desperate attempt to locate Ethan somewhere in the melee. She sucked in her breath when his head broke the water, not far from the boat. One of the ferrymen rushed to crouch at the edge of the flatboat and extend his pole within Ethan's reach. The blood pounding in her ears, Elizabeth watched him grapple to seize the lifesaving pole only to be dragged under by the cattle crushing around him. A seeming eternity passed before he surfaced yet again. This time he managed to clamp both hands to the pole and hold fast as the ferryman pulled him toward the boat.

Stumbling through the thick mud, Elizabeth fought her way to the landing. As the ferrymen poled the boat toward the dock, she could see Ethan lying on the deck. His bare chest rose in fitful jerks, laboring for each breath. Elizabeth pressed a hand to her mouth at the sight of the dark red stain spreading over the lower left leg of his breeches. She clambered onto the dock and shoved past the gaping drovers to join Gray Bear at the edge of the dock. When the boat touched land Ethan tried to sit up, but the impact sent him sprawling onto his back. With the agility of a man half his age, Gray Bear sprang onto the ferry and knelt beside him.

"Be still, Ethan." Gray Bear spoke calmly, his voice belying the concern reflected in his hooded dark eyes.

"I think my leg's broken," Ethan managed to get out between rough gasps for air.

Gray Bear only nodded as he helped Noble and one of the ferrymen lift Ethan and carry him to shore. Elizabeth followed the men up the bank, trying not to look at Ethan's leg dangling at a sickeningly unnatural angle. Only when a light hand closed around hers did she notice Dolly, who had fallen in step with her on the path. Elizabeth clasped the young woman's hand, taking comfort from its warmth against her own icy fingers. As they approached the tavern she released Dolly's hand to rush ahead and open the door wide.

Drawing a long, deep breath to steady her nerves, Elizabeth glanced around the public room and then beckoned to one of the workmen. "Joseph, bring one of the mattresses downstairs and lay it on the floor over there." While the man hurried to do her bidding, she dispatched Dolly to the well for water and collected linen from the basket. Elizabeth quickly prepared a bed, then stood aside as the men lowered Ethan onto it and covered him with a sheet.

Pain had drained his face of its naturally warm color, replacing it with an unwholesome sallow sheen. His jaw was clenched, so tightly the sinews rose like welts along his neck. As he gulped uneven drafts of air, his mouth quivered slightly in mute testimony to the agony racking his body. When his eyes met hers, his lips parted as if he wanted to speak, but a wince cut short his effort.

"Don't try to talk, Ethan," Elizabeth whispered, fighting to control the quaver in her voice. "Just lie still." She gently smoothed the wet hair from his forehead, her fingers grazing the deep furrows that creased his brow.

Dipping a cloth into the bucket of cold water Dolly had fetched, she sponged Ethan's face while Gray Bear cut away his sodden breeches. As Noble lifted the sheet to bare the injured leg, a grimace displaced his normally stoic expression. At first glimpse of the jagged bone protruding through the flesh, a cold blackness engulfed Elizabeth and the room began to recede. She swallowed to curb the violent wave of nausea rising inside her.

"It's broke clean through, Ethan." Noble hesitated, his solemn eyes traveling from the shattered limb to Ethan's damp face. "Ain't no way we can set it proper without pullin' it 'round straight first."

Ethan nodded without lifting his head. "Do whatever you have to do."

Noble's broad hand rested briefly on Ethan's arm. Then he turned to Gray Bear, but the older man had already risen and started for the door.

"I am going to make splints," Gray Bear said. "We will need something to bind them."

Elizabeth pushed to her feet and hurried to overtake the elderly ferryman. She caught his elbow as he started down the porch steps. "Shouldn't we summon a doctor?" she asked in an urgent, low voice.

Gray Bear shook his head slowly. "The closest doctor is a good day's ride from here, if he still lives at New Echota. Ethan cannot wait that long." He continued down the steps, his broad shoulders hunched beneath an invisible burden.

Elizabeth felt dazed as she returned to the tavern and rummaged through the linen basket. She mechanically tore a sheet into long strips, refusing to let her mind stray from the task at hand. When Gray Bear returned bearing a sheaf of stout, flat sticks, she knelt beside Ethan once more. His breathing had grown shallow now, his face suffused in a clammy sweat. He was staring at the ceiling, his dark eyes so clouded with pain that Elizabeth wondered if he could still distinguish any of the people moving around him. When she bent over him, however, he tried to smile.

"This is some mess I've gotten myself into, isn't it?"

"Yes, it is." A constricting tightness grabbed at Elizabeth's throat, but she refused to let her own smile falter.

"Those damned cattle will swim all the way to the Coosa River fork if someone doesn't round them up." Ethan's voice caught, and he swallowed in an effort to regain control.

Elizabeth could tell he was trying to talk only to distract himself from the ordeal he was about to undergo, and she was determined to do her part to that end. "I suspect most of them headed for shore pretty quickly," she said, lightly stroking his brow. "The drovers probably have them penned by now."

She was adjusting the cool cloth on his forehead when Ethan winced with a violence that made her start. Elizabeth glanced behind her and saw Gray Bear standing with Ethan's foot braced against his own knee. He exchanged glances with Noble, who was clasping the injured leg just below the hip, and then nodded. As the men attempted to straighten his leg, Ethan's body arched, rebelling at the suffering inflicted on it. He was panting now, his breath coming in short spurts, and Elizabeth realized how badly he must have wanted to scream.

"It's almost over, Ethan." Elizabeth lifted his hand, clenched in a fist, and held it tightly. "They're almost done."

Ethan's feverish eyes widened for a moment, and a low moan escaped his lips. Then Elizabeth felt his hand relax inside hers as his head sank to one side. Her own body sagged with relief at the merciful oblivion that had delivered him from his torture.

"He's passed out," she told Gray Bear and Noble over her shoulder. She continued to hold Ethan's unmoving hand while the men rotated the broken leg and stabilized it with splints.

"He will sleep for a while, I think. That is good," Gray Bear said. "We should take Ethan home before he wakes up. At least he will be spared the misery of a rough ride."

Elizabeth nodded numbly. "We can carry him in my wagon."

As the men prepared to lift Ethan, she roused herself to her feet. For a moment she swayed unsteadily, overcome by the smell of river water, blood and pain filling the room. She closed her eyes to regain her equilibrium, forcing back the terrible memories that gaped like livid wounds in her mind. Elizabeth quickly collected fresh linen and then hurried outside to the wagon. With Dolly's help she fashioned a pallet in the back of the wagon. She stood back, nervously clutching her elbows, while Gray Bear and Noble eased Ethan's seemingly lifeless body onto the makeshift bed.

Gray Bear stepped back from the wagon bed, his eyes still lingering on Ethan's pallid face. "I will see if Martin Early can spare a servant to look after Ethan until he is well again."

Elizabeth gave the elderly man a surprised look. "Ethan doesn't have a housekeeper who can care for him?"

A faint smile relieved Gray Bear's somber expression. "Ethan has never taken to having people wait on him. He lets old Maum Betsy cook for him and clean house because it is what she always did for his folks. She still thinks of him as a little boy and would be very hurt if he told her she was not needed. But since her husband has been down with the palsy, she spends most of her time tending to his needs."

Elizabeth frowned as she followed Gray Bear to the front of the wagon. When he lifted the reins she reached out and abruptly grabbed one of the lines, causing Midnight to toss his head in confusion. "Let's take Ethan to my home, Gray Bear." Without waiting for his agreement she climbed onto the seat beside him. "I've Dolly and Jephtha to help me, so he need never be left alone. It makes perfect sense."

Gray Bear glanced over his shoulder at Noble, who was already helping Dolly clamber into the wagon bed. When the two passengers were seated alongside Ethan, he clucked to the horse. "You are right, Elizabeth," he said at length. "Your home is the best place for Ethan."

Gray Bear drove slowly, checking Midnight's natural inclination to pick up his pace now that he was homeward bound. As soon as he halted the wagon in the yard, Dolly scrambled to the ground and hurried into the house. By the time Elizabeth caught up with her, she was returning from the chiffonier, her arms laden with lavender-scented linen.

"It gets mighty hot upstairs in the daytime. I expect Mr. Woodard might be most comfortable if we were to put him in that nice corner room with the big windows."

"That's an excellent idea, Dolly." Elizabeth followed the young woman up the stairs. She paused midway to beckon to Gray Bear and Noble when they appeared in the doorway carrying the still-unconscious Ethan.

As the men edged their way up the staircase, Elizabeth helped Dolly make the bed, then she adjusted the curtains to shield the room from the brunt of the early-afternoon sun. She hovered by the window while Gray Bear and Noble lifted Ethan onto the bed. As the two men retreated toward the door, Elizabeth reluctantly started to follow, but Gray Bear waved her back.

"I will tend to the tavern today, Elizabeth," he told her on his way to the landing.

"Thank you," she whispered, but the ferryman only shook his graying head as he ambled down the stairs.

Turning back to the room, she found Dolly standing beside the bed with one hand resting lightly on Ethan's brow. When Elizabeth approached, she looked up. "His fever's rising. 'Course, that's to be expected," she was quick to add. "I remember when my little brother broke his arm. He had such a raging fever Mama thought he'd set the mattress afire before it finally broke." She laid a reassuring hand on Elizabeth's arm. "I'd best fetch some fresh water."

Elizabeth nodded. As Dolly disappeared into the hall, she reached to touch Ethan's forehead. His skin felt hot and dry, seared to the texture of paper. Her fingers drifted down his face, slowly tracing the contour of the oblique cheekbone. When she heard Dolly's quick steps on the stairs she caught herself and hastily walked to the door.

"I've quite lost track of time, but I imagine Jephtha will be in from the fields in an hour or so, and he's certain to be hungry. Why don't you start supper? I'll sit with Ethan for a bit, just to make sure he's resting quietly, and then I'll join you."

Dolly reluctantly surrendered the bucket of water, giving the darkened bedroom a final inspection over Elizabeth's shoulder. "You let me know if you need anything, ma'am," she said in parting.

"I will," Elizabeth promised. She waited until Dolly had started down the stairs before she stepped back into the room and pulled the door closed behind her.

Elizabeth filled the washstand basin and soaked a linen towel in the cold water. Folding the towel into a compress, she walked to the bedside and leaned over Ethan. As she began to bathe his heated face, she murmured soothingly to him. Although Ethan gave no indication that he was aware of anything around him, the sound of her own quiet voice seemed to soften the atmosphere and relieve the tension that clotted the air as oppressively as the afternoon heat.

"You're so warm. We need to bring your fever down." Elizabeth blotted his throat, pressing the cool cloth into the cleft where his neck and shoulder joined. "There. Doesn't that feel good?" Her lips quivered as she smiled down at him. "Remember that afternoon on the dock when you did this to me?" She carefully turned one of his bare arms and dabbed his wrist with the cloth. Feeling the weak pulse throbbing beneath the hot skin, she bit her lip to still its trembling.

So much misfortune had since come to pass that that beautiful sun-blessed day now seemed to belong to the remote past. Elizabeth had assumed that her memories of the fleeting intimacy that she and Ethan had enjoyed would dim as well, that time would deaden the intense emotions he had awakened in her. Yet now she need only touch his hand to recall its sensuous feel against her cheek, need only gaze at the still, closed eyes to remember the warmth of their dark caress. If bitter circumstance had not intervened, she could have grown to care for him deeply.

She *did* care for Ethan still, regardless of how he felt about her. Looking down at his face, its handsome features scarred by pain, Elizabeth realized that her feelings for him stemmed from factors far more profound than a transient flirtation. Ethan had befriended her at a time when she had felt desperately alone in the world. He had been fair with her, something she had not even gotten from her own kin-by-marriage. Most important, he had respected her spirit and intelligence enough to give her the chance to build a new life for herself.

Glancing away from the bed for a moment, Elizabeth remembered their first encounter in that very room. He had seemed so harsh and intimidating she had been a little

frightened of him. Fearing a man as kind and generous as
Ethan Woodard had proven himself to be now seemed pathetically foolish, as ridiculous as Josiah's bigoted assump-
tions.

"I will always be your friend, Ethan," Elizabeth whispered. "I cannot make the world right, but nothing will ever
change the way I feel about you. I promise you that by everything that is sacred to me."

Elizabeth dampened the cloth with fresh water then
placed it on Ethan's brow. She walked silently to the side
chair angled next to the window and sank onto its tapestry
cushion, her eyes lingering on the tall figure delineated beneath the sheet. The light was beginning to wane when Dolly
knocked softly at the door. Elizabeth thanked the solici-
tous young woman for the dinner she had delivered, but after Dolly had withdrawn she put the tray aside, leaving the
food untouched. As night gathered outside the curtained
window she rose to freshen the cloth and bathe Ethan's fe-
ver-racked body, repeating the ritual until only the full moon
lighted her path between chair and bed. Resting her head
against the windowsill, Elizabeth closed her eyes and let the
sound of Ethan's breathing lull her into a fitful sleep.

Dawn crept stealthily over the yard, its arrival trumpeted
only by the doleful call of mourning doves. Elizabeth
frowned as she awkwardly lifted her head from the hard sill
and squinted into the gloom. She had not intended to sleep
long, certainly not until daybreak, but fatigue had apparently subverted her good intentions. Massaging her stiff
neck muscles, she rose as quietly as possible and tiptoed to
the bed.

The white linen towel still lay across Ethan's brow, while
another cloth covered one wrist, exactly where she had
placed it. Indeed, his appearance seemed not to have altered in the slightest during the night. As Elizabeth watched
the rise and fall of his chest, she tried to persuade herself
that his breathing had become more regular. Carefully lifting the folded towel from his brow, she rested her hand on
his forehead to gauge its warmth.

Ethan murmured and rolled his head to one side. When he opened his eyes, he grimaced, straining to focus in the sparse light. "Elizabeth? What...where am I?" Lifting his head unsteadily from the pillow, he attempted to rise onto his elbows.

Elizabeth caught his shoulders and tried to ease him back onto the pillow. "You mustn't stir, Ethan. You've had a dreadful fever, and you need to rest." When he continued to frown in confusion, she smiled gently. "After Gray Bear and Noble set your leg, we brought you to my house. Dolly and Jephtha are going to help me look after you until you're on your feet again."

Ethan's dark eyes traveled to his rigid left leg, silhouetted beneath the sheet. For a moment he resisted the pressure of her hands, his will struggling against the limitations that his body sought to impose on it. Then he reluctantly sank back onto the bed.

Elizabeth lightly grazed his cheek with the back of her hand. "You still feel as if you have a touch of fever." She turned to the washstand and filled the shaving cup with water. Bending over the bed once more, she slipped one hand behind his head and raised it slightly. "Here. You must be terribly thirsty."

As Elizabeth guided the cup to his mouth, Ethan reached for it, covering her hand with his. He drank greedily until he had drained the cup. Licking his parched lips, he closed his eyes for a few seconds as if he were waiting for the cool water to restore his depleted strength.

"Would you like some more?" Elizabeth asked, stepping toward the washstand.

"No, thank you."

Ethan drew a measured breath. Shifting his weight to one side, he gingerly prodded his left thigh through the sheet covering it. When he stretched to touch the tips of the splints extending over his knee, the sheet slipped from his chest to bare his taut waist. As Ethan hastily snatched at the sheet, Elizabeth pretended not to notice, focusing her attention on filling the basin and soaking a fresh towel. When she turned back to the bed he was leaning on one shoulder with an expression of annoyed constraint on his face. He stiffened his neck, evading her attempt to place the cloth on his brow.

"I can't just lie here like a helpless infant, Elizabeth," he protested.

Elizabeth gave him a perplexed look. "I don't see that you have much choice in the matter, Ethan."

Ethan shook his head, as impatiently as his weakened condition would permit. "At the very least, I've got to talk with my men. It's so dry, if they don't cut hay this week, we might as well burn off the pasture. And that little cow with the white star on her face needs to be penned. She's about to drop a calf, and the last time she had trouble."

"Don't worry about your fields and stock, Ethan," Elizabeth interrupted. When he once more defied her effort to lay the cloth on his forehead, she added, "I'll make certain that they receive proper attention."

"I can't expect you to manage the tavern and see that six field hands do their jobs, as well," Ethan argued.

"Why not? I thought you always wanted me to give farming a try," Elizabeth reminded him. At last she anchored the towel on his forehead.

As she wheeled toward the washstand, Ethan tried to roll onto his side, wincing from the toll it exacted on his injured limb. "This is different."

"In what way?"

Ethan took a moment before replying, tacitly betraying his consternation. "My farm is my responsibility, not yours."

Elizabeth dipped another towel into the basin of water. Lifting the cloth, she gave it a shake and then folded it into a compress. "If I were to break my leg, would you still expect me to run the tavern?"

"Of course not. And you know that's an absurd question."

"But the tavern is my responsibility." Placing the compress in the middle of his chest, Elizabeth gently pushed Ethan onto his back. He said nothing while she sponged his chest and shoulders, only frowning up at her in frustration. Elizabeth retrieved the cloth that had fallen from his brow and clamped it over his forehead again. "I know it goes against your grain, Ethan, but you're going to have to depend on other people until your leg has mended. Gray Bear can certainly operate the ferry alone for a while, and you've often said that Noble manages hands better than any man you've ever known. I'm sure he'll be able to see that your hay is mowed and that your cow delivers without undue difficulty." A slight smile played on her lips as she slid one finger beneath a lock of his black hair and lifted it free of the compress. "If you're half as stubborn about getting well as you are about most things, you'll be up and about in a short while."

For a moment Ethan's smile relieved the tense lines that pain had etched into his lean face. "I'm no more stubborn than you are, Elizabeth Merriweather."

Elizabeth stepped back from the bed, folding her arms across her chest. "I should hope not." She straightened the hem of the sheet before starting for the door. "Rest well, Ethan. I promise to make note of everything that could possibly concern you about the ferry and your farm. When I get home this evening I will give you all the news you wish."

True to her word, Elizabeth made a point of stopping at Ethan's house on her way to the tavern. Before she had even dismounted, a wizened woman with wiry white hair curling from beneath a turban rushed across the yard to meet her. Elizabeth took pains to reassure Maum Betsy that while Ethan's injury was as incapacitating as the ferrymen's gossip had implied, his life was in no danger. After asking the aged woman to be especially kind to Blue until his master returned, she went to the stable to check on Ethan's horses. She was pleased to find a slender fellow of about eighteen forking fresh straw into the stalls. Satisfied that the animals had been fed and watered properly, Elizabeth promised the lad that Noble would come by later to direct the day's work in the fields.

When she reached the tavern, Gray Bear had already cooked breakfast for the cattle drovers who had been forced to spend yet another night at the public house. Elizabeth joined him on the dock while he and Noble completed repairs on the damaged ferryboat. Both men agreed that for the time being, Noble would divide his time between Ethan's farm and the ferry, with Gray Bear assuming primary responsibility for the latter.

Before the day was over, however, Elizabeth realized how difficult it would be to compensate for Ethan's absence. While Gray Bear and the ferrymen were transporting the cattle across the river, four drovers arrived with a sizable herd of pigs, which required penning and fodder for the night. No sooner had Elizabeth served the men food and drink than a frightened-looking girl burst into the tavern to announce that her father, who worked for Ethan, was lying abed with a festered snakebite. Elizabeth had no choice but to accompany the girl to her family's cabin and minister to the ailing man. When she returned to the public house over an hour later, she found the mail coach pulled up in the yard. After cooking a meal for the driver and the six travelers he had delivered, Elizabeth hurried to the stable and tended the stage horses as best she could without Gray Bear's help. By the time she had prepared sleeping quarters for the travelers and tidied the public room, dusk was descending on the yard. Her whole body felt weighted with fatigue when she at last saddled Midnight and set out for home.

As Elizabeth dismounted and led the horse to the stable, she gazed up at the tall windows of the corner bedroom. The evening breeze billowed the drawn damask curtains to reveal a sliver of the darkened room hidden behind them. Elizabeth made short work of removing Midnight's tack and filling his water pail before heading for the house. She closed the front door carefully behind her, taking pains not to disturb the stillness hanging over the house. A mixture of eagerness and apprehension filled her when she spotted Dolly hurrying down the stairs, her quick tread silently skimming the steps.

Elizabeth met the young woman at the foot of the stairs. "How is Ethan?"

"Resting pretty easy now," Dolly assured her. The anxious glance she cast overhead, however, did not escape Elizabeth's notice. The smile she forced was only slightly less suspect. "I swear but I've never seen a man so set against having folks do for him. Every time he'd consent to me bringing him a cup of water, you'd have thought he was asking for the world." As Elizabeth started up the stairs, she called after her in a loud whisper, "You tell him he needs to start eating, what with all that food Mr. Early brought by." When Elizabeth looked back at her, Dolly shook her head appreciatively. "A ham and two fresh-killed chickens, a crock of sweet butter, a whole bushel of corn and enough rice to last us until next year. He's a strange man, not that I mean it unkindly, mind you. When I tried to thank him for the food, he didn't say nothin' but 'I expect you'll be needing this.' Then he just up and rode off."

Still pondering Martin Early's unexpected largess, Elizabeth walked to the corner bedroom and tapped softly on the door.

"Don't trouble yourself, Dolly. I'm fine." Ethan's subdued voice cast doubt on its assertion.

"It's only me." Elizabeth pushed the door ajar a few inches and peered into the room. When she caught sight of Ethan's face, its haggard aspect thrown into relief against the white pillow, she almost winced, but she managed a smile for his benefit. "I thought you'd be impatient to hear how well we muddled through without you, but if you'd like, I'll come back later."

"No, no, please stay." Ethan struggled to pull himself into a sitting position. He grimaced when the injured leg forced him to compromise.

Elizabeth hastened to the bedside and adjusted the pillows behind his back. As she smoothed the sheet over his chest, her hand brushed the hot, bare skin. "You're burning up with fever."

"It's no worse than earlier. I'd be surprised if the fever didn't last for a day or so." Ethan tried to dismiss her concern, but he offered no resistance when she dampened a towel and sponged his face. He swallowed with some difficulty. "So tell me all of your news. Did Gray Bear and Noble finally rid us of that infernal herd?"

"Yes, indeed."

While Elizabeth launched into an account of the day's activities, she bathed Ethan's fever-ridden neck and arms with cool water. She tried to enliven her narrative with amusing details—faithful Blue's downcast mien, the coachman's unfailingly ravenous appetite, the argumentative couple traveling on the stage—and was heartened to see a smile ease the drawn lines of his face. Taking advantage of the distraction her chatter provided, she walked to the foot of the bed and lifted the sheet to inspect the splinted leg. In spite of her resolve, she faltered when her eye fell on the blood-soaked linen framed between the splints.

"How does it look?" Ethan's tight voice made clear that he would settle for nothing less than the truth.

"You need a fresh dressing," Elizabeth replied.

She took a deep breath in an effort to appear calm, avoiding the fevered eyes fixed on her. As Elizabeth carefully peeled away the sodden crimson cloth, however, she was alarmed not only by the severity of the wound, but also by the painfully inflamed flesh surrounding it. She fostered a brisk manner to conceal her uneasiness, gingerly swabbing the gash and then covering it with a clean towel. Only after she had adjusted the linen strips securing the splints did she risk looking up at Ethan. He had closed his eyes, his head sunk back against the pillow as if this latest painful assault inflicted on him had exhausted his last reserve of strength.

"I'm sorry if I hurt you," Elizabeth said.

Ethan's face was glistening with sweat, but he shook his head. "You have such a gentle touch I scarcely felt anything." He tried to smile. "I'm just tired. That's all."

"Then I'll let you rest." Elizabeth started for the door. She backed into the hall. "Good night, Ethan. If you can sleep undisturbed tonight, I expect you'll feel much better tomorrow."

"I expect so." Ethan's voice faded to a hush as muted as the waning light filtering through the drawn curtains. "Good night, Elizabeth."

Pulling the door closed, Elizabeth paused outside the bedroom. She listened to the silence for a long moment before retreating slowly down the hall.

* * *

Contrary to Elizabeth's hopeful prediction, however, Ethan showed little sign of improvement when she visited him the following evening after her return from the public house. He ate a few bites of the rice pudding Dolly had prepared, but Elizabeth suspected the gesture was prompted more by a desire to humor her than by any real appetite. More troubling still, his fever had not abated in the slightest, and his injured leg was now so swollen it looked as if the distended flesh would burst the splints binding it. When she changed the dressing she was distressed to discover the skin surrounding the gash grossly discolored. Although the bleeding had stopped, an unwholesome discharge had now taken its place. As she had the previous evening, Elizabeth did her best to cheer Ethan and make him as comfortable as possible. After she had left him for the night and retired to her own room, however, she lay awake into the early predawn hours, unable to rid her mind of the worries haunting it.

Elizabeth rose at first light. She dressed quickly, tarrying at the dressing table only long enough to pin up her hair and splash water on her face. She hurried down the corridor and then paused outside the corner bedroom. Since it was early, she had no wish to awaken Ethan from his rest, and she took care to open the door as noiselessly as possible. As she hovered on the threshold she listened to his shallow, uneven breathing, and her hands unconsciously tightened into nervous fists. In the meager light he appeared to be sleeping, his chest lifting the sheet slightly as he labored for breath. Only as she tiptoed closer to the bed did she see that his eyes were open, their dark luster veiled by a feverish glaze. When she bent over the bed he blinked without comprehension and murmured in his native language.

"Ethan, it's Elizabeth." She silently cursed the quaver rippling through her voice, pressing her lips together as she reached to touch his face. The skin felt desiccated, parched by the fever consuming him.

"Elizabeth. For a moment I thought...I must have been dreaming." Ethan turned his head toward her, his dry lips curving into a faint smile. "You should try to get some sleep.

You work so hard you can't afford to waste the night sitting here with me."

"I did sleep, Ethan. It's morning now," Elizabeth told him. She clasped his arm tightly for a moment and then turned to the washstand to dampen a fresh towel and fill the shaving cup with water.

Elizabeth held the cup to Ethan's cracked lips, lifting his head enough to allow him to drink. When she placed the cool cloth on his forehead, he closed his eyes. "That feels good." His voice sounded as if he was too spent even to mutter those three short words.

"You'll be much cooler in just a little time. I'll change the cloth the second it starts to get warm. If you want a drink of water, you need only ask." Elizabeth realized that she was almost babbling, but talking was her sole defense, however feeble, against the dreadful sense of helplessness that gripped her. "I'm going to stay with you until the fever breaks."

"And who's going to tend the tavern?" When Ethan looked up at her, a flicker of his once-familiar grin penetrated the pain clouding his face. "You promised to look after things while I'm down, remember?"

Elizabeth shook her head, not trusting her trembling lips to speak. She was grateful for the shadows that sheltered her damp eyes from his gaze.

"Go on, now. Dolly will take good care of me." When she hesitated, he smiled once more. "Only promise that you'll come back tonight with lots of stories to amuse me."

"I promise, Ethan."

As Elizabeth retreated toward the door she turned her face to shield it from his scrutiny. In the corridor she wiped her eyes with her apron, forcing herself to take several deep breaths. Yielding to her emotions served no purpose, she reminded herself sternly. Ethan's grave condition demanded calm, careful attention, not useless tears and handwringing. The best she could do for him right now was to honor his wishes and see that his farm and ferry continued to flourish in his absence.

With this resolution in mind, Elizabeth tried to resume her normal routine. After stopping briefly at Ethan's house to give Maum Betsy his regards and console the forlorn Blue, she rode to the tavern and plunged into the day's chores. Her efforts to distract herself with work, however, utterly failed to dispel the distressing thoughts oppressing her. As sunset approached and she at last led Midnight from the stable, Elizabeth felt as if she had been holding her breath all day, fighting the burgeoning tension pent up inside her. Once they were on the road, she let the horse have his head and gallop the short distance to the house.

When she reined Midnight into the yard, Elizabeth immediately noticed a sturdy gray horse tied to the hitching rail in front of the veranda. Guessing that one of Ethan's hands had called to pay him a visit, she tethered Midnight beside the strange horse and entered the house. As Elizabeth passed the parlor, Dolly's melodious voice drifted through the open window, humming a song while she cooked supper in the summer kitchen. The wistful tune followed Elizabeth up the stairs, gradually fading to a vague murmur.

On the landing she started when the door of the corner room unexpectedly opened. For a moment Elizabeth and Martin Early only stared at each other. Early turned slightly to pull the door closed behind him and then walked to the landing.

"Good evening, Mr. Early." Straightening her shoulders, Elizabeth forced herself to meet his direct gaze. "I appreciate very much the food that you brought us. That was very kind of you."

Martin Early halted a few feet short of her, close enough, however, for her to recognize the concern reflected on his angular face. "You've taken Ethan in. I wanted to help you," he said simply.

Elizabeth glanced toward the closed door. "How is he?" She was surprised by how obstinately that question balked in her throat, shying from the answer she feared.

Early hesitated. "When I walked into the room today, he didn't recognize me at first. I looked at his leg, Mrs. Merriweather." His jaw tightened in a futile effort to bridle its insidious quiver. "The skin is starting to turn black."

Elizabeth's hand flew to her mouth. She bit her lip, fighting to regain control of herself. "You think—"

"The poison won't stay in his leg, Mrs. Merriweather. It will spread through his whole body." Early's black eyes followed hers for a moment, silently reading her fear. Then he started down the stairs. "I'm riding to New Echota to fetch the doctor," he announced.

"What if he doesn't live there any longer?" Elizabeth called after him in an anxious whisper.

Martin Early glanced back at her from the foot of the stairs. "I'm going to find a doctor if I have to ride all the way to Milledgeville," he vowed. "And then I'm going to bring him back here."

Elizabeth watched his tall figure stride down the corridor. She heard the front door close, followed shortly by the throb of cantering hooves against the yard's packed earth. Elizabeth waited until the accelerating hoofbeats had disappeared into the distance before she turned and slowly walked to the corner room. She hesitated before opening the door, steeling herself to face Ethan's worsened condition. As she approached the bed, however, Elizabeth realized that nothing could have prepared her for the sight of his fever-dazed eyes or his body shivering uncontrollably beneath the sheet.

Elizabeth bent over the bed. "Ethan," she whispered softly. With some effort she succeeded in keeping her voice even. "I've come back, just as I promised."

Ethan looked up at her, struggling to smile. "I knew you would. You always keep your word."

"I try to. And this time I'm not going to let you run me away until your fever is all gone." Elizabeth gently smoothed the damp hair from his forehead. "You'll never guess what Noah Gilmer tried to sell me today."

"Bad whiskey?" Ethan tried to laugh, but an involuntary shudder cut short his effort.

Without thinking, Elizabeth stroked his cheek with the back of her fingers. "No, he knows better than that. A bear trap. Can you imagine that?"

Still smiling, Ethan closed his eyes and rested his face against her hand. "What did you tell him?"

"That our tavern's mice were a trifle small to snare with such a monstrous contraption and, in any case, I wouldn't know what to do with a bear if I caught one." Elizabeth turned her hand to pillow his cheek with her palm. She continued to talk softly, recounting the most minute details of the day's activities until Ethan had drifted into sleep.

Elizabeth rose once, when Dolly tapped lightly at the door to offer supper. To placate the concerned young woman, she made a show of sampling the food and drank a cup of tea. As soon as Dolly had departed, however, she put the tray aside and pulled the chair up to Ethan's bed. Elizabeth had no idea how long she had kept vigil by his side when he once more drifted into consciousness.

"Elizabeth, are you there?"

"Of course I am." Elizabeth leaned forward in her chair. "Do you need anything?"

"No, just for you to be here. I feel so cold."

Elizabeth tucked the sheet over his chest, then lifted his hand, enfolding it in both of hers. She grappled for any means to comfort him. "Martin has gone to fetch a doctor, Ethan."

His head jerked in a nod. "I know. He told me he was going to ride out tonight, even though I tried to talk him out of it." He fell silent, his breath coming in fitful gasps. "The doctor is going to want to take my leg off, Elizabeth."

"What nonsense, Ethan! Of course he won't!" Elizabeth insisted, hating the doubt that shadowed her assertion. She tightened her grip on his hand. "I remember when I was a girl," she began, lowering her voice to a soothing level. "How I hated the doctor's visits! I suppose I was what people call sickly, but it seemed as if the doctor was forever calling on me. He never left without prescribing some foul-tasting concoction for me to take or forbidding me to do something that I enjoyed. I wasn't supposed to ride or walk outdoors unless the weather was absolutely perfect. I dared not touch any creature with fur on it. And never under any circumstances should I get my feet wet."

Ethan's fingers curled around her wrist. "Tell me more about you when you were little. Your voice sounds so sweet in the dark."

Elizabeth lightly caressed his hand. "Well, I went to a horrid boarding school for a year, but my asthma became so troublesome I had to return to my uncle's plantation. For once I didn't mind being sick! He hired a tutor for me, a Mr. Washburn from Richmond, but the man drank like a fish and chased after the servant girls. Needless to say, Uncle dismissed him without delay. My next teacher was a wonderful lady, so wonderful, in fact, that my cousin ended up marrying her. They have two beautiful children now— Emma and Nathaniel. Did I ever tell you that my cousin has Cherokee blood?''

When Ethan said nothing, Elizabeth realized that he had faded from consciousness once more, even as the tremors convulsed his fever-ridden body. She felt a great mass swelling in her throat, and she choked to hold it in check. Elizabeth rose and fled the room. Only when she reached the veranda did she at last give vent to the flood of tears that had been building inside her for the past two days. Sinking onto the wooden floor, she leaned her head against the veranda rail.

"Please, God, Ethan is a good man. He's kind and strong and generous. And he's much too young to die. I don't think I can stand to see another good, young life slip away from me, God.'' Clutching her arms across her waist, Elizabeth rocked forward, her whole body racked with sobs. "Please just let him live. Just let him live.''

Elizabeth lay with her face buried against her knees, crying until her tears dissolved into empty shudders. Her head was pounding so fiercely she at first did not recognize the hoofbeats drumming on the road. When she looked up she detected two blurred figures galloping across the yard, their dark silhouettes etched against the breaking dawn. She stumbled to her feet as Martin Early pulled his horse up at the rail and sprang from the saddle. His companion, a portly fellow with disheveled gray hair billowing from beneath a broad-brimmed hat, dismounted more slowly. As he followed Early up the steps, Elizabeth noticed the tail of a white nightshirt protruding from beneath his frock coat.

Elizabeth hurried to meet Martin Early. "I didn't expect you back until late tomorrow,'' she began.

"Nor did I,'' he told her on their way down the corridor. "I rode like the devil until I reached Adair's public house.

When I stopped to water my horse I discovered that, by some remarkable stroke of luck, a doctor was passing the night there. I persuaded him to leave his bed and come with me.'' Martin took the stairs two at a time, impatiently beckoning his stout companion to follow. "This way, Dr. Howell.''

Martin flung open the door to Ethan's room and ushered the doctor inside. When Elizabeth caught up with him, she gasped, clamping her hand over her mouth. In contrast to the state in which she had left Ethan, he was now lying very still without the slightest trace of movement. As still as if he were dead. The doctor must have heard her gasp, for he wheeled to peer over his lopsided spectacles with undisguised annoyance.

"Perhaps you should escort the gentleman's wife elsewhere, Mr. Early," he suggested.

"Let's go downstairs, Elizabeth." Martin gently slipped his arm around her shoulders and guided her out of the room. She let him lead her down the stairs, her will too battered to resist. He pulled her toward the horsehair sofa, and she obediently sank onto it. As she began to cry silently, she heard him walk out of the room and then return a few minutes later. She looked up when he seated himself on the edge of the sofa, balancing a cup on his knee.

"Take a deep breath and hold it for a moment," Martin told her in a low, even voice.

Elizabeth's shoulders jerked as she inhaled, but she managed to quell the sob rising in her throat.

"Let it out slowly." His dark eyes resting on her face, Martin nodded his approval. "There. Now drink this." He took each of her hands and curved them around the cup he held. He watched while she sipped the cool, fresh water. Then he stood. She felt him clasp her shoulder briefly before he turned and walked to the window.

They both started when the doctor appeared on the stairs some time later.

"How is he?" Martin voiced the question Elizabeth could not bring herself to ask.

Dr. Howell took his time rolling down his sleeves. "I did the best I could for him."

But it was not good enough. As the unbearable thought loomed in Elizabeth's mind, a ringing filled her ears, the sound of the entire world ebbing away from her, and her limbs went numb.

"I whittled away that morbid flesh on his leg," the stocky physician went on, tugging at the straining buttons of his waistcoat. "So don't be surprised if his fever comes up again. Leastways, he won't have to worry 'bout blood poisonin'. I'm afraid there's nothin' I can do 'bout the way his leg's set, though. That young fellow's probably goin' to have a stiff leg for the rest of his life."

For a moment, Elizabeth could only stare at Dr. Howell, unsure whether she had understood him correctly. Ethan was alive. He was going to recover. As the realization settled over her, she gasped, "Thank God!"

The doctor gave her a quizzical look. "Pardon me for sayin' so, ma'am, but I been at my practice nigh on thirty years now, and you're the first I've seen that's felt like thankin' the Lord for a bad leg."

Elizabeth only shook her head and smiled through her tears. "Thank God!"

Chapter Eight

Elizabeth pulled the front door closed behind her and then leaned back against the smooth, hard surface. She drew a leisurely breath of the corridor's cool air, relishing the relief it offered from the withering August heat. Fanning herself with one hand, she loosened the button securing her collar and ran a finger between the damp fabric and the prickling skin imprisoned beneath it. She abruptly straightened herself when a thump sounded from overhead.

Pushing away from the door, Elizabeth hurried to the foot of the stairs. Her eyes widened in alarm when she spotted Ethan working his way toward the landing on one crutch. To judge from his startled expression, he was equally disconcerted to discover her glaring up the stairwell at him, but he recovered himself quickly enough to smile.

"What on earth are you doing?" Elizabeth demanded as she started up the stairs.

"Taking a walk," Ethan replied matter-of-factly. To Elizabeth's dismay he anchored the tip of the crutch on the top step and levered himself forward.

"For heaven's sake, Ethan, do take care that you don't fall!"

"I'm not going to fall," he assured her. "Although it would help if you could give me a bit more room."

Seeing that he had no intention of retreating to the landing, Elizabeth hastily pulled her skirts to one side and flattened herself against the wall. After he had edged past her, she glanced up the stairs and frowned. "Where is Jeptha?"

"When I saw him this morning, he mentioned wanting to repair the corncrib today," Ethan informed her. "I suppose he's still at it."

"You can't mean that you've gotten up and about with no one in the house!" Elizabeth gathered her skirts and hurried down the stairs after Ethan.

"Dolly and Jephtha have enough to do without playing nursemaid to me all day."

"Helping you until you've regained your strength and fully recovered is not playing nursemaid," Elizabeth insisted.

"And that they've both done admirably. But I'm certainly fit enough now to venture a few feet from that wretched bed on my own. In any case, I'm tired of having other people draw my bath, fetch my clothes and wait on me as if I were an invalid. I thought you said you were going to the Birdsong place this afternoon to buy a calf," Ethan went on, as if their disagreement had been laid to rest once and for all. "When I got up, I wasn't expecting to find you here."

"I could say the same of you," Elizabeth remarked dryly. Arms folded across her chest, she followed him down the corridor. Despite her cautionary protests, she was pleased by how easily he kept ahead of her. "After I left the tavern this afternoon I did ride to the Birdsongs'. Unfortunately, the cow had broken out of the paddock sometime during the day and taken her firstborn with her. Little David went looking for them, but I didn't want to chance waiting half the evening while he chased the wily creatures through the forest."

"That's just as well. Give me another week and I'll be happy to ride over and fetch the calf for you," Ethan told her over his shoulder.

"If I didn't know you better, I'd assume you were joking," Elizabeth retorted, winning a chuckle from Ethan.

At the end of the hall he pivoted neatly on the crutch to face her. Elizabeth drew up short, her face a scant few inches from the midpoint of his chest. Catching his amused grin, she felt her own mouth relax into a smile. "You do get around quite well," she conceded.

"So you don't intend to banish me to my room again?" Ethan's deep brown eyes twinkled with mirth.

"At least not right away." Elizabeth took a sufficient number of steps backward to establish a decorous distance between them. She glanced through the dining room's open door, in part to evade the dark eyes playing such unapologetic havoc with her attention. "Since you've come this far, why don't you have dinner downstairs tonight? It's really quite pleasant in the dining room of an evening with the breeze blowing through those big magnolias outside the windows." She unclasped her hands to gesture in the direction of the summer kitchen. "I've no idea what Dolly has prepared, but her cooking is always fit for a celebration."

"You don't have to persuade me, Elizabeth," Ethan interrupted. "Stale corn bread would seem like a feast to me if I could eat it sitting at a proper table with you to share it."

"I'm certain we'll dine far better than that," Elizabeth demurred. "If you'd like, you can sit on the veranda while I see when Dolly plans to serve supper." She half turned toward the rear of the house and then hesitated. "You're sure you can manage?"

Ethan laughed as he performed an adroit about-face and started toward the door. "Considering that I've gone up and down those stairs a good dozen times without falling on my face, I'm fairly confident I can handle dropping into a rocking chair."

Elizabeth gaped at the tall figure poised in the doorway. "A *dozen* times? You mean, you've done this before?"

"I had to find some way to amuse myself while you were away all day." Ethan glanced over his shoulder to give her a thoroughly unrepentant grin. Then he swung over the threshold and nudged the door shut with the tip of the crutch.

Elizabeth sighed and shook her head as she headed out the back door. She found Dolly seated on the kitchen step, fanning her face with the hem of her apron. The young woman rose when she noticed Elizabeth coming up the path.

"Lord, but it is hot today," Dolly said by way of greeting. "Every time I baste those chickens I've put to roast on the spit, I feel like I'm about cooked to the bone myself."

"So we're having chicken tonight?" Elizabeth smiled in anticipation.

"Yes, ma'am, the big, plump ones that Mr. Early sent over yesterday. I've boiled some rice and cooked a mess of fresh beans and stewed corn to go with them. I thought I'd best bake another pound cake and cook a custard sauce, too, before the butter and cream went bad in this fearsome heat."

"It all sounds wonderful, but you know no one expects you to spend so much time in the kitchen while it's this hot," Elizabeth felt bound to chide her.

Dolly gave her a good-natured frown. "I don't mind cooking big meals, never mind the weather, so long as I have hungry folks to eat 'em. Since Mr. Woodard's appetite's picked up, I never have to worry on that count. 'Course, I can always rely on Jephtha to put away his share, too," she added with a chuckle.

"I wanted to tell you that Ethan will be eating in the dining room this evening. I had no idea until today, but apparently he's learned to negotiate the stairs with the crutch." Elizabeth eyed Dolly closely to gauge her reaction.

Dolly squared her slim shoulders, and her chin rose slightly. "Now, I know what you're thinking, ma'am, and it's only natural that you should worry 'bout Mr. Woodard, what with all you went through when he was doing so poorly. But now that he's mending, there's just no way to keep a headstrong man like that flat on his back in bed, leastways not without tying him down. Maybe he's been a bit reckless getting a feel for that crutch, but that's his nature. Jephtha and me both tried to tell him to take it easy, but I saw real early that he was just going to smile and keep right on doing what he wanted. He thinks the world of you, ma'am, but I do believe not even you could convince him to stay abed when he wants so bad to be back to his old self."

"No, I suppose you're right," Elizabeth admitted. "Do you need any help with dinner?"

"Not a bit, ma'am. You just freshen up, and I'll have everything on the table in an hour's time."

Heeding Dolly's advice, Elizabeth returned to the house. She paused in the dining room to peek through one of the windows that opened onto the veranda. Ethan was seated on the rail with his back propped against the column, his splinted leg extended. A peaceful smile had settled on his handsome face as he watched the squirrels chasing one another through the magnolias' interwoven branches. Ethan had endured so much pain and uncertainty, the freedom to enjoy such simple pleasures once more must seem like a precious gift to him. Taking care not to stir the lace curtains, she stepped back from the window and went upstairs to her room.

Dolly was right, Elizabeth reflected as she pulled the tin foot tub from beneath the bed and emptied the ewer of fresh water into it. Accustomed as Ethan was to an active and independent life, he had chafed under the confinement his injury had imposed. No one could blame him for hastening his convalescence behind her back, however imprudent his actions may have been.

Not that Ethan had ever seemed ungrateful for her attempts to brighten his sojourn in the corner bedroom. He had never failed to thank her when she brought him a new book she had managed to borrow or surprised him with coffee and cake on a rainy Sunday afternoon. Elizabeth smiled to herself as she recalled the time she had brought Blue to the house for a visit. The big, clumsy dog had been so overjoyed to see Ethan that he had promptly lunged onto the bed to lick his face, leaving a trail of clay-colored paw prints on the white counterpane, but neither of them had had the heart to scold him. Blue had finally settled down, curling up on the rug while Ethan ate supper. As she did almost every day, Elizabeth had joined him, taking her own meal from a tray while she sat by the window. Afterward they had talked until the last glimmer of the enduring summer sun had faded from the sky. She would have been hard-pressed to remember all the ordinary, homely little things they had discussed—the fawn Rebecca and Ben had discovered hidden in the cornfield, the new settle Gray Bear was building for the tavern, perhaps some amusing childhood memory—but the evening had ended all too quickly. She would miss spending that kind of time with Ethan, more than she had dared allow herself to think.

At the first hint of pensiveness Elizabeth sternly redirected her attention to the practical matters at hand. She slipped out of her clothes and stepped into the tin tub. The water felt wonderfully refreshing as she lapped it over her heated body, and she took her time bathing. Elizabeth blotted herself with a towel, then padded to the dresser. After she had pulled on fresh linen and a starched petticoat, she seated herself at the dressing table.

She started to brush her hair but stopped short, her attention arrested by her own image reflected in the looking glass. With the ferry and Ethan's farm claiming most of her waking hours during the past three months, Elizabeth had given little thought to her appearance, devoting only enough time to her toilette to satisfy cleanliness and basic civility. Until this evening, she had not fully appreciated the startling alteration that the summer had wrought in her aspect. Exposure to the sun had burnished her normally pale cheeks to the color of ripe peaches, dusting her nose with a faint sprinkle of freckles. Not only had her fashionable pallor vanished, but her face looked fuller, its former hollows now conspicuously softened.

Elizabeth's eyes traveled to her bare arms and across the gently rounded front of her camisole. No, it was not her imagination. Although she was, by most standards, still quite slim, she had definitely gained weight. That should come as no surprise, she reflected, for she now returned home from a long day's work as hungry as she was tired. Then, too, chatting over dinner with Ethan encouraged her to relax and eat more than she probably would under other circumstances.

Shaking back her hair, Elizabeth ran the brush through the thick reddish-brown waves. She sectioned the sun-lightened hair into a neat part and then swept the sides into soft curves over her ears. Weaving the length into a braid, she secured it in a coil at the back of her head. She gave her hair a quick final inspection before pushing away from the dressing table.

Elizabeth walked to the wardrobe and pulled out her clean frock. Although freshly laundered and pressed, the black poplin dress looked little better than its soiled counterpart lying on the bed. The hem's edge was frayed, and the hopelessly faded fabric hung in limp folds, proof that even well-made dresses did not last forever. She had worn those two day dresses for almost a year and a half now, ever since she had put on mourning following Samuel's death.

Replacing the worn dress in the wardrobe, Elizabeth was about to remove the black silk gown when her eye fell on the pale lavender print hanging beside it. She had clothed herself in black for over a year now, longer than propriety required, but for some reason she had not thought of putting away her widow's weeds until this evening. Elizabeth withdrew the cotton print dress from the wardrobe and held it up in front of her for a moment. It was a lovely dress, with graceful leg-of-mutton sleeves and a large white collar with points reaching nearly to the waist. Ages seemed to have passed since she had last worn that dress, so much time that she now felt almost as if she were a different person.

Elizabeth carefully stepped into the lavender print frock and then fastened the row of tiny mother-of-pearl buttons curving down its back. She turned in front of the mirror, indulging herself in the feel of the crisp skirt furling around her. She paused long enough to select a moss green bow from her bandbox and pin it to the center of the collar before heading downstairs.

When she reached the dining room Elizabeth halted in the door. Although Dolly always put great store in serving meals properly, the sumptuous table she had prepared tonight exceeded even her normal impeccable principles. By some unknown wizardry she had managed to locate not only Elizabeth's finest white damask tablecloth but the heirloom silver candlesticks, as well. Two beeswax tapers flickered in the holders, adding their sweet odor to the scent of the magnolia blossoms spilling from the silver urn. Elizabeth's eyes swept the table, delighting in the sparkle of crystal and china. Only when she stepped across the threshold did she notice Ethan standing in front of the empty fireplace.

"You should be careful when you use the word *celebration* around Dolly," he remarked. "She's set a table fit for a banquet."

Elizabeth circled the table, giving the fine details the appreciative attention they deserved. "Marking your recovery is an occasion that deserves as much."

Ethan shrugged, but his pleased smile confirmed that Dolly's efforts had not been wasted. He made his way to the table and then rested his weight on the crutch to pull out a chair for Elizabeth. After she had taken her seat, he stood behind her for a moment, watching her smooth her skirts. His eyes lingered on her as he edged to the opposite side of the table and sank onto the chair. He continued to regard her, an enigmatic half smile hovering on his lips.

Elizabeth glanced down at her lap, feeling suddenly awkward. "Is something wrong?"

"Not that I know of. Why do you ask?"

Elizabeth toyed with one of the tiny buttons fastening her sleeve. "You're looking at me so curiously."

"Forgive me. I was only thinking how pretty you look tonight." The intense eyes fixed on her face were as frank as his unhesitating response.

"Thank you. I've always liked this dress," Elizabeth remarked modestly.

Ethan laughed softly. "I wasn't talking about the dress, although it is quite nice, now that you've brought it to my attention."

Meeting his gaze over the lush centerpiece, Elizabeth smiled, but she was grateful for the candle's glow, which muted the color rising to her cheeks.

As if an invisible spy had informed her of the need for diversion, Dolly appeared in the doorway at that moment, bearing a platter of roasted chicken surrounded by spiced crab apples and sprigs of watercress. Like a sorceress working a charm, she left Elizabeth and Ethan to admire the perfectly browned fowl while she hurried back to the kitchen and then returned with a tray laden with equally tempting side dishes. After she had served them, she lingered long enough to decant a portion of homemade mulberry wine into each goblet before withdrawing from the room.

Elizabeth lifted her glass. "We must drink to your health."

Ethan raised his goblet, smiling over its rim. "I've no desire to hold a monopoly on our good wishes. Why not just say 'to health and good fortune' and let us both share in any luck it might bring?"

"To health and good fortune, then." Elizabeth gestured with her glass, her eyes joining with Ethan's across the table. She took a sip and placed the crystal goblet on the table. "If I remember correctly, that was the toast we made the day we sampled Noah Gilmer's whiskey. Perhaps we should have been more specific about health and requested no broken limbs, please."

Ethan chuckled as he reached for the knife and fork. "There's another way of looking at the matter, of course. I am on my feet again. And I do feel very fortunate."

"So do I," Elizabeth said, slicing a sliver from the chicken breast Dolly had served her. She hesitated, then rested her fork on the plate. "I am very grateful for your giving me a chance to run the tavern, Ethan."

Ethan shook his head. "You've worked so hard you've no one to thank but yourself, Elizabeth."

"But you could have turned me away," she insisted, leaning forward slightly.

When Ethan looked up, an earnest expression had tempered his affable smile. "It would have been my loss," he said quietly. He glanced across the room and cleared his throat, looking uncharacteristically self-conscious. "I mean, you've done a remarkable job turning the tavern back into a respectable place. So, tell me what sort of traffic we had at the ferry today." He fostered a smile as he offered Elizabeth the basket of yeast rolls and then selected one for himself.

"Not a great deal," Elizabeth began. "But the stage finally arrived with a letter for Miss Ballard from her sister in Boston. I rode by Martin's farm on my way to the Birdsongs' and delivered it to her. She was so delighted she was almost speechless."

Ethan chuckled and launched into a discussion of the strong-minded teacher and the new school over which she would be presiding in the fall. Although talking with Ethan of an evening had become as much a part of Elizabeth's daily routine as eating and sleeping, she still marveled at how a seemingly uneventful day could yield hours of conversation and laughter for them. When Dolly arrived to clear the plates and offer dessert, Elizabeth felt as if they had scarcely touched on the day's news.

"Would you all be wanting cake and coffee here, ma'am, or in the parlor?" Dolly asked, holding the tray just close enough to the table to tempt them.

"Why don't we have dessert in the parlor?" Elizabeth glanced at Ethan, but he only smiled and nodded his approval.

Resting the tray on the table, Dolly rearranged the coffee service before nestling the two candlesticks between the cream pitcher and the two cups. She led the way into the parlor and then arranged the tray's contents on the occasional table, within reach of the sofa and the armchair. After placing the two candlesticks on either end of the mantel, she gave the room a quick inspection from the doorway.

"Will you be needing anything else, ma'am?"

"No, thank you, Dolly. And please don't worry about clearing away here later. I'll take care of that," Elizabeth told her.

Dolly looked a trifle doubtful, but she dutifully retreated into the hall. Just as she was about to turn, Ethan called after her. "Thank you, Dolly, for everything."

"You've no account to thank me, Mr. Woodard," Dolly demurred, shaking her head. "But that's very kind of you," she added, quickly enough to forestall Ethan's protest. She glanced at Elizabeth before gathering her skirt and hurrying down the corridor.

Elizabeth gave Ethan an appreciative smile, but he pretended not to notice as he reached for the plate of cake sitting on the occasional table. They sat in silence for several minutes, savoring the delicious sweet and the humid night breeze wafting through the open windows. When Ethan had finished his cup of coffee, he pushed up on the crutch and walked to the fireplace. He studied the Seth Thomas clock ticking placidly in the center of the mantel, stepping back to survey the porcelain shepherdess poised alongside it.

"I kept the things that were left in the house," Elizabeth felt bound to explain. "It seemed a shame not to. Most of them are far finer than anything I own."

Ethan turned slightly to give her a gentle smile. "I don't think Jonathan or Susanna would object to your using what they couldn't take with them." He levered his way across the hearth and paused in front of the bookcase. "I see you have your Swift and your Goethe, too," he remarked.

Elizabeth laughed softly. "We have a lot of the same books, which is one reason I found it so hard to bring you anything new to read while you were ill." Putting her coffee cup on the table, she rose to join Ethan.

"Your parents?" Ethan inclined his head toward the two oval portraits hanging over the shelves.

"Yes. Those pictures were painted shortly after they were married."

Ethan smiled, rocking forward on the crutch for a closer look at the two solemn faces enshrined in the ornately carved frames. "You favor your mother a great deal, although no one could mistake where you got that wonderful chestnut hair." He nodded toward her father's likeness.

As Ethan continued past the bookcases, Elizabeth accompanied him, matching her pace to his. He scanned the collection of prints depicting exotic plants with their Latin names, not halting until he reached the tiny wooden chair angled in the corner.

Placing his weight on his sound leg, Ethan gestured with the crutch. "I'll bet this chair was yours when you were a little girl."

"No, actually a man made it for us when we lived in Auraria. My husband had done some legal work for him, trying to settle a mining claim. The poor fellow didn't have enough money to pay Samuel, but he had been a joiner before coming to the goldfields, so he offered to build something for him as a way of settling his debt. I wanted a chair for little Ned." Elizabeth swallowed slowly, resisting the old tightness that threatened to paralyze her throat. "He died before he was big enough to sit in it."

"I'm sorry, Elizabeth. I didn't realize you had lost a child."

Elizabeth shook her head, looking down to avoid Ethan's intense gaze. "How could you have known? I don't talk about Ned often now—although not a day passes when I don't think of him. I suppose it was foolish to keep the chair, but I couldn't bear to part with it."

"It wasn't foolish," Ethan said in a low voice.

Elizabeth's shoulders rose in a helpless shrug. "I'll always remember the way he would smile up at me when I tucked him in his crib at night, how his little fingers would curl around one of mine. He was such a dear baby, so sweet, so quick to laugh. That first winter in Auraria was terribly harsh and cold. It seemed everyone we knew was ailing. I asked Samuel if we might go back to Milledgeville, just until the spring, but of course, he couldn't leave his practice. Then Ned took sick—" She broke off, unable to trust her trembling lips.

Elizabeth turned abruptly in an effort to conceal her brimming eyes from Ethan's scrutiny. Keeping her back to him, she began to collect the empty plates and cups. "It's getting quite late. I'd best take these things out to the kitchen."

"Elizabeth," she heard him say as she started for the door with the tray, but she dared not look back. She rushed down the dark corridor, careless of the teaspoon that bounced off the tray to clatter onto the floor. Only when she reached the dark kitchen did she halt. Shoving the tray onto the table, Elizabeth covered her face with her hands in a futile attempt to stay the tears streaming down her face.

Whatever had possessed her to try to talk about Ned? She knew all too well the peril of giving expression to those aching, bittersweet memories locked inside her heart. As it was, she had barely managed to excuse herself in time to avoid breaking down in front of Ethan.

Elizabeth's shoulders began to shake, and she bent over the table, unable to stifle the sobs racking her body. When a tentative hand touched her shoulder she pressed her lips together and shook her head.

"Elizabeth." When she refused to turn, Ethan shifted his weight to his good leg and propped the crutch against the table's edge. Elizabeth felt his arms close around her shoulders as he gently pulled her around to face him. His palm covered her damp cheek, guiding her face to rest against his chest.

"I'm sorry to go on like this," she managed between sobs. "It's only that . . . that I miss him so much."

"Of course you do, Elizabeth," Ethan said softly. Holding her close, he stroked her hair. "You don't have to be strong all the time, to keep the pain bottled up inside you. Let yourself cry all you need."

"I think I would give anything if I could only hold Ned one more time," Elizabeth whispered hoarsely against his chest.

Without thinking, she locked her arms around Ethan's waist, holding fast to the warm, strong feel of his body. He let her cry until she was too exhausted to weep, never slackening his embrace. When Elizabeth at last lifted her head to look up at him, his eloquent dark eyes drifted slowly over her face, seeming to read even the subtlest emotion reflected on it. His hand hovered over her cheek, so close she could feel the slight tremor pulse through it. His lips parted as if he wanted to speak but was unable to summon the words. Then he stepped back to slip from her grasp. Ethan took both of her hands in his and held them together tightly for a moment.

"Good night, Elizabeth." His voice sounded husky against the still night air. Then he seized the crutch and abruptly pivoted toward the door, leaving her alone in the dark kitchen.

Chapter Nine

"For heaven's sake, Mr. Woodard! The way you're tearing out of this house, folks would think it was burning down around you," Dolly called over the bundle of clean clothing she clutched to her chest. When her complaint failed to slow Ethan's rapid progress down the corridor, she sighed in resignation. "'Course, I suppose if I was going back to my own place after nigh on two months of being away from it, I'd be in a right big hurry, too."

Elizabeth smiled as she paused to adjust the ribbon securing her summer bonnet. "I imagine it seems a far longer time to Ethan."

She glanced behind her, her thoughts involuntarily returning to that terrible afternoon when Gray Bear and Noble had borne Ethan's insensate body up the stairs. In the dark hours that had followed, Elizabeth had often been too frightened to think beyond the few small comforts she could offer him as he lay trapped in a web of fever and pain. That Ethan was now able to walk with only limited dependence on a crutch seemed nothing short of a miracle.

When Dolly and Elizabeth emerged onto the veranda they found Ethan waiting beside the wagon Jephtha had drawn up in front of the house. He grinned as they joined him in the yard, looking only slightly less eager to be under way than Midnight, who was stamping and pulling at the bit. Before the young housekeeper could protest, he relieved her of the folded clothes that she was carrying and deposited them in the back of the wagon. He waited for Elizabeth to climb onto the driver's seat and then braced his crutch firmly against the wagon's tracing. Without giving Jephtha a chance to offer assistance, Ethan grabbed the frame of the seat and hoisted himself alongside Elizabeth with surprising ease.

"You take care of yourself now, Mr. Woodard. I don't want to hear about you getting throwed by some crazy horse next week or anything like that," Dolly chided, her mouth set in a valiant smile.

"I promise." Ethan leaned over the side of the wagon seat to clasp first Dolly's hand, then Jephtha's. "How can I ever thank you both enough?"

"You've done that already. Go on, now, 'fore that nasty-tempered horse busts a hamstring." Dolly stepped back, reaching to cover Jephtha's hand, which rested on her shoulder.

Elizabeth slapped the lines against Midnight's glossy back, causing the wagon to lurch forward abruptly. As she reined the horse onto the road, she glanced back to see Dolly and Jephtha waving from beneath the magnolias. She held Midnight at a walk to give Ethan a chance to return the gesture. When he twisted around in the seat once more, she smiled at him.

"Would you care to do the honors?" Elizabeth offered him the reins.

Ethan shook his head, laughing under his breath as he took the lines from Elizabeth. "My God, how long has it been since I've held reins in my hands?" He whistled to the horse, and Midnight broke into a brisk trot.

Although the first days of September had brought little relief from the stifling summer heat, the trees lining the road formed a dense bower overhead, penetrated by only a few thin stalks of sunlight. A light breeze blowing off the river refreshed them with the scent of verdant growth and rushing water. As they approached the fork in the road, Ethan slowed Midnight to a reluctant walk.

"Would you mind if we drove upriver a ways, just to the north pasture?" he asked. "I've been anxious to see how my cattle have fared over the summer."

"I wouldn't mind at all," Elizabeth told him.

Ethan guided the horse onto the road that skirted the tree-shrouded riverbank. When Midnight resumed his jaunty trot, Elizabeth peeked from beneath her bonnet's deep brim to observe Ethan. The light filtering through the woodland canopy cast a shadow play on his handsome features, accentuating their sculpted contours. As he deftly worked the reins, a contented smile settled over his face, the look of someone who, for the moment, is doing exactly what he pleases.

Presently the trees lining the road thinned to permit an unobstructed view of a fenced pasture. Ethan pulled Midnight to a halt and shifted in the seat, craning for a better look at the cows lazily browsing the belly-deep grass. His lips moved silently as he counted and then recounted heads.

"Twelve calves!" Ethan turned to Elizabeth, his brow knit in disbelief. "I'd no idea the herd had grown that much over the summer."

"You must have lost count, then, for I'm certain I told you every time a new calf was born," Elizabeth insisted. She touched Ethan's wrist lightly and pointed toward a cluster of animals grazing beneath a spreading oak. "See the cow with the star on her forehead, the one you were worried about?" When Ethan nodded, she went on. "That plump little heifer over to the right is hers. Her mama did just fine bringing her into the world, too, although she kept Noble and me up all night trying to make up her mind when to do it."

Ethan's eyes shifted from the placid herd to Elizabeth. "You never mentioned sitting up with that cow."

Elizabeth shrugged. "I knew you were concerned about her. In any case, her delivery was nothing to compare with the difficulties the poor brindled cow had. I thought she'd been in labor a terribly long time, so I told Noble to pen her away from the rest of the herd. As it turned out, her calf was born feetfirst. What an ordeal that was! The little fellow was so weak I feared he wouldn't survive, but as you can see, he proved me wrong." She gestured toward a strapping young bull butting his poll against his mother's flank. "We didn't lose a single calf this summer and had only one stillbirth," she concluded proudly.

Ethan glanced from Elizabeth to the herd and then back again, shaking his head slowly. "I knew you were working your hands to the bone all day with the tavern and the ferry this summer, but I had no idea you spent the nights playing midwife to my cattle."

"Just a few nights," Elizabeth corrected him. "Besides, I learned a lot that I'm sure will stand me in good stead if I ever decide to try my—"

"Hand at farming," Ethan concluded for her with a dismissive nod. He leaned back slightly, as if to allow himself a more accurate assessment of the woman seated next to him. "You know, you never cease to amaze me, Elizabeth. Every time I think I've figured you out, you turn around and surprise me. I remember the first time I saw you. You looked so fragile and pale in your fine black dress. I imagined you would be only too glad to head back to some place where you could drink tea with other ladies and stitch samplers all day long. Even when you agreed to run the tavern, I half expected you to get your fill of country life after a few weeks and change your mind. Not that I would have blamed you, but I don't think giving up ever entered your mind, did it?" When Elizabeth shook her head, Ethan laughed softly. "And now, just when I've gotten accustomed to seeing you haggle with Noah Gilmer and shame drovers for spitting on the floor, I discover that you apparently have an equal talent for managing a farm."

"You put far too much stock in my helping to deliver a few calves," Elizabeth protested with a modest smile.

"You've done much more than that, Elizabeth," Ethan countered. His dark eyes drifted slowly over her face, lingering on one feature, then another as his fancy prompted him. "I guess I've just never known a woman who could look so delicate and yet be so strong."

Elizabeth glanced down, her hand rising reflexively to cover her warm cheek. "I don't imagine I look all that delicate with a sunburn and freckles."

Ethan tilted his head to peer beneath the bonnet's sheltering brim. "I would say that you have a nice bloom on you."

Elizabeth watched his hand stir where it rested on his knee, not trusting herself to look up at him. Ethan's lengthy convalescence had given them the opportunity to restore the comfortable familiarity of their relationship, and she was deeply grateful for the warm friendship they once more enjoyed. At the same time Elizabeth was acutely aware of every occasion when their contact threatened to overstep the bounds of friendship—not least of all because Ethan, too, now seemed unsure in such instances. Where he had once touched her hair or her face with a natural ease, he now appeared to weigh carefully even the slightest brush of their hands. Perhaps Ethan sensed the tumultuous emotions even such casual intimacy kindled in her and did not wish her to mistake lighthearted flirtation for something more profound. Whatever the case, she released the breath she had been holding and eased back in her seat when he abruptly lifted the reins and clucked to Midnight.

They followed the river road, heading south at a fast clip, slowing only when the tree-shaded white frame house rose into view. No sooner had Ethan reined the horse in front of his house than a jubilant baying erupted from somewhere behind the stable. Elizabeth grinned as Blue charged across the yard, long, floppy ears blown back from his face. In a bounding leap the hound sprang onto the wagon seat to nuzzle his master's face.

"That's right, old fellow. I've come home at last." Ethan wrapped both arms around the squirming dog and gave him a fond hug. He gently held the ecstatic animal still with one hand while he reached for the crutch. "See this thing, Blue? I'm going to be hobbling around on it for a month or so, so you'll have to be patient with me."

Elizabeth clutched the hound around the neck to restrain him and give Ethan a chance to climb to the ground. As if he understood the nature of his human friend's handicap, Blue accompanied Ethan along the path at a sedate pace. Elizabeth collected the clothes from the wagon bed and then followed them to the house. As they approached the veranda, Maum Betsy appeared in the doorway.

"Lord, but you finally come home!" Tears glistening in her russet brown eyes, the tiny woman rushed across the veranda to embrace Ethan. Given her diminutive stature, the top of her turban barely reached the midpoint of his chest, but in spite of the crutch he managed to stoop and encircle her shoulders with one arm.

"It's so good to see you, Maum Betsy. How is Josephus?" Ethan asked, guiding the wizened little woman back up the steps.

"Waitin' right in the front room of this house to see you," Elizabeth heard Maum Betsy say as they disappeared into the hall.

Not wishing to intrude on what had become an emotional homecoming, Elizabeth deposited Ethan's clothes on one of the veranda chairs and retreated to the yard. Although Ethan's stablehand had proven himself to be a reliable lad, she always made a point of checking the horses' supply of water and hay whenever she visited the farm. She was cutting across the paddock where Inali, Ethan's favorite saddle horse, passed his days when she happened to notice the gate standing open. Elizabeth dashed into the stable, only to find the gelding's stall empty.

Returning to the yard, she hesitated for a moment. In all likelihood the escaped horse would have headed for an attractive grazing area rather than for the open road. With any luck she would find him cropping the lush grass that flourished along the river's edge. As she descended the slope leading to the river, Elizabeth shaded her eyes from the sun and scanned the bank in hope of locating the big bay horse. She paused a few yards short of the river and looked in both directions. She was elated when she spotted the gelding grazing on the edge of the forest.

"Easy, Inali! There's a good fellow," Elizabeth crooned as she picked her way through the tangle of blackberry bushes.

Forcing herself to move slowly and deliberately, she edged toward the horse. Just as she reached for the halter, however, the animal pivoted out of her reach and jogged into the forest. Elizabeth brushed a dangling strand of honeysuckle vine out of her face and trudged after the horse. When Inali at last stopped to nibble at a low bush, she waited a few moments before trying her luck once more. To her relief she managed to grasp the halter before the gelding could swerve away from her.

"A fine way to behave on the very day Ethan comes home again!" Elizabeth scolded the horse as she led him through the deep underbrush. "As if there wasn't enough grass—" She stopped suddenly, her attention fastened on a shadow gliding between the trees.

Her hand nervously fingering the halter's leather straps, Elizabeth peered into the forest. Since assuming management of the tavern she had heard enough hunters brag about their exploits to know that bears still populated the foothills surrounding the Oostanaula River. Although Gray Bear claimed that the creature whose name he shared was too wise to venture near human settlements, the summer's surplus of new lambs and calves might have tempted a hungry bear to violate that principle. Whatever the case, Elizabeth had no desire to risk a face-to-face encounter with a potentially dangerous animal.

Hiking her skirt with her free hand, Elizabeth tugged at the horse's halter and began to retrace her path as quickly as the tangled undergrowth would permit. The gelding had led her deeper into the woods than she had at first realized, a fact that did nothing to calm the uneasiness creeping over her. As she stumbled through the forest, she glanced over her shoulder, wary of any sign of movement. Nothing stirred, however, save for a few squirrels skittering through the trees. Reminding herself that an animal as large as a bear would surely make some noise thrashing through such close woods, Elizabeth began to relax slightly. Perhaps she had only allowed the shifting morning light to deceive her.

When a vine bristling with tiny briars snagged her hem, Elizabeth stooped to pull her skirt free. As she was straightening herself, she froze, her eyes riveted on the screen of overlapping branches not more than a few feet from where she stood. It was not her imagination. Something behind those bushes had moved. With both hands latched to the halter, she was backing away from the clump of bushes when a faint rustle caused her to turn. She had stared at the dense wall of evergreen for several seconds before she distinguished a man's scarred face half-hidden by the branches.

Elizabeth screamed, causing Inali to jerk free of her grasp. She was too terrified, however, to think of anything but getting out of the isolated forest. She flailed at the low-hanging branches that snatched at her bonnet, stumbling through the snarled creeper that threatened to trip her with each step. By the time she reached the clearing her side ached from exertion, but she did not slow her pace. She was running up the slope when she almost collided with Ethan.

He caught her arm, leaning on the long rifle he held at his side in lieu of the crutch. He anxiously scanned her face. "I heard a scream. Are you hurt?"

Elizabeth shook her head as she tried to catch her breath. "Inali broke out of the paddock, and I followed him into the forest. A man startled me. I can't be sure, but he seemed to be trying to hide. He had this terrible scar across his cheek." She shuddered at the still-vivid image.

Ethan's lean face darkened as he surveyed the close-standing trees lining the riverbank. "Was he an Indian?"

Elizabeth frowned. "I couldn't see him very clearly, but I think he was a white man." When Ethan started down the bank she snatched at his sleeve, but he eluded her grasp.

"Go to the house, Elizabeth, and stay with Maum Betsy and Josephus. I'm only going to have a look, and then I'll be right back," Ethan told her over his shoulder.

Ethan hurried toward the forest as quickly as his limp would permit, using the long rifle as a walking stick. Ignoring his order, Elizabeth followed from a distance to watch him disappear among the trees. For what seemed an interminable length of time she kept her eyes trained on the spot where he had entered the forest. When Ethan at last emerged from between the pines with Inali in tow, Elizabeth ran along the river to meet him.

Ethan shook his head in anticipation of her question. "I didn't see anyone. Chances are you stumbled on to someone with a mind to steal a chicken or two. Your scream was probably enough to convince him to try his luck elsewhere." Despite his assurances, the wary glance he cast toward the woods did not escape Elizabeth's notice.

"He moved so quietly, almost as if he were a ghost. I saw his shadow slipping between the trees, and then the next moment he appeared in an entirely different spot." Seeing Ethan's hand tighten on the gun, Elizabeth hastened to add, "At least he didn't get away with any of your chickens." The strain of pressing through the woods on his weakened leg had exacerbated Ethan's limp and left his face covered in a light film of sweat, and she was determined that he not make another painful and potentially hazardous foray into the forest.

To her relief, Ethan only nodded as they continued up the path to the paddock. She waited while he released Inali in the paddock and then joined her in the yard.

As they walked to the house, Elizabeth glanced up at the sun, which was now suspended almost directly overhead. "It's nearly midday, and I've cooked nothing to serve at the tavern. I suppose I must be on my way," she admitted reluctantly. She halted beside the wagon. "You should try to rest a bit."

Ethan smiled as he helped Elizabeth climb onto the driver's perch with his free hand. "I've been resting for two months now, Elizabeth. But I promise to do as Maum Betsy says, at least for today." When she lifted the reins, he stepped back from the wagon. "Tell everyone at the ferry that I'll be by tomorrow."

"I'll tell them you'll be by soon," Elizabeth amended.

She shook the reins, setting Midnight into a brisk walk. As they approached the bend, Elizabeth looked back at Ethan, intent on waving, but he had already turned his back to the road. Leaning on the rifle propped at his side, he was staring along the river at the great, silent forest.

"Deerkiller is not the only man to bear a scar on his face, Ethan." Gray Bear tamped his pipe, his blunt finger carefully pressing the tobacco into the clay bowl.

Ethan glanced at the husky man seated beside him on the step. "Why would someone be hiding in those woods?"

Gray Bear shrugged and kept his eye on the tiny ember glowing among the brown shreds of tobacco. "To wait for the right time to steal a chicken or maybe even a horse." He paused to draw on the pipe. "He could have been one of those that General Wool has talked into leaving their homes to go west. I have seen many such people on the road this summer, following the soldiers with their wagons. Perhaps this man changed his mind and decided he did not want to go after all, so he hid himself until he was sure the soldiers would not see him return to his home."

"Elizabeth said he looked like a white man," Ethan countered.

Gray Bear puffed on his pipe for a minute, savoring the transparent cloud of fragrant smoke. "There are many white men living in our country now."

"But I don't believe that this man was one of them." Ethan shifted on the step to face Gray Bear. "Only think of everything Elizabeth told me about him. He looked white, which Deerkiller does, thanks to his Scottish grandfather. And she said he could move through the forest as if he were a spirit." He paused, his eyes searching the older man's face for the glimmer of a reaction.

"Deerkiller is a Creek, Ethan. He would have gone west when his people did. If he was still alive," he added as an afterthought.

"He's still alive. He swore he would avenge his father's death, and he won't let himself die until he does so." Ethan was surprised by the strength of his conviction, an instinctive certainty that gnawed at his gut like an ulcer. "Deerkiller is a man obsessed with revenge. I'll never forget the night he overtook my father outside the tavern. While we were grappling for the knife, I looked into his eyes. What I saw there frightened me more than his bowie knife, for I realized that he had passed caring about even his own life. The only thing that still had any meaning for him was his hatred."

"Deerkiller was full of hate, but his life still meant enough for him to run from you when he had the chance," Gray Bear pointed out. His hooded eyes followed the threads of smoke drifting across the darkening night air. "That was almost fifteen years ago. In all those years you have not seen

Deerkiller again. Time can change a man, Ethan, even one who is ruled by hate."

"I would like to believe that. But what if it *was* Deerkiller in the woods today? What if he still holds to the blood oath he swore over his father's body?" Ethan frowned, his gaze fixed on the shadowy billows of vapor rising from the river in the distance. "Maybe you're right. Fifteen years is a long time. It's only when I think that Elizabeth might have been hurt because of me—" He abruptly fell silent.

"It is only natural that you should worry about Elizabeth, Ethan. That was the way I felt about my Mary. You should be with her so that you can look after her," Gray Bear went on, as matter-of-factly as if they were discussing some mundane aspect of running the ferry.

"Mary was your wife, Gray Bear. It's a very different situation with Elizabeth and me," Ethan reminded him in a voice calculated to sound even and deliberate.

"So very different?" Gray Bear gave Ethan a skeptical look before turning his attention back to his pipe. "Elizabeth is a good woman who loves you. You are happier when you are together than when you are apart. What more do you want in a wife?"

"I can't think of marrying, not with the way things are now," Ethan said, evading the elderly man's question. He looked down at his hands clasped in front of him. "We've both seen the federal troops on the road. In the past year they've flooded into our country, and you know as well as I that they aren't going to abandon their forts and go away just because some of us refuse to acknowledge the treaty." He hesitated, swallowing to relieve the dry-dust taste on his tongue. "I've given a lot of thought to what I would do if they came to force me to leave. I can't say I really know yet. Maybe I won't until the time comes. But I'm certain of one thing. I have no right to involve Elizabeth in a life as uncertain as mine."

"Elizabeth is already involved in your life, Ethan, and there is nothing you can do about that," Gray Bear remarked quietly.

Ethan looked up at his old friend. "But she isn't legally tied to me. As far as the state of Georgia is concerned, she is the widow of a white man, with a legal claim to the land on which she lives." He shook his head. "Elizabeth has a secure home and for the first time in her life, I think, a measure of peace. She would be foolish to throw in her lot with me and risk losing everything."

Gray Bear rested one of his big, callused hands on Ethan's shoulder. "Perhaps you should let Elizabeth decide what is best for her."

The ferryman stood up slowly. He stooped to tap his pipe against the side of the steps, emptying the spent remains of tobacco into the grass before tucking it into his pocket. Ethan watched Gray Bear amble to the hitching post where his aged chestnut mare patiently waited. He swung into the saddle and then turned his horse to face the house.

"Good night, Ethan." Through the gathering darkness Ethan saw the elderly man's mouth draw into a smile. "It is good to see you sitting on those steps again."

"It's good to be sitting here. Good night, Gray Bear." Ethan managed a smile of his own.

As the chestnut mare's hoofbeats faded down the dark road, however, a deep melancholy sank over him. Although not a day passed without his reminding himself that he could never, in good conscience, be more than a friend to Elizabeth Merriweather, Ethan had not shared his agonizing dilemma with another person until tonight. Much as he respected Gray Bear's wisdom, he had taken little comfort in his old friend's advice regarding Elizabeth. She had already given up far too much in the course of her short life to be asked to make yet another sacrifice.

Leaning his head against the porch rail, Ethan recalled Elizabeth's wrenching account of losing her little son. She had followed her husband to a godforsaken mining town, endured hardship that he might pursue his ambitions, and yet when their infant fell ill he had refused her plea to return to a more hospitable place. Ethan felt a wave of rage at the self-centered, unthinking man whom he would never meet and the needless suffering he had inflicted on Elizabeth. Whatever his opinion of Samuel Merriweather might be, however, he was powerless to alter the past. He could only vow that he would never ask Elizabeth to make such sacrifices on his account. Even as he made his private pact, Ethan winced at the thought of what he must ask himself to give up if he were to keep his word.

Chapter Ten

"Elizabeth, I've a surprise for you!"

Elizabeth looked up from the apple pie that she was lacing with strips of pastry dough. Dusting the flour from her hands, she hurried to the kitchen door in time to see Ethan rein Inali just short of the well. Her eyes widening in amazement, she watched as he kicked his feet free of the stirrups and then swung his right leg over the horse's rump. He leaned across the saddle to balance himself and dropped to the ground, letting his sound leg take his weight.

"You're riding again!"

"Yes, indeed." Ethan braced both hands on the saddle and agilely vaulted into the saddle. Still grinning at Elizabeth, he executed another adroit dismount.

Elizabeth shook her head as he led the horse toward the kitchen. "I'm afraid to ask how long you've been doing this behind our backs," she scolded him, not quite managing to contain her smile.

"Only a little over a week. Since I've finished with the crutch, I couldn't see any point in not giving it a try. Poor Inali was getting as restless as I was. Will has been giving him a few short rides a week, but that's hardly enough for a high-spirited horse. In any case, I'd had my fill of driving myself about in the wagon. My leg's still stiff, so I've had to let the stirrup out a good bit, but otherwise I feel the way I always have on the back of a horse—good." Ethan laughed and gave the horse's neck an affectionate pat.

Elizabeth extended her hand to allow Inali an inquisitive sniff. She stroked the animal's head, leaving a light trace of flour on the satiny coat. "When you were still bedridden I used to close my eyes and imagine you doing all the ordinary things that we never give a second thought to until they're taken away. I swore that if I could just see you ride up to the ferry the way you once did, I'd never take any of those things for granted again."

"Nor will I." Ethan tickled the horse's velvet-soft nose, his fingers grazing Elizabeth's. "See what you've done?" He laughed softly as he brushed the white handprint from the animal's dark brown coat. "You have flour on your face, too." Smiling down at Elizabeth, he dabbed the tip of her nose with his little finger.

Elizabeth looked up into the intense eyes resting on her. A wave of heat swept through her, augmenting the warmth emanating from Ethan's vigorous, masculine body, now standing less than a footstep from her. For a moment she let herself imagine how it would feel to have his hands cradle her face, gently tilt it as he lowered his mouth to hers. Her lips parted in an involuntary response to the fantasy drifting through her mind. She caught herself and straightened her shoulders when Gray Bear appeared in the tavern's back door.

"There is a man here to see you, Elizabeth," the ferryman announced as he approached them on the path.

"Who is he?" Elizabeth asked.

Gray Bear shook his head. "I have never seen him before, and he did not seem to want to talk much. He only said that he had been told he could find Mrs. Merriweather here."

Ethan gave Elizabeth a wry smile. "It sounds to me as if someone has decided to give Noah Gilmer a little competition. Drive a hard bargain, Elizabeth," he admonished her teasingly as he started for the stable.

"Don't I always?" Elizabeth called after him. She smiled at the sound of his laughter carrying across the yard.

Gathering her skirt, Elizabeth followed Gray Bear to the tavern. She pulled up short in the doorway when she spied the frock-coated man who waited impatiently by the window. Elizabeth hastened to remove her wrinkled apron and toss it onto the settle just before Josiah Merriweather wheeled to face her.

"Josiah! I had no idea you were planning to visit." Elizabeth fostered a smile that only partially disguised her consternation.

"Winter is fast approaching, and I prefer to travel before the cold weather sets in. In any case, I do not intend to tarry long."

Josiah was regarding her with such severity, Elizabeth wondered if her face bore a splotch of flour that Ethan had neglected to blot. "Did you receive the letter I wrote you this summer?" she asked.

"Yes, but based on its content, I assumed that you had not received mine." Josiah's protruding eyes traveled to Gray Bear with unconcealed disdain. "Can we perhaps talk in private?"

"Yes, of course." Elizabeth gestured toward the table situated nearest the fireplace. As they seated themselves she was secretly pleased to see Gray Bear take his time putting away the rifle he had been cleaning and amble to the door without the slightest haste.

Josiah frowned over his shoulder, waiting until the gray-haired ferryman had disappeared through the door before he twisted in the chair to face Elizabeth. "I will get right to the heart of matters, Elizabeth. I can say in all honesty that I have not been favored with a single night's restful sleep since I learned of your intentions to relocate to Samuel's land lot. I wrote you immediately to offer my assistance in settling with the Indian, but I realize that my letter must have gone astray, for you made no mention of it in your own letter, which I received last month. My offer, however, still stands. I will treat with this obstinate Indian and secure you full title to the property in question."

Elizabeth forced herself to meet the unsmiling blue eyes glaring reproachfully across the table at her. "If you have worried on my account, Josiah, I am sorry, but I can assure you that your concern has been in vain. As I told you in my letter, the arrangement I have made with Mr. Woodard has proved quite satisfactory."

Josiah's gaze swept the tavern, his lip curling slightly at what he saw. "Elizabeth, I know that you are a selfless woman, willing to sacrifice greatly rather than burden your loved ones. I cannot in good conscience, however, allow my own brother's widow to be reduced to servile labor in a place such as this."

"I am not making any great sacrifices, Josiah. I have a comfortable home, and I am able to meet my material needs," Elizabeth insisted. "And I enjoy the work I do here," she added with a trace of defiance.

Josiah's brief laugh dripped derision. "What can you mean? That you relish waiting on the scoundrels and ruffians who frequent a place like this? That you take pleasure in allowing that Indian to exploit your desperation? I mean no insult, Elizabeth, but I scarcely recognized you when you walked through that door with your hair flying about and your face scorched as red as one of these Indians."

"Josiah!" Elizabeth interjected hotly. She broke off when she noticed Ethan standing in the doorway.

As he started across the room he winked at her, taking advantage of Josiah's turned back. Ethan no doubt supposed that the portly man seated at the table was intent on selling them liquor or tenpenny nails, a potentially disastrous assumption, and Elizabeth moved swiftly to avert an unpleasant encounter. She jumped to her feet before Ethan reached the table, causing Josiah to swivel in his chair.

"Ethan, I'd like for you to meet my brother-in-law, Josiah Merriweather." Elizabeth gave Ethan a meaningful look over the top of Josiah's generously pomaded head. "Josiah, this is Ethan Woodard."

She noticed Ethan's hand stir at his side and then relax, his impulse to offer it apparently forestalled by a quick appraisal of Josiah's belligerent mien. "Good afternoon, Mr. Merriweather."

Josiah nodded curtly. "Good afternoon."

Ethan looked at Josiah for a long moment, giving Elizabeth the rare pleasure of seeing her normally domineering in-law avoid someone's gaze. Then he turned to Elizabeth. "Why don't you take the rest of the day, Elizabeth? I'm sure you'll want to visit with Mr. Merriweather. We can manage here just fine. I'll saddle Midnight for you," he offered, turning to the door.

"Thank you, Ethan." Elizabeth smiled at him before glancing at Josiah. "If you'll excuse me, I only need to tidy the kitchen and then we can go to my house."

Josiah shifted his considerable bulk in the chair, signaling his resignation to a tedious wait, but he said nothing as Elizabeth retreated out the back door. While she stored the unbaked pie beneath an upturned bowl and cleared away the apple parings and scraps of dough, she tried to quell the unsettled feeling that her brother-in-law's unannounced arrival had aroused in her. Her encounters with Josiah had never had a soothing effect on her, but his open hostility to Ethan now added a particularly galling barb to their relationship. As Elizabeth walked back to the tavern she realized that anger, rather than discomfiture, was responsible for the tight knot lodged in the pit of her stomach.

"Shall we go, Josiah?" Elizabeth did her best to sound cordial.

Josiah roused himself from his seat to accompany her to the door. From the porch Elizabeth noticed that Ethan had tethered Midnight at the hitching post beside Josiah's well-fed dun gelding. She let Josiah help her mount and then held Midnight steady while he hoisted himself into the saddle.

They had ridden only a short way along the road when a wagon pulled into sight, drawn by a team of fat roans. As the wagon drew even with the two horses, Elizabeth threw up her hand in greeting.

"Good afternoon, Mr. Birdsong. I hope David's cough is better."

When the driver nodded, the heavy silver discs suspended from his ears captured sparks of the late autumn sun. "He is well enough to go to school again."

"That's good to hear. Please give Mrs. Birdsong my regards, and do thank her again for the muscadine jam."

"I will, Mrs. Merriweather." The man smiled as he slapped the lines against the horses' broad backs, urging them into a trot.

"Really, Elizabeth! If I didn't know you better, I would think you had become an apologist for these savages." Josiah jerked the reins, venting his annoyance on his luckless mount.

Elizabeth cast an apprehensive glance over her shoulder, but fortunately the wagon's rumbling wheels had prevented James Birdsong from overhearing Josiah's mean-spirited comment. Goading Midnight alongside her brother-in-law's horse, she frowned at Josiah.

"These people are not savages, Josiah," Elizabeth told him sharply. "Many of them still dress as their ancestors did and keep their customs, but that is no reason to scorn them. My neighbors in this valley are as decent and upstanding as any of the people I knew in Auraria—or in Milledgeville, for that matter," she added.

Seeing his scowl darken, Elizabeth drew a deep, calming breath. Arguing with someone as opinionated as Josiah Merriweather rarely yielded anything but grounds for further discord. If she hoped to amend his prejudice against the Cherokees even slightly, she would have to choose another tactic. As they approached the fork in the road, an idea occurred to Elizabeth.

"I'd like to show you something, Josiah. It's only a short distance from here."

Elizabeth let Midnight take the lead, giving Josiah little choice but to follow. Invigorated by the crisp fall weather, the spirited horse took full advantage of his mistress's encouragement and broke into a swift canter. Only when they had passed Martin Early's attractive two-story house did Elizabeth tighten the reins. As she turned Midnight onto the narrow trail, she glanced back at Josiah. His face was flushed—whether from consternation or the brisk ride, Elizabeth was unsure—but she smiled to herself as the clapboard schoolhouse came into view. She halted Midnight beside the hitching rail and waited for Josiah to follow suit.

"Why have you brought me here?" Josiah's suspicious eyes swept the quiet orchard as if he expected to find the Indians of his worst imaginings lying in wait behind the gnarled trees.

"I wanted you to see our school." After tying Midnight to the rail, Elizabeth led the way to the little building's single door. She waited while Josiah grudgingly trudged after her, and then tapped at the door.

"Miss Ballard?" Elizabeth peeked around the half-opened door to find fifteen pairs of young eyes trained on her. She smiled apologetically as she stepped into the schoolroom. "I'm sorry to interrupt your class, but I've a guest who very much wanted to see the school. May we visit with your class for a few minutes?"

"Certainly you may, Mrs. Merriweather." Miss Ballard rounded the oak desk situated at the front of the room, her doll-like face beaming with pride.

Elizabeth introduced Josiah to Abigail Ballard. In her best schoolmistress fashion, the teacher rallied her pupils to their feet and coaxed them to welcome their honored guest. Faced with a chorus of "Good afternoon, Mr. Merriweather," Josiah looked decidedly perplexed, but he listened with seeming good grace to Miss Ballard's brief history of the school.

"All of these children are enrolled in the school, then?" Hands clasped behind his back, Josiah surveyed the rows of small faces like a drill sergeant inspecting conscripts.

"Every one of them, Mr. Merriweather," Miss Ballard assured him.

Josiah stepped between two rows of desks, adopting the portentous stride he had perfected during his years of successfully arguing before juries. He halted abruptly and wheeled to face a slender black child of about eight years of age.

"What is your name, boy?"

"George Corey, sir."

"And who is your master, George Corey?"

A frown creased the youngster's even-featured face for a moment as he considered the question. "Why, no one, sir. My papa is a free man. He works the ferry, but Mr. Woodard pays him a wage," he added helpfully.

Josiah's bristling brows drew together as if he were mulling over exceedingly complex information. "Do you learn well?"

"Yes, sir," the child replied with an eager nod. "I can already read from the fourth primer and do sums."

"Indeed," Josiah remarked. He continued to the back of the schoolroom. He paused at the door and turned. "Thank you, Miss Ballard. This has been a most enlightening experience." He held the door for Elizabeth, indicating his readiness to depart.

Elizabeth thanked the teacher once more and then accompanied Josiah into the yard. "Ethan's brother-in-law wanted an education for his children so badly he built this schoolhouse and brought Miss Ballard here at his own expense. Isn't that admirable?" She gave Josiah a triumphant look as she stepped onto the mounting block and then swung into the saddle. To her dismay he only frowned.

"I suppose you realize that woman is engaged in illegal activity." Josiah's lips tightened into a smug line.

"Whatever do you mean?"

"Teaching that black boy to read is in direct violation of the laws of this state," Josiah informed her in a self-righteous tone.

Elizabeth bit her lip, censuring the scathing rebuke forming on her tongue. If she had learned anything in nearly thirty years of living, it was to recognize a hopeless situation. Josiah had arrived at her new home with the worst expectations, and nothing she could do or say was going to alter his opinion. While they rode the short distance to her house, Elizabeth resolved to avoid any further serious discussion with him and somehow get through the remainder of his visit as best she could.

To that end, she hurried to the kitchen as soon as they reached the house and instructed Dolly to set an extra place for dinner. After entrusting the horses to Jephtha's care, Elizabeth mustered as gracious a manner as possible and dutifully showed Josiah around the house. For his part, Josiah seemed content to avoid further controversy, chatting over dinner about his law practice and his decision to run for public office. Nonetheless, Elizabeth was relieved when he declined dessert, pleading fatigue from his long journey.

Leaving Dolly to clear the table, she led Josiah upstairs to the corner bedroom. She gave the room a quick inspection and silently blessed the efficient housekeeper for the fresh linen and ewer full of water.

"I trust you will be comfortable here, but if you require anything, please let me or Dolly know," Elizabeth told him, smoothing a wrinkle from the white counterpane.

"Thank you, Elizabeth. Perhaps an extra blanket would be in order. The nights are getting quite cool."

As Elizabeth rummaged through the folded quilts stored on the wardrobe shelf, Josiah deposited his saddlebag beside the chair, then tested the mattress with one hand. Stifling a yawn, he casually flipped open the book lying on the nightstand. "*Clarissa?* I had no idea your taste in literature ran to risqué novels."

"It's Ethan's book. He owns quite an extensive library," Elizabeth explained. Although she would normally have taken issue with such an obtuse judgment of Richardson's masterpiece, her only desire at this point was to conclude the evening as expeditiously as possible.

Josiah's short laugh reeked with condescension. "And you've taken to dabbling in this library, I gather?"

Elizabeth frowned at the wool blanket she was shaking out and tried to hold her temper in check. "I fetched it for him to read while his leg was healing, and I suppose he forgot it when he went home," she snapped without thinking. She caught herself, but Josiah's aghast expression warned her that she would pay dearly for her lapse.

"You can't mean to say that you had that Indian *here!*" Josiah almost choked on his words.

Elizabeth raised her chin to meet his livid gaze. "Yes, I did. Ethan had no one else to care for him after he broke his leg. He helped me when I was in need. It was the least I could do for him."

"My God, Elizabeth!" Josiah's bulging eyes darted to the four-poster. He grimaced, recoiling from the bed as if it were contaminated by some dread disease. "Have you no shame?"

"I've done nothing to be ashamed of!" Elizabeth insisted indignantly.

An apoplectic flush began to creep up Josiah's fleshy cheeks. "I suppose you consider bringing that red savage into your bed—"

"Enough, Josiah!" Elizabeth was shaking with fury, and her breath was coming in rapid gulps. "I'll not have you impugn my character in my own home. And I will not tolerate your insulting Ethan Woodard. Ethan is a far better man than many who would call themselves gentlemen. He has never treated me with anything but respect and consideration. Think what you will of me, but I will not stand by and permit you to malign him.''

"As you please, Elizabeth." Josiah's low voice was thick with anger and contempt. "But mark me. In these times you cast your lot with an Indian at your own peril. I warn you. You will live to regret your folly."

Chapter Eleven

"The way those old hens have been laying, you'd never suspect the weather was so cold. I guess they figure since it's getting close to Christmas, they better give us enough eggs for a proper eggnog, or they just might end up on the Christmas dinner table." Dolly chuckled as she rose on tiptoe to tie a sprig of evergreen to one of the wall sconces mounted over the mantel. Then she stepped back from the hearth to give her handiwork a critical appraisal.

Elizabeth looked up from the pine boughs she was binding into a garland and smiled. "It's perfectly beautiful, Dolly. You've such a knack for making things look pretty. I used to marvel at how fine you could make that shabby little house in Auraria look at Christmas with just a few scraps of ribbon and some greenery."

Dolly's eyes shone as she stooped to warm her hands over the open fire. "I've always loved Christmas. Seems to me if there's one day in the year worth celebrating, it's when folks can put aside their cares, feel kindness toward one another and thank the Lord for their blessings." She jabbed the simmering logs with the poker, releasing a spray of fiery sparks, before turning to Elizabeth. "I hope you won't think I'm speaking out of turn, ma'am, but I do wish you'd ask Mr. Woodard about taking a few weeks away from the tavern so you could visit with your cousins over Christmas. He's such a kind man, I'm certain he'd be willing to oblige."

"I'm sure he would, too, Dolly, but as I've told you, I wouldn't feel right asking him. Ethan has worked so hard this fall, to make up for the time he lost over the summer.

Now that the harvest is in and his fences are repaired, he at last has a chance to rest a bit. I would feel very selfish asking him to manage the tavern while I was away at Prospect enjoying myself.''

Dolly looked only partially won by Elizabeth's argument. "I just hate to think of you spending Christmas without some family to share it.''

Elizabeth rose to shake out the garland, releasing a faint whiff of the forest's perfume into the air. "Don't worry, Dolly. I intend to celebrate Christmas this year in the best fashion. And I shan't do it alone.''

Dolly gave her an inquiring look, but Elizabeth only smiled as she carried the thick swag of evergreen to the bookcase and carefully arranged it along the top shelf. She heard the young housekeeper sigh behind her back. "Well, I expect I'd better feed the chickens before it gets dark. The days are getting mighty short now.''

After Dolly had retreated down the corridor, Elizabeth took a few minutes to sweep up the stray pine needles and toss them onto the fire. As she started for the door, she paused to take stock of the gaily decorated room. Spending the afternoon trimming the house with Dolly had put her in high spirits, as if the gay festoons had at last banished the aura of malice that Josiah had left in his wake.

The morning after their ugly row, Elizabeth had awakened to find that her brother-in-law had risen before daybreak and departed without a word. Despite her efforts to put his vicious slurs out of her mind, however, her anger had been slow to subside. She had been grateful for the onset of the holiday season and the diversion it provided.

Right now she was in far too festive a mood to squander even a moment recalling the unpleasant confrontation with Josiah. Then, too, a critical step in her preparations for the holiday still remained to be done. With this thought in mind, Elizabeth dashed upstairs to collect her mantle, bonnet and gloves and then hurried to the stable. Wresting the reluctant Midnight away from the sweet hay Jephtha had forked into his manger, she quickly saddled the horse and set out for the ferry. As she approached the dusk-shrouded tavern, she was pleased to find Gray Bear enjoying his pipe on the steps, oblivious to the chill sharpening the air. The elderly ferryman rose and smiled in greeting.

"Good evening, Gray Bear. I hoped I would find you here. Has Ethan gone home yet?" Elizabeth asked, reining Midnight at the foot of the steps.

The ferryman shook his iron gray head. "Right after you left this afternoon, old Gideon Broom drove up and wanted his whole team shod. Ethan finished with the last horse only a little while ago. He is washing up now." He turned at the sound of footsteps coming from inside the tavern.

Ethan paused in the doorway to shake down his sleeves and fasten the buttons. "Elizabeth, what on earth are you doing out at this hour?"

"I needed to ask you both something, and I didn't want to wait until morning." Elizabeth shrugged self-consciously, glancing down at the reins she held.

Ethan grinned as he sauntered across the porch. "It must be a pretty important question." When Elizabeth said nothing, he prompted, "Well, then, aren't you going to ask?"

Elizabeth cleared her throat. "Do you keep Christmas?" Not giving the surprised-looking men a chance to respond, she hurried on. "Because if you do, I should like very much for you to share my Christmas dinner and join me in celebrating the day. I've always felt the best part of the holiday was having your family and friends around you, and since I shan't see my relatives this year..." She hesitated, weaving the reins between her fingers. "It would mean a great deal to me to have you in my home."

For a moment Ethan looked as if he did not know what to say. "I would be very pleased to accept your invitation," he told her quietly, but his voice carried a husky undercurrent that betrayed how genuinely touched he was. "I think I can speak for both of us." He glanced at Gray Bear, who nodded without hesitation.

"Good. Then I shall expect both of you at my table next week." Elizabeth smiled down at them. Her eyes lingered on Ethan, withdrawing only reluctantly from his intense dark gaze. "I should be going while I've still some light."

Gathering the reins, Elizabeth backed Midnight away from the porch. She bade the men good-night and then turned the horse toward the road. As she approached the fork she tightened the lines to counter the headstrong gelding's ingrained habit to veer left in the direction of his stable. After Elizabeth had turned Midnight onto the road leading to Martin Early's home, she held him at a walk mindful of the unfamiliar terrain underfoot.

The yard surrounding the Early house appeared deserted, but a warm glow shone through the drawn curtains of two downstairs windows. Elizabeth tied Midnight at the hitching rail and climbed the veranda steps. She had knocked at the front door and was awaiting a response when she heard someone approaching from behind the house. Elizabeth turned to see Martin Early trudging up the steps, his arms laden with split logs. When he noticed her standing in the shadows, he pulled up short.

"Good evening, Elizabeth." Martin juggled the firewood he held and gave her a brief nod.

"Good evening, Martin."

Although Elizabeth would be forever grateful to Martin for his quiet support the night of Ethan's crisis, a reserved courtesy had continued to characterize their encounters. Elizabeth felt awkward—as she usually did in Martin's presence—as she stepped to one side, permitting him to deposit the logs beside the door. "I didn't mean to disturb you. I only called in hopes of speaking with Miss Ballard for a few minutes."

Martin dusted the flecks of bark from his sleeves. "I'm afraid she isn't in just yet. She took the children to the Birdsongs' this afternoon to pull taffy. I expect them shortly." He reached for the door and then hesitated. "You're welcome to wait inside if you like."

"Oh, no." Elizabeth bit her lip, repenting the haste with which she had replied. "I mean, I only wanted to ask Miss Ballard if she would like to celebrate Christmas with me. With the holidays so near, I know she has been pining to see her sister and her nephews in Boston, and I thought she might appreciate the hospitality."

"I'll be sure to tell her." A smile briefly relieved the sober cast of Martin's angular face. In contrast to Elizabeth's earliest impression of him, the black eyes resting on her face appeared not hard, only sad, the wistful gaze of someone whose heart has been wounded too deeply to mend.

"Thank you." Elizabeth turned to go and then stopped. "Martin," she began, halting him in the doorway. When he faced her, she took a deep breath. "I don't know what you might have planned with Rebecca and Ben, but I'd be very honored to have you and your children as my guests on Christmas, too."

Martin stared at Elizabeth for several seconds, as if he were unsure he had understood her. "That's very kind of you, Elizabeth."

"That means yes, I hope." Elizabeth pressed her luck.

"Yes, it does." Martin's mouth slowly drew into another smile, one that lingered as he watched Elizabeth follow the path to her waiting horse.

Elizabeth pulled herself into the saddle and then turned Midnight toward the road. Just as she nudged the horse into a trot, she heard Martin's voice carry across the yard. "Thank you, Elizabeth. And Merry Christmas!"

Although Elizabeth cherished many fond memories of Christmases from her childhood, she could remember none that had dawned more auspiciously than that cold, bright day in 1837. An early snow had fallen during the night, gilding the trees with an icy patina that glistened like crystal in the morning sun. Inside the house, a roaring fire blazed in both of the downstairs fireplaces, adding the fragrance of smoldering hardwood to the tempting mélange of scents that filled the dining room.

As Elizabeth hurried between kitchen and house, helping Dolly transport the formidable array of covered dishes, she concluded proudly that none of the banquets gracing her mother's Savannah sideboard had exceeded today's bountiful feast. At one end of the dining table lay a platter of roast venison, garnished with spiced peaches and plums, while the opposite end boasted a golden brown turkey so large Jephtha had been obliged to carry the tray. Elizabeth had chosen her finest linen tablecloth for the occasion, but not more than a few inches of the delicately embroidered fabric remained visible, thanks to the multitude of side dishes and relishes arranged on the table. There were candied yams and corn pudding, buttered carrots and greens steamed with a splash of vinegar, souffléed potatoes and glazed beets, baked rice and dressing seasoned with herbs, wheat rolls and beaten biscuits, as well as a half-dozen dishes of pickles and conserves. The sideboard bore its own burden of sweet delights—layer cake with boiled frosting, hickory nut tart, chess pie, a tiered silver tray displaying all manner of confections and a dark fruitcake studded with dried peaches, apples and pears.

As she always did on Christmas, Elizabeth relieved her servants of their duties, giving them the day to spend together in their own home. After shooing Dolly back to the kitchen with strict orders to take extra generous portions of the food for herself and Jephtha, Elizabeth rushed upstairs to change into the dark green velvet gown she had chosen for the occasion. She was fastening her mother's heirloom pearl choker around her neck when she heard a knock at the door. Elizabeth paused long enough to put on the matching drop earrings and then hurried downstairs.

As she opened the door, Ethan greeted her with a smile as brilliant as the clear winter sun. "Merry Christmas, Elizabeth!" He presented her with a cloth-wrapped bundle that suspiciously resembled a smoked ham.

"Thank you, and a Merry Christmas to you!"

Clutching the ham with both hands, Elizabeth smiled up at Ethan. Although she had always appreciated his exceptional good looks, he had never appeared quite as dashing as he did today. Accustomed to seeing him clad in clothing suited for hard work, Elizabeth took admiring note of the light gray breeches and midnight blue coat he wore. Expertly tailored, the well-fitted attire emphasized both his height and the superb proportions of his lean, muscular body, while the startlingly white shirt and stock accentuated his naturally warm color.

Catching the amused twinkle in his eyes, Elizabeth hastily pushed the door open wide. "Please do come in."

Ethan stamped the snow from his boots before he stepped over the threshold. As he accompanied her down the corridor, she was mindful of his gaze on her, and she felt her cheeks color ever so slightly. Ethan halted in the dining-room door to survey the bounty displayed on the dining table and the sideboard.

"How many guests did you invite, Elizabeth? You've cooked enough for at least fifty," he exclaimed.

"That's the way Christmas dinner is supposed to look," Elizabeth defended herself with a laugh.

Hearing voices in the yard, she glanced out the window to see the Earlys, Miss Ballard and Gray Bear all converging on the veranda. Elizabeth rushed down the corridor to open the door and welcome her guests. In the pleasant confusion that characterizes Christmas gatherings the world over, Elizabeth found herself besieged with smiles and good wishes along with each guest's contribution to the holiday table.

In his usual generous fashion, Martin had brought two smoked pheasants and a bottle of mulberry cordial, while Gray Bear contributed a large basket of polished red apples. When Miss Ballard presented Elizabeth with a covered dish, she took pains to explain that the sweets included not only chocolates that her sister had sent from Boston, but also sugared pecans and molasses drops that Rebecca and Ben had helped to prepare.

Soon the house was filled with the sound of laughter and voices talking all at once as everyone admired the beautifully decorated rooms and sipped the cordial that Elizabeth had insisted on opening. After Ben and Rebecca had finished their mugs of hot cider, Elizabeth let them light the candles and then summon their elders to dinner.

As they gathered around the dining table, all attention was focused on Ethan, who had gallantly volunteered to carve the turkey. Elizabeth took advantage of the distraction, letting her eyes slowly wander over the little assembly. To her right sat Miss Ballard, dressed in her best black silk with a lace fichu, smiling like a schoolgirl while she reminisced about the Christmases of her youth. Martin was seated next to Miss Ballard, and Elizabeth was touched by his kind attention to the spinster schoolmistress. Perhaps because of the strained circumstances surrounding their earliest meeting, Elizabeth had never before marked how attractive Martin was, especially when he smiled, as he was now doing freely.

Contributing to her father's amusement was Rebecca, who had chosen the chair beside him. In a pale blue frock with her dark hair bound in satin ribbons, the little girl leaned forward in her seat to grin shyly at Elizabeth. Ben sat across from his sister, his eyes fixed intently on the slices of turkey accumulating on the platter in front of him. Elizabeth's gaze came full circle to rest on Gray Bear, who occupied the seat to her left. Dressed in the traditional Cherokee tunic and sash, the elderly ferryman had never looked more dignified.

Elizabeth looked the length of the table at Ethan. He was occupied with serving the turkey, teasing Ben about saving room for dessert and cajoling Miss Ballard into taking two slices. When he caught Elizabeth's eye, however, he winked at her, so quickly she was certain that no one else noted the gesture. It was the sort of private communication that passed between the best of friends. *Between husband and wife.* This last thought struck Elizabeth with such impact she hastily glanced down, lest anyone discern a glimpse of the errant musings revealed on her face.

In the best tradition of Christmas dinner, everyone seemed inclined to linger at the table long after the final helping of dessert had been offered and reluctantly declined. Elizabeth's announcement that there was eggnog yet to be sampled earned a chorus of good-natured groans, but the lure of Dolly's nutmeg-scented concoction proved irresistible. Armed with cups of the rich drink, the party adjourned to the front room to enjoy the treat in front of the fire.

Elizabeth tarried in the dining room, ostensibly to cover the remaining dishes. As soon as she was alone, however, she removed two small packages, wrapped in blue sugarcone paper, from the sideboard cabinet. As she went to join her guests she found Ethan waiting for her in the hall. When he saw the two presents he only smiled, but his hand resting on her shoulder tightened for a moment, and he gave her a little hug before they entered the front room.

Elizabeth crossed the room and stooped over the two children cracking nuts on the hearth. "See what I found?" She held up the blue paper parcels, instantly earning the attention of both youngsters. She pretended to study the names inked on the paper. "Let's see. I believe this one is for Ben." She handed the little boy one of the presents. "And this says For Rebecca, so it must be yours." She placed the remaining gift in the girl's eager hands.

Elizabeth stepped back to watch while the children opened their gifts. In the week since she had invited the Earlys to share Christmas with her, she had racked her brain for suitable presents for Ben and Rebecca. An accomplished carver, Jephtha had been happy to fashion a team of wooden horses, although he had chafed at the payment Elizabeth had insisted on giving him in return. A thorough search of the bedroom wardrobes had yielded the abandoned doll that Elizabeth had discovered on her first inspection of the house. After refurbishing the doll's features with ink, she had plundered her sewing box and found enough scraps of muslin and lace to stitch a tiny frock.

"She's so beautiful, Mrs. Merriweather." Rebecca cradled the doll in her arms, gently smoothing its ruffled skirt with her small hand.

"I like my horses, too," Ben put in. He trotted one of them across the hearth to nudge his sister's foot.

Catching their father's glance, both children chimed, "Thank you, Mrs. Merriweather."

"Oh, you mustn't thank *me*. You see, Father Christmas left those gifts. I only delivered them for him," Elizabeth explained, winning giggles from both children. As she retreated to the settee, however, she felt a warm glow for which the blazing fire was only partially responsible.

As with every happy Christmas in Elizabeth's memory, the normal means of measuring time seemed suspended for the day, the hours' passage marked only by the need to light more candles or toss yet another log on the fire. As evening wore on, Elizabeth slipped away from the cozy circle to fetch more eggnog and a plate of sweets. When she returned, she found Ethan occupying the seat she had vacated. He smiled as she sank down beside him, shifting to stretch his arm along the settee behind her. Elizabeth sat back comfortably, grateful for the soft light and relaxed atmosphere that permitted such closeness with him.

After Ben had helped himself to a small chunk of fruitcake, he scooted onto the settee beside her. Elizabeth felt Ethan's hand pull her closer to him to make room for the child, and she willingly complied. With the innocent contentment that adults can only envy, Ben snuggled his head against her arm and closed his eyes. Elizabeth gently cradled the boy's smooth cheek and sighed, treasuring the sweet smell of a happy child drifting off to sleep. She glanced at Ethan and found him smiling down at both of them, his face blessed with an expression of rare peace. This is what it means to be happy, Elizabeth thought, to feel warm and secure and surrounded by love.

"I fear it's time we went home." Martin gently lifted his sleepy-eyed daughter off his lap and then rose. Rebecca leaned against her father, making a heroic effort to stay her drooping lids.

As Martin bent over the settee to scoop Ben into his arms, Elizabeth looked at the mantel clock. She was startled to discover the curved black hands poised just before midnight. "I had no idea it was so late."

"Nor I," Martin whispered, smiling at the small boy dreaming against his shoulder. "I can remember few days that have ever passed so quickly."

After graciously accepting another round of compliments from her guests, Elizabeth accompanied them down the corridor. As she opened the door a piercing gust of wind swept the hall, causing the wall sconce candles to flicker. Shielding herself behind the door, Elizabeth watched Martin, Rebecca and Miss Ballard cross the snow-blanketed yard. When they reached the stable they threw up their hands and waved.

"Merry Christmas, Mrs. Merriweather!" Rebecca's little voice carried on the brittle night air.

"Merry Christmas to you all!" Elizabeth called. "And to you, too," she added to Gray Bear.

The aging ferryman inclined his head in a gesture that could only be described as courtly, a twinkle shining in his ageless dark eyes. "Good night, Elizabeth. You have given us all a day we will never forget."

As Gray Bear started for the stable, Elizabeth felt Ethan's hand at her waist. When the Earlys' gig appeared in the stable yard, they walked onto the veranda. They watched the black trap roll swiftly down the road, followed by Gray Bear on his stout chestnut mare. The hoofbeats gradually faded into the night until only the pristine winter stillness remained.

"You're going to get cold out here." Ethan slid his arm up her back to pull her into his protective embrace.

Elizabeth leaned against him, savoring the feel of his solid, warm body. "I don't care. It's such a beautiful night."

"I wish it could go on forever," Ethan said in a soft voice, his eyes fixed on the glistening white landscape. "I wish..." He hesitated, and Elizabeth could feel a slight tremor catch in his chest. "I wish things could always be like this."

"So do I." Elizabeth stared at the sparkling white carpet covering the yard, not daring to face him.

"I suppose I ought to be going, too," Ethan said reluctantly.

As he surrendered his hold on her, Elizabeth fought the urge to reach for his hand and draw him back. She swallowed to loosen the tightness binding her throat. "Good night, then, Ethan."

Elizabeth watched him adjust his collar against the wind, half-turning away from her. He hesitated, then spun so abruptly she almost started. Without a word Ethan took her face in both his hands and lifted it. For a moment Elizabeth could only gaze into the deep, wine-dark eyes that held her as fast as the warm palms molded against her cheeks. As he lowered his mouth to hers, she closed her eyes, surrendering to the delicious sensation of his lips lightly teasing her own. Ethan wove his head to one side, then the other, letting the pressure of his mouth build with tantalizing slowness. Driven by the emotion swelling inside her, Elizabeth's hands slid up his arms to his shoulders and drew him to her while her lips parted to welcome his kiss.

Ethan rested his forehead against hers. The sound of his accelerated breathing mingled with her own against the cold night air. Still holding her face in his hands, he straightened himself to look down at her, his eyes full of wonder as if he were seeing her for the first time. "Can you have any idea how long I've wanted to kiss you?" he murmured.

Elizabeth's hands tightened around his arms, struggling to convey the powerful feelings yearning for expression. "Oh, Ethan... I—"

Shaking his head, he touched her lips with two fingers to gently silence her. For a very long moment he only gazed at her, an expression of exquisite tenderness working on his face. Then he leaned to graze her forehead with his lips.

She felt his arms slip from her grasp as he stepped back. Then he took her hands in both of his and clasped them tightly. "Good night, Elizabeth." His voice sounded husky against the cold night air. Releasing her hands, he turned and then dashed across the moonlit yard.

"Good night, Ethan," Elizabeth whispered just before he disappeared into the dark stable.

A snowstorm was brewing in the mountains. Deerkiller had spent too many winters in the Western Territories to ignore the frigid wind that whipped at his bones. He leaned forward in the saddle, trying to stifle the violent cough tearing at his chest like a raging animal caged inside him. Gripping the horse's withers, he steadied himself until the spasm had subsided. In his youth he had weathered many such a night on horseback, braving cold that stiffened his buckskins and froze the breath in his pony's nostrils. That was before the sickness had begun to gnaw away at his lungs. The hardships that had once affirmed his capacity to endure harsh conditions could now easily kill him. Deerkiller was not ready to die, not yet.

Goading his horse into a stiff-legged trot, he followed the road cutting through the close forest. At the crossroads he headed south, his narrowed eyes fixed on a pinprick of light in the distance. When the public house loomed into sight, he halted his mount on the road, taking advantage of the darkness to survey the run-down log building. Four horses stood tethered at the hitching rail, rawboned bodies crowded together against the sharp wind. The sound of a drunken argument penetrated the greased paper covering the tavern windows.

Deerkiller dismounted and tied his horse at the end of the rail. His hand instinctively traveled to his bowie knife, relishing its lethal feel as he crossed the sagging porch. When he pushed open the door, he stood on the threshold for a moment to take stock of the tavern and its patrons. This public house, like so many other places he had seen since his return to the Cherokee Nation, had apparently fallen into a white man's hands, by fair means or foul. A burly man with hair the color and texture of dirty straw was presiding over the bar, while four other white men sat hunched around one of the tables.

The bartender looked up from a tankard he was swabbing with a rag to shout at him. "Come on in or git out, but either way shut the door!"

Deerkiller kicked the door closed behind him, winning sullen glances from the men drinking at the table, and walked to the bar.

The bartender performed only a quick study of his new customer, making note of the ragged scar that disfigured his face and little else. "What you drinkin' tonight?" The grizzle-faced man sounded gruff but not unfriendly, and Deerkiller could tell that, as was often the case, his red hair and hazel eyes had fooled the bartender into thinking he was white.

"Whiskey."

The bartender shook his head as he complied with Deerkiller's request. "It's cold enough out there to freeze the hide off a mule, ain't it?"

Deerkiller only nodded and dropped coins onto the counter. Collecting the bottle and the greasy glass, he carried them to a table beside the fireplace, not far from the one where the four men were seated. They were either too drunk or too engrossed in their conversation, however, to pay him any mind as he pulled out a chair and poured himself a drink.

"If I'd had a few good men beside me, I'd have learned that son of a bitch a lesson he'd not be like to forget. I'd have whipped his red hide clean off him!" The speaker's small eyes cut to each of his companions in turn in an obvious play for support. When none was forthcoming, he tossed back his drink and wiped his mouth on his sleeve. "'Course, don't look to me like none o' you's got the stomach for showin' a worthless savage his place."

"You callin' me a coward, Johnson?" The rat-faced man seated opposite him sprang from his chair, his hand closing over the knife sheathed at his waist.

Deerkiller smirked into his uplifted glass as Johnson squirmed in his seat, his bleary eyes fixed on the wicked-looking blade. "I'm sayin' that Indian's got it comin' to him, that's all," he amended grudgingly. The knife wielder sank back into his chair, but he waited a few tense seconds before returning his weapon to its sheath. "Anyone who'd help me, there'd be plenty in it for him," Johnson went on. "Woodard looked to have a good-sized herd of cattle and some horses that'd fetch a handsome price."

Deerkiller held the whiskey in his mouth, letting the fiery liquor sear his tongue, as he strained to follow the conversation that had taken an unexpectedly interesting turn.

"I'm up for takin' some stock if we can do it a-night and run 'em across the Alabama line 'fore this Indian's any the wiser," the man with the pointed chin volunteered. He glanced at his two companions, who nodded their general agreement.

"What about Woodard?" Johnson licked his lips, glazing them with a film of whiskey.

The rat-faced man reached for the bottle and refilled his glass. "He's goin' to find himself a sight poorer with his cows gone, I'd say." He regarded Johnson coldly. "If you want him killed, that's another thing. From what I hear, old General Wool's set on talkin' the redskins into leavin' peaceful-like, and he's not too patient with white folks who'd help his job along with a few bullets. Mind you, I'm no Indian lover, but I'm not willin' to land in a federal stockade for a land lot that ain't even mine."

"You can have every stinkin' cow Woodard's got!" Johnson insisted, his already florid face deepening to a violent flush.

Deerkiller pushed back his chair and stood. When he halted beside the foursome's table, the men looked up at him in surprise, but he ignored them all, save Johnson. "I'll help you kill Ethan Woodard."

Johnson blinked, then narrowed his bloodshot eyes, apparently not trusting his alcohol-dimmed senses. "Did I hear you right?"

"I'll help you kill Ethan Woodard," Deerkiller repeated in the same flat, emotionless tone. "And I don't want anything for it, not his cattle or his horses. Nothing." He looked into Johnson's wary eyes, taking pleasure in the glimmer of fear reflected in them. "All I want is to watch him die."

Chapter Twelve

Ethan kicked his feet free of the stirrups and swung out of the saddle before Inali had slid to a full halt. A sharp pain shot up his left leg, the price exacted for his impatient dismount, but he managed to clear the tavern steps with two strides. He shoved open the door, causing Elizabeth to look up with a start from the quilt she was mending by the fire.

"Is something wrong, Ethan?" Elizabeth put aside her needlework to follow him to the bar.

Ethan propped his rifle against the wall, then rounded the bar. He frowned as he rummaged beneath the counter. "Someone made off with over half of my herd last night. Martin, Noble and I are going after them."

Elizabeth warily eyed the box of percussion caps that Ethan had just placed on the counter. "Do you have any idea how many men there are?"

"Two, maybe three, to judge from the tracks in the pasture. One thing is certain. They headed south on the river road. They have a good start on us, but thirty head of cattle are going to slow them down. If we ride hard we should be able to overtake them." Ethan slipped the percussion caps into his jacket pocket, his mouth set in a grim line. Catching the stricken look in Elizabeth's eyes, he mustered a smile that he hoped looked confident and reassuring. "Don't worry, Elizabeth. I'm not looking for a fight. I just want my cattle back. Chances are, these thieves are going to scatter when they see they're outmatched. It's still early. With any luck we'll be back this evening."

"I hope you're right." Elizabeth did not sound at all convinced.

Ethan clasped her shoulders and stooped slightly to look down into her face. "Come, now. You aren't going to send me off with such a sad look, are you?"

"I can't help it, Ethan. I'm frightened." Elizabeth shook her head, gesturing in frustration toward the rifle. "These days we hear such awful stories about the dreadful things happening in this country, bands of ruthless men burning houses and slaughtering stock, people being dragged from their homes and flogged. When I think what could happen to you..." Her words trailed off and she pressed her lips together.

"I'm not going to do anything foolish, Elizabeth. I may be hardheaded, but I've sense enough to value my life and those of my friends over a few head of cattle." Ethan grasped her arms tightly. Then he reached with one hand to lift her chin. "Let me see that pretty smile before I go." When she glanced away, he added, "Please."

Elizabeth forced her lips into a shaky curve. "Just do promise me that you'll be careful." A quaver rippled through her voice.

"I've already said that I will. I've never lied to you, have I?"

Elizabeth shook her head. "No."

"And I'm not about to start now."

Ethan's finger stirred against her chin, lightly stroking the smooth skin. He took a step closer to her and halted. She looked so vulnerable, her large gray eyes full of unspoken care, that he longed to take her in his arms and hold her deep in his embrace until he felt the tension ease from her slender body. He would kiss first her brow until all the furrows had vanished. Then his lips would caress her eyelids to brush away the tears she could now scarcely hold back. As his imagination progressed to her soft lips, Ethan abruptly drew himself up short.

"I'll be back as soon as I can." He gave her arms a firm squeeze and released his hold. "Take good care of the tavern." When he forced a smile, he was surprised by how untrustworthy his mouth felt. He slung the rifle over his shoulder and headed for the door before his feelings could give him away.

Elizabeth followed Ethan onto the porch and watched him swing onto Inali's back, then pivot the horse toward the road. He cantered a short distance before reining the gelding. Elizabeth had walked to the hitching rail, her arms folded anxiously across her chest. When she saw him check Inali she gave a valiant little wave. The spirited horse pranced from side to side, but Ethan held the lines tight long enough to fix that parting image of her in his mind. Then he let the gelding have his head and gallop the scant two miles to Martin's place.

As they had planned, Ethan found Martin and Noble waiting for him, mounted, armed and ready to ride. They set off without further delay, maintaining a hard pace for most of the morning in an effort to overtake the cattle thieves. As the miles passed, however, Ethan's thoughts began to stray to Elizabeth.

After yielding to his emotions on Christmas night, he had relived their kiss in his mind often enough for the memory to become a private ritual, one that both fueled his desire for her and taunted him with the cruel realities separating them. Although Ethan had governed his impulses with a martinet's severity in the three weeks since Christmas, he had only to see Elizabeth to be reminded of how undiminished his passion remained. Only this morning he had been within a heartbeat of kissing her again.

What harm could come of a kiss? After all, he had kissed a number of women in his life, with some had given and taken even more intimate pleasure. Frowning, Ethan angrily crushed the insidious thoughts, for he knew all too well that he wanted far more than merely to kiss Elizabeth. He wanted to make love to her, with his body, heart, soul, entire being. More sobering still, he realized that he would never be satisfied with a lighthearted dalliance. Once he had loved her, he would want her with him always.

Yet what kind of life could he offer Elizabeth? A hard-scrabble existence in an unknown wilderness, without benefit of even modest comforts? The uncertainty of facing yet another host of hostile white settlers and Indian tribes for whom the Cherokees were only unwelcome interlopers?

And even if, by some miracle, he managed to remain on the land that his family had occupied for generations, could he honestly promise Elizabeth any real security? As she had pointed out that morning, violence was now rife in the country as lawless gangs of ruffians attempted to hound the Cherokees from their homes. Only last week the stage-coach driver had told him of the atrocities inflicted on a family living near Spring Place. While the flames had reduced their home and fields to ashes, the couple had been stripped and beaten in front of their children. The woman had been violated. As a result of the abuse—or so the stage driver believed—she had lost the baby she had been carrying. Ethan knew he could never forgive himself if Elizabeth were to suffer such an outrage simply because she was his wife.

Anger and despair welled inside him, flooding his mouth with a taste as bitter as gall. Digging his heels into Inali's flanks, he goaded him into a gallop that churned the earth, leaving the echo of furious hoofbeats in their wake.

Elizabeth flinched at the sharp crack of gunfire in the distance, almost dropping the basket she was carrying.

Dolly placed a reassuring hand on her wrist. "There now, ma'am. It's only someone hunting in the woods over yonder." Linking her arm through Elizabeth's, she led the way up the steps to the veranda of Ethan's house. "I know you're worried about Mr. Woodard, but chances are, he's going to bring those cows of his back without firing a shot. And when he gets home, he'll be mighty pleased to find the nice chicken pie and biscuits we brought him."

Elizabeth only nodded and unlatched the front door to admit them to the house. Since Ethan's departure early that morning, she had silently repeated to herself the same assurances that Dolly had just offered her, with little effect. The hours had dragged, and with the approach of evening Elizabeth had alternately rejoiced that Ethan would soon return home and feared that he would not.

Her anxiety accompanied her after she had left the tavern for the day. Unable to contain her restlessness, she had decided to prepare supper for Ethan and deliver it to his home. With Maum Betsy ailing, Ethan had taken most of his meals in the tavern of late, and he would surely appreciate a decent dinner after a long day's ride. Then, too, Elizabeth preferred any action, however feeble, to sitting in her parlor and watching the creeping progress of the mantel clock's hands.

While Dolly went to the front room to bank the fire for the night, Elizabeth carried the basket to the dining room and placed it in the middle of the table, where Ethan would be sure to see it. She parted the curtain to glance across the yard. Through the winter evening gloom she could make out Jephtha's slender silhouette as he walked to the stable to check Ethan's horses. She let the curtain fall back into place and drew a deep breath. It was early yet, and depending on how rapidly the thieves had been able to drive their booty, tracking them could have taken longer than Ethan had anticipated.

A muffled cry from behind the house abruptly interrupted Elizabeth's thoughts. She wheeled away from the window and ran into the corridor. When she opened the back door she discovered a bucket of ash overturned on the path. Elizabeth dashed into the yard, then froze, arrested by the sight of her housekeeper grappling with Cephas Johnson.

"Let go of her!" Elizabeth shouted.

Johnson ignored her demand, only tightening the heavy arm he had clamped around Dolly's waist while his other hand yanked her head back by the hair. Undaunted by his efforts to subdue her, Dolly kicked and flailed at her captor. When one of her small fists found its mark on Johnson's unshaven jaw, he released his hold on her hair to land a vicious blow to her head.

Now frantic, Elizabeth tore back into the house in search of a weapon. Ethan had taken his rifle with him, but the military sword still hung over the bookcase. In desperation, Elizabeth yanked the sword from the wall and rushed back to the yard. Grasping the hilt with both hands, she lifted the sword, still encased in its scabbard, and swung with all her strength. When the heavy blade connected with Johnson's back, he let out an oath and lurched forward onto the ground. The blow had only stunned him, but it gave Dolly a chance to scramble from beneath his prostrate figure. Before he could weave to his feet, Elizabeth wrestled the sword from its scabbard.

"Stay where you are!" she ordered.

With his unkempt hair and beard, Johnson resembled a shaggy beast as he lowered his head in a belligerent stance. "You goddamn bitch, I'll teach you—"

"Another step and I'll take your head off! I swear I will!" Elizabeth brandished the heavy sword as best she could and succeeded in holding Johnson at bay.

"Jephtha, help us!" Dolly cupped her hands around her mouth to shout across the yard.

Elizabeth cut a darting glance toward the stable and swallowed hard, trying to hold on to her nerve. *Hurry, Jephtha! Oh, do please hurry!* she silently prayed, her whole body rigid with fear and anger. She almost sagged in relief when she spotted Jephtha's wiry figure running across the yard toward them.

Without any warning a shot pierced the cold evening air. Elizabeth watched in mute horror as Jephtha staggered and then sprawled facedown onto the ground.

"Jephtha!" Dolly's voice rose in an agonized scream. She ran to her husband's side and sank to her knees. "It's me, honey! Do you hear me? Say something, Jephtha, anything! Oh, please!" In her anguish, Dolly wove from side to side as she pleaded and wept over him. When she began to smooth his face, Jephtha moaned. He still clung to life, however tenuously.

Elizabeth's eyes darted from the horrific scene to Cephas Johnson. An ugly smile began to spread across his face, warning her to tighten her grip on the sword. Elizabeth stiffened when she felt something hard and cold jab her between her shoulder blades.

"Put down the sword." The voice was calm and dispassionate—and all the more frightening for it.

Elizabeth let the hilt slide from her damp palms and winced as the honed blade rattled against the brick path.

"Now I'm gonna show you!" Cephas Johnson reached for his rifle lying on the ground and started for her, his small eyes glistening with malice.

"No, Johnson," the flat voice ordered in the same empty tone.

Cephas Johnson scowled his displeasure as he retreated, but Elizabeth noted a glimmer of fear in his pale eyes.

"Turn around slow and walk back to the house." The man nudged Elizabeth's back with the gun.

Her limbs numb with fright, Elizabeth started to turn, then gasped. She stood stock-still, too startled to do anything but stare into the expressionless, scarred face. Brief as her encounter with the man hiding in the woods had been, his ruined visage and the rough red hair surrounding it had left a lasting impression in her mind. She had no doubt that he and the man now holding a gun on her were one and the same.

"I need to see to my manservant," Elizabeth protested.

The stone-colored eyes fixed on her were so devoid of any spark of human kindness that, for a moment, Elizabeth feared he might kill all three of them and be done with it. She realized that she had been holding her breath when he jerked his head toward the spot where Jephtha lay with Dolly kneeling over him. "Help her get him into the house," he said.

Elizabeth hastened to Dolly's side. Together they managed to lift Jephtha to his feet. Draping his arms over their shoulders, they half carried, half dragged him into the house. The man with the gun followed them down the corridor, with Cephas Johnson trailing behind him like a cur vying for a scrap.

"Put him in there." The gunman gestured toward the front room with the barrel of his rifle.

Elizabeth and Dolly eased Jephtha onto the floor beside the desk and tried to make him as comfortable as possible with the meager means at their disposal. They were forced to inspect his wound without benefit of a candle, but mercifully the bullet appeared to have passed through his side without lodging. The gaping tear was still bleeding, however, copiously enough to alarm both of them. Dolly ripped a length from her petticoat and finally managed to stanch the flow with the makeshift bandage. While they ministered to Jephtha, Elizabeth strained to overhear the men talking at the other end of the room.

"She's got it comin' to her, too. She's his woman, ain't she?" Cephas Johnson was grumbling.

The scar-faced man pulled a chair up to the window and seated himself. "You will have your time with her," he assured Johnson, not shifting his eyes from the window. "Later, when Woodard can watch."

Johnson began to laugh, a gurgling, obscene titter. He broke off, however, when the scar-faced man gave him an icy look. Slinking back to the hearth, Johnson dropped onto the settle and stretched his feet in front of the still-warm grate.

"They mean to kill Mr. Woodard?" Dolly rasped under her breath.

"I fear. But we'll find a way to warn him," Elizabeth whispered. She cut a nervous glance over her shoulder. When the gunman looked their way she went on in a less hushed tone. "There now, Jephtha, you're going to be fine." Her stomach lurched when the man rose and walked toward them.

"Get up." He jabbed her back with the rifle.

Elizabeth slowly pushed to her feet. Obeying the gun barrel's prodding, she walked to the other side of the fireplace. As she sank onto the floor, she avoided Cephas Johnson's leering gaze. Drawing her knees up beneath her skirt, she folded her arms across her chest and leaned back against the wall. She closed her eyes and tried to think calmly, but the steady tick of the mantel clock only reminded her of each passing minute that brought Ethan closer to the evil men lying in wait for him.

As the last embers beneath the grate faded, a thick darkness filled the room, throwing into relief the few random sounds that intruded on the stillness. From across the room Elizabeth could hear Jephtha's labored breathing and occasionally the indistinct murmur of Dolly's voice as she tried

to comfort him. She was aware of Cephas Johnson shifting
and turning on the settle, whether from drowsiness or im-
patience, she could only guess. At one point, Blue returned
from his hunting excursion to scratch and whine briefly at
the back door. Twice a convulsive cough seized the gunman, doubling his shadowy form over in the chair.

Not long after the clock struck eleven, Elizabeth stiffened, her senses attuned to the vague cadence of hoofbeats
on the road. Fear surged through her as she watched the
gunman shove back his chair and then hover to one side of
the window.

"It's him, ain't it?" Cephas Johnson jumped to his feet
and stumbled over the iron bootjack resting on the hearth.
With an angry curse he kicked the offending jack across the
room.

Elizabeth gasped as the heavy iron struck her ankle, but
she recovered herself quickly enough to grab the bootjack
and thrust it beneath her skirt.

"Quiet!" the gunman ordered. Keeping his eyes on the
yard, he backed away from the window. "Stay here and
watch them." He gestured toward Dolly and Jephtha with
the rifle.

"You gonna kill him all by yourself?" Cephas Johnson
sounded disappointed, like a churlish youngster excluded
from a game.

The red-haired gunman shook his head. "You will have
your chance." Turning toward Elizabeth, he motioned with
his rifle. "You come with me."

Elizabeth's legs felt so unsteady she feared that they
would give way beneath her as she rose to her feet. The
gunman seized her arm and roughly shoved her toward the
door. She stumbled across the corridor into the dining
room. As the gunman approached her, she instinctively
cringed and backed away from him until the dining table
forced her to halt. He stopped a few feet short of her, close
enough to press the end of the rifle barrel against her throat.
He lifted the gun, forcing her chin up.

"One move, one word from you, and I vow that both
Woodard and you will beg me to kill you before I am finished with you. Do you understand?"

"Yes."

Elizabeth's eyes followed the rifle barrel as the scar-faced man slowly pulled it away from her chin. Clutching the edge of the table, she watched him walk to the window and station himself behind the curtain's protective cover. She could easily discern the steady clip-clop of hooves now, a sign that Ethan had slowed Inali to a trot and turned into the yard.

Gauging each breath that she drew, Elizabeth inched along the table. Fortunately the gunman was too intent on monitoring Ethan's movements to allow his gaze to stray for even a moment. Her whole body rigid with tension, Elizabeth hesitated at the end of the table. She could see the yard from the window, and in the bright moonlight clearly distinguish Inali drinking from the trough. She almost winced when she glimpsed Ethan's dark head over the horse's back. Any moment now he would step from behind the horse, directly into the gunman's firing line.

Elizabeth slid her hand into her pocket. She grasped the bootjack she had secreted there, getting the feel of it in her hand before slowly drawing it out of her pocket. Holding the jack poised at her side, she took a deep breath and then hurled it at the window. The glass shattered, spraying the veranda with shards.

The gunman was startled and hesitated for only a split second, but it was enough time for Elizabeth to throw herself to the floor and crawl beneath the table. A shot exploded from his gun to splinter the floor not far from where she had stood. Then the gunman pivoted to fire through the broken window. Elizabeth almost cried out in relief when she heard a rifle return fire from the yard, but she kept working her way the length of the table until she was within a few feet of the door. Springing from beneath the table, she lunged into the corridor to come face-to-face with Cephas Johnson.

"Where you think you're goin', gal?" Johnson seized her wrist and twisted it.

"Let go of me!" Elizabeth aimed a kick at Johnson's shin, winning an animal-like yelp from him. Seeing him draw back his hand, she tried in vain to dodge his blow. The hard slap sent her reeling onto her back against the staircase and knocked the breath out of her. Unable to move, she steeled herself for another onslaught from Johnson, but his attention was now focused on the dining room door. After a moment's fearful hesitation, he glanced wildly from one end of the hall to the other, then bolted toward the rear of the house.

Clutching her throbbing midriff, Elizabeth managed to slip into the niche beneath the stairs just before the scar-faced man emerged into the hall. Pressing herself against the wall, she watched through a crack in the wainscoting as he lurched toward the back door. When he drew even with her hiding place she could see that he held his hand clamped to his breast in a futile attempt to stay the dark stain spreading over his buckskin shirt.

Elizabeth listened to the sound of his footsteps staggering down the hall until only the rasp of her own irregular breathing remained. Moving as stealthily as possible, she at last summoned the courage to venture into the dark corridor. Although she longed to call to Dolly, the danger that one or both of the men might still be lurking near the house kept her quiet. When she spotted the young housekeeper standing on the threshold of the front room, she pressed her finger to her lips and pointed toward the back door, signaling her intention to confirm the men's departure. Both women started when the front door suddenly opened to admit a wedge of moonlight into the hall.

Elizabeth spun around to discover Ethan's tall figure outlined in the doorway, his rifle propped against his shoulder. He lowered the gun slowly, as if he was unwilling to trust his eyes. "Elizabeth?"

Elizabeth nodded, at first unable to coerce words from her constricted throat. "You're...you're all right?" she finally managed to get out as she dashed down the hall to him.

"Yes." Ethan closed his arms around her to pull her into his embrace but hesitated, his dark eyes fixed on her reddened cheek. "My God, what happened to you?" he asked in a voice thick with anger. His hand trembled slightly as he reached to touch the throbbing bruise.

"Cephas Johnson slapped me," Elizabeth explained.

"So it was Johnson who tried to gun me down!" Ethan interrupted.

"He and that man I found hiding in the woods the day Inali escaped," Elizabeth told him. "They were hiding in the house when I stopped by this evening with Dolly and Jephtha to leave some food for you and check the horses. After you wounded the man with the scar, Johnson got scared, I think, and fled. I was hiding under the stairs and couldn't see too well, but the scarred fellow seemed to have been hurt pretty badly. He could barely walk as he headed for the back door." She reached to cover Ethan's hand, which still rested against her cheek, then cradled it in both of hers. "Jephtha was shot when he tried to help Dolly and me. I need to see about him."

His arm still encircling her shoulders, Ethan accompanied Elizabeth down the hall. Dolly met them in the doorway to the front room.

"Mr. Woodard, thank the Lord you're safe!" Dolly clasped Ethan's wrist for a moment, tears of relief unabashedly flowing down her cheeks.

"How is Jephtha?" Ethan craned to see over the housekeeper's head.

Her hands twisting anxiously, Dolly glanced at the still figure lying beside the desk. "The bleeding has stopped, and he seems to be resting pretty easy for now."

"Then it's probably best that we don't risk moving him just yet. You can both sleep here tonight," Ethan offered. He tightened his hold on Elizabeth's shoulder and then released it. "I'm going to stable Inali for the night and have a quick look around outside. I promise I'll be right back."

Before Elizabeth could protest, Ethan headed down the corridor to the back door. Resisting the renewed fear gripping her, Elizabeth helped Dolly carry a mattress downstairs and prepare a bed for Jephtha. To her relief, however, Ethan returned to the house as they were easing the injured man onto the pallet.

"I don't think we have anything to worry about tonight," Ethan said. "I followed the trail of blood from the back door to the place in the woods where they had apparently hidden their horses. As far as I can tell, both of them rode off in the direction of the federal road."

While Ethan went to board up the broken dining-room window, Elizabeth made certain that Dolly would be comfortable for the night and then withdrew into the hall. She found Ethan bolting the front door.

"Did you get your cattle back?" Elizabeth asked softly, clutching both elbows.

"Eight of them," Ethan replied as he settled the heavy bar into place. "We ran into a contingent of federal troops south of the Coosa River fork, and they wouldn't let us go any farther. 'In the interest of preventing strife between the Cherokees and the whites that would harass them,' so the commanding officer informed me," he added sarcastically. "We rounded up the few animals that had strayed from the herd into the woods and then headed back here."

"At least none of you was hurt." Elizabeth leaned her back against the wall, suddenly overwhelmed by a marrow-deep fatigue. When she reached to press her aching temple, her hand threatened to shake, and she quickly balled it into a fist.

Without a word Ethan took her tightly knotted hand and drew her to him. Gently lowering her face to his chest, he smoothed her hair. "There, it's all over now. I don't care about the damned cattle or anything else. All that matters to me is that you're safe." She felt him rest his cheek against the top of her head for a moment. Then his arm slipped around her shoulders to turn her toward the stairs. "Come, you need to get some rest. You can sleep in what used to be my sister's room."

Elizabeth let Ethan guide her up the stairs and into the bedroom at the far end of the hall. He led her to the four-poster and waited until she had sunk onto the edge of the bed. After he had lighted the candle on the nightstand he adjusted the pillows. "Just lie back and close your eyes." When Elizabeth had complied, he started for the door. "I'll get some fresh water. A cold cloth will make that bruise feel better."

Ethan returned a few minutes later carrying a white iron-stone ewer. Elizabeth shifted her head on the pillow to watch while he filled the basin and dampened a towel. Easing onto the side of the bed, he gently brushed the loose strands of hair off her face. When he reached to place the folded cloth on her swollen cheek, however, his hand faltered. At the sight of the purplish blotch that discolored her face, a tremor passed through his clenched jaw. Ethan turned his face away in an effort to master the rage contorting it.

"When I think that bastard dared to lay a hand on you—" Ethan looked down.

"It isn't as bad as it looks, Ethan," Elizabeth insisted, sliding her hand across the quilted coverlet to clasp his.

Ethan shook his head, still staring at the coverlet. "It could have been far worse. You don't know Deerkiller the way I do."

"Deerkiller?"

Ethan turned to look at her, his solemn dark eyes full of anguish. "That is the name of the man with the scar. I put that scar on his face, Elizabeth, almost fifteen years ago." He glanced across the room as if the specter of the memory were lurking among the shifting shadows, taunting him with its grim reminder. "I told you that my father saved Colonel Kilpatrick's life at Horseshoe Bend. The Creek warrior he killed in doing so was Deerkiller's father. Deerkiller swore a blood oath of revenge against my family over his father's body.

"One night he surprised my father outside the tavern, attacked him from behind like a coward and struck him over the head. He would have killed him if I hadn't been working in the stable and heard the dogs bark. When I ran into the yard all I could see was my father lying facedown on the ground with someone standing over him. The only thing that's still clear in my mind is how terrified I was that he might be dead. I remember lunging for Deerkiller and having blood all over me and then seeing him run away.

"For a long time I waited for him to return. But the years passed, my father died in peace and I lulled myself into thinking I would never see Deerkiller again. The day you followed Inali into the woods, I knew I had been wrong, but I didn't want to believe he had come back." Ethan's voice dropped, and a shadow seemed to pass over his face, throwing a somber cast over his handsome features. "I don't know how he and Cephas Johnson came to join forces, but I would never have forgiven myself if either of them had hurt you badly, had—"

Elizabeth tightened her grasp on Ethan's hand. "You mustn't blame yourself for Deerkiller's or Cephas Johnson's actions."

"I should have killed them both when I had the chance!" Ethan said bitterly.

"Don't say that, Ethan!" Elizabeth rose on her elbow to face him. "If you had shot Johnson that day when he first came to your house, the soldiers would have arrested you, and you would very likely have had to pay with your own life. I don't think..." She hesitated, swallowing to control the wrenching emotions her words had evoked. "I don't think I could have gone on living if that had happened."

Ethan looked into her eyes, holding her with his dark gaze as he reached to touch her face. His finger slowly traced the single tear trickling down her face. Then he bent to kiss her, letting his mouth follow the damp trail still glistening on her cheek. "I don't want to leave you tonight, Elizabeth," he whispered, his lips caressing the curve of her jaw.

Elizabeth drew back slightly. Taking his face in her hands, she savored the feel of the warm skin beneath her palms. "I don't want you to leave me."

She was startled by how steady her voice sounded, free of any hesitancy or doubt. As she looked into Ethan's tender eyes, all the strictures that uncertainty, convention and her own innate shyness had imposed on her emotions fell away, leaving only one guiding truth—that she loved him with all her heart.

Ethan turned his face to kiss first her palm, then her wrist, and caressed her face. Elizabeth let her own hand's movement mirror his, first skimming the oblique slant of his cheekbone, next stroking the firm outline of his jaw, then grazing the sensuous curve of his lips. When he kissed the tips of her fingers, she responded in kind.

As Ethan leaned forward to cover her mouth, Elizabeth closed her eyes, abandoning herself to the sweet pleasure of his kiss. While his tongue and lips performed their magic, his hand traveled down her back and began to unfasten the row of tiny buttons. A draft of cool air teased her skin as her bodice fell open. Ethan's hands glided down her arms, peeling away the sleeves to bare her arms.

His mouth traveled from her lips to her chin and down her throat. Elizabeth felt his hands graze her breasts through the chemise's thin muslin, and she drew in her breath. When she reached to encircle his neck, he caught her hand and gently guided it down the front of his shirt, pausing to allow her to unfasten each button.

Now governed by her own impulses, Elizabeth opened his shirt and began to explore the exquisite contours of his bare chest. As her hand drifted over the firm pectoral muscles and then to his back, she felt a shiver of excitement ripple beneath the heated skin. With deliberate slowness, Elizabeth eased her hands inside his sleeves to knead the hardened muscles of his shoulders and arms. The rise and fall of his chest accelerated as she slid the shirt away from his shoulders and down to his waist.

Ethan curved his arm around her back and pulled her closer to him until less than an inch separated his bare chest from her breasts. He slipped his fingers beneath the straps of her chemise to ease them from her shoulders. Elizabeth felt the soft fabric float over her taut breasts as the chemise fell to her waist. She moaned softly as Ethan pressed his body to hers, teasing the straining points of her nipples with the solid muscles of his chest.

He nuzzled the cleft of her jaw, his breath fanning the fine strands of hair curling over her ear. "I've never wanted anything as much as I want to make love to you."

Elizabeth locked her arms around his neck to hold him close against her, responding with her whole body to his desire. His hands cradling her shoulders, Ethan lowered her onto the bed. When he pulled back to look down at her, his dark eyes glowed with passion and wonder.

"Everything about you is so beautiful, Elizabeth."

Ethan loosened the pins binding her hair and then carefully uncoiled the thick tresses. He let the waves sift through his fingers to fall over her bare shoulders and breasts. His hand slid beneath her back once more, lifting her slightly so he could slip her gown and petticoat down her hips. Ethan tossed her dress and linen onto the floor, then rose for a moment to strip off his remaining clothing. A warm surge of desire coursed through Elizabeth as her eyes drifted over his perfect masculine form delineated in the flickering candlelight.

When Ethan stretched himself alongside her on the bed, she murmured with pleasure at the feel of his skin against hers. Shifting his body even closer to her, he kissed the tip of her chin, then her throat. His mouth worked its way to the smooth plane below her collarbone. With maddening leisure, Ethan deposited a trail of kisses along each of her arms, from the shoulder to the wrist and then back again.

Elizabeth dug her fingers into his thick black hair as his lips caressed the soft mounds of her breasts. Only after his tongue had aroused the sensitive nipples to hard, throbbing points did he began to edge farther down her body. Elizabeth's breath quickened as Ethan kissed first her midriff, then her flat belly, then the soft curve of her thighs. When his hand slid between her legs to gently part them, she gasped at the sensual delight elicited by his touch. Her head rolled to one side, then to the other as his lips and tongue reached the apex of their exploration. An uncontrollable spasm of ecstasy seized her, and she cried out, unable to contain the sweet bliss that filled every part of her.

When Ethan's body covered hers, Elizabeth slid her hands down his back to clasp his lean waist and guide him to her core. Another crest of passion started to build inside her at the touch of his hard arousal, and her hips rose to welcome the fusion of their bodies. Borne by the sensuous rhythm of their union, Elizabeth felt a tingling wave break over her, its peak coinciding with the ecstatic shudder rippling the length of Ethan's body.

His breath still coming in ragged drafts, Ethan sank onto the bed beside her. Enfolding Elizabeth in his arms, he molded his body to hers and rested his cheek against her hair.

Elizabeth closed her eyes and snuggled her face against his shoulder. "It feels so good when you hold me," she murmured.

"Then I'll hold you all night." Ethan kissed the part of her hair, his hand lightly stroking her back. "I'll hold you as long as you want me to, Elizabeth," he added, his voice dropping to an even softer whisper.

Elizabeth looked up at him. In the uneven light of the guttering candle she could see her own tiny image, held a willing captive in the dark depths of his gaze. "Even if that was forever?" A great swell of emotion filled her throat, muting her words.

"Forever wouldn't be long enough." Ethan grazed her forehead with his lips as he reached to snuff the candle. Then his hand passed over her eyes to close them once more. Pressing her head against his shoulder, he tightened his embrace. "Every night when I lie down to sleep I want you in my arms. And when I wake up in the morning I want to open my eyes and find you there beside me. I want to love you for the rest of my life, Elizabeth. Just as I want you to love me. For as long as we both live."

Chapter Thirteen

Stretching beneath the quilt, Elizabeth smiled through the sleepy fog still damping her senses. In her dream, Ethan had been kissing her, and she was reluctant to surrender that blissful image too readily to the waking world. Only when she felt something brush her face, light as the touch of a butterfly's wing, did she open her eyes.

Ethan's lips drew into a smile against her cheek. Supporting himself with one hand, he reached to brush the loose tendrils of hair from her forehead. "I'm sorry I woke you, but you looked so pretty in your sleep I couldn't resist the temptation to kiss you."

Elizabeth pushed up against the pillows and looped her arms around his neck. He willingly obeyed the pressure of her hands as she drew him close enough for their mouths to join in a lingering kiss. Hands still locked at his nape, she gently smiled at him for a few moments. Equal to the sweet delight of sharing a kiss with Ethan was the pleasure she took in seeing him look as happy as he did right now, the lean lines of his face free of tension, his fine dark eyes unclouded by worry or pain.

"Good morning." Ethan bestowed a light kiss on the tip of her nose.

"Good morning." Elizabeth glanced the length of him, taking stock of the deep crimson shirt and buff breeches he wore. "Have you been up long?"

"Not as long as Dolly. It was still dark when I went downstairs, but she had already made coffee. Would you like some? I brought you a cup." When Elizabeth nodded,

Ethan gently extricated himself from her embrace and twisted to retrieve the cup and saucer sitting on the nightstand.

"How is Jephtha?" Elizabeth asked before taking a sip of Dolly's strong, fragrant coffee.

"Dolly said he had a restless night, and I suspect he's still in quite a bit of pain, although he did his best to hide it when I stopped in to see him. He's lucky the bullet cut clean through him, but he's still going to need some time to recover." Ethan's expression darkened as he pushed up from the bed. "I'm going to do everything I can to see that Deerkiller and Johnson pay for what they've done."

Elizabeth replaced the coffee cup on the nightstand, then swung her legs over the side of the bed. "I know the injustice of it all makes you angry, Ethan, but please, I beg you not to do anything rash. Putting yourself in danger won't make Jephtha well, nor will it compensate for those awful men threatening Dolly and me."

Ethan sank onto the bed beside her and encircled her shoulders with his arm. "I have to do something, Elizabeth, or we'll never live without the fear of their coming back someday." He gave her shoulders a comforting squeeze. "While I was feeding the horses this morning I thought about what I should do. Even if Martin and I could afford to leave our farms untended while we searched for Deerkiller and Johnson, we would run the risk of having the troops disarm us or, even worse, of returning to find our homes plundered. Our nation once had a militia to enforce the law, but it was forced to disband when the Council was dissolved. Now the federal troops are supposed to keep the peace, and whatever his faults may be, General Wool has tried to make good on that claim. I'm going to ride to the garrison near Dahlonega and report the incident. I believe that it's our best chance that Deerkiller and Johnson will be brought to justice."

"You're right, Ethan." Elizabeth clasped his hand, looking down at the long, tanned fingers laced through her much smaller ones.

Ethan bent to kiss her cheek. He gave her a prolonged hug, then stood. "Why don't you get dressed, and then we

can have something to eat before I take you all home. I want
to leave for Dahlonega as early as possible."

Elizabeth reached for her linen and frock that he had laid
on the foot of the bed. While he went downstairs to hitch the
wagon, she quickly washed and dressed. She was pinning up
her hair when Dolly knocked softly at the door to summon
her to breakfast.

After serving Ethan and Elizabeth bacon and corn cakes,
the young housekeeper retreated to the front room to coax
her ailing husband to eat. When Elizabeth joined her a short
time later she was pleased to find Jephtha propped on pillows, his face drawn but still capable of a resolute smile.

Dolly and Elizabeth prepared a pallet of folded quilts in
the back of the wagon and then helped Ethan carry Jephtha out of the house. As they set out for Elizabeth's house,
Ethan held the horses at a slow walk, easing the wagon over
the ruts channeling the road. He glanced over his shoulder
frequently to banter with the injured man in an obvious effort to distract him from the discomforts of the ride. When
they reached the house he halted the wagon as close to the
porch as possible. At Elizabeth's insistence they carried Jephtha upstairs to the corner bedroom where she had nursed
Ethan through his convalescence.

"Jephtha is going to need us both to look after him, and
it makes no sense for us to run back and forth between the
house and your cabin to do so," Elizabeth explained to
Dolly. "The room is large enough to accommodate the
trundle bed, so you can sleep here, too," she added, placing a gentle hand on the young woman's thin wrist.

Leaving Dolly to lay a fire in the chilly bedroom, Elizabeth went downstairs. Ethan met her in the corridor.

"I suppose you'll be riding to Dahlonega now?" Although Elizabeth could not dispute the sensible argument he
had presented earlier, a vague uneasiness continued to nag
her, undermining her matter-of-fact tone.

Ethan nodded. "But first I need to show you something."

Elizabeth gave him a puzzled look, but he only beckoned
her toward the door. Throwing her shawl over her shoulders, she followed Ethan into the yard. She watched as he

reached beneath the wagon seat and removed the rifle stowed there. Hefting the gun in his hands, Ethan turned to Elizabeth.

"Do you know how to shoot?"

Elizabeth shook her head, instinctively shrinking from the firearm.

"It's time you learned then." Ethan examined the firing mechanism of the gun and held it out to Elizabeth. "Don't worry. It isn't loaded." When she reluctantly took the rifle, he nodded encouragement. "Just relax and let yourself get the feel of it."

Elizabeth grimaced, still holding the gun at arm's length. "I'm sorry, Ethan," she apologized, biting her lip. "But Samuel lost his life in a hunting accident, and I've been frightened of guns ever since."

"That's nothing to be ashamed of, Elizabeth. Any sane person has a healthy respect for a dangerous weapon." Ethan rested his hand on her shoulder. "I would just feel better if I knew you had some means of protecting yourself when I'm not around." When she only continued to regard the rifle with undisguised aversion, he stroked her shoulder lightly. "Come, now. What if I told you I had decided to take the sword with me instead of the rifle when I rode out today? You would have a fit."

Elizabeth drew a deep breath. "Very well. Show me."

"First you need to turn a little to this side." Elizabeth took a shuffling step to comply, and Ethan walked behind her. "Hold the rifle in your left hand like so." Shadowing her small figure, he reached to slide her hand down the barrel. "Your other hand should be right here at the trigger. Good. Now bring the butt up to your shoulder. No, that's too high." Ethan closed his arms over hers to rearrange her awkward grip on the rifle. "Loosen up a bit. Remember, you're in charge, and the gun isn't going to do anything you don't want it to." He massaged her shoulders, gently jostling her. "That's better. Now bring your face down close to the stock. That's how you're going to sight, right along here." His finger skimmed the long bore. "Fire off a shot."

Elizabeth glanced at Ethan's face hovering only a few inches from hers. Then she pulled the trigger, wincing at the sharp snap.

"Do it again."

Following Ethan's direction, Elizabeth fired the rifle repeatedly.

"Would you like to try hitting a target?" Ethan asked when she paused between shots.

"I guess that's the whole point, isn't it?" Elizabeth replied.

Ethan chuckled. "I'll take that for a yes. Let's go around back so we won't startle the horses. I'll show you how to load and then you can practice your aim."

They followed the footpath leading to the spring house located at the rear of the kitchen. With the rifle braced against his knee, Ethan demonstrated the proper technique for loading and priming it, pausing several times to give Elizabeth a chance to repeat each procedure. She watched apprehensively as he selected a stout log from the kitchen woodpile and balanced it on the fence.

Brushing the bits of bark and dried moss from his hands, Ethan stepped away from the fence. "Let's see what you can do with the log. It's big, and it's not going anywhere. If you miss too wide, that old pin oak behind the fence will stop the lead."

Swallowing her distaste for the task at hand, Elizabeth forced herself to repeat the steps she had practiced earlier in the front yard. When the rifle discharged, she was unprepared both for the loud report and the recoil that jolted her backward. As she was regaining her balance, Ethan clapped her on the shoulder.

"Good for you!"

"You mean I hit it?" Elizabeth frowned in disbelief at the splintered gash torn in the log.

"You surely did. Load again, and have another shot."

Encouraged by her modest success, Elizabeth reloaded the rifle and fired once more. Although she realized that hitting such a substantial target required minimal marksmanship, she was pleased that the gun no longer felt so threatening and unpredictable in her hands. She managed a reserved smile when Ethan at last called an end to the lesson.

"Later on, you can practice hitting something smaller." When Elizabeth attempted to hand Ethan the gun, he shook his head. "I'm giving you that rifle to keep for now. I have another one at the tavern that I can take with me to Dahlonega." He glanced up at the bright morning sun cutting through the web of barren branches overhead. "I'd best be on my way if I'm to cover any ground before nightfall."

Cradling the rifle across her arm the way that Ethan had shown her, Elizabeth fell in step with him as they walked back to the front yard. When they halted beside the wagon, she propped the rifle against the hitching post.

"I should be back in a couple of days, depending on how long it takes me to find a receptive ear at the garrison. I'll tell Martin and Noble to keep an eye on your place, and you know you can always turn to Gray Bear if you need help." Ethan took her hands and chafed the backs of them lightly. "I'll come home to you just as soon as I can."

"I know you will." Elizabeth looked down at their joined hands, trying to sort through the cavalcade of thoughts crowding her mind. Only a few hours earlier they had made the most tender, passionate love she had ever experienced, and yet now circumstances demanded that she simply say goodbye to him and resume her daily routine. Then, too, Elizabeth dreaded Ethan's departure on a journey that would take him across the state line, into a caldron seething with violent animosity toward the Cherokees.

Elizabeth pulled her hands free of his grasp to put her arms around him and hug him with all her might. "Please keep yourself safe, Ethan. That is all I ask."

Ethan took her face in his hands and stooped to kiss her, slowly and deeply. Still cradling her jaw, he nestled his cheek against hers. "I promise you I won't do anything reckless, Elizabeth, not now," he vowed in a whisper husky with emotion. "I have too much to live for."

He stepped back and looked at her for a long, solemn moment. Then he turned and climbed onto the wagon seat. Through blurred, stinging eyes, Elizabeth watched Ethan set the horses into a trot and drive out of the yard.

* * *

"Damnation, Hezzie! How many times do I have to remind you not to disturb me at my work!" Josiah Merriweather flung the pen onto the desk, spattering the sheet of creamy vellum with blotches of black ink.

The servant cringed, instinctively turning her face out of range of her master's unpredictable and sometimes punitive right hand. "I'm sorry, sir, but it's nigh on eight o'clock, the time you'll usually be wanting your toddy." She proffered the small silver tray she carried, displaying the hot drink for his approval.

"Very well. Put it on the desk and be off with you." Josiah nodded curtly toward the door, not looking up from the ruined sheet of writing paper that he was crumpling into a ball. He scarcely noticed the maid as she curtsied, then scurried into the hall.

Although Josiah prided himself on brooking no slack with his slaves, the housemaid's ill-timed interruption had only fanned an irritability that had been vexing him since he had retired to his office after dinner that evening. Accustomed as he was to writing voluminous legal arguments, Josiah normally dispatched a personal letter with little time or exertion. Tonight, however, he had made at least a half-dozen false starts on his letter to his widowed sister-in-law, with nothing to show for his effort but a desk littered with dulled nibs and scraps of torn paper.

In truth, Josiah was uncertain exactly what sort of approach he should take with Elizabeth. While visiting her in the fall, he had threatened and railed with no discernible effect, and he suspected the same technique rendered on paper would yield equally dismal results. Much as the idea went against his natural inclinations, he had considered adopting a conciliatory stance, begging her forgiveness for his precipitate judgment, and offering, once more, to deal on her behalf with the Indian. Following such a strategy, however, ran the risk that she would accept his apology, decline his help and continue on the misguided path down which the miserable Indian was leading her.

Josiah drummed his fingers against the leather blotter, his eye traveling to the almanac calendar lying open on the desk.

He could, of course, say nothing more to Elizabeth and simply let events take their course. January was fast drawing to a close. Less than four months remained until the treaty would be enforced, and the recalcitrant Indians remaining in the country—Woodard among them—would be removed, once and for all. The ferry would become Elizabeth's by default, regardless of any ridiculous agreements she had made with the Indian. With Woodard no longer able to exert his insidious influence, Josiah imagined that Elizabeth would be far more receptive to his own suggestions.

Every time Josiah weighed the wisdom of doing nothing, however, he quickly reminded himself of how much mischief could be worked on a weak-willed and impressionable woman in four months' time. He shifted uneasily in his chair at the memory of Elizabeth's normally serene face grown livid with anger when she had leaped to the Indian's defense. He had never seen her as excited or irrational as she had appeared that evening. If he did not still reserve a modicum of respect for his sister-in-law's character, he might even be inclined to think that she had fallen in love with Woodard.

Josiah's fingers abruptly ceased their martial tap against the blotter. The very notion of his brother's widow submitting herself to a red savage filled him with revulsion, but his lawyer's instinct forced him to weigh every possibility, however repugnant. What if Elizabeth were, indeed, enamored of Woodard? What if she were guilty of the misconduct of which Josiah, in his agitation, had accused her? What if she were to marry the Indian?

This last thought struck Josiah with such sobering impact that he shoved himself violently away from the desk, nearly upsetting the toddy mug in the process. If the Indian were to seduce Elizabeth into marriage, all her property, including Samuel's land lot, would become his. Samuel's single bit of good fortune would be for naught, for after the Cherokee had been removed to the West, his land would fall into the hands of the first squatter greedy enough to grab it.

A fiery flush began to creep up Josiah's neck, heating the flesh trapped inside the high, stiff collar, as he recalled the

Indian's unseemly familiarity with Elizabeth. He had encountered redskins like Woodard before, those with enough white man's learning to make them arrogant and calculating. Josiah could see clearly now what Woodard had been scheming all along. Worse still, Elizabeth showed every indication of being susceptible to the Indian's nefarious plan. She would squander everything that his poor brother had worked to attain unless someone intervened.

Straightening his damp collar, Josiah sank back onto the desk chair. As he reached for a fresh nib and a clean piece of writing paper, a lucid calm settled over him, as it always did when he knew exactly what he must do. Dipping the pen into the inkwell, Josiah bent over the desk and began to write.

"Wait here." The heavyset sergeant gestured indifferently toward a crude wooden bench facing the garrison yard. He adjusted the hem of his tunic, hoisting the belt above his rounded belly, before swaggering through the open door.

Ethan pretended to watch the soldiers unloading a sutler's wagon on the far side of the yard, but he looked over his shoulder in time to see the stocky sergeant salute an officer bent over a low table.

"It's another Indian with a claim, sir," he heard the sergeant explain.

The officer took a while before answering. "Send him in, then," he said without looking up from the papers he was examining.

"Lieutenant Mayes'll see you now," the sergeant told Ethan as he brushed past him on his way to the yard.

Ethan stooped beneath the low doorframe and paused to give Lieutenant Mayes a chance to acknowledge his presence. When the officer only continued to frown over a map, Ethan stepped forward. "Lieutenant Mayes?"

The lines creasing the lieutenant's weather-beaten face deepened as he reluctantly straightened himself to face Ethan. "Can you write?"

Ethan blinked, caught off guard by the unexpected question. "Yes," he began, but Lieutenant Mayes cut him short.

"Good. List the property in question and its value." The officer pulled a sheet from one of the many stacks of paper and thrust it into Ethan's hands, along with a quill. "You can have a seat outside. When you're finished, leave the claim on the chair by the door, and I will see that it is forwarded to the proper authorities for compensation." He turned back to his map, apparently satisfied that he had done the job required of him.

Ethan leaned over the desk and placed the paper on the map, squarely in the line of Mayes's vision. "I didn't come to see you about a property claim, Lieutenant Mayes."

Hands still planted on the desk, Mayes cut his red-rimmed blue eyes up at Ethan. "Then I'm afraid I can't help you."

"You're here to enforce the treaty, aren't you? That includes preventing violence and harassment directed at the Cherokees," Ethan insisted.

"I'm aware of my duty," Mayes snapped. The hue of the sun-scalded skin rimming his collar deepened noticeably.

"Then hear me out. My name is Ethan Woodard. I own a ferry on the Oostanaula River along with other substantial improvements and stock. Last Monday two men broke into my home in my absence with the expressed intent of killing me on my return. While in my house, they threatened and struck a white woman, mistreated her maid and severely wounded her manservant. I know that one of them, Cephas Johnson, holds the lottery title to a portion of the land that I occupy." Ethan paused, waiting for Lieutenant Mayes to make some kind of response.

Mayes drew a deep breath that sounded more bored than exasperated. "You say this occurred on Monday?"

Ethan nodded. "Monday evening."

"That was almost three days ago." The lieutenant shook his head, his gaze drifting back to the map. "They could be in Georgia now or even Alabama. My jurisdiction extends only to lands presently designated as Indian Territory."

"You can't know where those men are unless you look for them. I want them apprehended, Lieutenant Mayes." Ethan caught his voice rising, and he hesitated, struggling to master his anger. "Are the federal troops not charged with the

protection of white settlers in the territory?" he went on in
a tightly controlled tone.

Mayes nodded in annoyance. "Of course. Everyone
knows that—"

"Then consider the woman who suffered a blow from the
hand of Cephas Johnson. Does her safety not merit your
concern?"

Lieutenant Mayes made no effort to conceal the contempt mirrored in his pale eyes as he sank onto the chair
behind the table. He reached for the paper and quill, however, apparently resigned to recording Ethan's complaint.
"Give me a full report of the incident."

Ethan forced himself to speak slowly, pausing frequently
to let the quill scratching across the page overtake his narrative. He took special care to give an accurate description
of Johnson and Deerkiller, as well as a thorough account of
the threats that they had both leveled at Elizabeth.

"What was the occasion for this white woman to be in
your house?" Mayes asked as he reached to dip the pen into
the inkwell.

"She and her servants had come to leave some food and
tend my horses while I was away."

Mayes glanced up at him abruptly, one wiry eyebrow
cocked at a skeptical angle.

"Elizabeth Merriweather is a neighbor." Ethan swallowed, before adding, "She is my friend."

"I see." As Mayes blotted the paper, his mouth drew to
one side in a malicious imitation of a smile.

Ethan clenched his hands at his sides, suppressing the urge
to grab the insolent man by the collar and shove him across
the room. When Mayes turned the document and presented it for his perusal, Ethan read it carefully. He was
signing his name below the officer's signature when the
thickset sergeant appeared in the door.

"Colonel Kilpatrick is preparing for inspection, sir," he
announced, snapping a salute.

"Thank you, sergeant." Mayes glanced past Ethan to note
his dismissal. He was busy strapping his sword to his waist
and only shrugged as Ethan flung the pen and paper on the
desk and dashed out of the office.

Ethan caught up with the sergeant in the yard. "Is that Colonel William Kilpatrick?"

"That's his name. What's it to you?" the truculent sergeant added, but Ethan had already rushed off in the direction of the sutler's wagon.

He edged through the labyrinth of kegs and crates surrounding the wagon, elbowing around the men trundling provisions into the single-story log building. He managed to come within a few feet of the entourage escorting a tall, impeccably turned-out officer past the store.

"Colonel Kilpatrick! May I have a word with you?"

The imposing-looking man turned, his wiry iron gray brows drawn together in puzzlement. Ethan tried to side-step the soldier blocking his path, but the fixed bayonet pulled him up short. Drawing back from the razor-sharp blade angled toward his throat, he managed to catch the tall officer's eye.

"I'm Ethan Woodard, sir. David Woodard was my father."

Colonel Kilpatrick's steel gray eyes narrowed, as if he could not quite accept the image they had conjured before him. Slowly the aging soldier's stern expression began to fade into one of amazement. "My God! For a moment I thought you *were* your father!" He cast an irritable glance at the soldier pointing his bayonet at Ethan. "Let this man pass, private!" he ordered in a tone that won instant compliance. As Ethan shouldered past the bayonet-wielding soldier, Colonel Kilpatrick waved aside the officers surrounding him. "Were it not for this man's father I would not be here today," he told them, clasping Ethan's shoulder with a firm hand. As he guided Ethan away from the crowd into the store, a smile cracked the severe cast of his face. "Ethan Woodard! By God, but you are the image of your father! But tell me. How is he?" he asked.

"He will have been dead nine years this fall," Ethan told him.

Colonel Kilpatrick shook his head sadly. "I'm sorry to hear that. I had always hoped to see my old friend again someday. There never lived a braver, truer man than your father, Ethan."

"He thought a great deal of you, too, Colonel Kilpatrick."

The colonel laughed under his breath, a brief, wistful chuckle. "So what brings you to the garrison today?"

Ethan quickly recounted the report that he had given Lieutenant Mayes. "I don't know how he met Cephas Johnson, but I'm convinced that Deerkiller will be back, with or without his henchman," he concluded.

Colonel Kilpatrick nodded his agreement. "I would advise you to take precautions to safeguard your family. You've a wife and children?"

"No, sir, not yet."

"I suppose that is just as well." Colonel Kilpatrick glanced across the store at the barrels of flour stacked in the corner, and Ethan had the distinct impression that he was avoiding his gaze.

Ethan shifted slightly, prompting Kilpatrick to look at him. "Will the federal troops make an effort to apprehend Johnson and Deerkiller?" When the colonel said nothing, Ethan felt his chest tighten, as if an invisible claw was trying to crush the breath out of him. "I need to know, Colonel Kilpatrick."

Kilpatrick slowly turned to face him. "Do you have any idea how many reports such as yours reach this garrison every week?" His hand shook slightly as he gestured toward the door. "How many miserable people pass through those gates, each with his story of a beating, a looting, a farm laid waste? I shudder when I think of the evil visited on your unfortunate people, Ethan. It will be a blessed day when the Cherokees remove far from these scoundrels who bedevil them!"

Ethan stared at the colonel in stunned silence. "A blessed day, you call it?" He swallowed to subdue the ragged catch in his voice. "Why should we be forced to abandon our land because others will not obey the law?"

Kilpatrick stiffened, obviously unaccustomed to having his word challenged. "You people talk of this land as if it were the last few acres in the country. There is plenty of land in the West, good land!"

"Tell that to the white men who would dispossess us, Colonel Kilpatrick."

The colonel's eyes darkened to the color of a honed saber as they met Ethan's uncompromising gaze. "I respected your father, Ethan, and because you are his son, I could not wish you ill. But hear me. The treaty will be enforced, regardless of what you or any other Indian thinks is right. The wise men among you will recognize that and act accordingly."

Without another word Colonel Kilpatrick turned his back on Ethan and strode out the door.

Gathering her shawl around her shoulders, Elizabeth walked to the edge of the tavern's porch and peered across the yard. She narrowed her eyes in an effort to distinguish the horseman approaching on the road. When she recognized David Birdsong cantering by on his sturdy white mare, she waved and then leaned one shoulder against the column, letting her head rest against the rough wood. She roused herself from her dejected stance at the sound of Gray Bear's even footsteps behind her.

"Do not worry, Elizabeth. Sekakee's farm is not far from here. Ethan and Martin will be back before nightfall with the cattle they have bought."

Elizabeth nodded, mustering a smile for the kindly ferryman. "You're right, Gray Bear. It's still quite early." She cut one final glance toward the road before forcing herself to turn to the tavern door. "Would you like some coffee, Gray Bear? We've had no trade today, and the better part of a pot is still warm."

"A cup of coffee would be nice." Gray Bear held the door open for Elizabeth, then followed her into the empty common room.

He sank onto his favorite chair near the window and resumed work on the harness he was repairing while Elizabeth collected cups and filled them from the pot simmering on the grate. After carrying her own cup back to the bar, she poured water into a bowl and began to wash and sort a batch of dried field peas. She tried to focus on her task, let the monotonous chore dull the tension plaguing her. Despite her resolve, however, her restless eyes wandered repeatedly to the window and the quiet yard beyond, watchful for any sign of Ethan's arrival. Given the present turmoil in the Cherokee Nation, she was never at ease when he ventured abroad.

When Ethan had ridden to the garrison two months earlier, Elizabeth had passed what seemed an interminable four days awaiting his return. With accounts of violence directed against the Cherokees now a staple of the gossip reaching the tavern, she had little difficulty imagining the evils that could befall Ethan, and she had wept with relief on the cold, rainy morning when he had at last come home.

Wrapped in his comforting embrace, Elizabeth had tried to convince herself that the nightmarish assault on their tranquillity had come to an end. In the weeks that followed, Ethan had canvassed the valley, inquiring at every stock stand and public house in hope of picking up a lead on Deerkiller or Cephas Johnson. No one recalled seeing either man, however, and he had abandoned his search to prepare for spring planting. With the arrival of an exceptionally clear and balmy March, and Jephtha continuing to make steady improvement, life regained a semblance of its previous normalcy.

Reminders of how fragile and illusory that calm had become, however, were never far removed. The passage of numerous and well-armed federal troops on the road was now commonplace, although their presence seemed to have little impact on the disorder rife in the country. Every time the stagecoach driver called at the tavern, he brought with him fresh accounts of Cherokee families terrorized and dispossessed by merciless white men. Even Noah Gilmer, whose lax principles usually allowed for considerable chicanery, expressed revulsion at the widespread brutality and pillage. To be sure, neighbors still returned from trips to the mill or a relative's wedding bearing rumors of some new treaty that Chief John Ross was negotiating, but in recent months such hearsay had taken on a note of wishful desperation.

Elizabeth's anger and frustration at the cruel treatment of the Cherokees was exceeded only by her personal concern for Ethan. Although he avoided burdening her with his problems, she knew him too well to mistake the sadness that haunted his dark eyes. He showed her so much tenderness and affection, Elizabeth longed to give of herself as generously, but Ethan guarded his private pain closely, she suspected, out of a desire to spare her worry.

Elizabeth halted at her work, overwhelmed for the moment by the memory of the one night they had spent in each other's arms. During four years of married life Samuel had often told her that she was a good wife and, less frequently, that he loved her. Never, however, had he made love to her with such ardor, such consuming passion as Ethan had. More precious still, Ethan had said that he wanted to love her for the rest of his life, wanted her to love him in like fashion. In these hard times, Elizabeth clung to the belief that those words, whispered softly in the dark, still held as much meaning for Ethan as they did for her.

Putting aside the bowl of peas to soak, Elizabeth walked to the chair that Gray Bear had vacated and scooted it next to the table. At the sound of hoofbeats on the road she leaned to glance out the window. Her heart sank as the drumming grew louder, for she realized that a party far larger than that of two men was approaching. She started when a burst of gunfire punctuated the throb of the horses' galloping hooves. Elizabeth rushed to the door just as the band of horsemen pelted into sight.

They were about fifteen strong, she guessed, and armed with rifles that a few fired at random into the air. Although the breakneck pace of their mounts permitted only a cursory assessment of the riders' appearance and manner, Elizabeth was struck by the slovenly character of their dress and the abundant curses interspersing their warlike whoops. Her relief when the uncouth men had ridden past was short-lived, for they wheeled at the bend in the road to set off in the direction of Martin Early's farm.

Elizabeth hesitated only a second before knotting her shawl across her chest and running to the stable. She had saddled Midnight and was leading him into the yard when she spotted Gray Bear jogging toward her. Noting the long rifle he carried at his side, Elizabeth guessed that he, too, had seen the band of dissolute-looking men while he was working on the ferry. She managed to clamber into the saddle and turn the horse toward the road before Gray Bear could stop her.

"Stay here and look after the ferry! I only want to see where they're going," Elizabeth called over her shoulder.

Gray Bear's protest was wasted on her as she prodded Midnight into a canter. She had no trouble following the party of horsemen, for their raucous shouts carried through the woods separating Martin's homestead from the public road. As she approached the clearing, her heartbeat quickened with fear. To her immense relief, however, the horsemen had apparently taken no interest in either the fine two-story house or the improvements surrounding it. Instead, they had turned onto the narrow trail winding through the orchard to the schoolhouse.

Through the branches of the budding fruit trees Elizabeth could see that the horsemen had surrounded the little clapboard building. One of the riders leaned in the saddle to shatter a window with the butt of his rifle, winning frightened cries from the children inside the school. Elizabeth reined her horse just as Abigail Ballard appeared in the yard, her diminutive stature underscored by the two burly men on either side of her. Elizabeth gasped when one of the men seized the tiny schoolmistress by the arm and roughly shoved her.

Anger now superseding her fear, Elizabeth jumped from the saddle and dashed across the yard. "Who are you, and what do you think you're doing?" she demanded.

A rawboned man with a coarse black beard edged his horse forward to block Elizabeth's attempt to reach Miss Ballard. "Captain Clements, Georgia Guard, *ma'am,*" He gave the tattered brim of his hat an insolent nick. "I've got orders to put this here lady under arrest."

"Under arrest?" Elizabeth could not believe she had heard correctly. "For what?"

"Teachin' a darkie to read." Beneath the sheltering hat brim, the man's yellowed eyes cut toward Miss Ballard. "She don't deny it. And even if she was to, we seen the boy sittin' right there in the middle of them Indians she was teachin' when we rode up.''

Elizabeth glanced past Clements at Miss Ballard. The teacher wore a stoic expression, paying as little attention to the men towering over her as if they were gnats that had inadvertently flown into her classroom. Elizabeth noticed, however, that her face had lost much of the meager color it normally possessed, and her small hands were clasped anxiously at her waist. A sickening knot twisted in Elizabeth's stomach at the sight of Miss Ballard's pupils clustered beside the schoolhouse, witnessing with terrified eyes the abuse of their beloved teacher.

Clements pivoted his horse, signaling an end to his exchange with Elizabeth. ''Git her on that pack horse!'' he ordered.

Elizabeth watched in horror as the two men flanking Miss Ballard grabbed the teacher's arms and hoisted her onto a horse as summarily as if she were a sack of potatoes. Unaccustomed to riding stride, the schoolmistress clung to the pommel when the horse shied to one side.

''You can't just take her away like this!'' Elizabeth circled Clements's restive horse, demanding his attention.

''I reckon I can if she broke the law.'' Clements's mouth drew into a spiteful smile. ''Lady or no, she's gonna stand trial in Milledgeville for what she done.''

He jabbed his horse with his spurs, and the animal lunged forward. A cloud of dust rose around Elizabeth as the Georgia Guard stormed out of the schoolyard, taking Abigail Ballard with them.

Chapter Fourteen

"They arrest a woman for teaching a child to read while the thieves and murderers who maraud our country go unpunished." Ethan's low voice choked with anger and contempt.

"The Georgia Guard is no better than a band of outlaws, Ethan. Damn them all to hell!" Martin broke off abruptly when he spotted Rebecca and Ben, dressed in their nightclothes, hovering outside the door in the hall.

Elizabeth rose and lightly touched Ethan's shoulder as she started for the door. "I'll look after the children."

Rebecca and Ben had retreated into the shadows, aware that they had been caught eavesdropping on their elders. Tonight, however, Elizabeth could detect no spark of mischief in their wide eyes, only a fear that cruelly mocked their innocence.

"Papa's very angry, isn't he?" Rebecca leaned to peer around Elizabeth's skirt into the front room.

"Yes, he is, sweetheart, and he has good reason to be."

"Are those men going to hurt Miss Ballard?" the little girl asked in a voice as grave as her gaze.

"No, Rebecca. They're terrible men, but they wouldn't harm Miss Ballard. They're just going to make her stay in another town for a little while." Elizabeth tried to infuse her words with a confidence she could not feel. She forced a reassuring smile as she reached to take the little girl's hand. A pang grabbed at her when she felt the small fingers cling tightly to hers. "Let's go back upstairs now. It's time you both were in bed.'' She offered her other hand to Ben and then started up the stairs.

"When is she coming back?'' Ben tugged at Elizabeth's hand, demanding an answer.

Elizabeth thought for a moment to frame her response carefully. Although she wanted to avoid further upsetting the children, she knew that lying to them would only create more heartbreak in the long run. "I don't know exactly how long Miss Ballard will be gone, Ben, but I'm certain she misses you all a great deal. She will want to be teaching again just as soon as she can.'' She was relieved when the little boy only nodded solemnly.

From the landing Elizabeth let the children lead her down the corridor. "This is my room,'' Rebecca explained, pointing to the door on the right. "And that one right across the hall is Ben's. But sometimes when it storms and there's lots of thunder and lightning, Ben sleeps on the trundle bed in my room,'' she added, her damp fingers weaving between Elizabeth's.

"Why don't we pull out the trundle bed tonight?'' Elizabeth suggested. As she had expected, both Rebecca and Ben seemed pleased with the idea.

Elizabeth followed the children into the bedroom overlooking the orchard. After lighting a candle on the nightstand, she adjusted the curtains and filled the basin with water. While the children washed their faces, she slid the trundle bed from beneath its larger counterpart and turned down the coverlets on both. With Ben seated next to her on the side of the big bed, Elizabeth unwound Rebecca's braids and brushed her hair until it shone like black silk. She tucked Ben into the trundle bed, then adjusted the quilt over Rebecca and the doll cuddled inside the curve of her arm.

"Good night. May you have sweet dreams.'' Elizabeth stooped to kiss both children. She stood smiling down for a moment at the two drowsy faces nestled against the pillows before snuffing the candle and retreating into the hall.

When Elizabeth returned downstairs she found Ethan and Martin still seated in front of the fireplace. They interrupted their conversation when she appeared in the doorway.

"I thought it best that the children share Rebecca's room tonight. They were very nearly asleep when I left them," Elizabeth told Martin as she crossed the room to warm her hands over the fire.

"I'll look in on them later." Martin shifted on the settee, as if his tall frame were unable to reach an acceptable truce with the stiff horsehair cushions. "Elizabeth, I've a favor to ask of you." He hesitated, obviously unpracticed in appealing to anyone for help. "I would appreciate your spending some time with the children while I'm away in Milledgeville. The housekeeper is a reliable woman, and they'll have Ethan, of course. But seeing Miss Ballard taken away has been very hard on Rebecca and Ben, and they're so fond of you, I thought—"

"No, Martin," Elizabeth interrupted, shaking her head. When he frowned in surprise, she went on. "I, not you, am going to Milledgeville."

"I won't hear of it!" Martin insisted. "Abigail Ballard came here at my behest. She was arrested in a school that I built for her, while teaching my children. It's my responsibility to help her now."

"The state of Georgia won't even allow you to testify in a case involving a white person. Once you're in Milledgeville, they'll only find an excuse to arrest you, too," Elizabeth reminded Martin. Seeing the anguish reflected on his angular face, she continued in a gentler tone. "I know how you feel, Martin. You are an honorable man, and you want to do what is right. But you must see my point. In a way, I am to blame for Miss Ballard's arrest. If I had not taken Josiah to the school when he visited last fall, this terrible thing would never have happened. I never thought he could be so spiteful, but I am certain he informed the authorities in Georgia that she was teaching a freedman's child. I can travel to Milledgeville safely, and once I am there, I will persuade Josiah to intercede on Miss Ballard's behalf."

"Do you think he will listen to you, Elizabeth?" Ethan sounded dubious.

Elizabeth looked down at the stone hearth. "I am convinced that Josiah made trouble only to punish me for refusing to let him run my life. I do not believe, however, that he is totally without shame. When he truly realizes what he has done, I think he will have a change of heart. He is a powerful man, and he will be able to influence the right people to win Miss Ballard's release." She straightened herself to face the two men. "Before I go home tonight, I would like to pack some of her things to take with me. Then I can depart early in the morning."

Martin reluctantly rose to his feet. "I'll fetch her trunk."

Elizabeth gave Martin a grateful smile. After he had disappeared into the hall, she turned to Ethan, who had stood and walked to her side. "You mustn't worry about me while I'm away, Ethan," she said.

"I don't intend to, Elizabeth. I'm going with you."

"And in the meantime who will take care of your farm?" Elizabeth protested.

"Who is going to look after yours?" Ethan retorted. "At least I have four able hands, but you know Jephtha is still far too weak to have any real demands placed on him."

"Then let one of your men come with me. You won't have to worry about my being alone on the road, and you can stay here where you're needed." When Ethan said nothing, Elizabeth took both his hands in hers and gave them a firm shake. "Please trust me, Ethan. This is something I must do alone." She paused and then dropped her voice, speaking very slowly and carefully. "If you were to come with me, Josiah would be so angry I can only imagine what he might do. But I am certain things would not go well for Miss Ballard or me or you." Elizabeth bit her lip, hating the bitter admission as much as the cruel, senseless circumstances surrounding it. Not giving Ethan time to speak, she released his hands and fled into the hall.

Elizabeth rushed up the stairs and closed herself inside Miss Ballard's room. Working quietly to avoid disturbing the children sleeping next door, she sorted through the schoolmistress's Spartan belongings and filled the trunk that Martin had placed at the foot of the bed. When she ventured into the hall, she found Martin waiting on the landing. She followed him as he carried the unwieldy trunk downstairs.

"I want you to take my trap to Milledgeville. I've already spoken with Ethan, and he's going to drive it over to your place in the morning," Martin told her over his shoulder. "You'll make better time with a light gig than with a wagon," he added before she could object.

"Thank you, Martin." Elizabeth arranged her shawl over her shoulders, unconsciously peering down the dark hall for some sign of Ethan.

Martin was quick to interpret her glance. "Ethan has already left for home. He wanted to see about having one of his hands drive for you. I expect he'll say his goodbye in the morning." A slight smile softened the whetted angles of his face.

"I'd best be off, then, I suppose. It's getting late, and I still need to talk with Dolly and Jephtha and pack a few things of my own."

Martin nodded as he escorted Elizabeth onto the veranda. When they reached the steps she turned to face him once more. "Goodbye, Martin."

"Goodbye, Elizabeth." Martin bent to lightly kiss her forehead. "May we all see you safely home again soon."

"I put your wool shawl in your bag 'fore I took it downstairs, ma'am. You know how cool these spring nights can get." Standing in the doorway of Elizabeth's room, Dolly clasped and then unfolded her arms as if she were uncertain what to do with them. "I told Mr. Woodard's fellow to park the trap out front."

"Thank you, Dolly." As Elizabeth collected her bag, she gave the dressing table a final inspection and turned toward the door. She looked into Dolly's solemn brown eyes for a moment before putting her arms around her and giving her a warm hug. "Be sure to take good care of Jephtha while I'm away."

Pressing her lips together, Dolly nodded. "You just see that you take care of yourself, ma'am."

Elizabeth gave Dolly's shoulders an affectionate squeeze, then hurried downstairs. She had never enjoyed leave-taking, especially when it preceded a journey as fraught with troubling circumstances as the one she was about to undertake. When she caught sight of Ethan on the veranda she was reminded that the most difficult farewell remained yet to be said.

As Elizabeth closed the front door behind her, Ethan pushed away from the rail and turned. "I put your things in the back of the trap with Miss Ballard's trunk," he said.

"Thank you."

Ethan glanced across the dark yard. "I don't suppose you've changed your mind about letting me come with you." His eyes lingered on the faint halo of silvery light framing the treetops.

"If I could, you know I would." When Ethan continued to stare at the dawning sky, Elizabeth rested her hand on his back. "You shouldn't make so much of my going away, Ethan. Think how many times I've had to say goodbye to you," she chided, forcing her unsteady mouth into a smile. "It isn't as if I weren't coming back."

"I know." Ethan drew an uneven sigh, but still did not look at her. "It's just that everything seems so unsettled these days, so horribly out of joint. Sometimes I feel as if the whole world were collapsing around me, and all I can do is watch. Nothing seems certain anymore except..." Ethan caught his breath before turning to look at Elizabeth. "Except the way I feel about you." His lips quivered with emotion as he reached to touch her cheek. "I love you, Elizabeth, more than I ever imagined I could love another human being. I want to take care of you, make you happy, share all the good things in life with you." He hesitated, his dark eyes caressing her face with a palpable ardor. "I want you to be my wife."

"Oh, Ethan, nothing could make me happier than to be married to you!" Elizabeth's voice caught. Wrapping her arms around his waist, she willingly surrendered to his fervid embrace. Her lips parted as he lowered his mouth to hers. She closed her eyes, shutting out everything but the indescribable pleasure of their kiss. Shifting her head to one side, Elizabeth whispered against his cheek, "How I do love you! I shall come home, Ethan, just as soon as I can, and when I do, I never want to be separated from you again, ever!"

Ethan clasped her arms to hold her in front of him. "You'd best go now, while I still have the strength to let you."

Elizabeth gazed up into his handsome face, engraving every minute detail of its image in her mind. When she stepped back she felt Ethan's hands tighten briefly, and she almost faltered. Wrenching herself free of his hold, she turned and fled down the steps to the waiting trap.

"Mind you, Mrs. Merriweather, the prisoner is not supposed to have visitors excepting kinfolk."

The warden had reminded Elizabeth of that fact at least a dozen times since she had appeared in his office that morning, armed with a parcel of clean clothes for Abigail Ballard and an obstinate determination not to be turned away. He appeared bound to repeat his objection at least once more, however, as he escorted Elizabeth down the dank corridor leading to the cell block.

"Miss Ballard has no family living nearby who can supply her wants." Elizabeth restated her own argument, whose recitation had by now become rote. "Surely, Mr. Bursome, you would not deny a lady the comfort of her Bible at a time such as this." Elizabeth leveled her eyes at the grizzle-faced warden and was rewarded when he frowned and looked away.

At the end of the corridor she stood to the side while the warden knocked on a thick wooden door girded with rusty iron braces. He conversed briefly with the matron before turning back to Elizabeth.

"Fifteen minutes, and not a second longer." Fostering a stern expression, Bursome wagged a big-knuckled finger in front of Elizabeth's face.

"Thank you, Mr. Bursome." Elizabeth gave him a stiff smile.

She surrendered the bundle of clothes to the matron and watched while the dour-looking woman pawed through them. Without bothering to refold the clothes, the matron thrust them back into Elizabeth's hands and then pushed open the reinforced door.

"This way." The matron marched briskly down the ill-lit corridor, ignoring the curses emanating from one of the cells.

As they drew even with the foulmouthed inmate's cell, a sallow face framed by a mass of unkempt red hair appeared in the cell door's barred window. Elizabeth started when the woman spit through the bars, narrowly missing the hem of her skirt. At the end of the corridor the matron selected a key from among those suspended on the large iron ring she carried, and unlocked a wooden door with a barred window set in it.

"You got someone here to see you," the matron announced as she wrenched open the balky door. Glancing at Elizabeth, she jerked her head toward the cell's gloomy interior. "I'll be back for you in fifteen minutes."

Clutching the bundled clothes to her chest, Elizabeth halted just inside the doorway. She heard the door slam noisily behind her, but her attention was now focused solely on the tiny woman seated on a bare cot in the corner.

For a moment Miss Ballard only blinked at her uncomprehendingly. "Mrs. Merriweather! My goodness, what are you doing here?"

"I've come to look after you." Elizabeth rushed to the cot and sank down beside Miss Ballard. When she put her arm around the teacher's shoulders she was startled by how fragile the bones felt beneath the sparse layer of flesh. "How . . . how have they treated you?"

"Far better than many prisoners, I would imagine." A coughing fit jolted Miss Ballard's frail body, and she covered her mouth with both hands. When she regained her breath, she straightened herself, looking as much the capable schoolmistress as her disheveled condition would permit. "Those brigands who delivered me here are unworthy to be called men, but they did not mishandle me. But tell me. How are the children?"

"Rebecca and Ben miss you very much, as I'm sure all of your students do. We tried not to alarm them, of course, but we've all been terribly worried about you. I had to fight Martin to prevent him from coming here himself."

A wistful smile drifted across Miss Ballard's pale face. "Mr. Early is such a good-hearted man." She looked up at Elizabeth, revealing a bead of moisture rimming her weary-looking eyes. "It was very kind of you to travel so far on my behalf."

"I brought you some clothes and a few personal things that I thought you might want." Elizabeth released Miss Ballard's shoulders to open the bundle resting on her knees. "See? Here's your Bible and your hairbrush and a cake of the nice lavender soap that your sister sent you for Christmas."

"*That* will certainly prove most useful," Miss Ballard remarked, managing a smile. "I never imagined such a filthy place existed on the face of the earth!" She grimaced in distaste as her eyes swept the dirty, stained walls around her.

Elizabeth took Miss Ballard's hands in hers. "I know all of this has been so dreadful for you, but trust me. You are going to be out of here very soon. My brother-in-law is a lawyer of considerable influence, and I'm confident that he will be able to win your release. He is away from home on business right now, but I plan to speak with him the minute he returns next week." At the metallic sound of the key scraping in the lock, she glanced anxiously toward the door. "Have faith, Miss Ballard." Elizabeth tightened her grasp on the teacher's small hands. She reluctantly rose when the matron threw open the door. "I shall call again soon, and when I do I'm certain I will have good news."

In the days that followed, Elizabeth often rued the overly optimistic assurance she had given Miss Ballard in parting. After relenting once, the warden had apparently galvanized his resolve and decided to forbid Elizabeth further visits until a date had been set for the teacher's hearing. Enlisting Josiah's aid had proved an elusive goal, as well. Contrary to the information that the housekeeper had given Elizabeth when she had called at his home on her arrival in Milledgeville, two weeks had passed without any sign of his return from Savannah.

Elizabeth tried to assuage her growing frustration with what little useful activity she could find. She brought fresh fruit and bread to the prison every day and prayed that the matron would be honest enough to deliver at least a portion of it to Miss Ballard. Twice she had been allowed to post letters that the schoolmistress had written, one to her sister and another to a minister in Massachusetts. Without fail, she stopped at Josiah's home daily to inquire about his anticipated return.

Elizabeth was elated when she approached her brother-in-law's imposing white house one afternoon and discovered two servants polishing his carriage in the stable yard. Taking time only to adjust her bonnet and lace collar, she hurried up the walk and smartly rapped the brass knocker mounted on the front door.

"Is Mr. Merriweather in?" Elizabeth asked the moment the housemaid opened the door.

"Yes'm, but he's talkin' with Mr. Briggs and Mr. Clayton right now." The young woman cast a meaningful glance behind her. "He just returned last night from a right long journey, and he's had an awful lot of important business to attend to today."

Elizabeth had no idea who Mr. Briggs or Mr. Clayton might be, but she was certain that her business was no less important than theirs. "He will want to see me," she insisted. "Please let him know that his sister-in-law is here, and that I shall wait until he is free."

The servant sighed, anticipating, no doubt, the ordeal of facing her irritable master, but she dutifully ushered Elizabeth into the parlor and then trudged off to do as she was bid. Elizabeth seated herself on the green brocade settee and folded her hands in her lap, trying to collect herself for the unpleasant encounter to come. She glanced frequently at the elegant mahogany casement clock, watching the long hand edge slowly around the dial. Over an hour had passed when she at last heard masculine voices in the hall, interspersed with outbursts of hearty laughter. Elizabeth listened to the sound of the front door firmly closing, followed by determined footsteps on the corridor floor. When Josiah flung open the parlor door she stifled the impulse to spring to her feet.

"Good afternoon, Elizabeth." Josiah strode into the room, bearing with him the faint odor of expensive tobacco and arrogance. "My apologies if I have kept you waiting," he went on without the slightest glimmer of remorse. "I regret, however, that I could not interrupt my conference with the gentlemen who will be advancing my campaign for the state senate this fall." Josiah could not resist preening himself as he paused to admire his robust image in the mirror mounted over the fireplace.

"I understand," Elizabeth told him. "I will not require much of your time."

Josiah half turned to regard her with mock surprise. "Surely you have not traveled all the way from Indian Territory for only a brief visit."

Elizabeth fixed him with a steely stare. "You know very well why I am here, Josiah. I want you to have the charges against Miss Abigail Ballard dropped."

"Miss Abigail Ballard?" Feigning a frown, Josiah stroked his chin, but Elizabeth cut short his charade.

"Do not make light of this matter, Josiah. I know you instigated Miss Ballard's arrest for teaching a black child to read, and I know why."

Josiah's stout shoulders rose in an indifferent shrug. "Perhaps I may have let slip in passing to a colleague of mine that a teacher in Indian Territory was engaged in unlawful activity." When he smiled, he reminded Elizabeth of a sadistic child pulling the wings off a fly. "You say she has been arraigned?"

Elizabeth felt the color rising to her cheeks, and she struggled to hold her temper in check. "That poor woman has been subjected to untold indignities in the past month. As we speak, she sits languishing in a barren cell, surrounded by the foulest of human beings. She is not young, and her health is suffering. I want you to see that she is released as soon as possible."

Josiah leaned back on his heels and folded his arms across his expansive chest. "I am afraid I cannot simply twist the law to suit your purposes, my dear Elizabeth."

Elizabeth rose to face Josiah, her hands clenched so tightly she feared her snug kid gloves would burst at the seams. "You know influential men, Josiah, men who owe you favors. We both know that worse transgressions than Miss Ballard's have been overlooked when the right people wished them to be."

"If I did not know you better, Elizabeth, I would think you were begging for my help." Josiah cocked an eyebrow, looking for a moment like the very devil himself. "You now expect me to perform a great favor for you, and yet you turned a deaf ear to my entreaties regarding Samuel's property and that wretched Indian who would possess it." He shook his head. "No, Elizabeth, life does not work that way. You insisted on handling your affairs yourself. I suggest you do so now."

Elizabeth could feel her heart pounding inside her chest. "I shall, then, Josiah, since you leave me no choice."

For a split second Josiah looked crestfallen, as if he were disappointed that she had not wept and groveled as he had expected her to do. His laugh was short and contemptuous. "No one is going to listen to your sentimental pleading, Elizabeth."

"Perhaps not. Perhaps there is nothing I can do to save Miss Ballard from standing trial, being convicted and sentenced for a trumped-up crime. But I shall try my best. And I swear to you one thing, Josiah. By the time I am finished, everyone in this county will know that you have a madwoman in your family. I will make sure of that."

Josiah's eyes narrowed into reptilian slits. "What do you mean?"

"That I intend to do everything within my power to embarrass and humiliate you. I shall rant and rave wherever I can find an audience, and I shall make sure that everyone knows who I am. When you take your campaign to the man in the street, rest assured that I shall be there on the opposite corner, making a spectacle of myself."

"Have you lost your mind?"

Elizabeth's lips tightened into a brief smile. "I suppose that is what people will think."

"You can't do such a thing," Josiah sputtered. "I won't allow it. I'll—I'll have you put somewhere where you can't harm yourself or anyone else."

Elizabeth shook her head. "I doubt that you will want to have your brother's widow committed to an asylum in the midst of a political campaign. No, Josiah, you are doomed to have me haunt you if you refuse to help Miss Ballard."

Josiah was breathing hard now, his chunky body heaving like some powerful engine gone awry. "You're bluffing! You wouldn't dare!"

Elizabeth lifted her chin to meet the choleric blue eyes glaring at her. "There is one way for you to find out."

"Damn it all!"

Elizabeth flinched in spite of herself when Josiah's fist crashed onto the mantel, upsetting the candlesticks and a small marble bust of Socrates. For a few moments he only stared at the wreckage scattered around his feet, his breath coming in erratic gulps. When he looked up at Elizabeth, his eyes were full of such hatred she knew she had won.

"I will do what I can for this miserable teacher." Anger had reduced Josiah's voice to a low growl. "Now get out of my sight! Go back to your vile Indian and never darken my door again!"

Much as Elizabeth yearned to return home, she mistrusted Josiah too deeply to leave Milledgeville until she was certain that he had, indeed, kept his word. With nothing to do now but wait, Elizabeth missed Ethan more acutely than ever. Confined to her cramped boardinghouse room, she took comfort in conjuring images of the life they had shared in the beautiful Oostanaula River valley. She often imagined sitting with him of an evening on the ferry landing, gazing across the river at the woods that would be laced with white dogwood at this time of year. His arms would draw her close against him, and she would nestle her face against his chest, feeling happy and loved in his warm embrace. She had written Ethan several long letters since her arrival in Milledgeville, but the effort of reducing her feelings to mere words on paper had only underscored the distance separating them, and she ached for the day when they would be reunited.

Elizabeth was encouraged when, two weeks after her confrontation with Josiah, she was permitted to see Miss

Ballard again. The schoolmistress had lost a noticeable amount of weight and her nagging cough had worsened, but she was in good spirits, thanks to the arrival of her sister from Boston the preceding day.

"Mr. Early had written to tell her of my misfortune, and she and her husband departed for Georgia the very day they received the letter," Miss Ballard explained to Elizabeth. "So you see, you needn't fret over me any longer." Her thin hand clasped Elizabeth's. "You have remained here far too long on my account, Mrs. Merriweather. Now you must go home."

Elizabeth rubbed the teacher's bony wrist. "Not until you are released. My brother-in-law has assured me that he is exerting every pressure at his command, but I won't rest until you are free."

Privately, Elizabeth was beginning to fear that after Josiah had had time to consider her threats at length, he had deemed them hollow after all and had decided to renege on his promise. She was both startled and immensely relieved when she called at the prison three days later and discovered that Miss Ballard had been released into her relatives' custody the previous afternoon. Elizabeth tarried in the warden's stuffy office only long enough to learn the name of the hotel where Miss Ballard's family was staying. She found the schoolmistress in the hotel sitting room, looking bewildered and surprisingly sad.

Elizabeth rushed across the room to hug the little woman. "What wonderful news! I am so happy for you." She stepped back, still clasping the teacher's narrow shoulders. "Is something wrong?"

"They made me sign a statement swearing that I would leave Georgia and the contested Cherokee lands forever!" Miss Ballard blurted out. She bit her lip, trying to bridle the unaccustomed display of emotion. "At first I refused, but Sarah was so upset that I would be returned to jail, I finally relented. We are departing for Boston today." She gestured toward the luggage stacked beside the door, then let her hand fall helplessly to her side. "Oh, Mrs. Merriweather, I feel as if I have betrayed Mr. Early and all of the children."

"You've done no such thing," Elizabeth insisted. "I am certain that if Martin was here he would have done everything in his power to persuade you to sign that document. You are a good, selfless woman, Miss Ballard, but you must go home with your sister and recover your health. That is what all of us who care for you would want you to do."

Miss Ballard's shoulders trembled slightly as she drew a deep breath. "I should like for Mr. Early and his children to have my books. Perhaps he can find another teacher for the school someday."

Elizabeth enfolded Miss Ballard's hand in hers and squeezed it tightly. "The work you began among the Cherokees will go on, Miss Ballard. I promise you that from the bottom of my heart."

Chapter Fifteen

"Easy, Inali! There's a good fellow."

Still holding the horse's hoof braced between his knees, Ethan reached to stroke the animal's tensed neck. He gently massaged the rigid muscles until they began to relax beneath his hand. Removing a thorn embedded in a horse's foot was not a pleasant task, but Inali seemed to have an uncanny way of knowing that he would never intentionally hurt him. Ethan grimaced as he yanked the sharp barb from the cleft of the V-shaped frog where it had lodged. Then he lapped his arm over the horse's back and gave it a reassuring pat.

"That wasn't so bad now, was it?"

Inali only snorted and turned back to the sweet-smelling hay cascading from the manger. Ethan was pleased to see the horse place its weight on the injured foot, a sign that the thorn had done no damage serious enough to lame him. In the last letter Ethan had received from Elizabeth, she had said that Josiah had relented and agreed to secure Miss Ballard's release. She hoped to return home soon, and when she did, Ethan wanted to spend a day riding through the foothills with her, just the two of them sharing the glorious spring and each other's company.

As was always the case now when Ethan thought of Elizabeth, a poignant longing filled him, an ache so tangible it almost made him wince. In the weeks since her departure for Milledgeville he had been grateful for the sunup-to-sundown labor demanded by spring planting, and had relied on the exhausting work to dull his yearning. When he at last fell into bed at night, however, he had never been too tired to conjure her lovely face in his mind just before he drifted off to sleep. As Ethan began to brush Inali's glossy coat, he vowed to himself that he would never say goodbye to Elizabeth again.

Ethan was combing the horse's mane when Blue roused himself from the pile of straw where he had been napping and trotted into the yard. The dog started to bark, at first intermittently, then building to an excited yelping. Ethan paused at his work to listen to the hoofbeats in the distance. His elation that the drumming thud might herald Elizabeth's arrival quickly faded as the sound grew progressively more thunderous. To judge by the commotion their horses raised, a good number of riders were approaching on the road.

In these troubled times Ethan usually carried the long rifle with him whenever he ventured from the house. He glanced at the empty corner of the stable where he normally propped the gun while he worked, and cursed himself for neglecting to bring it with him that morning. Not bothering to pull on his waistcoat, he secured the stall gate, then dashed into the paddock. He was running across the yard to the house when the mounted soldiers stormed into the yard, their fixed bayonets gleaming in the midday sun.

The troops surrounded Ethan so closely he had to flatten himself against the paddock fence to avoid being trampled. He made another break for the house, but one of the soldiers pivoted his horse to cut him off. Ethan jumped to one side before the charging horse could knock him off his feet, but not quickly enough to evade the cavalryman bearing down on him from behind. The horse's shoulder clipped him in passing and sent him sprawling facedown on the ground. Ethan struggled to his feet to see the troops divide, one detachment flanking the stable while another formed a line in front of the house. He felt as if all the blood were ebbing out of his body as he watched an officer wearing a plumed hat trot his mount across the yard toward him.

The man halted a few feet short of Ethan and leaned back in the stirrups. "You're the Indian presently occupying this property?"

Ethan swallowed, trying to cleanse the dust from his constricted throat. "Yes."

The officer rested one gloved hand on the saddle pommel as he looked down at Ethan. "By order of the United States government, I am charged with effecting your removal from this property. You are to surrender all firearms, which will be restored to you upon your resettlement in the West. You will be compensated for any improvements or livestock that you are unable to dispose of prior to your removal." The officer droned his announcement in a bored monotone, hinting at how frequently he had been called upon to repeat it. "You have one hour to assemble any personal effects that you may wish to retain," he concluded, starting to turn his horse.

A numbness filled Ethan, draining his body of all sensation save a sickening dread. "One hour?"

The officer checked his horse to glance over his shoulder. "You people have already had a year to remove of your own accord. Be grateful we're giving you another hour." He spurred his horse, stirring a cloud of choking dust in his wake.

For a few minutes Ethan felt too dazed to do anything but stare across the yard, now filled with uniformed men sitting astride their horses. Through the pin oaks' lush branches he could see the river, its flow as peaceful and unhurried as he could ever remember it. *My whole life I've spent in this place, and now I'm being asked to take leave of it in one hour.* The thought struck Ethan with the devastating violence of a dagger ripping through his heart.

Blue nudged Ethan's hand with his cold nose and whimpered, as if to remind him that he could not afford to waste the remaining hour standing immobilized beside the paddock. If he could now do nothing for himself, he needed to think of others whom he could still help.

Ethan pushed through the close ranks of mounted men guarding the stable, to the far end of the paddock. As he had anticipated, his hands had abandoned their labor in the adjacent field to gather by the fence and watch the events unfolding in the yard. When Ethan waved to Will, the stablehand, the young fellow swung between the fence rails and ran across the paddock.

"I'm going to be leaving in an hour, Will." Ethan's voice caught, and he paused to draw a deep breath that shuddered through his chest. "I'm going to see that you and the other men won't have to come with me. You've been the best of help to me, and you shouldn't be punished on my account."

The groom's anxious eyes traveled from Ethan's face to the cavalry filling the yard behind him. "Them soldiers can't just take your place, Mr. Woodard!"

Ethan shook his head. "They have enough guns to do anything they want, Will. But listen to me. I need you to do something important for me right now. Run to Elizabeth Merriweather's house and ask her maid to come here as fast as she can. Then when you get back, I'd like for you to saddle Inali for me."

The youthful stablehand nodded before tearing off across the field as if his very life were at stake. As Ethan turned and walked to the house, he could hear the soldiers talking among themselves, laughing at raw jokes and grousing about the unseasonably warm weather. They took as little notice of him as if he were one of the gnats swarming around their horses' legs.

When Ethan reached the veranda he was forced to edge past the men who had dismounted and posted themselves around the front door. In the hall he met a soldier carrying his own long rifle along with the powder horn and pouch of shot. The man regarded him as if he were an intruder, but he allowed Ethan to pass. Overhead he could hear booted footsteps and the sound of drawers and doors being opened and closed. When he turned toward the front room the buck-toothed private stationed by the door lifted his rifle chest high and stepped into the door to block his way.

"I have some business I need to settle." Ethan looked over the man's shoulder at the room beyond, fighting back his rage at being denied access to a room in his own home.

The man's close-set eyes narrowed in mistrust, but he stepped aside to permit Ethan to pass. He ambled across the room, posting himself by the fireplace to watch as Ethan seated himself at the desk. Turning his back on the soldier, Ethan opened the desk drawer and rummaged through its contents. As he placed writing paper on the desk and reached for the inkwell, a strange calm settled over him. When he dipped the quill, his hand was as steady as if he were taking time out of an ordinary day to note some purchase for the tavern.

In a clear, even hand, Ethan composed a document for each of his hands, stating that they were freemen, unencumbered by the bonds of slavery, and giving the date of their manumission. After blotting each sheet carefully, he put them aside and then selected a clean piece of paper. He wrote Bill of Sale at the top of the page, followed by a concise description of the ferry, whose title he was transferring to Elizabeth Troup Merriweather for the sum of five thousand dollars. Ethan signed the deed, then hesitated before dating the transaction March 30, 1838, the last day he had seen Elizabeth. *The last day I will ever see her.* Looking at the stark black figures inscribed on the paper, Ethan realized that he had never felt more empty or alone in his life.

When he reached to dip the quill once more, his hand faltered, but he forced himself to go on. Bending over the desk, Ethan stared at the pristine white paper for a long, solemn moment. Then he began to write.

My beloved Elizabeth, The time allotted me to settle my affairs is fast drawing to a close, so I hope you will excuse the brevity of this letter. Even if I had an eternity at my disposal, I know I still could not find words adequate to express my love for you. In the precious time we shared, you have given me more happiness than any man could deserve in a lifetime, and I will never cease loving you. The ferry is yours now, as it ought to be. I ask only one favor of you in parting. Please look after Maum Betsy and Josephus. My father granted them their freedom before his death, but they are both getting on in years, and I fear for their well-being once I am no longer able to provide for them. Know that you will always be a part of me, Elizabeth, just as I hope a part of my spirit will remain with yours forever.

"What you think you're doin' here, gal?"

Ethan started as the soldier's lazy drawl interrupted his thoughts. He turned in the chair to see the man brandishing his rifle, barring Dolly's entrance. Ethan jumped to his feet and hurried to the door.

"This woman has come to convey a payment that I owe her mistress, a white woman recently settled in this country," Ethan told the sentry.

After balking the obligatory few seconds, the soldier lowered his gun to allow Dolly to pass. To Ethan's immense relief he wandered into the hall, leaving Dolly and Ethan alone in the room.

"Lord, Mr. Woodard! What've they done to you?" Dolly's gentle face contorted in horror as she glanced the length of Ethan, taking in his dirt-smeared face and clothes.

"It's nothing. I just fell." Ethan brushed aside her concern. "I don't have much time, Dolly, but there's something I must give you." He walked back to the desk, beckoning her to follow. He folded the bill of sale inside the letter and then pressed the papers into her hands. "This is a deed giving Elizabeth full title to the ferry. Please put it in a safe place and see that she gets it when she returns."

Dolly stared at the folded papers clasped in her hands. When she looked up at Ethan the tears began to spill from her wide-set dark eyes. "Oh, Mr. Woodard..." She bit her trembling lip, shaking her head in anguish.

Ethan put his arm around her shoulders and gave her a firm hug. "I shall miss you, Dolly, and I'll never forget your and Jephtha's kindness." He drew an uneven breath and stepped back. "Take care of Elizabeth for me, please." Dolly only nodded, blinking through her tears. "You'd best leave now. The soldiers won't try to stop you while I'm still here."

Dolly backed a few steps, her glistening eyes lingering on Ethan as if the finality of turning was too much for her to bear. Then she wheeled and fled through the door. Ethan walked to the window and watched until he was certain that she had safely negotiated the gauntlet of soldiers. He hurried back to the desk and jerked open the lower right drawer. He glanced over his shoulder before lifting the false bottom from the drawer and removing a small pouch concealed in the hidden compartment. Ethan opened the pouch, quickly counted the gold pieces, then secreted the bag in the leg of his boot.

"Time to move out, Injun." The private loomed in the doorway, hefting his rifle to compensate for his paltry height.

Ethan collected the documents confirming his hands' freedom and joined the soldier in the hall. Trying to ignore the man's galling smirk, he started for the front door before the soldier could goad him on with another thrust of his gun. "I need to get my horse," he said, giving the self-important private no chance to object.

Ethan wove through the cavalrymen still congregated in the yard. He spotted Will standing solemn faced at the paddock fence with Inali in hand. Keeping his back to the soldiers, Ethan handed the young man the documents.

"Put these papers inside your shirt, and don't let anyone see them until the soldiers are gone. There's a document for you as well as one each for Laban, Cuffy, Thomas and Zachary. The papers state that you're all free. I know you read well, so you'll have no trouble distributing them. If anyone tries to force you into service after I'm gone, show him that paper." Hearing someone yell across the yard, he glanced over to see a soldier trotting his horse toward him. "I wish I could talk with the men before I go, but I have to leave now."

As he handed Ethan the reins, Will opened his mouth, his lips silently forming words that he was too stunned to speak.

Ethan placed a hand on the young fellow's wiry shoulder. "Goodbye, Will."

Gathering the reins, he vaulted into the saddle and then circled Inali away from the paddock. As the mounted soldiers closed around him, the spirited horse flattened his ears in annoyance. Ethan reached to stroke the nervous animal's neck before twisting in the saddle to look back at the tree-shaded house. The spirits of everyone who had ever loved that quiet, beautiful place seemed to rise before him—

his grandparents, wrinkled and kindly as they were in his memory; his father, still tall and dignified in his prime; his mother, her dark eyes smiling at him; and Sally, running across the yard with the sun rippling through her hair. Ethan wrenched his gaze from the yard, and in that terrible instant he knew what it meant to die inside.

As the cavalrymen trooped onto the road they goaded their horses into a brisk trot. Ethan held the reins slack in his hands, letting Inali match his pace to the animals surrounding him. Up ahead on the road another smaller group of soldiers waited for the main contingent, their ranks drawn to encircle about twenty Cherokee men, women and children. Ethan recognized the Birdsong family among the captives. The mother clung to her children, all of them weeping openly save for young David, who was making a manly effort to emulate his father's stoic expression. When the soldiers escorting Ethan delivered him into the band of Cherokees, he avoided looking at his old friends, sparing them yet another witness to their misery.

When they turned at the fork in the road leading to Martin's home, a cold sickness gripped Ethan. As if he were trapped in an awful nightmare without end, he saw the white house loom into sight, watched the guards circle the captives on the road while their comrades galloped across the shady yard to surround Martin's house and outbuildings. After the cavalry had halted their horses, a curious stillness fell over the yard. Ethan frowned into the strong western sun, searching the landscape for some sign of Martin. Even if his brother-in-law was working in his fields, he could not help but have noticed the arrival of such a large body of horsemen. When the housekeeper appeared on the porch with Rebecca hovering in the door behind her, Ethan lifted a hand to shade his eyes.

"Mr. Early's gone to the sawmill, sir, and done took his little boy with him," he heard the servant explain to the officer wearing the flamboyant plumed hat. "I don't rightly know when he'll be back."

"Does he have a wife, children, or other dependent Indians on the premises?"

"Just Miss Rebecca." The housemaid edged toward the door to place a protective hand on Rebecca's dark head.

As the officer turned his horse, he signaled a burly private to dismount. "Take the girl into custody. Then search the house."

The soldier trudged up the veranda steps and swaggered to the door. When he reached for Rebecca's arm she shrank back, clinging to the maid's skirt.

"Oh, please, mister! You can't just take this child away without her daddy! She ain't nothin' but a baby!"

The soldier shoved her roughly to the side and grabbed Rebecca by the shoulder. The little girl tried to wriggle free from his grasp, but he only seized her around the waist, hoisting her off her feet as if she were some inanimate thing to be moved about at will.

"Let me go! I won't go with you! I won't!" Rebecca screamed, kicking and flailing at her captor.

The man clamped a beefy hand over her mouth to silence her. He yelped in pain as Rebecca lunged free of his hold. "You little bitch, I'll teach you to bite me!" He drew back his hand and slapped her across the face, knocking her to the floor.

"No!" Ethan's voice rang in his ears as he shouted across the distance.

The soldier hesitated a second to glance in his direction. Then he shrugged and turned back to the child cringing at his feet. Tears streaming down her face, Rebecca scrambled onto her knees only to earn another blow on the opposite cheek. "I'll knock your stinkin' teeth out!"

Without thinking, Ethan dug his heels into Inali's flanks. The horse lunged forward, breaking through the startled mounted soldiers. He saw two of the cavalrymen spur their horses to head him off, but he managed to swerve Inali in time to evade them. As the horse drew even with the veranda, Ethan leaped out of the saddle to clear the rail in a single motion. Before the stocky private could react, Ethan's fist connected with his jaw to send him reeling back against the rail. He could hear shouts now, accompanied by the sound of sabers and bayonets rattling, but Ethan paid them no heed as he threw himself onto the still-stunned soldier.

"You goddamn bastard! I'll kill you!" he shouted, hammering the man's head against the veranda floor.

When two soldiers grabbed Ethan from behind, he tried to pull free, but they managed to drag him off their prostrate comrade. They pinioned his arms behind him while the private staggered to his feet. His face flushed with humiliation and rage, the soldier clenched his hands into fists and drew back to land a series of brutal blows to Ethan's chest and midsection. Ethan doubled over, as far as the men holding him would permit, but the private's fist smashed into his face to jerk him erect. He could hear Rebecca screaming and sobbing while the punishment continued. When the men restraining him at last released their hold, he collapsed on the floor, too nauseated and dizzy to stand.

"Get him on his horse!" a voice ordered somewhere in the distance.

A booted foot nudged Ethan's heaving side, and he struggled to push himself to his knees. He swallowed and almost gagged on the sickly-sweet taste of blood filling his mouth. "Rebecca, come here." Ethan opened his arms, beckoning to the little girl.

With tears streaming down her swollen face, the child ran across the veranda to lock her arms around his waist. "They hurt you. I want Papa. I want Ben." Her small shoulders jerked as she sobbed inside Ethan's embrace, burying her face against his bruised chest.

Ethan held her close, gently stroking her tumbled hair. "It's all right, baby. I'm with you now, and no one is going to take you away from me. Don't worry about your papa and Ben. They're safe, and we're all going to be together soon."

Ethan felt a bayonet prod his shoulder, releasing a warm trickle of blood down his back. By sheer will he managed to weave to his feet and carry Rebecca into the yard. He seated her on the saddle pommel and then pulled himself onto Inali's back. As Inali followed the horses trotting out of the yard, Ethan encircled the child's shoulders with his arm. He pressed her face close to him, shielding her eyes from view of the big white house they would never see again.

Chapter Sixteen

"Gettin' mighty close to home, Mrs. Merriweather."
Thomas shook the reins to urge the horse into a brisk trot.
His eyes briefly strayed from the road to give Elizabeth an
encouraging glance.

Elizabeth nodded, but her lips felt too stiff to form even
the meager smile she demanded of them. In the three days
since they had crossed the Chattahoochee River into the
Cherokee Nation she had seen little that made her want to
smile. Troops appeared to be everywhere, riding in forces so
large and heavily armed that an unknowing foreign traveler
might have thought the country was at war. On several oc-
casions Thomas had been forced to pull the trap onto the
side of the road to allow a contingent to gallop past.

Most sobering of all were the groups of Cherokees that
the soldiers herded along with them. Elizabeth's heart ached
as she watched these processions of sorrowing people—
proud men stripped of their dignity, weeping women, the
desolate-looking elderly and children with pathetic, un-
comprehending eyes—cursed and prodded with no more
consideration than if they were cattle being driven to
slaughter. Never far behind were the bands of ragtag civil-
ians bent on snatching the possessions that the unfortunate
Cherokees had been forced to abandon. After picking over
the remains, the scavengers left in their wake a trail of children's playthings they could not use, books they could not
read and ceremonial pipes and masks they deemed worthless.

As the trap rolled along the road winding into the river valley, a sickening apprehension weighed on Elizabeth, a heavy knot coiled inside her like a venomous snake. Near the Birdsong place she could see a woman in the front yard, boiling laundry in a huge iron pot set over a fire. Elizabeth started to wave in greeting only to catch herself when the woman turned toward the road. Her hand dropped to her lap as she stared across the distance at the unfamiliar wan face framed by a gingham bonnet.

Presently Thomas guided the trap onto the thoroughfare leading to the ferry landing. The closer they drew to Ethan's house, the harder Elizabeth had to fight the urge to close her eyes, lest she see some belonging of his discarded on the road.

"Pull into the yard," she told Thomas in a low voice made ragged by dread.

The young man did as she bade. He drew the reins to his chest to halt the horse and then sat stock-still on the driver's seat, his stunned gaze wandering helplessly over the littered yard. "Lord, Lord!" Elizabeth heard him murmur under his breath.

A numbing paralysis began to creep through Elizabeth's limbs, but somehow she managed to clamber from the driver's seat. She cut an irregular path to the house, stopping to pick up a broken china cup, then dropping it to retrieve a book with half of its cover ripped off. She let the book fall to the veranda floor, her heart pounding against the feeble ribs that confined it as she stared through the open door.

"Ethan!" Echoing through her head, Elizabeth's voice sounded as if it issued from the depths of a well. "Ethan!"

As she rushed into the hall, a man appeared in the doorway of the front room. When Elizabeth whirled to face him, he flinched slightly and backed into the room.

"I 'spect you're the lady who's won this place in the lottery." The man assumed a friendly tone. He scratched his chin, smoothing the sparse gray whiskers speckling it in an effort to appear nonchalant.

Elizabeth said nothing. She froze on the threshold, unable to do anything but stare at the horrific scene before her.

The room had been stripped of its furniture, save for the bookcases that lay overturned in a pool of shattered glass. Torn papers and broken candlesticks were scattered across the floor, while a few tattered books lay carelessly dumped on the hearth. In the corner where the desk had once stood, the portrait of Ethan's mother hung at a lopsided angle. Someone had used the picture for target practice, desecrating the once-lovely image with ugly black holes.

Without warning, Elizabeth spun toward the man. "Get out!" she ordered through gritted teeth. When the man only gaped at her, she took another step toward him. "I said get out!" she shouted.

"Ain't no need for you to get so riled up, now." The man raised his hands as he sidled toward the door. "I didn't take nothin', I swear it. Weren't nothin' left to take by the time I got here. Sorry Indians've been moved out for a good coupla weeks now, and other folks done got to their stuff afore me."

Elizabeth's eyes darted wildly around the room. When they settled on a large book lying at her feet, she grabbed the volume and hurled it at the man's head. He ducked in time to avoid the missile and hastily retreated into the hall. Snatching up the remnant of a broken platter, Elizabeth ran into the corridor and threw it at the man as he scurried to the veranda.

"You filthy scum! Get out of here!" She screamed so violently that her throat ached from the effort. "Get . . . out . . . of . . ." Her voice dissolved into a shuddering sob.

Tears pouring down her face, Elizabeth sank onto the floor at the foot of the stairs. She wrapped her arms around her knees and buried her face in her lap. When she heard footsteps in the hall she looked up and saw Thomas's blurred silhouette framed in the doorway.

"Mrs. Merriweather, you need to come with me now, ma'am," he said quietly.

Elizabeth only shook her head and waved him away. She leaned her head against the cool stairwell wall and wept, at last venting all the sadness and rage she had held bottled inside her for the past three days. She had no idea how long she had sat crying at the foot of the stairs when a light hand touched her shoulder. Elizabeth lifted her face and blinked her swollen eyes, trying to focus on the slender figure that stood over her.

"Dolly?"

"Thomas came to the house. He told me I'd find you here." Dolly sank down beside Elizabeth and put her arm around her shoulders. "There now, ma'am," she whispered soothingly.

Elizabeth clasped Dolly's wrist. "Oh, Dolly! If I had only been here when they came—"

"Don't go blaming yourself, ma'am. There wouldn't have been anything you could've done." Like a mother comforting her child, Dolly gently lifted Elizabeth's chin. She reached into her pocket and pulled out a folded letter. "Before he left, Mr. Woodard told me to give this to you."

Drawing an uneven breath, Elizabeth tried to steady herself as she took the letter from Dolly. With trembling fingers she unfolded the two pieces of paper. As she read Ethan's letter, silent tears began to course down her cheeks.

"Mr. Woodard wanted real bad for you to have the ferry," Dolly said softly. "I think it made him feel better that he could do that for you."

Elizabeth shook her head. "I don't want the ferry or anything else in this awful world. I just want Ethan," she said in a low, choking voice. She rubbed her eyes roughly against her sleeve and then looked at Dolly. "Do you know where they took him?"

"I talked with old Noah Gilmer when he passed this way last week. He seemed to think most of the folks in these parts were being held at a fort up near Spring Place," Dolly told her.

Pulling free of Dolly's arm, Elizabeth abruptly stood. "Spring Place is not terribly far. If I leave first thing in the morning I should be able to cover the distance in a day."

Dolly pushed to her feet to follow Elizabeth down the hall. At the door she caught at Elizabeth's hand, forcing her to face her. "I know you're hurting real bad, ma'am. You love Mr. Woodard so much you'd do anything to help him. But this isn't like what happened to Miss Ballard. The folks who took Mr. Woodard aren't just a band of scoundrels that Mr. Merriweather's put up to no good. They're the United States Army."

Leveling her eyes at Dolly, Elizabeth gently withdrew her hand from the young woman's grasp. "I'm riding to that fort, Dolly, and after I get there, I'm going to find a way to win Ethan's release."

After spending two months confined to the paddock with no one to ride him, Midnight possessed a surplus of energy. Elizabeth pressed the horse without guilt, covering the road winding north along the Oostanaula River at a rapid pace with only brief pauses to rest and water the animal. Thanks to the tardy summer sunset, a metallic pink light still glowed on the horizon when she reached Fort Hoskins.

From a distance the soldiers' encampment presented an almost cheerful aspect. Campfires burned brightly, while the mingled sound of song and laughter drifted through the trees. Only the big stockade looming against the darkening sky hinted at the sinister purpose underlying the troops' presence. At first glimpse Elizabeth was startled by the sheer size of the stockade, a massive enclosure of upright logs tall enough to bar any contact with the hapless people confined inside its walls. A sentry tower stood at each corner of the fenced compound, offering the armed guards an unobstructed view of the prisoners.

As Elizabeth walked Midnight along the outskirts of the camp, she ignored the knowing looks and occasional vulgar comment from the soldiers who looked up from their card games to mark her passing. When she spotted a group of officers congregated near a whiskey peddler's wagon, she halted the horse.

"Excuse me, but can one of you gentlemen please tell me how I might locate someone here at the fort?"

The officers turned to look at her, almost in unison. She was heartened when one of them stepped forward and swept off his hat. "Captain Matthew Blaine, at your service, madam." When he bowed slightly, his saber rattled at his side to add a chivalrous flourish to the gesture. "I would be honored to personally locate whomever you seek. May I ask if he is an officer or a man of the ranks?''

"Neither. His name is Ethan Woodard, and I have reason to believe he is being held in the stockade."

"This man is an Indian?" Captain Blaine's luxuriant golden mustache did not quite conceal the disdainful curve of his lip.

Elizabeth looked straight into the steel blue eyes fixed on her. "Yes, a Cherokee who was forcibly evicted from his home sixteen days ago." When the man only regarded her coldly, she added, "He is a friend of mine, and it would mean a great deal to me if I could speak with him."

The captain made a show of adjusting his hat band. "My job isn't to keep track of Indians once I've delivered them to the fort, ma'am. About all I can tell you is that we have a lot of them penned up inside that fence." He glanced at his companions, winning a chorus of guffaws from them. "In any case, no one is allowed to traffic with the Indians. As a matter of security," he added with a slight smirk.

Elizabeth watched Captain Blaine turn his back on her to rejoin his friends. As the men sauntered in the direction of the whiskey barrel, she heard the captain mutter something about a squaw, earning another outburst of laughter.

Her cheeks burning with anger, Elizabeth collected the reins and pivoted Midnight. She checked him sharply as a soldier stepped into the horse's path, avoiding a collision by only a narrow margin. The young man clasped the horse's bridle to steady himself and then stepped back. Looking down into his smooth, rosy face, Elizabeth realized that he was little more than a boy.

"Excuse me, ma'am, but I couldn't help but overhear what you was sayin' to the captain, that you was lookin' for a fellow up there in the stockade," the youthful private said in a low voice. He glanced in the direction of the officers and then back at Elizabeth. "If we was to go over by them pine trees, we could talk a mite better."

Elizabeth dutifully walked Midnight to the stand of trees, safely out of the officers' earshot. Leaning forward in the saddle, she dropped her voice to a whisper. "You've heard of a man named Ethan Woodard?"

The private shook his curly dark head. "No, ma'am, but I figure I can find him if he's here. You need to talk with him?"

Elizabeth nodded. "If at all possible."

The youth pursed his lips in scorn. "As many soldiers go up yonder every night trying to get to them Indian girls, I reckon there shouldn't be much problem for one lady to speak a few minutes with some fellow in there."

"If I could see Ethan, I should be grateful to you for the rest of my life!" Elizabeth told him. "You're very kind to help me."

"No, ma'am. I'm a lot of things, but I don't see how any honest soul could call me kind." As the young man looked across the field of white-peaked tents, his expression hardened, adding years to his unlined face. "I been soldierin' since I was fifteen, nigh on five years now, and this is the nastiest piece of work I ever seen. They say God is merciful, but I don't rightly see how he's ever gonna forgive me for the misery I've helped bring on these poor, wretched people." He heaved a sigh laden with sadness and remorse. Then he straightened himself and looked up at Elizabeth. "Give me an hour. Then ride 'round to the other side of the stockade. You'll see a log cabin with some kegs stacked alongside it. If I can find your fellow he'll be waitin' there."

As he turned, Elizabeth nudged Midnight forward, causing the young soldier to hesitate. "What is your name?" she asked.

"McGreer, ma'am. Private Lucas McGreer."

Elizabeth looked into the clear hazel eyes. "Thank you, Private McGreer. And may God bless you."

Elizabeth waited in the shadow of the pine trees until she had lost sight of the good-hearted private. She consulted her watch, chafing as the minutes sluggishly dragged by. After a half hour had elapsed she walked Midnight farther along the path, taking care to stay on the periphery of the encampment. She let another twenty minutes pass and then set out for the far side of the stockade. She immediately spotted the log cabin that Private McGreer had described, but her heart sank when she saw no sign either of him or of

Ethan. When the young soldier suddenly stepped from behind the kegs' protective cover, she started in surprise.

"He's inside the cabin," Private McGreer told her in a rasping whisper. He grabbed the reins and held Midnight still while she dismounted. "I'll take your horse 'round back. You got a good fifteen minutes 'fore the sentry comes by this way again. I'll knock on the wall when I see him startin' up the hill."

Elizabeth dashed between the kegs and pushed open the cabin's door. She hesitated on the threshold, giving her eyes a chance to adjust to the paltry light. Elizabeth cautiously pulled the door to behind her, leaving it cracked only enough to admit a slim wedge of moonlight. "Ethan?" she said in a tremulous whisper.

At the sound of halting footsteps in the near corner she spun to see Ethan step from the shadows. "Oh, Ethan!" Elizabeth ran to throw her arms around him and press her face against his chest. "I was so afraid I wouldn't be able to find you!" Her hands kneaded his back, greedy for the warm, solid feel of him.

Ethan's arms tightened around her shoulders, embracing her with a fierceness that matched her own hunger for him. "I thought I would never see you again." His rough whisper stirred the loose wisps of hair curling over her forehead.

Elizabeth shifted her face against his chest to look up at him. Only then did she see the bruises that discolored his face, their marks hideously delineated in the pallid light. "My God, what have they done to you?" Her hand trembled as it hovered over his inflamed cheek. She glanced down, her horror growing with the realization that the dark stains stippling his shirt were dried blood. "They can't beat you like this and go unpunished! They can't!" A catch in her voice checked its crescendo.

Ethan only shook his head. He covered her hand, clasping it tightly inside his own. "You shouldn't have come here, Elizabeth. There's so much sickness in the stockade, even the soldiers are starting to fall ill."

"I'm going to find a way to get you out, Ethan," Elizabeth vowed, but something in his anguished dark eyes caused her heart to lurch.

"No one can do that, Elizabeth, not you or anyone else." His voice was so quiet and controlled, the sound of it sent a shiver through her.

"Don't say that, Ethan! This is all so horribly unjust. There has to be a way...." Elizabeth snatched a shallow breath, fighting back the sob building in her throat.

Ethan released her hand and clasped her shoulders, looking directly into her eyes. "If you want to help me, you can, Elizabeth, but you must listen to me." He waited until she had nodded shakily before going on. "The day the soldiers came, Martin and Ben had gone to the sawmill. Rebecca had stayed behind at home with the maid, but the soldiers insisted on taking her anyway. She's with me now, but I have no idea where Martin and Ben might be. I can only assume that they've been taken to one of the other forts." He hesitated. "If you could find out where they are, somehow let Martin know that Rebecca is safe—"

"I promise I will," Elizabeth interrupted. "And then I'll come back here to you. I'll join you in the stockade, Ethan, before I'll say goodbye." Elizabeth broke off. Her whole face had begun to ache from the now-futile effort of holding back her tears.

Ethan pulled her into the curve of his arm. His hand guided her face to rest against his chest. Then he gently stroked her hair. "Please don't cry. You know I can't stand to see you cry."

"I love you so much, Ethan. I would do anything for you." Elizabeth's shoulders jerked as she choked out the words.

"Then smile for me and let me kiss you."

Elizabeth brushed the tears from her face and drew the deepest breath her constricted chest could accommodate. When she looked up into Ethan's sad, beautiful eyes, she faltered, but she managed to force her quivering lips into a faint smile. Ethan's hand cupped her jaw to tilt her face, and she fastened her hands behind his neck, pulling him to her. He kissed first her eyes, gently closing them with light pressure, then each cheek in turn, his mouth plying the damp skin with increasing urgency. When their lips met, he kissed her with an almost desperate desire, as if all the yearning of his heart and soul must find expression in that sweet, brief union. His arms tightened around her, drawing her yet more deeply into his embrace.

A brisk tap on the side of the cabin caused Elizabeth to start. She clung to Ethan, as if her arms were strong enough to meld their bodies into one and forestall the approaching separation.

"Sentry's comin'!" The private's urgent whisper rasped from outside the door.

"You must go now, Elizabeth." Ethan clasped her arms to loosen their hold, but his hands shook slightly as they closed over hers. He stepped back, still holding her hands, and looked at her for a long moment.

Elizabeth swallowed, trying to find the will to bid him farewell. "Good—"

Ethan touched her lips to silence her. "Don't say goodbye. Just go."

Elizabeth took an unsteady step backward. As her hands slid from Ethan's grasp she felt as if she were relinquishing everything in life that mattered to her. Without giving herself a chance to falter, Elizabeth turned and fled into the night.

"I can quite naturally appreciate your interest in collecting any money that this Indian might owe you, Mrs. Merriweather. I would advise you, however, to refer your claim to the proper authorities rather than to pursue matters on your own." The colonel lifted his chin in a feeble attempt to win his neck some reprieve from the tight collar imprisoning it.

"Your point is well taken, Colonel Mabry. Rest assured that, as a widow of severely reduced circumstances, I have learned to value a concerned gentleman's counsel. I would only feel more confident of resolving the debt with Martin Early if I could determine where he is presently being held." Elizabeth folded her hands in her lap, adopting the politely implacable expression that she had honed to perfection in the past two weeks.

While searching for Martin and Ben she had quickly learned that officers such as Colonel Mabry responded far more favorably to an impoverished widow desperate to collect money from a delinquent Indian than to someone seeking to reunite a Cherokee father with his child. Then, too, after traveling to four detention forts without finding any trace of Martin, Elizabeth was willing to tell as many lies as were necessary to advance her purpose. It had taken her two days merely to gain an audience with Colonel Mabry, and she was not about to squander her chance with scrupulous honesty.

She was pleased when Colonel Mabry excused himself and walked to the anteroom to confer with another soldier. When he returned some time later, she was elated to find him carrying what appeared to be a roster.

Colonel Mabry sighed as he sank onto his chair. He frowned across the desk at Elizabeth, looking like a man with little taste for the job he has been given and only slightly more will to get it done. "My records show a Cherokee male, Martin Early, thirty years of age, and his son, Benjamin, aged five, awaiting deportation here at Fort Campbell." He cleared his throat before adding, "That is, as of June 3. With the recent outbreak of scarlet fever, I cannot vouch for the absolute accuracy of this list."

Elizabeth felt the color drain from her face as the chilling implication of the colonel's disclaimer settled over her. "I should like to speak with Martin Early at the earliest opportunity," she told the officer in a tight voice.

Colonel Mabry shook his head. "I'm afraid that isn't possible, Mrs. Merriweather." Recognizing the dismay reflected on Elizabeth's face, he went on in a more accommodating tone. "I fear you distress yourself unduly, madam. If the Indian is no longer alive, restitution can be taken from any improvements or property belonging to him once you have filed claim."

"I wish to speak with him personally," Elizabeth insisted. "I have not traveled such a long distance only to be turned away, Colonel Mabry."

The colonel tossed the roster aside and half rose from his chair, bracing his palms flat on the desk. "I am very near having an epidemic on my hands, Mrs. Merriweather. It will only be by the grace of God if I can keep enough troops fit to transport these wretched Indians to the river port this month. I am doing everything in my power to contain the spread of disease outside the stockade, and I'll not compromise my better judgment to humor you or anyone else." He shoved up from the desk. "Good day, Mrs. Merriweather."

Elizabeth rose stiffly. "Good day, Colonel Mabry."

She whirled and marched out of the office, ignoring the stares of the junior officers in the anteroom as she brushed past them without a word. When she reached the hitching post where she had tethered Midnight, she took a few minutes to collect herself. It was early yet, with a good two hours remaining before dusk. With any luck, she might be able to find a sympathetic soldier who would contact Martin for her before the day was over.

With that thought in mind, Elizabeth pulled herself into the saddle and walked Midnight to the edge of the encampment. By the time campfires started to twinkle against the waning light, she had circled the camp twice and approached more soldiers than she cared to count, without finding one with the least inclination to help her. Elizabeth decided to return to the public house where she had spent the previous night and resume her quest in the morning. A ferocious headache had been pounding between her temples since morning, a condition that her snug bonnet did nothing to alleviate, and her whole body felt stiff and sore. Assuring herself that supper and a decent night's sleep would banish both her physical discomforts and the dejection oppressing her, Elizabeth trotted Midnight the distance to the modest tavern.

The innkeeper's wife seemed genuinely pleased by her return. After filling a plate with a generous portion of venison stew, she seated herself at the table while Elizabeth ate her meal. Elizabeth nodded politely while she listened to the lonely young woman's chatter, but she cringed inwardly at each gleeful comment regarding the expulsion of the red savages from the land. As soon as she had eaten, Elizabeth pleaded fatigue and fled upstairs to her room.

Thanks to its low ceiling and single minuscule window, the room was ferociously hot and stuffy. Elizabeth impatiently removed her frock and splashed her face with water before dropping onto the lumpy bed. She sank into a fitful sleep, bedeviled by disturbing dreams. She had no idea how long she had slept when she awoke, shivering so violently that her teeth chattered. Elizabeth stumbled out of bed and retrieved her dress from the chair where she had laid it. A wave of nausea rose in her stomach, but she managed to wrap herself inside the gown's voluminous skirt and crawl back into bed.

The venison stew had not tasted quite right, and Elizabeth felt certain she was now paying the price for consuming it. She closed her throbbing eyes tightly, promising herself that she would feel better in the morning. The next time she opened her eyes a pale gray light filled the tiny window. Elizabeth thrashed against the yards of cotton swathing her body, fighting free of the perspiration-soaked fabric. She felt as if a wildfire were raging inside her, threatening to consume her as she dizzily staggered to the washstand. She saw her hand move through the air, reaching for the ewer, just as the room began to sway around her. Elizabeth sank to the floor, aware of how cool it felt and nothing more.

Chapter Seventeen

"You're not hungry?" Ethan glanced at the tin dish lying on the edge of the blanket, exactly where he had placed it an hour earlier.

Rebecca shook her head, her joyless eyes staring across the clusters of people huddled together in the stockade field. "It's so hot," she said in a listless voice.

Ethan sank onto the blanket beside her. "I know, but it will get cooler now that the sun has gone down." As he smoothed the loose strands of damp hair off her forehead, she looked up at him.

"I want to go home and be with Papa and Ben."

Ethan placed a comforting arm around the little girl, his hand lightly rubbing her shoulder. "So do I, Rebecca. I promise you we're going to find them, and we'll all have a nice home again someday." He had repeated those assurances so often, without anything concrete to show for them, that he dreaded the day when Rebecca would challenge him. Mercifully, she only nodded and sighed tonight. "Why don't we get you ready for bed and then I'll tell you a story?"

Rebecca obediently turned her back for him to unbutton her frock. Ethan slipped the dress over her head and folded it into a makeshift pillow for the night. Dressed in her shift, the little girl looked cooler if not happier. She sat back on her heels while Ethan dampened a cloth in the remains of the day's water ration, then washed her face and hands. Stretching on her back, she propped her head against his leg in preparation for what had become their nightly ritual.

When Ethan rested his hand beneath her chin, she wove her small fingers between his.

"Tell me how the redbird got his color," Rebecca commanded, looking up at him.

Ethan smiled at her, feigning surprise. "You don't know that by now?"

"I know, but I want to hear you tell me how again anyway."

Ethan drew a deep breath before launching into the familiar Cherokee folktale. By now he knew which stories were Rebecca's favorites, and she never seemed to tire of listening to them. He nonetheless felt obligated to vary his rendering from night to night, embellishing details and heightening drama to amuse her. As was usually the case, Rebecca refused to be content with only one story, and Ethan willingly obliged her demand for more. He was pleased when she frowned up at the sky, trying to pick the Seven Brothers out of the stars twinkling overhead, and even giggled briefly at the escapades of the wily bear. By the time Ethan had finished the story of how strawberries came to be, Rebecca's eyes were growing heavy.

Ethan gently tickled the tip of her chin with his thumb. "You're getting sleepy."

"No, I'm not," Rebecca protested drowsily. "I want another story."

"All right. I bet I have one that you've never heard before." Ethan pulled her onto his lap and cradled her small body in the crook of his arm. As Rebecca snuggled her face against his chest, he kissed the top of her head. "There was once a very brave, very smart, very beautiful girl named Rebecca," he began.

"That's not a story," Rebecca interjected.

"Oh, yes, it is. Everyone who knew Rebecca loved her, for she was not only clever, but also kind and good. 'Rebecca can do anything she sets her mind to do,' the people would say. 'See how well she rides that big horse? To look at her galloping him across the field, you'd never guess he'd thrown every man who had ever tried to ride him.' 'And just listen to her sing,' a woman exclaimed. 'You would swear the mockingbird himself had taught her how.' 'She dances,

too, graceful and light as a butterfly,' a wise old man added.
'And once she taught a chipmunk to eat nuts out of her
hand, one at a time. If she can do that, she can do anything,' he insisted, 'for everyone knows how wary the chipmunk is.' 'Rebecca is the most wonderful girl in the whole
world,' her uncle agreed. 'But there is one thing she cannot
do.' When the people heard what Rebecca's uncle had said,
they all turned to look at him." Ethan paused for effect,
winning a heavy-eyed glance from his niece.

"What can't she do?" she murmured.

"'When she gets sleepy...no matter how hard she
tries...she cannot stay awake.'"

Rebecca smiled, but did not open her eyes. Ethan tenderly lifted her in his arms and laid her on the blanket. He
bent over her to kiss her cheek. "Good night, Rebecca."

When she said nothing, Ethan eased back on his knees.
Rebecca looked so sweet and innocent with her little face
pillowed against her hand. As he listened to her soft, even
breathing, he was grateful that sleep had delivered her, at
least for a time, from the hell surrounding them.

Nearly a month had passed since they had arrived at the
stockade, and in that time, living conditions had deteriorated to an appalling level. The food provided for the Cherokees was frequently spoiled and of such poor quality that
many people refused to eat to the point of starvation. In-
adequate water added to the suffering of the incarcerated
Indians, who were forced to pass the long summer days in
the open yard with nothing to shelter them from the blister-
ing sun. With the stockade crowded to the bursting point
and few provisions for even basic hygiene, disease flourished, taking an especially brutal toll on the elderly and the
very young.

Ethan had tried to safeguard Rebecca's health with the
limited means at his disposal, reserving for her the best food
he could scrounge and maintaining some meager semblance of cleanliness. So far, she had escaped the fevers and
fluxes raging among the imprisoned Cherokees, but Ethan
dared not think how much longer their luck could last. A
few parties of Indians had already been evacuated from
other stockades to begin their journey westward via river-

boat. The severe drought had made river travel impossible in places, however, and rumors were now growing that the final stage of removal would be postponed until the fall. Ethan's imagination balked at conceiving the horrors that would result if they were forced to remain in the stockade yet another two months.

Bracing himself on his hands, Ethan leaned back to gaze up at the star-sprinkled sky. He had always been fascinated by the enormity of the night's canopy, the multitude of glittering gems that lured the eye into infinity. Since he had been imprisoned in the stockade, looking up at the evening sky had taken on a deeper significance for him, had become a way of connecting with the greater world from which he was now barred. He liked to think that Martin and Ben, wherever they might be, were sheltered beneath the same heavens, that Elizabeth would mark the day's passage with the same evening star.

At the thought of her, a profound anguish filled Ethan, a pain more intense than any physical wound could ever cause. So many precious things had been wrested from him, but no loss could equal the agony of giving up Elizabeth and the life they could have had together. Ethan grieved to think of the love they could have given each other over the years and of the children that would have added to their happiness, just as he mourned all the countless simple pleasures—the first dogwood blossom of spring, the earthy smell of a summer rain, long walks through the autumn forest, hot coffee on a dark winter morning—that they would now never share.

Ethan abruptly pushed to his feet in an effort to extinguish the images torturing his soul. Regardless of how passionately he clung to his memories of Elizabeth and their time together, the world in which they had lived had been cruelly swept away. As much as he loved her, Ethan knew he could never allow her to join him in the hellish one that had taken its place.

He stooped to smooth the wrinkles from the edge of Rebecca's blanket and collected the plate of untouched food. Only a little over a month ago Ethan would have tossed the pathetic scraps of meat to his dog without a second thought.

A far different standard prevailed inside the stockade, however, one based on hardship and deprivation, and Ethan was chary to waste the few edible slivers of salt pork that he had managed to cull from the day's foul stew. Gray Bear had been fighting a fever for several days, and he would benefit from some extra nourishment.

After making sure that Rebecca was still sleeping soundly, Ethan carried the leftover meat to the blanket where Gray Bear rested, not far from the stockade fence. The aging ferryman was lying on his back, so still that at first Ethan thought he was asleep. Only when he sank onto his knees beside the blanket did he notice that his old friend's eyes were open, staring up at the sky.

"I brought you something to eat," Ethan said softly. "Rebecca didn't have much appetite tonight." He proffered the plate, but Gray Bear lifted his hand in refusal.

"You should eat it, Ethan. You have gotten thin."

"We've all lost weight, but I'm still fit." Ethan looked down at the plate, wishing he could think of something to say that would banish the disturbingly somber expression on the elderly man's face. He glanced at the battered tin cup resting within reach of Gray Bear's hand. "Would you like for me to get you some water?" As he started to rise, Gray Bear shook his head without lifting it from the blanket.

"I saw the Raven Mocker today, Ethan." Gray Bear's voice was so faint that Ethan instinctively leaned closer to him.

"I'll wager it was only a crow come to pick carrion from the soldiers' rubbish heap," Ethan scoffed. Like every Cherokee, he had heard the legend of the Raven Mocker for as long as he could remember. Not since his childhood, however, had the story of the frightening creature that portended death sent such a bone-deep chill rippling through him. He swallowed, testing his tight throat, before risking to speak again. "James Birdsong heard that we may not be leaving until the end of the summer. I suppose that would be better than traveling while the weather is so hot and dry." He paused, his eyes drifting across the shadowy forms dotting the yard. "It's strange. As bad as it is here in the stockade, part of me is still glad that we might have a little more time on our land.''

A sigh rustled inside Gray Bear's chest, and he closed his eyes. "I will stay here with my Mary.''

Ethan frowned as he reached to touch Gray Bear's forehead. His skin felt hot and dry, strengthening Ethan's fear that the elderly man's raging fever was making him delirious. "Mary's memory will always be with you, Gray Bear, no matter where you go,'' he said as gently as possible.

"I will stay with her,'' Gray Bear repeated. He opened his sunken eyes to look up, and only then did Ethan realize the true import of his words.

Ethan took his friend's work-roughened hand and clasped it tightly. "Don't say that, Gray Bear! You're going to get well. I'll look after you and see that you have the food you need to be strong again. And when we finally do reach the West, we'll help each other start over.''

Gray Bear shook his head again, this time scarcely moving it. His parched lips stirred to form a faint smile. "You are a good, brave man, Ethan. If I had been blessed with a son, I would have wanted him to be like you, a true *Tslagi*,'' he said, using the Cherokee word for their own people. "You have been as good to me in my old age as any son could have been." His chest rose jerkily with each labored breath. "I would have liked to see your children,'' he murmured, closing his eyes once more.

"And you will!'' Ethan insisted, tightening his hold on Gray Bear's hand. "Someday we're going to leave this godforsaken hellhole and find a place that no one can take away from us, ever. We'll have a home and decent food and live like human beings again. And then I'm going to find Elizabeth and marry her, and you'll watch our children grow up, the same way you watched me and Sally. I swear it will be so!'' His voice caught, checking the desperate torrent of words. Still gripping the elderly man's hand, Ethan stared down at his wrinkled face, watching its solemn features blur before his eyes. He bent to rest his ear against Gray Bear's motionless chest and listen to the terrible silence. "Goodbye, my old friend. You are free now,'' he whispered. "May your spirit rest among our ancestors forever.''

* * *

The air around Elizabeth was thick, so heavy she could feel its weight against her body. She frowned, trying to still the faces floating through her dream like disembodied masks. Her senses strained to hold one likeness together, only to have it fragment into a kaleidoscope of elusive features. Of late, her dreams had been filled with disjointed yet familiar images from her childhood—the garlands of pink roses covering the wallpaper in her old room at Prospect, the gauzy canopy arched over the bed where she had slept as a girl, the little china pug that had stood on her nightstand, next to the brass candlestick. When her mind's eye managed to form Dolly's gentle face out of the haze, Elizabeth struggled to pierce the dim membrane separating them.

"I'm right here, ma'am." The voice sounded remote, as if it belonged to someone else's dream and not her own.

When a light hand touched her forehead, Elizabeth blinked in an effort to focus. "Dolly?" The faint word clung to her dry, swollen tongue. Her eyes still narrowed against the unaccustomed light, she swallowed with difficulty. "What...what are you doing here?"

"I'm just taking care of you, ma'am. You've been real sick."

Elizabeth closed her eyes again, retreating from the harsh brightness. "The last thing I remember was falling. I must have slept for days. How did you ever find me?"

"You didn't make it easy on me, that's for sure." When Dolly chuckled, Elizabeth smiled, comforted by the warm, throaty sound. "No sooner than you had left home but Jephtha and I got to worrying about you traveling all by yourself, so I took Mr. Early's trap and set out after you."

"Alone?"

"Yes, but that's no worse than what you'd done," Dolly retorted. "With all the trouble brewing in the country, Jephtha had to stay and look after your place, or some of those squatters would have grabbed hold of it for certain. Anyways, I just kept asking folks at the public houses until I found you. I'll tell you, that poor innkeeper's wife was right glad to see me. She'd been tending you for two days, and you were still out of your head with a fearsome fever.

When I saw how bad off you were, I was scared, too, but I figured you needed to be someplace where a doctor could look after you. So I brought you here to Prospect.''

''Prospect?'' Elizabeth's eyes flew open, and she struggled to lift her head. For a moment she could only gape in disbelief. ''How long have I been here?''

''Almost a week now. Like I said, you've been real sick.'' Dolly's cool hand smoothed Elizabeth's brow, easing her head back onto the pillow.

''I've got to get in touch with Martin in the stockade,'' Elizabeth protested, resisting the pressure of Dolly's hand.

''Now you listen to me, ma'am.'' Beneath its gentle hush, Dolly's voice was uncompromisingly firm. ''You're still too sick to think about anything but getting your strength back. We've all been so worried about you. For a little while there, even the doctor was afraid to say if you'd pull through or not.''

''I promised Ethan.'' Elizabeth tried to lift her head again, but her neck felt as flimsy as a rag doll's, unable to support even the meager weight demanded of it.

''You're not going to do anyone any good by pushing yourself and getting all sick again,'' Dolly insisted. ''Mr. and Mrs. Stewart are going to be so happy to see you coming around, and you know they'll do everything they can to get word to Mr. Early. I know it goes against your will, but there's times when you've no choice but to let other folks do for you.''

''I have to let Martin know...that Rebecca is safe.'' Elizabeth licked her lips, her scant reserve of energy nearly exhausted. She closed her eyes, too weary to fight her heavy lids.

''You just rest now, ma'am.'' Elizabeth heard Dolly's voice ebb away into the still, dark void.

''You mustn't worry so, Elizabeth.'' Putting aside the pillow slip that she was embroidering, Lucinda Stewart leaned to place a comforting hand on Elizabeth's arm. ''I'm certain the commanding officer at Fort Campbell will respond to Charles's letter, if only out of respect for Charles's father. Major Stewart is still held in such high esteem, I'll warrant few officers would refuse a request made in his name, by his son *and* his niece, no less," she added encouragingly. When her assurances failed to lighten Elizabeth's pensive expression, she hesitated. "Before he left yesterday morning to deliver that mare to Savannah, Charles told me that if an answer to his letter had not arrived by the time he returned home, he was going to ride to Fort Campbell and insist that Martin Early be reunited with his little girl. He didn't want me to tell you because he thought you would worry," she admitted with a trace of guilt. "But I hate to see you so melancholy."

Elizabeth looked directly into her friend's luminous violet eyes. "I can't stand by and allow Charles to travel into the Cherokee Nation at a time like this."

"Charles's mother was Cherokee, but he is a citizen of this state, with legal title to his land," Lucinda reminded her.

Elizabeth shook her head. "At every public house I visited I heard rumors of volunteer militiamen who had swarmed into the country, vowing not to return home without killing an Indian first. If any of those men overtook Charles, I doubt if they would bother to inquire about his citizenship. I will do everything in my power to keep my word to Ethan, but if something happened to Charles on my account, I would not be able to live with myself."

Lucinda carefully knotted the periwinkle blue embroidery floss, then folded the pillow slip. "Perhaps a letter from Fort Campbell will come soon." She tucked the sewing basket beneath the side table and rose. "I'm quite tired. I think I shall look in on the children and then retire for the evening."

Elizabeth lifted the book that had been lying open on her knee for the past two hours. "I'm going to read a little while longer, at least until I get sleepy."

"Good night, then." Lucinda bent to give Elizabeth a sisterly hug. Still holding her shoulders, she smiled down at her. "I am so happy to see you improving. You will be well enough to go home by and by, but I must confess I will miss you dreadfully."

Elizabeth clasped her friend's arms fondly. "I shall miss you, too. And Charles and Nathaniel and Emma," she added. "You've all been so kind to me."

"That is because we love you." Lucinda stepped back, her face glowing with warmth and affection. "Don't tax yourself by staying up too late." She smiled at Dolly, who was seated in the comfortable wing chair, mending a camisole. "Good night, Dolly."

"Good night, Mrs. Stewart," the housekeeper replied as Lucinda started for the door. She continued to sew for a few minutes and then sighed. "I'm a bit tired myself. Will you be wanting anything before I go to bed, ma'am?"

Elizabeth glanced up from the book she had been pretending to read. "No, thank you." She was about to turn back to the book when she noticed Dolly removing her apron. For a moment Elizabeth could only stare in amazement at the gently rounded contour of the young woman's belly outlined beneath her gingham frock. "My goodness, you're going to be a mother!"

Dolly nodded, a little shyly. "Yes, ma'am, I do believe so."

Tossing the book aside, Elizabeth jumped up and rushed to embrace her. "That's wonderful news!" She held Dolly out at arm's length. "But why haven't you said anything? You should be getting more rest and not rushing about working so hard the way you do."

"You're a fine one to tell anyone to rest, Mrs. Merriweather," Dolly demurred. "I'm doing just fine," she added before Elizabeth could chide her further.

"We must get you home to Jephtha where you belong," Elizabeth insisted. "He doesn't know, I suppose?"

Dolly shook her head, a wistful look drifting across her deep mahogany eyes. "No, ma'am. I didn't know myself before I left to find you, and since I been here I didn't see much sense in having someone write to him, seeing as how he can't read."

"He will know very soon, I promise. He will be so happy." Elizabeth gave Dolly's thin arms a firm squeeze. "Are you hoping for a boy or a girl?"

"All I ask the Lord is that my baby come into this world strong and healthy." Dolly hesitated for a moment, her fine-boned face a palette of complex emotions. "And someday I want him to be able to hold his head up as proud and free as any man. That's what I want most for my child." She met Elizabeth's gaze, her eyes conveying their own poignant message. Then she gently slipped her arms from Elizabeth's grasp and turned for the door. "Good night, ma'am. You remember what Mrs. Stewart said about staying up too late."

"I will," Elizabeth promised. "Sleep well, Dolly."

Long after the young housekeeper had retreated upstairs, however, Elizabeth continued to sit by the conservatory window, gazing out at the dark orchard. Pleased as she was for Dolly, her mind refused to be distracted for long from the misfortune afflicting Ethan and his kin. Although she tried to conceal her despondency from her generous-hearted relatives, every passing hour only reminded Elizabeth of the steady erosion of time since she had last seen Ethan. Her heart ached when she recalled the livid bruises marring his handsome face, the pain and despair, betrayed in his eyes, that he fought so bravely to conceal. Over two months had passed since their cruelly brief reunion, but fear and uncertainty made it seem an eternity. As she closed the book and laid it on the hassock, Elizabeth realized that she could wait no longer.

Taking the candlestick from the side table, Elizabeth carried it to the desk and seated herself in the big high-backed chair. She rummaged through the drawers until she found writing paper and a pen nib. Elizabeth stared at the yellow pool of light cast on the paper for several minutes, composing her thoughts before she began to write. Although her hand felt unsteady, a result of the virulent fever that had ravaged her strength, the script laced across the white page was clear and precise. When she had finished, Elizabeth blotted the note carefully, then folded it and slipped it into her pocket.

She climbed the stairs quietly, shielding the candle's wavering flame with her cupped hand. Thanks to the late hour, not a sliver of light shone from beneath any of the doors lining the hall, but Elizabeth tiptoed to her room nonetheless. Once inside the bedroom, she assembled her few belongings with single-minded efficiency and bundled them into the carpetbag that Dolly had brought from home.

Elizabeth placed the folded note on her pillow, where Dolly or Lucinda would be sure to find it the following morning. With Midnight fresh and well fed, she would easily have reached the Chattahoochee River by then. Charles would not return from Savannah for another five days, far too late to overtake her and persuade her to return to Prospect. Much as she hated the idea of slipping away in secret, she knew that her cousins considered her far too weakened from her protracted illness for them ever to consent to her departure at this point. She would write Charles and Lucinda as soon as she could to reassure them that she was well. In the meantime, she could trust them to look after Dolly and see her safely reunited with Jephtha.

Elizabeth crept out of the room, closing the door behind her without a sound. Halfway down the stairs a slight lightheadedness forced her to pause, but she quickly recovered her equilibrium. Taking a deep, fortifying breath, she hurried down the hall as rapidly as her untested legs could manage. She was crossing the veranda when a ghostlike flutter on the edge of her vision caused her to start. Turning, Elizabeth was startled to see Emma, her cousins' daughter, step from the shadows. Tall and slim at fifteen, the girl resembled a graceful sylph in her flowing white nightgown.

"Emma! What are you doing here?" Elizabeth exclaimed in a rasping whisper.

"It was so hot I couldn't sleep, so I came downstairs for a breath of fresh air. I didn't mean to disturb anyone." Emma's gaze traveled to the carpetbag that Elizabeth held. "You're leaving us?" Her soft voice sounded more sad than reproachful.

Elizabeth nodded. "Yes, dear, I must." She placed the carpetbag on the floor and walked over to clasp the young girl's hands. "I love you and Nathaniel and your parents very much, Emma, and I will never be able to thank you all enough for taking care of me when I was sick. I know it seems selfish and ungrateful to leave like this, without saying a proper goodbye, but I can only hope that you will try to understand my reasons for doing so. There is someone very special to me who needs me right now, someone who stood by me and believed in me when I had almost lost faith in myself.'' She swallowed to dispel the sudden dryness impeding her tongue. "Someone whom I love with all my heart.''

As Emma's wide-set eyes swept her face, Elizabeth was struck by how wise she looked. "You're going away to be with him?''

Elizabeth nodded. "I must find him first.'' At the sobering admission an unseen hand seemed to grab her throat. "If I must travel to the ends of the earth, I am going to find him,'' she vowed in a low whisper, defying the quaver rippling through her voice.

Emma put her arms around Elizabeth and hugged her tightly. "You will find him, cousin. I know you will.''

Elizabeth stepped back and took Emma's slender hands in hers once more. "I have to go now.'' She gave the girl's hands a firm squeeze before relinquishing them to retrieve the carpetbag. "Goodbye, Emma.''

As Elizabeth started down the steps, Emma walked to the veranda rail. Elizabeth waited until she had reached the orchard separating the stable from the house before she looked back. She could see Emma clearly, her long white gown reflecting the waxen moonlight as she leaned over the rail. With her long brown hair billowing around her face and shoulders, she resembled an artist's rendering of an angel, and Elizabeth tried to fix the image in her mind, to carry with her as a talisman. Elizabeth raised her hand in farewell. Then she turned to disappear among the shadows of the spreading trees.

Less than a day's ride, and he would reach the Coosa River. The thought cheered Cephas Johnson as he goaded his horse along the narrow mountain road, and made the heavy clouds clotted around the peaks seem less threatening. He had spent a good number of his years wandering the backwoods, sometimes to outpace the law, more frequently because his luck had run out in one place and he could think of nothing better than to move on to another. He had resented this latest spell of living in the saddle, however, occasioned as it was by a worthless Indian that someone should have paid him to shoot.

The night Cephas had fled the Indian's house on the Oostanaula, his only thought had been to save his own skin. Occasionally, when he was in a speculative frame of mind, he wondered what had become of the strange, scar-faced fellow who had accompanied him on that ill-fated venture. The last time Cephas had seen him, dragging himself through a pool of his own blood, he had looked just about done in. Had he died there with his gun in his hand, leaving Woodard to find his body and crow over his defeat? Or had he somehow managed to survive? Cephas had no way of knowing, but in the short time they had spent together, the fellow had impressed Cephas as too crazy to be killed without considerable effort.

Reining his horse, Cephas squinted up at the dark clouds and sniffed the air. Rain was coming—it was just a matter of when. He could press on in hopes of finding a public house before nightfall, or he could make camp in the woods while he could still see well enough to stay clear of rattlesnakes and scorpions. After only brief consideration, Cephas opted for the latter. One more night of sleeping in the open—even a wet one—mattered little when he reminded himself that tomorrow evening would find him snug and settled in the house that he had won in the land lottery. Then, too, he could see little point in paying for lodging in some stinking hole, only to provide free meals for yet another host of lice and bedbugs.

Cephas guided the horse along a switchback until he found a sheltered spot beneath an outcropping. He made short work of hobbling the horse and cutting a few pine boughs to cushion his bedroll. He had finished the last of his hardtack and biscuit and was filling his pipe when a shadow fell across his shoulder. Cephas jumped inside his skin when he looked up to find the scar-faced man standing over him.

"You liked to scared me there!" he complained in a voice that was a couple of registers higher than usual. Cephas mustered a frown, but something in the man's unblinking expression made the cold sweat break out all over him. "When I saw you all shot up that night, I thought for sure you was dead," he lied. "I see you made it all right."

The man nodded. His curious stone-colored eyes did not waver in the slightest. "I see you did, too."

When Cephas's eyes darted to his rifle, propped beside his saddle just out of reach, the man's gaze moved in tandem. "Sit yourself down," Cephas said, trying to sound cordial. "I got some whiskey left, enough for a coupla swigs, anyhow." He pulled the flask from his coat pocket and started to open it, but the scar-faced man only shook his head.

"I won't be staying long."

Cephas was about to return his bottle to his pocket when he saw the man lift his rifle. A shot jolted the humid air, and an agonizing pain cut through his left knee. Cephas howled, writhing on his side as he clasped his bloodied leg. Another blast, and he rolled to the other side, vainly trying to hold his sundered right leg together.

"You left me to die," the man said, so quietly Cephas could barely hear him through his own moans.

"No, I swear! I thought you was dead 'fore I left! Don't kill me! Please don't kill me!" The words poured out of Cephas, as unchecked and wasted as the blood gushing from his wounds. When the rifle leveled with his face, he flattened onto his back, his arms moving like the legs of a helpless turtle trying to right itself. His eyes widened and his mouth formed a hollow O, just before his head exploded into a thousand bloody shards.

Chapter Eighteen

"Ain't nothin' wrong with your horse that a new set of shoes won't fix." Holding Midnight's leg firmly clamped between his knees, the blacksmith tapped the rim of the hoof with his rasp. "These here shoes are 'bout worn clean through."

"How long will it take to shoe him?" Elizabeth asked.

The smith released the horse's leg and straightened. He chuckled, absently scratching the tip of his chin with the rasp. "First question most folks asks is how much is it gonna cost." Catching Elizabeth's anxious look, he went on in a more serious tone. "Old Dooley left a sprung wagon wheel this mornin', and he'll have my hide if I ain't done with it when he comes back. I'll shoe your horse just as soon as I've fixed his wheel. It shouldn't take more than a coupla hours, all told. You're welcome to wait in the house," he offered, gesturing toward the door with the ever-useful rasp. "The missus won't mind none. She's used to takin' folks in."

"Thank you." Elizabeth sighed in resignation as she gathered her skirt above the dirty straw littering the stable floor and started for the door.

When she looked at the matter realistically, a two-hour wait should still leave her enough time to reach the town of Cadron by nightfall. In the past four months, however, her search for Ethan had been fraught with so many frustrating delays that she had come to resent even the smallest hindrance.

After leaving Prospect, Elizabeth had returned to her home in the ravaged Cherokee Nation only long enough to collect money and a few provisions before setting out for Fort Campbell. She had found the stockade deserted, and when she reached Fort Hoskins three days later, its detainees, too, had already been evacuated to Ross's Landing for transport to the West. Elizabeth had squandered over a week in the Tennessee River port town, trying to obtain information about Ethan's or Martin's circumstances, when the sympathetic wife of an army doctor had intervened on her behalf. She had learned that Ethan's band had departed for the West via an overland route at the beginning of September, while Martin's party had left the port aboard flatboats later in the month.

Hoping to overtake Ethan, Elizabeth had joined a group of settlers headed for Kentucky. Their progress westward had been slow, however, not least of all due to the huge parties of Cherokees that congested the road for miles on end. Few days passed along the route when they did not encounter displaced Indians, some numbering a thousand or more, escorted by armed soldiers, others amounting to only a handful of stragglers, too sick or enfeebled to keep pace. Elizabeth's heart ached at the sight of those unwilling migrants, ill-clothed, malnourished and often near exhaustion. More sobering still were the fresh graves that lined the road, often in numbers sufficient to constitute a small cemetery.

Elizabeth approached anyone who would listen, questioning English-speaking Cherokees and friendly soldiers and describing Ethan at every tavern and stock stand along the way. By late December she had traveled with three different groups of settlers to follow the Cherokees' trail into Arkansas, without finding any trace of Ethan, and Elizabeth now waged a daily battle with her growing despair.

She clutched her traveling cape close around her, resisting the icy wind that scoured the yard as she trudged from the blacksmith's stable to the boxy log house. Elizabeth stamped the clods of mud from her boots before rapping on the door. The woman who opened the door a few moments later was as tiny and brunette as the blacksmith was large and blond, with hair skinned tightly back from her face into a bun.

"Cal's workin' on your horse?" Despite her laconic phrasing, the smith's wife did not look at all displeased to find a strange woman standing on her doorstep. Before Elizabeth could answer, she beckoned her into the house. "Set yourself down by the fire." Stooping over the hearth, she jabbed the simmering logs with a poker, then retrieved one of the sadirons heating by the grate. "You travelin' all by yourself?" she asked, giving Elizabeth a look that was more admiring than dubious.

"Only since yesterday," Elizabeth told her, chafing her icy hands over the blaze. "I was traveling with a family from Missouri, but we parted company in Batesville. I should like to find a party journeying to the Indian Territory."

The woman eyed Elizabeth with mild curiosity as she licked one finger and then gingerly tested the iron. "There's plenty of folks headed that way, that's for sure, though I'm not certain you'd be wise to join company with 'em." She shook her head, skillfully gliding the iron over the shirt that she had spread on the table. "I don't care how a body might feel about Indians in general. I still say no one who calls hisself Christian could look at those poor Cherokees and not feel for 'em. Every bunch of 'em that comes down that road yonder looks worse than the last, ragged and froze stiff and some so sick they can hardly hold their heads up. Cal says you can't feed 'em all, but I couldn't sleep at night if I thought I hadn't shared what little I could spare with those poor, starvin' children. It'd like to break your heart if you could see how grateful they are for cold corn bread and a bite or two of salt meat."

In her eagerness to question the kindhearted woman, Elizabeth walked to the table where the blacksmith's wife stood ironing. "I'm looking for someone traveling with the Cherokees, a man about thirty years old." She proceeded to describe Ethan in detail. "He walks with a slight limp due to an injury. The last I heard he had a little girl with him, his seven-year-old niece. Do you recall seeing him among any of the Indians who have passed this way?" Accustomed to disappointment as she now was, Elizabeth nonetheless felt her heart sink as the woman began to shake her head.

"Not with any of them big bands." The smith's wife smoothed one of the shirt sleeves before attacking it with the iron. "I do recollect a fellow with a child who come by here, just yesterday. He had the young 'un all bundled up in a big blanket so I couldn't tell if it was a boy or a girl, but this fellow was an Indian, anyone could see that plain enough. Nice-lookin' man, too, like the one you was tellin' me 'bout, though he could've used some meat on his bones. He was walkin' kind of stiff legged like someone who's been ridin' a good long while, but I guess that could just as well have been from a bad leg, now that you mention it. Funny thing, *he* was askin', just like you was, about a Cherokee fellow travelin' with a child, only it was a little boy in his case."

"It has to have been Ethan!" Elizabeth clasped her hands, scarcely able to contain her excitement. "Did he say where he was headed?"

"When I couldn't tell him nothin' about the folks he was lookin' for, I think he said somethin' about goin' on to Little Rock."

"Thank you so much!" Elizabeth rushed to the door, misbuttoning her cape in her haste. "You're sure you saw him yesterday?"

The woman nodded resolutely. "Right before suppertime. You won't have no trouble catchin' up with him, honey," she assured Elizabeth as she followed her to the door. "That nag he was ridin' looked like it was 'bout to drop in its tracks."

Elizabeth ran across the yard to the stable, and burst through the door so suddenly the blacksmith almost dropped the huge hammer he was wielding. He frowned in confusion as she began to saddle Midnight.

"I ain't touched his feet yet, ma'am," he protested.

"Those shoes got him here from New Madrid, they can get him to Little Rock," Elizabeth told the smith as she led the horse out of the stall.

Leaving the blacksmith standing openmouthed in the door of the stable, Elizabeth clambered into the saddle and set Midnight into a trot. Once they were on the road, she pushed the horse as much as she dared, given his travel-weary condition. When she reached Cadron, shortly before dusk, she paused at a farmhouse to water Midnight and chat with a lanky boy splitting kindling near the well. Elizabeth was elated when the young fellow remembered seeing a man fitting Ethan's description ride by that morning, and she wasted no time resuming her journey. As the last precious glimmer of daylight faded into darkness, she was forced to slow Midnight to a walk. With only the vague murmurs from the forest to distract her from the sluggish clop of the horse's hoofbeats, Elizabeth rode through the night. Dawn was just beginning to break, spreading a rosy glaze over the wide brown Arkansas River, when she reached the outskirts of Little Rock.

Elizabeth followed the road curving along the waterfront, scanning the scattered assortment of unpainted warehouses and landings. If Ethan was traveling independently of a major contingent of Cherokees, he may well have sought shelter in a public house for the night. When Elizabeth spotted an elderly black man trundling a wheelbarrow across the road, she hailed him to ask directions to the nearest tavern. Following his guidance, she jogged her horse down a narrow road lined with naked sycamores and elms. Elizabeth dismounted and tethered Midnight at the hitching rail outside the stable, between a sorrel mare and a scruffy bay gelding. She was crossing the yard to the tavern when something caused her to halt midway and turn back to the horses.

Frowning, Elizabeth approached the bay gelding cautiously. The animal was pathetically thin, its ribs sticking out like barrel staves beneath its dull, staring coat. When Elizabeth reached to touch its drooping head, it seemed hardly to notice. She gently brushed aside the horse's forelock to expose the tiny white star concealed beneath it.

"Inali?" Elizabeth whispered. When one of the horse's ears shifted slightly, she ran her unsteady hand along the creature's neck. "You remember me, don't you, old fellow?" Emotion choked her voice, and she broke off. When she heard a bucket rattle behind her, she wheeled.

She found Ethan standing in the door of the stable, the pail of spilled corn scattered at his feet. For a moment he only stared at her, but in that brief time a myriad of emotions passed over his gaunt face.

"Elizabeth." Ethan's quivering lips formed the word, scarcely above a whisper, as if murmuring a private incantation would lend substance to the apparition looming before him.

Elizabeth tried to say something, but her dry tongue stubbornly refused to comply. As Ethan ran across the yard she rushed to meet him. When he swept her into his embrace, she clung to him with all her strength. Ethan took her face in his hands. His glistening eyes searched its every contour and feature, as if he were still afraid to accept as real the image that his senses had evoked.

"I can't believe you're here." Ethan's low voice caught.

"But I am." Elizabeth reached to touch his cheek, her finger trembling as it traced the sharp cheekbone delineated beneath the tanned skin. "My God, I've missed you so much!"

Ethan began to kiss her, his mouth moving over her face with a fevered ardor. As Elizabeth responded in kind, her hands slid the length of his back, then along his arms to his shoulders and chest, driven by an insatiable need to touch every inch of him, reassure herself that she had at last found him, alive and whole. During the long months when they had been separated, she had yearned for him as desperately as a drowning man craves air or a starving person sustenance, and her burgeoning emotions now threatened to overwhelm her. When Ethan cradled her cheek in his hand, Elizabeth turned her head to brush her tears against his palm. She felt a rough sigh shudder through his chest as he enfolded her in his arms and held her close against him.

"I was so afraid I might never find you," Elizabeth whispered, shifting her face to look up at him. "After I saw you that night outside the stockade, I started looking for Martin and Ben. I learned where they were being held, but then I got sick, and by the time I was able to travel, you had already started for the West. Every day on the road I saw more sad, starving people, sick children, old people too weak to walk. And so many graves...." Pressing her quavering lips together, Elizabeth closed her eyes for a moment. "I never let myself think that one of them was yours. I simply *couldn't!*"

Ethan's arms tightened around her. "That's what I've tried to tell myself about Martin and Ben, that if I keep looking for them long enough, I'll find them. I don't know if Rebecca still believes me."

"How is Rebecca?" Elizabeth asked gently.

"Better since we've been traveling on our own. At least she isn't coughing so badly. The harsh weather has been really hard on her. She fell ill while our party was camped, waiting to cross the Mississippi River into Missouri. When they finally arranged for flatboats to bring us across the river, I knew I had to do something, or Rebecca was only going to get worse. Once we were on the road again, it was easy enough to fall behind—people were always lagging behind one group and then joining up with the next. I'd managed to bring some money with me, so I bought a rifle from a whiskey peddler and started to hunt to feed us. The game has been pretty scarce, but even so, it's better than the wretched stuff the government provided." Ethan fell silent, and Elizabeth could tell that he was making an effort to understate the horrors they had suffered.

"Have you heard any word of Martin and Ben?"

Ethan shook his head. "I've backtracked a stretch of our party's route, hoping to find them, but when I'm honest with myself, I know they could be anywhere between Georgia and the Indian Territory."

Elizabeth loosened her grasp on Ethan's waist to clasp his arms. "Martin's party came west by river, Ethan." When he gave her a questioning look, she hurried to explain. "I learned that when I was at Ross's Landing. They departed around the end of September."

"Assuming they've gotten this far, they would have to follow the Arkansas River to reach the Indian Territory," Ethan said, instinctively glancing in the direction of the riverfront.

Elizabeth nodded and gave his arms an encouraging squeeze. "At least it gives us a place to start looking."

Ethan quickly kissed Elizabeth before dashing back to the stable to fetch another bucket of corn. After letting Midnight eat a few handfuls, Elizabeth poured the grain into a pouch to carry with them for later. She had watered the horses and tightened the saddle girths by the time Ethan returned from the public house with Rebecca in his arms.

The little girl was overjoyed to see her, but Elizabeth inwardly winced at the all-too-ample evidence of the child's ordeal. Her arms felt pitifully thin linked around Elizabeth's neck, and beneath the rough blanket swaddling Rebecca, Elizabeth was horrified to discover only a light summer dress to protect her from the cold. To spare the already overtaxed Inali, she offered to let the child ride with her. As she snuggled Rebecca's small body close to her in the saddle, however, Elizabeth imagined that neither horse would notice the girl's insignificant weight.

They left the tavern stable yard and rode back to the riverfront. At one of the landings Ethan halted to question the workmen and learned that a steamboat towing two keelboats carrying migrant Cherokees had docked at the port the previous week. Although they had no way of knowing if Martin and Ben had been among the hapless passengers, the possibility was too tempting to ignore. With only minimal haggling, Ethan arranged passage for Elizabeth and himself on a steamboat headed for Fort Smith.

Despite the brisk wind whipping across the river, the day was pleasant, blessed with bright midwinter sun that warmed the passengers huddled on the *Valiant*'s deck. While Ethan secured the horses, Elizabeth found a relatively comfortable place for them to sit near a row of barrels that would shield them from the wind. She cuddled Rebecca on her lap, tucking the blanket around the little girl to keep her warm. When Ethan sank down beside them, he put his arm around Elizabeth and drew her close.

As the steamboat made its way upriver, Ethan would occasionally nudge Rebecca to point out a heron gliding overhead or the quick flash of some animal darting through the dense forest closing on the riverbank. For the most part, however, they were content to pass the hours quietly. During the long, wearisome search for Ethan, Elizabeth had often whiled away the time by thinking of all the things she would say to him when she found him again. Now that they were reunited, however, she wanted nothing more than to rest her head against his shoulder, feel his fingers woven through her own, share the warmth of his body next to hers.

The boat put in to shore at Lewisburg, docking long enough to unload a hogshead of molasses and acquire a couple of rough-looking passengers headed for Kansas. Ethan took advantage of the brief pause to question the men working on the landing, but they could tell him nothing about the migrants who had passed by the port save that they were Indians in wretched condition.

By midafternoon Rebecca had dozed off, and Elizabeth closed her own eyes, letting herself drift in and out of sleep. Once when she awoke, she lay very still. She looked up at Ethan while he stared across the water, unaware that she was watching him. The fading afternoon light carved deep shadows on his handsome face, revealing without mercy the prominent bones beneath the tanned skin. More telling even than the gaunt angles of his face was the haunted expression in his eyes, one that betrayed a sadness too deep ever to be put into words.

A wrenching pain seized Elizabeth when she thought of the terrible suffering that Ethan must have endured in the seven months since he had been driven from his home, and she tightened her arm around him. Ethan glanced down at her, and for a few moments a gentle smile relieved the pensive cast of his face. That fleeting smile evoked such poignant memories of another, happier time that Elizabeth hastily pressed her face against his shoulder to hide the tears welling in her eyes.

Darkness had enveloped the river by the time they approached the next port town of Old Dwight Mission. As they neared the landing, however, they could see clearly the bright campfires dotting the distant shore. After coaxing the stiff-legged horses onto the dock, Ethan helped Elizabeth mount and then lifted Rebecca into the saddle in front of her. They rode single file along the narrow trail leading to the encampment, dismounting when they reached the edge of the clearing.

Although Elizabeth had visited countless camps such as this one on her way west, the sight of the haggard, miserable Cherokees hunched around their fires never failed to fill her with anguish. When Ethan stopped to speak with an old woman trudging up the riverbank with a bucket of water, Elizabeth held tight to Rebecca's hand and guided the little girl away from the heartbreaking scene.

"We'll find a warm place to sleep tonight, Rebecca," Elizabeth stooped to pull the blanket over the child's dark head. When Rebecca only continued to frown past her in the direction of the camp, Elizabeth took both her hands and squeezed them. "You won't ever have to go back to one of those places," she promised. Straightening herself, she tugged gently at Rebecca's hand. "Let's look after the horses while we wait for Ethan." She was startled when the little girl suddenly broke free of her grasp.

Throwing aside her blanket, Rebecca tore down the footpath leading back to the camp. Elizabeth ran after her, as quickly as her cumbersome skirt and the dark, vine-choked path would permit. She was relieved when Ethan interrupted his conversation with the elderly woman to dash after his niece. They at last caught up with her just short of a blanket-shrouded family clustered around a fire. When Ethan bent to lift Rebecca into his arms, however, the child resisted, pushing both small hands against his shoulders.

"I want Papa," Rebecca protested, her face contorting in genuine distress.

"I know you do, sweetheart, and we're going to find him and Ben. It's just going to take some time." Ethan attempted to hug Rebecca, but the little girl only redoubled her efforts to pull away.

"Papa!" she cried, loudly enough to earn a few glances from the people huddled by the fire.

"Rebecca, please listen to me," Ethan began. Then he suddenly fell silent.

He froze, his unblinking eyes transfixed by the shadowy, blanketed figure weaving stiffly to its feet beside the fire. When the blanket dropped to the ground Elizabeth, like Ethan, was too stunned to do anything but stare at Martin's wraithlike form. Hovering half-hidden behind his father, Ben clung to Martin's hand, startled dark eyes widening in his pinched face. Only Rebecca trusted her unerring senses enough to act. She ran to her father and flung her small arms around his waist.

"Rebecca. My baby," Martin gasped as he sank to his knees. He kissed the little girl, then embraced both children, rocking them in his arms. As Ethan approached, he looked up, his wet face glistening in the firelight. "I tried to get back to the house, but the soldiers caught me. When they got through with me, I thought—" His low voice caught, forcing him to pause. "I thought for a while that I might not make it. And then they told me that she was dead."

Ethan shook his head. "Don't think about it, Martin." He reached to clasp his friend's rawboned shoulder. "We're all alive, and that's all that matters now. For any of us."

Chapter Nineteen

∽∾∽∾∽∾∽

"Is it a long way to Fort Gibson?" Ben surveyed the adults seated around the table, his fretful expression making no secret that he hoped it was not.

"The man at the livery stable seemed to think we could make it in three days without pushing our horses, now that the weather has broken," Ethan told him. "Tomorrow I'm going to buy two more horses, so you and Rebecca will have your very own to ride," he added, seizing on one of the few positive aspects of continuing their journey.

Ben looked resigned if not overly eager as he resumed munching on his apple. In light of the hardships that the children had suffered on the long road westward, it was little wonder that they both dreaded leaving the relative comfort of the public house where their elders had taken rooms for the night.

After finding Martin and Ben at the encampment at Old Dwight Mission, Ethan had booked passage for them on the *Valiant,* and on the following cloudy morning they had all embarked for Fort Smith. Treacherous snags and sandbars had delayed their voyage, forcing them to sleep on the deck of the boat overnight, while a limited food supply and brackish water had added to their discomfort.

When they had at last reached the ragged little border town the next day, the riverfront public house had seemed like a palace fit for kings. Mrs. Bastrop, the tavern's plain-spoken proprietress, had provided hot baths and as much venison stew and corn bread as her famished guests were able to consume. She had seemed to take a special liking to

Ben and Rebecca, treating them to the first apples they had eaten since leaving home, and advising Elizabeth on the best place to outfit them with new clothing.

As Ethan glanced around the table he was grateful for the salutary effect that the past few hours had worked on all of them. To be sure, Martin looked worn and thin, his clean clothes hanging on his angular frame like sheets hung out to dry, but when his eyes traveled to the children seated on either side of him, they bore the expression of a man who has come back from the dead. Ben and Rebecca were both relishing the affection and attention of the adults surrounding them, and smiles now occasionally brightened their hollow-cheeked faces. Rebecca still clung to Martin, refusing to be separated from him for long, but Ethan assumed that only time would blur her memory of the nightmare from which she had just emerged.

When Ethan's gaze settled on Elizabeth, he took advantage of the conversation she was carrying on with Ben to observe her, unnoticed. The long months on the road had taken a toll on her, as well, whittling her already slim figure to a willowy silhouette and casting a weary shadow over her lovely face. Elizabeth had undertaken a journey in the harshest weather at her own expense, endured poor food and bad water, braved the dangers of the wilderness—and for no other reason than to be with him.

Ethan loved Elizabeth so deeply, no sacrifice, no risk seemed too great to ensure her welfare and happiness. Not until that moment when he had found her standing outside the stable in Little Rock, however, had he considered that she loved him in equal measure, without qualification. The realization both sobered him and filled him with a yearning that made his whole body ache. Since Elizabeth and he had been reunited, Ethan was acutely aware that they had not had any time alone together, and he was pleased when Martin gently nudged the sleepy-eyed children to their feet.

"I want you to come with me to the stable tomorrow morning," he told Martin as they pushed away from the table. "I found two horses that I can get for a good price, but the legs of one look a little spavined, and I'd like your opinion."

Martin nodded. "Fine." As Ethan started up the stairs, he caught his arm. "I'd like to talk with you, Ethan, if you have a few minutes." He cast an apologetic glance at Elizabeth, but she had already taken the children in tow.

"I'll get Ben and Rebecca ready for bed," she offered, joining hands with each of the children.

"Thank you, Elizabeth." Martin smiled at her, but he quickly sobered when he turned back to Ethan.

Ethan searched his friend's grave dark eyes. "What is it, Martin?"

"While you were having the horses shod this afternoon, I started talking with a fellow at the mercantile, a half Creek who's been scouting for the army. He'd just come from Fort Gibson. Things are very bad there." Martin looked down as if he held himself culpable for the bad news he was obliged to bear. "The federal government has kept none of its promises. There isn't enough food, and what little they supply is usually half rotten. This man said that none of the Cherokees has gotten any money yet. They haven't even provided the rifles they said they would give us to hunt with. People are starving, Ethan."

"You know I was able to bring some money with me," Ethan reminded him. "And eventually we'll get something for our improvements that we had to abandon back home."

"Perhaps, but we can't afford to count on it. Just think of your cousin. Jonathan removed over two years ago, and yet you told me that in his last letter he complained that he had still not received all the money due him." Martin drew a deep breath that seemed to tax the limits of his slender frame. "When we cross the border tomorrow, we will have no place to live. Assuming we can find some decent land, we won't be able to plant for another two months anyway, and then there will be nothing to harvest for yet another three. With so many people pouring into the country, the game is already depleted. It's going to be a very hard time, especially for the children." Martin's voice dropped to a near whisper. "I've been thinking that it might be best if I were to find someone to take them, until I can do better for them myself. Maybe some missionaries would be willing to look after them. I don't know. The woman who runs this place was telling me how much she missed her own children now that they're grown. She seems fond of Ben and Rebecca....'' He swallowed with noticeable difficulty.

Ethan grasped both of Martin's arms. "I know you're worried about the future, Martin, just as I am. But after all Ben and Rebecca have been through, I don't think they could bear being separated from you."

"When I think about parting with them, I don't see how I could stand it, but I have to do what is best for them." Martin's lips tightened. "I can't let them starve."

"Nor will you. This is no time to stand on pride, Martin. I can see us all through until we get settled."

Martin's black eyes locked with Ethan's. "I know you would do anything for me and my children, Ethan, for you are like a brother to me," he said slowly. "But even you can't make food and shelter out of thin air."

"Don't force yourself to do anything now," Ethan pleaded. "At least wait until we get to Fort Gibson. Then, if it's necessary, we'll find some way to make arrangements...." His voice trailed off, unable to carry the statement to its awful conclusion.

Martin managed a hesitant nod. "It's getting late," he said as he turned toward the stairs. "I'd like to spend some time with the children before they go to sleep."

Ethan stood at the foot of the staircase, staring numbly across the empty common room. Martin had been stripped of his property, banished forever from the land where his beloved wife lay buried, beaten within an inch of his life when he had sought to recover his daughter. Ethan's mind rebelled at the thought that after suffering so much, Martin would now be forced to give up the children he loved more than anything else in the world. Never had he wished to defy a more terrible injustice, and never had he felt more powerless to do so.

As he started up the stairs Ethan felt as if a ponderous weight had descended onto his shoulders. The landing was so dark that he did not at first see Elizabeth standing in the alcove. She was gazing out the narrow window overlooking the river, but she turned as he joined her.

"There's a full moon tonight. The river looks like glass with the moonlight shining on it." Her soft voice reached out to him like a caress. "I can't remember the last time I've taken notice of the moon or the stars or anything beautiful in the world." She tentatively touched his hand where it rested on the rough sill.

Ethan took her hand and held it tightly. When she looked up at him, her gray eyes shimmered in the indistinct light. He let his fingers slowly drift along the curve of her cheek. "You're so beautiful, Elizabeth, so good and kind," he murmured. "Sometimes the world seems like such a lonely, desperate place. But then I always remember that you're in it, and that makes everything seem bearable."

Without speaking, Elizabeth curved her hand to clasp his. When she turned, Ethan followed her to the corner room. He closed the door behind them and then led her to the window. In the shaft of cool moonlight her face took on an ethereal glow, the fine wisps of hair framing it like spun copper. Ethan reached to loosen the pins binding her hair, letting the thick waves spill over her shoulders. Her lips parted as he unbuttoned her gown and gently eased the bodice to her waist. He ran his fingers through her hair, reveling in the silky texture as the strands tumbled over her creamy skin.

"This is how I always imagined you in my dreams, with your hair falling around your bare shoulders." Ethan slid his arms around her and pulled her to him. "I don't think I passed a single night when I didn't dream about you, Elizabeth," he whispered against her hair, swaying her in his arms. "There were times when the only thing that kept me alive was the belief that, someday, somehow, I would find a way to be with you again."

"I don't ever want to be apart from you. Oh, Ethan, I love you so much!"

As Elizabeth reached to encircle his neck, her breasts rose beneath the thin camisole to caress his chest. At the exquisite contrast of their pliant softness against his hard chest, a wave of heat flooded Ethan's body, firing his passion. He freed her from his embrace only long enough to cast off his shirt.

When he reached to take her in his arms once more, she surprised him by catching his hand. Not taking her eyes off his, Elizabeth unhooked her stays and dropped them onto the floor. As she lifted her camisole to draw it over her head, he sucked in his breath at the sight of her naked beauty bathed in the pale moonlight. Ethan marveled at how perfectly her breasts fit in each of his hands as he gently cupped them. He bent to kiss the delicate mounds of flesh, relishing the prick of her aroused nipples against his face.

When Elizabeth slowly slid her hands over his shoulders and down his chest, an almost unbearable ache surged through his limbs. Ethan closed his arms around her back and began to work her skirt and petticoat down her hips. She edged her feet between his, moving closer to him as he impatiently shucked the remainder of his clothing. Her small hands skirted his waist, then glided over his backside and around his hips, causing his body to throb with desire. When her palms drifted across his taut belly to follow the warm crease of his thighs, he moaned with pleasure.

Ethan's hands followed the slope of Elizabeth's back to grasp her hips and lift her to him. Arms wrapped around his neck, she let him guide her as he stepped back to the bed. Still keeping their bodies as one, he sank onto the bed and pulled her on top of him. His body arched beneath her, responding to the feel of her hands against his inflamed skin as they sculpted the contours of his chest and sides. Her breath quickened to short gulps as the rise and fall of his hips increased in urgency. Ethan felt Elizabeth tense, her hands tightening around his arms. Then her head fell back, her long hair tumbling over her flushed shoulders, and she gasped with pleasure. An ecstatic tremor rippled through her, sending a sensual pulse coursing through his own body. No longer able to contain his burgeoning passion, Ethan felt an explosive release shudder through him.

His chest still heaving, he rolled onto his side and curved his body around Elizabeth's. She placed her arms over his and wrapped them close around her. As he nestled his cheek against her hair, she sighed and eased her shoulders more deeply into his embrace. Ethan lay very still, shutting his troubled mind to everything but the warm feel of her body next to his. Closing his eyes, he let the sound of her soft, even breathing lull him off to sleep.

Ethan rested his shoulder against the window frame, his unfocused gaze wandering over the ill-defined shapes stirring in the predawn darkness. He had no idea at what time he had awakened and crept out of bed or how long he had been sitting by the window, staring down at the riverfront. The faint creak of a loose floorboard behind him caused him to turn.

Clutching the blanket around her shoulders, Elizabeth smiled gently and smoothed the hair at his nape. "You're all dressed. You can't sleep?"

Ethan shook his head, reaching to cover her hand. "No. When I woke up I started thinking about what we'll do after we get to Fort Gibson." He hesitated, looking back to the heavy mist rising from the river. "Martin talked with a man who's just come from there," he went on. "It sounds even worse than the stockade was."

Elizabeth clasped his shoulders. "But we won't be forced to stay at the fort. We'll find a place to make a homestead, buy some stock, start to plant as soon as the spring thaw comes." Her fingers dug into his muscles, forcing him to look at her. "I know you're concerned, Ethan, but we'll manage." She kissed him tenderly. "Please don't worry so. We have each other now, and that matters more than anything."

Ethan reached to touch her face. When his mouth threatened to quiver, he forced a slight smile. "Go back to bed. We have a long day ahead of us, and you need to get some sleep. I'll call you when it's time to get up. And don't worry about me. I'll be all right."

Elizabeth took an uncertain step back, her hands reluctantly relinquishing their hold on him. "I love you, Ethan."

"I love you, too, with all my heart." Ethan caught her hand abruptly and held it fast. "You must always know that, Elizabeth, regardless of how hard things may seem."

"Of course I do." She bent to kiss him once more, cradling his cheek with her free hand.

Ethan turned his face to caress her warm palm with his lips. He closed his eyes for a moment, clinging to every minute detail of her touch, the faint salty taste of her skin, the light pressure of her fingertips, the smooth texture of her wrist. As her hand slipped from his grasp, an invisible vise closed around his throat with such palpable violence he almost winced. He shifted toward the window, fixing his gaze on the river until the vague rustle of the straw mattress assured him that Elizabeth had returned to bed. Ethan waited until her breathing had subsided to a deep, steady rhythm before he turned back to the room.

He could see her sleeping form outlined beneath the blanket, the lush mass of chestnut hair spread across the pillow, and for an agonizing moment he yearned to turn his back on the unfeeling world outside, quietly slip beneath the cover beside her and pretend that nothing truly did matter but their love. At one time he could have done so, before the trail west had taught him its cruel lessons. Ethan had watched too many parents weep over their dying children, had helped too many men bury wives and loved ones to have any faith left in the power of wishes. Much as he loved Elizabeth, he knew that would not be enough to provide her with decent food, shelter her from the cold, protect her from sickness and the dangers of a frontier life.

Ethan forced himself to his feet and silently walked across the room. He paused beside the bed to gaze down at Elizabeth. Her lovely face looked so serene, too gentle and good for the hard world in which she lived.

"I don't want to give you up, Elizabeth." Ethan's mute lips formed the bitter protest he dared not speak. He closed his eyes, wrenching himself from the image that he would carry in his mind for the rest of his life. Then he abruptly turned and fled the room.

"Good morning, Mrs. Bastrop." Elizabeth leaned over the banister to hail the woman briskly sweeping the hearth with a straw broom. "Have you seen any of my traveling companions this morning?"

Mrs. Bastrop shook the broom over the fire, releasing a shower of lint onto the crackling flames. "They were up before dawn, the lot of 'em, and done with their breakfast before I could wink. When the good-lookin' fellow paid up, he told me just to let you sleep. He said they were goin' to buy a couple of horses and some provisions, and then he'd come back by for you when they were ready to head out." She propped the broom beside the stone fireplace and dusted her hands on her apron. "You must be hungry. How about some eggs and coffee?"

"Thank you. That would be very nice." Elizabeth seated herself at the plain wooden table and placed her traveling bag on the floor beside her chair. She turned toward the window, keeping an eye on the riverfront road while Mrs. Bastrop busied herself over the open hearth. She took her time eating the hot biscuits and fried eggs that the tavern's proprietress had prepared for her, and was sipping her second cup of coffee when a gangly boy of about twelve threw open the door.

"Wipe your feet and shut the door," Mrs. Bastrop ordered, looking up from the potatoes she was peeling to gesture with an impressive-looking knife.

The boy complied, sweeping his hat off his straw-colored hair as an added gesture of good deportment. "I got somethin' for a lady stayin' with you, Miz Bastrop." Frowning, he began to slap his pockets, and at last produced a folded sheet of ledger paper. "A Miz E. Merriweather," he added helpfully.

Elizabeth pushed up from the table. "I am Mrs. Merriweather." As she reached for the paper the boy proffered, an uneasy feeling began to stir in the depths of her stomach, one that the sight of her name scrawled in Ethan's familiar hand did nothing to relieve. She walked to the window and unfolded the note.

My dearest Elizabeth, I beg your forgiveness for writing what I could not say to you, and pray that you will understand my reasons for doing so. I would not blame you if you accuse me of cowardice, for whenever I think of looking into your sweet face to take leave of you for the last time, I know my will would surely falter. Much as I love you and have wished to make you my wife, I cannot condemn you to a life in exile, in a hostile land where I will be unsure of providing even the most basic necessities for your well-being. You have a comfortable home and, with the ferry now in your hands, the means of insuring yourself a prosperous future unclouded by fear and uncertainty. To ask you to exchange your secure life in the East for one of poverty and struggle in the new territory would not be an act of love, but one of the most shameful selfishness. I have arranged passage for you on the steamship *Mercury* as far as Montgomery Point. You need only show the captain your name on this letter, and he will see to your safe conduct. Elizabeth, I know it is presumptuous to ask for your compassion, but please know that I act only out of the deepest love for you. I will always carry your memory in my heart, and hope that a time will come when you will remember me with kindness and forgiveness.

For a few moments Elizabeth felt too numb to do anything but stare at the sheet of yellowed paper she held in her hand. Then she turned and dashed out of the tavern. She overtook the towheaded boy in the muddy yard skirting the livery stable.

"Where was the gentleman who gave you this note?" In her agitation, Elizabeth shook the paper in front of the boy's startled face.

The lad jerked his head toward the stable's open door. "Right over yonder." When Elizabeth started for the barn he hastened to add, "But that was a good long while ago. He told me to wait a few hours before I was to bring it to the tavern. I seen him ride out of town a while back, with another Indian-lookin' fellow and a couple little children all wrapped up in blankets."

Elizabeth glanced the length of the riverfront road, although she knew that Ethan had planned his actions too carefully for her to entertain any hope of spotting him now. In retrospect, she cursed herself for not having recognized the agonizing dilemma tormenting him when he had been unable to sleep that morning. Ethan had felt morally bound to spare her a difficult fate, which he himself had no choice but to face. Elizabeth knew, too, that despite his profession of cowardice, he had avoided telling her of his decision only because he realized she would never have agreed to return east without him.

Shoving the note into her pocket, Elizabeth hurried back to the tavern. She found Mrs. Bastrop trimming tallow from a ponderous chunk of beef, alternately tossing the lean meat into an iron pot and the scraps to a hound curled at her feet.

"Excuse me, but can you recommend a lawyer in this town?" she asked.

Mrs. Bastrop screwed her thin lips to one side, regarding the hunk of meat critically. "Me myself, now, I've never had any use for a lawyer's services, but some folks think highly of Nestor Beale. Which is to say, most of the time he's sober." She pointed with a greasy finger, anticipating Elizabeth's next question. "You'll find his office right next to the jail, real convenient-like."

Elizabeth thanked Mrs. Bastrop before gathering her bag and hurrying out of the tavern. She had no trouble locating the office of Nestor A. Beale, Esquire, attorney-at-law, thanks to a lopsided sign displayed within easy view of the jail's single barred window. Elizabeth knocked at the unpainted wooden door before gingerly pushing it open.

A thin man with the soulful eyes of a scolded bloodhound half rose behind his desk. "Good day, madam."

"Good day, sir. You are Mr. Beale?"

"That I am, indeed." He adjusted his lapels, shifting his narrow shoulders inside a black frock coat that had seen better days. The drooping eyes did a quick study of her, and Elizabeth guessed she was not the typical client to appear on his doorstep. "How may I be of service to you?"

"I should like to settle my affairs back East. Can you help me with that sort of thing, Mr. Beale?"

"The law is my business, ma'am, in all its manifestations," Nestor Beale assured her. He scooted around the desk to pull up a chair for Elizabeth, then hovered behind her until she was settled. He returned to his seat and began to carve out a space among the papers scattered over the desk. "Now, what exactly do you wish to do?"

"First of all, I should like to grant freedom to two slaves whom I inherited from my late husband." Elizabeth watched while Nestor Beale dipped his pen into the inkwell and then poised it with a flourish over a clean piece of paper. Her eyes followed the attorney's hand as he drew up a document immediately freeing Dolly and Jephtha and transferring to them title to forty acres of the land lot including the house. "My only stipulation is that they continue to care for Josephus and Maum Betsy for the remainder of their days, although I know that will be no problem."

"Josephus and Maum Betsy," the lawyer repeated, vigorously striking a line through the *t.* "I will need to have this document witnessed, of course, and then there is the matter of conveying it to the proper party back East."

"I understand," Elizabeth told him impatiently. "I am not finished. I also wish to divest myself of an additional one hundred twenty acres and a ferry."

Nestor Beale eyed her with surprise, as if he doubted a woman dressed as shabbily as Elizabeth could own any property at all. He cleared his throat as he reached for another piece of paper.

"I wish the remaining acreage to be divided between my cousin's children, Miss Emma Stewart and Master Nathaniel Stewart, with them to share equally in any profits derived from the ferry. Until they reach their majority, I would like for their father, Mr. Charles Stewart, to manage the property as he sees fit."

"To manage said property until such time as . . ." The attorney mumbled to himself, his muttering punctuating the rapid scratch of the pen.

When he had finished writing, he scanned the two documents and then read them aloud for Elizabeth's approval. She waited, somewhat impatiently, while he prepared duplicates. Mr. Beale excused himself briefly and returned a few minutes later with an earnest-looking young man in tow. After Elizabeth had signed both papers, the young fellow placed his signature below hers, exactly where Nestor Beale had indicated. As soon as the documents had been executed, the attorney dispensed with the witness as summarily as he had pressed him into service. He jotted figures on a paper and checked his arithmetic before presenting Elizabeth with a bill for his services.

"I should like you to forward both documents to Mr. Stewart as soon as possible," Elizabeth told the attorney as she returned her purse to her traveling bag.

"By the next post, Mrs. Merriweather, by the very next post." Smiling officiously, Nestor Beale escorted her to the door.

Elizabeth bid the lawyer a hasty farewell, not bothering to look back as she set off in a jog toward the livery stable. She shoved past the men loitering in the door of the stable and quickly saddled her horse. The extra ration of corn that Midnight had eaten the previous night had done much to restore his spirit, and he impatiently pulled at the bit. As soon as they were on the open road, Elizabeth let him set his own pace, a long-strided canter that rapidly covered the miles. With Ethan enjoying a good three-hour lead on her, Elizabeth was counting on his party's traveling slowly to spare their horses. The pale winter sun was sinking toward the horizon, however, when she at last spotted three horses halted on the side of the road. Ethan was picking out one of Inali's hooves, his back turned to her as she reined Midnight and jumped to the ground.

"Ethan!" Elizabeth cupped her hand around her mouth to call to him.

Ethan released the horse's foot and turned. For a few seconds they only stared at each other across the distance. Then, dropping the reins, Elizabeth started toward him and he ran to meet her. Ethan caught her shoulders and looked down at her, the pulse quivering beneath his lean jaw betraying his feelings.

"You shouldn't be here." Ethan's low voice was charged with emotion. "You should be on your way home, where you belong."

"I am."

Ethan shook his head, his dark eyes desperately pleading with her. "You have a place to live where you'll never be hungry or cold, Elizabeth, where you won't be worn down with hard work and old before your time, where you can have a family some day and see your children grow up healthy and happy." His voice caught, and he swallowed. "I can't let you turn your back on your home in the East, not when you have the freedom to go back there."

"But I don't, Ethan."

When he only frowned at her, Elizabeth pulled her copies of the legal documents from her pocket and handed them to him. Ethan glanced at her with uncertainty before he unfolded the papers and read them.

"You—you can't give away everything you have in the world," he stammered.

"I haven't, only the things I can live without." Elizabeth lifted her chin to look deep into his glistening eyes. "You once told me that you wanted to love me for the rest of your life, just as you wanted me to love you. All I need to know is if you still feel that way."

Ethan looked away for a moment, his handsome face working with emotion. "My God, you know I do!" He enfolded her in his arms and held her close against him. "I want to marry you, Elizabeth, and spend the rest of my life with you. I love you so much I only wish I had more to offer you."

Elizabeth reached to hold his face in her hands. "You couldn't give me anything more precious than your love, Ethan." As he lowered his mouth to hers, she closed her eyes, joining him in a lingering kiss that celebrated their union that would never again be broken.

Chapter Twenty

They reached the Grand River in the first week of February. Although Ethan was determined not to burden his already strapped cousin, he had persuaded Martin that, for the children's sake, they should spend a few days with Jonathan before striking out on their own. Conditions at Fort Gibson had been as dreadful as they had feared, and they had arrived at Jonathan Woodard's modest farm hungry and near exhaustion.

The Woodard family had received them warmly, sharing unstintingly of their winter food supply and mustering much-needed clothing for the ragged refugees. Elizabeth deeply appreciated their kindness but, like Ethan, she was eager to find a place that they could call their own. She had been pleased when he had interrupted her one afternoon while she was mending a quilt and asked her to ride out with him to look at some land. They had followed a trail through the woods scarcely wide enough to allow the horses' thin bodies to pass, but when they reached a knoll overlooking the winding river, Elizabeth knew that they had at last found a site for their home.

Ethan and Martin had set to work the following week, clearing enough of the virgin land to accommodate a small house on each of their respective homesteads. A heavy snowfall had forced them to interrupt their work for three days, but by the end of the month they had constructed two single-room log houses, each with a detached shed to provide storage space and shelter for their horses.

Elizabeth and Ethan were married in a traditional Cherokee ceremony on the day they were to move into their new cabin. Outfitted in a blue muslin gown that Susanna Woodard had hastily refurbished for the occasion, Elizabeth joined Ethan in celebrating with their friends and relatives, feasting on wild turkey and an opulent cake that had depleted the Woodards' dwindling reserve of wheat flour. At the conclusion of the festivities, Martin accompanied Ethan to the center of the Woodards' front room, while Susanna escorted Elizabeth. The bridal couple exchanged the symbolic gifts that their attendants provided, Ethan presenting Elizabeth with a venison ham while she offered him an ear of corn and a blanket. With each of them holding a corner of the blanket as a sign of their commitment, they listened to Jonathan pronounce them united as man and wife. Still carrying the blanket between them, Elizabeth and Ethan walked out of the house to their waiting horses. With the congratulations of the wedding party ringing on the crisp night air, they mounted and rode through the woods to the home where they would begin their married life.

When they reached the cabin sequestered among the trees, Ethan halted Inali in the dark yard and quickly swung to the ground. He caught Elizabeth around the waist as she attempted to dismount and lifted her out of the saddle. She rested her hands on his shoulders, smiling down at him, her face radiant in the frosted moonlight. Ethan slowly lowered her to the ground, letting her body slide the length of his own. He embraced her and kissed her, first on her chin, then on each cheek, then full on the mouth.

"I need to put the horses up for the night." Ethan reluctantly stepped back, still holding her hand. He was pleased when she laced her fingers tightly through his.

"I'll come with you."

They led the horses to the small shed located at the rear of the cabin. As Ethan pushed open the door he was startled to hear a distinct rustle in the darkness. When he swung open a window to admit enough light for further inspection, he discovered a small brown cow daintily browsing hay in the corner stall.

"Isn't that one of Jonathan's herd?" Elizabeth asked, squinting at the animal.

Ethan nodded. "Jonathan kept saying we were entitled to a wedding gift, but he can ill afford to part with a cow, especially with four children to feed."

Elizabeth squeezed his arm. "Don't worry. I'll see that they have all the butter and cheese they can eat. We certainly won't be able to use as much milk as one good cow can produce. At least, not for a while," she added, giving him a demure smile.

With Elizabeth leaning against the stall barrier, Ethan made short work of bedding Inali and Midnight down for the night. They walked back to the cabin arm in arm. Elizabeth waited in the open doorway while Ethan knelt on the hearth to kindle a fire. As the flames began to curl around the split logs, she closed the door behind her and joined him by the fire. Clasping Ethan's arm, Elizabeth turned to survey the small, sparsely furnished room.

"It isn't much of a house now, but by and by we'll add on to it," Ethan assured her.

Elizabeth linked her arms around his waist, holding him tightly for a moment. "I don't care if we have fifteen rooms and a veranda and the grandest staircase in the country. For me, this little room will always be the heart of our house." She shifted to face him. "Because this is where we started our life as husband and wife."

Ethan slipped one arm around Elizabeth's shoulders while the other curved beneath her knees to scoop her off her feet. With her head resting against his shoulder, he carried her to the bed and laid her gently on the sweet-smelling straw mattress. When he sank onto the bed beside her, she sat up and began to unbutton his coat.

"I want to undress you," she whispered, leaning to kiss his throat beneath the curve of his jaw.

His breath quickened as she slowly removed his clothing, piece by piece. Her small hands explored each part of his body they laid bare while her shimmering eyes added an equally exciting caress of their own. Submitting to the pressure of her hands on his shoulders, he stretched on his back to revel in the heady power of her touch. A shiver of delicious pleasure rippled the length of Ethan's body, following Elizabeth's hand as it glided from his naked shoulder to the arch of his bare foot.

Pushing onto his elbow, Ethan reached to unfasten the tiny buttons closing Elizabeth's collar. "Now it's my turn to make you feel good," he murmured.

He took his time undressing her, enjoying the leisure to stroke and kiss and taste every mystery of her lovely body. All his senses felt heightened, keyed to the exquisite delights of her closeness—the scent and silky feel of her hair as it brushed his bare skin; the sound of her laughter in the dark, throaty and sensual; the sweet flavor of her soft, moist lips.

Their excitement driven to an almost unbearable peak, they made love with abandon, clinging to each other with a feverish passion. When they were at last sated, they curled beneath the quilt to share the warmth of their heated bodies. Ethan curved his arm around Elizabeth, encouraging her to snuggle against him.

"I feel so loved and happy and safe with you." Elizabeth sighed with contentment as she pillowed her face on his chest.

Ethan closed his eyes, resting his face against her soft hair. "And that is the way I will always feel with you, Elizabeth."

Ethan rubbed his eyes with the back of his hand and stretched his legs beneath the heavy quilt. He smiled as he glanced at Elizabeth, still sleeping peacefully in the crook of his arm. Taking pains not to wake her, he carefully inched his arm from beneath her shoulders and then rolled to the side of the bed.

Although thin slits of light appeared through the shuttered windows, it was still quite early. Ethan decided to feed the horses and the new milk cow before brewing the fragrant coffee that would surely waken Elizabeth. He dressed quietly, then tiptoed to the door.

A light snow had fallen during the early-morning hours, blanketing the yard and surrounding trees with a pristine white cloak. Pulling his collar up against the cold, Ethan trudged through the icy crust. As he opened the shed's door, Inali greeted him with a low nicker. Ethan only patted the horse's neck in passing, however, as he hurried to inspect the empty stall where they had found Jonathan's cow last night. Cursing himself for not having spent a few minutes the previous evening to make sure that the stall gates were secure, Ethan hastily distributed grain to the two horses. He collected a length of rope and hurried out of the shed.

The fresh snow had efficiently covered any tracks the cow had made as she wandered away from the shed. Ethan frowned at the forest surrounding the clearing and scanned the close-standing trees for any sign of the path the animal might have taken. When he spotted a trampled cluster of brush he set off in search of the escaped cow. He followed the trail of low, broken branches, shaking the snow out of his hair as it tumbled from the heavy limbs overhead. For some reason known only to the cow, she had decided to climb the ridge overlooking the river. Ethan's breath formed vaporous puffs in the cold air as he grappled his way through the thick underbrush to scale the cliff.

At the top of the ridge his efforts were rewarded by the sight of the cow nibbling at a clump of dry brush. Approaching the animal slowly to avoid frightening her, Ethan slipped through the woods. Only when he was within a few feet of the cow did he notice the leather line tethering her to a nearby pine tree.

Ethan turned just as a shot cut through the icy morning air. He dove, flattening himself against the snowy ground. Crawling on his belly, he worked his way behind the protective cover of the brush bank. He held his breath, helpless to do anything but watch as Deerkiller emerged from among the trees.

Elizabeth's eyes shot open, her whole body jolted from its blissful slumber by the crack of gunfire in the distance. She sat up in bed and peered around the dimly lighted room. As her senses regained their waking acuity, she noticed that Ethan's clothes were no longer piled beside the bed where she had discarded them last night. Guessing that he had risen early in hopes of bagging a squirrel or two to supplement their meager supply of meat, Elizabeth climbed out of bed and dressed. With any luck, she would have the fire blazing and breakfast under way by the time he returned.

Elizabeth had gathered a handful of kindling from the stoop and was returning to feed the fire when she happened to notice Ethan's rifle propped beside the door. Still holding the kindling in her arms, she paused. Although the remote area was sparsely settled, either Martin or Jonathan could be hunting in the woods, close enough to the cabin for her to have heard their gunfire. But if Ethan had not taken his rifle into the forest to hunt, then where was he?

Elizabeth wasted little time pondering the question. Dumping the kindling on the hearth, she threw on her cloak. She was headed for the door when another gunshot reverberated through the forest. Elizabeth hesitated only a moment before grabbing the rifle. She drew a deep breath, trying to keep her hands steady as she loaded the weapon. Slipping the box of percussion caps into her pocket, Elizabeth shouldered the gun and raced out of the house.

She followed the clear trail of tracks leading to the shed. "Ethan?" Elizabeth called his name as she pushed open the shed door. When she discovered only the two horses munching their morning's hay ration, she quickly retreated into the yard. Tracing his footprints in the crisp snow, she impatiently thrashed through the thick undergrowth that caught at her skirt. The unwieldy rifle slowed her progress as she began to climb the ridge, but she managed to scramble up the slope. Her foot sank into a crevice concealed by the snow, causing her to stumble, and she dropped the rifle. She gingerly probed her throbbing ankle, and grimaced when a sharp pain shot up her leg.

Elizabeth was struggling to regain her footing when she glimpsed a man slipping among the trees. The sickening taste of raw fear flooded her mouth as she recognized the unmistakable shock of dark red hair. Deerkiller was moving stealthily, as if he were stalking something, but when he halted, Elizabeth realized that he had seen her. As he turned toward her, she could hear her heart pounding in her chest, feel the blood gushing into her head.

"Deerkiller!" Ethan's piercing cry echoed through the snow-covered trees.

Deerkiller stopped abruptly. In an instant that seemed to last a lifetime, Elizabeth saw him wheel in the direction of the shout and lift his gun. She was dimly aware of her own body mirroring his movements. When the rifle discharged, the recoil was too much for her injured ankle, and she fell back into the snow.

Elizabeth pushed to her knees in time to see Ethan lunge for Deerkiller. The blood trickling from Deerkiller's shoulder spattered the snow as the two men grappled on the ground. Dragging the rifle at her side, Elizabeth fought her way through the snarled vines and brush. As she neared the embattled men, she recognized the bright metallic flash of the knife that Deerkiller clutched in his hand. Elizabeth quickly reloaded and lifted the rifle, but the men were locked in too close combat for her to aim with any certainty.

She caught her breath as the men rolled within a few perilous feet of the steep drop-off overlooking the river. Deerkiller fought furiously, but the wound had weakened his arm. He grunted as Ethan forced him onto his back to jar the knife from his grasp. With an animal-like surge of strength he managed to shove Ethan off his prostrate body. Deerkiller dove for the knife.

"Throw me the gun!" Ethan shouted to her.

Elizabeth hurled the rifle to Ethan, and he caught it with one hand just as Deerkiller clambered to his feet. Ethan raised the gun to his shoulder, but Deerkiller suddenly lurched to one side, his footing undermined by a treacherous pocket of snow. Arms outstretched, he struggled to regain his balance as the ground beneath his feet fragmented into loose stones and chunks of ice. Deerkiller toppled backward, his cry following him into the ravine below. A deathly silence fell over the ridge, broken only by the soft patter of melting icicles dripping from the trees.

Ignoring the pain in her ankle, Elizabeth ran to Ethan's side. He dropped the rifle to take her in his arms. Only when he pressed her to his chest did she realize that she was shaking.

"I don't know what I would have done if you hadn', ten here when you did." Elizabeth felt Ethan's lips ve against her forehead as he smoothed her hair.

Elizabeth lifted her face to look up at Ethan. She tou ed his cheek, her fingers still trembling slightly. "He could have killed—" She stopped, her tight throat damming the terrible words. Her eyes inadvertently traveled to the ridge overlooking the ravine, and she shuddered.

Ethan cradled her face with his palm, guiding it to rest against his shoulder. "It's all right. It's all over now." Slipping his arm up her back, he gently turned her away from the overlook. "Let's go home."

Epilogue

❦

"Look, Mama! See what I've got for you?"

Elizabeth looked up from the letter lying open on her lap to smile at the small boy running across the yard. The child's wide-set dark eyes sparkled as he held out his hands, cupped together to conceal his gift.

Elbows folded on her knees, Elizabeth leaned forward on the veranda step. "Is it something special, David?" she asked in a voice hushed with excitement.

The little boy nodded emphatically.

"It's a wild plum," Elizabeth guessed.

Her son solemnly shook his head.

"A robin's egg, all pecked through where the little bird hopped out?"

"Uh-uh." A dimple dented the four-year-old's tanned cheek.

"I know!" Elizabeth exclaimed. "It's one of the Little People that you surprised in the forest."

David giggled, unable to contain his amusement any longer. "See?" He opened his hands to reveal a firefly nestled in his palm. The little insect crept along his arm, then suddenly took flight.

"How wonderful!" Elizabeth encircled her son's small shoulders, giving him a hug as they watched the tiny beacon flit across the dusky sky.

"I'm going to catch another one," David announced. He slipped from his mother's embrace and scampered back to the yard.

Elizabeth leaned her head against the column and watched David chase the elusive fireflies, relishing the sound of his carefree laughter carrying on the humid summer air. When she heard footsteps on the veranda behind her, she turned slightly and smiled up at Ethan.

He sank onto the step behind her and then lightly kissed the back of her neck. Ethan covered her arms with his own and crossed them over her breast. Pulling her back close against his chest, he rested his chin on her shoulder. "It's a beautiful night, isn't it?"

Elizabeth nodded. "Too beautiful to stay indoors. I wanted to read Charles and Lucinda's letter before it got too dark to see out here on the veranda."

"What did they have to say? Good things, I hope."

"Lots of good things." Elizabeth chafed the backs of Ethan's hands, settling comfortably into his embrace. "It's hard to believe that Emma is twenty-one now. Lucinda says she's grateful that Emma is so levelheaded, for she is fairly plagued with beaux. Nathaniel is doing well at his studies and is as handsome as ever. Both he and Emma rode with Charles to look at the ferry early last month. Charles insists that we would both be proud of the job that Jephtha is doing as ferryman."

"Did they say anything about little Stephen?" Ethan asked.

"Of course. Charles can't decide if he favors Dolly or Jephtha more, but everyone seems to agree that he is as bright and sweet natured as can be. His parents have high hopes of his getting an education, and Charles is determined to help them. When I answer their letter this week, I'll be sure to mention that Martin has persuaded Miss Ballard to come out here next year, if her health permits."

"That isn't the best news we have, you know." Ethan smoothed the gently rounded swell beneath the waistband of her apron.

Elizabeth turned her head to brush Ethan's cheek with her lips. "No, it isn't. Not by far." She straightened herself slightly as David came running up to the steps.

"Look how many I caught!" The little boy separated his clasped hands, and four fireflies darted free. He rested one chubby hand on Ethan's knee, rocking back on his heels to watch the zigzag path that the flickering insects cut across the dark sky. "When they go up high, they look just like stars."

Still keeping one arm around Elizabeth, Ethan slid onto the step beside her and then reached to pull David onto his lap. "See those stars? There are six of them. I bet you can count them, can't you?" He pointed to describe an arc overhead, smiling as David squinted and silently counted to six. "It wasn't until I was about your age that my father told me how they got there."

"How did they?" David wanted to know.

"A long time ago there were seven boys who liked to play a game called *gatayusti* more than anything. Their mothers had to nag them even to get them to come in for supper of an evening. Finally their mothers decided they would teach their sons a lesson, so they put some of the stones the boys used in their game into a big pot and cooked them for dinner. Well, you can imagine what the boys thought when their mothers gave them stone soup to eat. They were so annoyed they decided to go some place where their mothers couldn't find them. Now, they didn't really want to leave home forever, but you know how children feel sometimes. Anyway, they danced around the council house, and as their mothers watched, the boys started to rise slowly off the ground. The mothers ran after them, but the boys were already out of reach. They floated higher and higher, right over the treetops and into the distant sky. One boy tumbled to earth, and where he fell the first pine tree sprang up. The other six finally came to rest up there." Ethan gestured toward the constellation. "And there they remain to this day."

"Do they miss home?" David asked gravely.

"Not with everyone looking up at them and knowing where they are," Ethan assured him. "And they look down on the people here, of course. They shone down on my father many years ago when he was just a boy back East, and when I came along, they were still up there." He cuddled the little boy against his chest. "And just think. They've kept right on shining for you."

David thought for a moment, his lustrous dark eyes scanning the heavens. "The very same stars?"

Ethan's arms tightened around Elizabeth and David, drawing his family together in his embrace. "The very same stars."

*   *   *   *   *

Harlequin® Historical

First there was **DESTINY'S PROMISE**...
A woman tries to escape from her past on a remote Georgia plantation, only to lose her heart to her employer's son.

And now **WINDS OF DESTINY**...
A determined young widow finds love with a half-breed Cherokee planter—though society and fate conspire to pull them apart.

Follow your heart deep into the Cherokee lands of Georgia in this exciting new series from Harlequin Historical author Laurel Pace.

WINDS

1994 MISTLETOE MARRIAGES
HISTORICAL CHRISTMAS STORIES

With a twinkle of lights and a flurry of snowflakes, Harlequin Historicals presents *Mistletoe Marriages*, a collection of four of the most magical stories by your favorite historical authors. The perfect way to celebrate the season!

Brimming with romance and good cheer, these heartwarming stories will be available in November wherever Harlequin books are sold.

RENDEZVOUS by Elaine Barbieri
THE WOLF AND THE LAMB by Kathleen Eagle
CHRISTMAS IN THE VALLEY by Margaret Moore
KEEPING CHRISTMAS by Patricia Gardner Evans

Add a touch of romance to your holiday with
Mistletoe Marriages Christmas Stories!

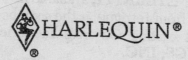

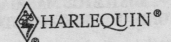

HARLEQUIN®

Weddings, Inc.

EDGE OF ETERNITY
Jasmine Cresswell

Two years after their divorce, David Powell
and Eve Graham met again in Eternity,
Massachusetts—and this time there was magic
between them. But David was tied up in a
murder that no amount of small-town gossip
could free him from. When Eve was pulled into
the frenzy, he knew he had to come up with
some answers—including how to convince her
they should marry again…this time for keeps.

EDGE OF ETERNITY, available in
November from Intrigue, is the sixth book in
Harlequin's exciting new cross-line series,
WEDDINGS, INC.

Be sure to look for the final book, **VOWS,** by
Margaret Moore (Harlequin Historical #248),
coming in December.

WED6

Relive the romance.... This December,
Harlequin and Silhouette are proud to bring you

by Request™

Little Matchmakers

All they want for Christmas is a mom *and* a dad!

Three complete novels by your favorite authors—
in one special collection!

THE MATCHMAKERS by Debbie Macomber
MRS. SCROOGE by Barbara Bretton
A CAROL CHRISTMAS by Muriel Jensen

When your child's a determined little matchmaker,
anything can happen—especially at Christmas!

Available wherever
Harlequin and Silhouette books are sold.

HARLEQUIN®   Silhouette®

HREQ1194

HARLEQUIN®

Georgina Devon

brings the past alive with

Untamed Heart

One of the most sensual Regencies ever published by Harlequin.

Lord Alaistair St. Simon has inadvertently caused the death of the young Baron Stone. Seeking to make amends, he offers his protection to the baron's sister, Liza. Unfortunately, Liza is not the grateful bride he was expecting.

St. Simon's good intentions set off a story of revenge, betrayal and consuming desire.

Don't miss it!

Coming in October 1994,
wherever Harlequin books are sold.

REG2

"HOORAY FOR HOLLYWOOD" SWEEPSTAKES

HERE'S HOW THE SWEEPSTAKES WORKS

OFFICIAL RULES — NO PURCHASE NECESSARY

To enter, complete an Official Entry Form or hand print on a 3" x 5" card the words "HOORAY FOR HOLLYWOOD", your name and address and mail your entry in the pre-addressed envelope (if provided) or to: "Hooray for Hollywood" Sweepstakes, P.O. Box 9076, Buffalo, NY 14269-9076 or "Hooray for Hollywood" Sweepstakes, P.O. Box 637, Fort Erie, Ontario L2A 5X3. Entries must be sent via First Class Mail and be received no later than 12/31/94. No liability is assumed for lost, late or misdirected mail.

Winners will be selected in random drawings to be conducted no later than January 31, 1995 from all eligible entries received.

Grand Prize: A 7-day/6-night trip for 2 to Los Angeles, CA including round trip air transportation from commercial airport nearest winner's residence, accommodations at the Regent Beverly Wilshire Hotel, free rental car, and $1,000 spending money. (Approximate prize value which will vary dependent upon winner's residence: $5,400.00 U.S.); 500 Second Prizes: A pair of "Hollywood Star" sunglasses (prize value: $9.95 U.S. each). Winner selection is under the supervision of D.L. Blair, Inc., an independent judging organization, whose decisions are final. Grand Prize travelers must sign and return a release of liability prior to traveling. Trip must be taken by 2/1/96 and is subject to airline schedules and accommodations availability.

Sweepstakes offer is open to residents of the U.S. (except Puerto Rico) and Canada who are 18 years of age or older, except employees and immediate family members of Harlequin Enterprises, Ltd., its affiliates, subsidiaries, and all agencies, entities or persons connected with the use, marketing or conduct of this sweepstakes. All federal, state, provincial, municipal and local laws apply. Offer void wherever prohibited by law. Taxes and/or duties are the sole responsibility of the winners. Any litigation within the province of Quebec respecting the conduct and awarding of prizes may be submitted to the Regie des loteries et courses du Quebec. All prizes will be awarded; winners will be notified by mail. No substitution of prizes are permitted. Odds of winning are dependent upon the number of eligible entries received.

Potential grand prize winner must sign and return an Affidavit of Eligibility within 30 days of notification. In the event of non-compliance within this time period, prize may be awarded to an alternate winner. Prize notification returned as undeliverable may result in the awarding of prize to an alternate winner. By acceptance of their prize, winners consent to use of their names, photographs, or likenesses for purpose of advertising, trade and promotion on behalf of Harlequin Enterprises, Ltd., without further compensation unless prohibited by law. A Canadian winner must correctly answer an arithmetical skill-testing question in order to be awarded the prize.

For a list of winners (available after 2/28/95), send a separate stamped, self-addressed envelope to: Hooray for Hollywood Sweepstakes 3252 Winners, P.O. Box 4200, Blair, NE 68009.

CBSRLS

OFFICIAL ENTRY COUPON

"Hooray for Hollywood"
SWEEPSTAKES!

Yes, I'd love to win the Grand Prize — a vacation in Hollywood —
or one of 500 pairs of "sunglasses of the stars"! Please enter me
in the sweepstakes!

This entry must be received by December 31, 1994.
Winners will be notified by January 31, 1995.

Name _____

Address _____ Apt. _____

City _____

State/Prov. _____ Zip/Postal Code _____

Daytime phone number _____
(area code)

Account # _____

Return entries with invoice in envelope provided. Each book
in this shipment has two entry coupons — and the more
coupons you enter, the better your chances of winning!

DIRCBS

- -

OFFICIAL ENTRY COUPON

"Hooray for Hollywood"
SWEEPSTAKES!

Yes, I'd love to win the Grand Prize — a vacation in Hollywood —
or one of 500 pairs of "sunglasses of the stars"! Please enter me
in the sweepstakes!

This entry must be received by December 31, 1994.
Winners will be notified by January 31, 1995.

Name _____

Address _____ Apt. _____

City _____

State/Prov. _____ Zip/Postal Code _____

Daytime phone number _____
(area code)

Account # _____

Return entries with invoice in envelope provided. Each book
in this shipment has two entry coupons — and the more
coupons you enter, the better your chances of winning!

DIRCBS